dream wide awake

.........was she born with a gift or a curse?.........

a novel by

cj zahner

author of the suicide gene

To Maryjane,
Thanks for reading!
Love your book club.
Cyndie
1-28-2020

This is a work of fiction. The names, characters, places, programs, projects, and incidents are either a product of the author's imagination or are used fictitiously, and any resemblance to actual persons living or dead, business establishments, events, locales is entirely coincidental.

Dream Wide Awake

For information contact Cyndie Zahner
www.cyndiezahner.com

Cover Art by Amanda Filutze

Published 2018
Printed in the United States of America
Print ISBN: 9781717993472
First Printing, 2018
www.cyndiezahner.com

Dedication

To Jeff,
my husband and soul mate,
you are the glue and sanity behind my crazy,
imaginary world. Your love and support gave
me the courage to pursue my dream of writing novels.

To my children, Jessie, Zak, and Jilly,
may you be half as proud of me as I am of you.
Always remember, no one loves you like your mother.

And to my sweet Layla Grace,
whom my entire being
now revolves around.
The world is at your fingertips.

Foreword

Trust in dreams, for in them is hidden the gate to eternity. Khalil Gibran

The Four Project Dream Dreamers

#1 Lenny Emling
#2 John Michael Turnbull
#3 Todd Kennedy
#4 Rachel Callahan Kennedy

The Callahan Sisters' Families

The Dalys

Jack Daly
Lisa Callahan Daly
Mikala Daly
Twins Jaden and John Daly

The Kennedys

Todd Kennedy
Rachel Callahan Kennedy
Jeffrey Kennedy

The Dream Chasers

Chief Ben Morgan
Detective Billy Mackentire
Detective Jack Daly

The Dream Snatchers

The American Government

1 Jack

He felt her eyes on him before she spoke.

"Daddy?"

Her breath warmed his cheek. She stood so close that the remnants of last night's snack—her mom's favorite, watermelon gumdrops—mingled with mint toothpaste and reminded him she was a little Lisa, only fearless.

He kept still. Held the sweet smell for a moment and waited for the familiar poke. The prod came. One miniature finger pecking three times, knocking at his shoulder.

"Daddy? Are you in there?"

He loved that she pictured him inside his own head. Yet, he hated it, too.

"Yes, Mikala." He stretched his legs, being careful not to wake Lisa. "I'm in here."

"Marky is close now."

His eyes snapped open.

"How close, sweet pea?"

"In my room."

Jack Daly sat up and swung his legs over the bed, feeling for his shorts on the floor with his toes. He placed his feet in the leg holes, stood, and pulled them over his boxers.

"I can see the movie better," she said softly, shuffling her pink puppy slippers backward to give him room.

"Quiet, darling, let's not wake Mommy," he whispered, but the request was in vain. The covers rustled as Lisa rolled over. She tugged a pillow over her head to muffle their words. She didn't approve of their morning chats.

"Okay," Mikala whispered softly from the doorway. A ray of moonlight cheated its way through the corner of a window blind and fell faintly on her eager form. She stood, hands raised, fingers wiggling.

He whisked her up in his arms, her one-size-too-big flannelled pajamas bunching over wiry arms and legs, and her long blond locks cascading over tiny shoulders. He turned and backed out of the room, closing the door behind him. When he released his hand, the doorknob clunked to the floor, and the door drifted ajar.

"Damn it," he whispered, tucking Mikala close as he leaned over to look for the handle. "Oops, sorry, sweetie."

"It's okay, Daddy."

Normally, he refrained from swearing around the kids, but his procrastination had thrust him into a parental slip of the tongue. Shirking home-upkeep chores naturally accompanied tough work cases. Plus, he hated odd jobs. Twirling a screwdriver and dipping a paint brush had never been his forte. He hoped the knob-less door didn't remind Lisa he hadn't patched the wall in the boys' bedroom or touched up the kitchen backsplash. Their homey little tri-level needed a makeover.

For lack of vision, he swirled one foot over the hall carpeting until he felt the knob against his foot, and then he kicked the nuisance to the side and glanced down the hall toward the fluorescent yellow lights of the cartoon clock in Mikala's bedroom. 4:44. The time was always about the same when the dreams called her from the night. His fingers found the hall light switch, and their world lit up.

"Let's go downstairs, so we don't wake your brothers."

"Daddy?"

"Yes?"

"We don't have time for coffee."

He smiled. She knew the routine: milk and coffee in their favorite mugs at the kitchen counter. He shouldn't be amused. He knew what was coming, but despite all, her youthful wisdom still grabbed him.

"Okay, sweetie." He sat down at the top of the staircase, and her little frame collapsed into his lap. One of her arms landed squarely around his shoulder. "You said Marky is in your room?"

"Yes, he played the movie, bigger."

Her voice tickled his eardrums. He loved its young, high-pitched tone that hadn't kept time with her six years. He savored the youthful shrill, knowing that when she grew older, like Lisa, the years would age her sweet voice, and life would cloud her innocent interpretation of the dreams.

He yawned and threaded the thick, caramel-colored hair garnishing his forehead with his fingers, smoothing an annoying clump to the side. The tuft bounced back defiantly. He frowned. "Can you see the other little boy yet?"

"Yes, but I didn't look at his face. I wanted to wait, so I am safe with you."

"You're safe, sweet pea."

"I'm scared." Her fingernails pressed into the skin on his shoulder.

"Scared?"

Her dreams seldom frightened her. He could lead her away from the bad parts, talk her around the actual crime, so she didn't experience the horror. He wasn't completely sure about all this. Her psychologist said she didn't seem damaged in the least from her nightmares, but then they hadn't been completely truthful about everything. These weren't really nightmares. "Why? You aren't normally afraid."

"Because I recognize the room in the movie."

He turned to face her. "It's familiar?" He scratched an itch at the back of his neck with his free hand and yawned again.

She nodded.

"What do you recognize about it?"

"It's Danny's room."

He stopped breathing.

Doubting his daughter's words had long escaped him. Since she first explained about the movies—dreaming wide awake, she called the phenomena—their accuracy had dissolved any disbelief. But this couldn't be. She must be wrong this time. Marky, the boy in her dreams, relayed movies of strangers. Visions that remarkably resembled abductions in their hometown.

Years before, he merely suspected she had inherited her mother's gift. Now, he knew. She was Lisa's replica. The one difference? Mikala was strong willed like her aunt Rachel, grounded at age six. Lisa couldn't handle the dreams. Mikala could more than handle them. Like a miniature newscaster, she announced each scene to him until she came too close to the scary parts, and he nudged her by them.

As an investigator promoted within the police force three years ago, the fact that his own daughter had a sixth sense was anything but coincidental. After all, his occupation and this curse of a trait so alive in his in-law's family is what had led him to Lisa in the first place.

But this was different. Now the gift—curse—befell his daughter.

"Danny? As in your cousin Danny?"

"Yes. Can I close my eyes now?" She poked her chin out and shut her eyes before he responded.

"Sure, sweetie, but I think you're confused."

"No, I'm not confused." She scrunched her eyelids tighter. "I can see Danny's Superman bed."

"There are lots of Superman beds." He kept his arms around her still while she concentrated. As if absence of movement could clarify her vision, erase his nephew from her mind's eye.

"No, it's Danny's. I can see the three Batman stickers. The ones Aunt Janice yelled at him for putting on his bed."

This wasn't normal. Typically, she described streets, houses, faces of strangers, never people or places she knew.

A week ago, two months after Marky Blakley turned up missing, she'd described the boy's lisp to perfection. Said he appeared to her. Showed her the scar on his finger where the spokes of a neighbor boy's tricycle had cut a piece off—a bit of information never released by the department. Then Marky began showing her movies of two other little boys. In her head. Scenes of an abductor targeting children of single mothers flooded her mind.

But this couldn't be. This was Danny, his sister's son.

"The bad man broke the glass of Danny's window and then held up the white washcloth—the sleepy cloth."

Chloroform.

"Mikala, look at the boy in the bed, his face. You're confused."

She was quiet, still, her expression soft. Lip relaxed against lip. Then her eyes opened.

"He can see me."

At first, because of her casualness, he thought he'd surely heard her wrong.

"Who can see you?"

"The bad man."

His calmness faded to confusion. He tightened his eyebrows. Premonitions, they called these episodes. His wife experienced them, now his daughter. But they were never interactive.

"What do you mean he can see you?"

"He said my name. He has a guide."

"A guide?"

"You know, Daddy, someone who shows him movies. He knows who I am."

"No, Mikala, the bad man does not know who you are."

"Yes, he does, Daddy." For the first time, he heard panic in her voice. "That's the reason he is at Danny's house."

A creak in the floor behind him grabbed his attention, and he turned his head. Lisa darted from the bedroom, ripped

Mikala from his arms, and handed him something in her place.

"I told you not to allow this. I said you were playing with fire."

"Lisa, she's wrong. He can't see her."

"Yes, he can, Daddy."

"No, he can't, Mikala." He lowered his voice to sound stern.

"Yes—yes he can. He's with Danny right now. Run, Daddy. Get Danny!"

"Go." Lisa screamed so loud one of the boys in the next room woke crying.

Jack glanced at his lap—at the ratty sneakers Lisa had placed there. For the moment it took him to put them on, he wondered if he should run or drive the block and a half to his sister's house. He decided, descended the stairs, and bounded out the front door bare-chested, leaving Lisa behind switching on lights and talking into the scanner. She would call for a cruiser to go to Janice's house, to her own house. But Mikala was wrong about Danny. She had to be. He was going to be in a heap of trouble with the chief later.

He ran down the driveway and disappeared into the black night within seconds. His legs turned over like an Olympic sprinter's, his breath labored, and sweat beaded on his upper lip. He rounded Third Street and nearly slipped in the wet grass on Nevada Drive but caught himself. He saw her house in the distance. Janice, four months separated from her husband, was alone there with her son. Alone like the others. Three single mothers of three abducted little boys.

His mind raced. The police would be at his house in two minutes. At Janice's in three. They protected each other's families.

When he was four houses away, he began screaming his sister's name. Trying to scare anyone off. Make the bad man drop the child? Leave without the child? He didn't know why he screamed. By the time his feet hit her driveway her light had turned on. The front bedroom window opened.

"Jack?" Janice's voice slithered through the screen.

He passed her window and ran toward the back of the house, toward Danny's room. He could see broken glass on the ground shimmering with the reflection of a street light.

Dear God, no.

This couldn't be. These abductions could not have hit his family.

"Danny!" he yelled.

When he reached his nephew's window, the whites of Danny's two little eyes glowed in the dark room. He was there. Standing and looking out the bare, open window back at him. Waiting.

"Hi, Uncle Jack," Danny said, his little face peeking over the window ledge, his stuffed bear, Tony, nudged under his chin.

Jack leaned his hands on the house and huffed, trying to catch his breath. Trying to digest that Danny was okay. Alive. Mikala was wrong.

"Thank God, thank God," he uttered out loud. When he caught his breath, he gazed up at his nephew.

That's when horror seized him. Above Danny's little face, secured on the broken glass, a scribbling on Christian stationery paralyzed him. It was the abductor's fourth message, but the first to make Jack's blood circulate like an electric current. The words he read flowed over his lips in a whisper, expelled with terrifying breath.

"One mulligan for Mikala."

2 Lenny; dreamer #1

Lenny stuttered.

His eyes barely ever made contact with humans and one occasionally wandered. The skin on his face bragged of a bad case of childhood chicken pox, and his pores reeked a glandular smell even after he bathed. His long scaly thighs bled because his thick fingers, which dangled below two long arms, never stopped scratching. Always scratching. Occasionally burrowing right through wax-coated jeans.

His gait was fine. In fact, he could run with the litheness of a cheetah, but when he stood still, he swayed. One foot positioned itself a bit in front of the other, one massive shoulder pointed downward, and he rocked slowly in a slight, nervous seesaw.

He hated mirrors, glimpsing his frightening guise. Because of his ugliness, he ran to the dark-screened porch or hid in the tree garden when children came near. He tried not to scare the little ones. Often found excuses to go inside when he heard the dismissal bells sound at the nearby grade school.

Yet, he did enjoy standing on the wide sidewalk when sixth-grader Robby Redgrave strolled home after Friday detention. He liked planting his feet in the middle of the walkway and rocking harder when he spotted Robby bouncing down the street. Even grunted a bit, as he neared. Robby was the neighborhood bully, born of a bully. Lenny remembered Robby Senior—Rob Robby, he called him—at age eleven, throwing punches at the smaller boys, lifting little girls' skirts, and bullying him into his stuttering ways.

Rob Robby never bullied him anymore. In fact, he and his son crossed the street if they saw him. Everyone did, except the little ones. And LeeLee, of course.

His face reddened and his pox scars deepened. He grew calm and sweet when he thought of her. For the rest of his life he would lurk in the shadows just to catch a glimpse of her, protect her as she had done for him when he was a child.

Life was funny. He laughed when he thought about it. How his scrawny little arms and legs had grown such mass and muscle. How sometimes people who looked big to you when you were little, looked little to you when you were big. And how one punch of a fist could forever stop the name calling, the badgering, and the pranks that he would take to his grave because he could never forgive or forget those boys, like Rob Robby, who did not know he would grow so big.

He could protect LeeLee now. There was a time he couldn't. But that was before they sent him away to the prison that wasn't a prison. To the pale building on the flat, hot land with the other children who were different. Kids like him and LeeLee's big sister and the boy from New Jersey and the girl from Kalamazoo, Michigan. A place where the scorching sun spilled onto miles of barren land around you, and the night sky lit Orion up so brightly you felt you could stretch an arm upward and touch Rigel with your fingertip. A makeshift village where you could almost taste the sandstone dust of the buildings and smell the burning sage and honeysuckle left over from the Indians. A phrontistery of square, bleak structures with basic rooms, their ceilings so low you felt entombed. And when you sat in them for hours and watched the movies in your head of bad places and bad planes and bad, bad men, you believed the vibration of your thoughts might dislodge the sun-dried bricks of the adobe walls.

There were secrets he could not tell and anger he could not tame. But for now, he could not think of such things. It was time.

He climbed the old cherry staircase and entered the first bedroom.

"M-Ma, I'm leaving for w-w-work." He set a glass of water on the faded antique bed stand, leaned over, and kissed his mother's cheek.

"Lenny? Already? I must have dozed off."

"Here, t-t-take your p-pills." He took her knuckle-cramped hand in his, gently turned her wrist, and slipped two pills into her palm.

"Okay, thank you," she said, then propped herself up on one elbow, clumsily placed the pills on her tongue, and reached stiff-shouldered for her water.

"G-good night, Ma, sweet dreams," he said and made his way toward the door, the floorboards of the old home creaking beneath each step. "I'll b-be sure to set the s-s-security alarm."

"Lenny?"

He turned and glanced at her small frame in the king-sized four-poster bed. She seemed tiny. Looked lost in the brocade coverlet that matched the big roses on the fading wallpaper and the lavish drapes that concealed the old beveled windows.

"Yeah, Ma?"

"Promise me something?" She asked as she lay her head back down on the silky pillow and drew the quilt to her chest. "Promise me you'll stay away from the boys?"

He sighed.

"M-ma, I don't know what you're t-talking about."

"Lenny," she said, but Lenny was closing the door behind him. "Lenny—"

"It's ok-k-kay, Ma," he said and wrenched the door shut.

He descended the stairs quickly, grabbed his gear, set the alarm, and went out the front door, so he could not hear her call after him. He threw his backpack of clothes and sandwiches and coke over his shoulder and started down the dark street.

Working the graveyard shift had advantages for a man with an ugly face. He walked three houses, jogged three houses, and then took off in a sprint. The night air made his big ears tingle and his blood shot eyes water, but the feeling of freedom he experienced while running beneath the stars far outweighed any discomfort. No one gawked at him. No one tried not to stare. The distance was a mere three miles from his home, eighteen minutes. Sometimes, if the wind pressed his back, he could run the route in seventeen.

He rounded the corner and picked up his pace as he turned onto the empty four-lane street. He would stop and check on the boys after work. His ailing mother wouldn't be awake until late morning, so he'd have time. He glanced down the street toward the corner store and stretched his lips into a wide smile. Three teenage boys leaned against the store's brick facade, yelling and guffawing, throwing profanities at each other. When they heard the loud click of fast feet against pavement, they looked up and squinted their eyes to see who was coming. When they saw him, they silenced, and then scattered into the dark like cockroaches running from light.

Lenny smiled and scratched and ran after the boy with the fastest dash. How much grander it was to be feared than to fear.

3 1995 – LeeLee

On the night LeeLee met fright, the smell of fresh plaster mingled with sawdust and lingered in the air around her. A small gas heater, positioned at the top of the staircase, warmed the upstairs sitting area and two bedrooms that had no doors. The small tiled bathroom with the claw-foot tub did have a door, and they had to remember to shut it after they used the toilet because PopPops didn't want the attic's warm air to escape up the long ceiling vent and outside into the black night.

Three days before, eight little children had helped LeeLee celebrate her fourth birthday. Five came to the Chuck E. Cheese party from her old neighborhood—the hoodlums-will-get-you area, PopPops called it—and three from PopPop's neighborhood—the good-families-live-here place.

Only a dim light from the streetlamp squeezed through the small front window and into her new bedroom, but LeeLee didn't mind the darkness. She felt safe and warm, and she loved sleeping upstairs beside her sister in her grandparents' attic with the new walls and cushy carpeting that felt springy when you jumped out of bed in the morning. She and Sissy moved there with her parents shortly after her grandmother—G'Ma, Gee for short—came home from the hospital. Mama had to be close to Gee to help her.

PopPops had explained the situation to LeeLee.

"G'Ma went under the knife," he said, fists clenched. "That bastard of a doctor cut her spine, and now she'll never walk again."

"Dad." Mama put a hand on her forehead. "Please don't swear in front of the girls."

But he didn't hear her. PopPops hardly ever heard anyone. His head was full of hot wind that swirled around and made too much noise between his ears, her dad said.

"Because of that son-of-a-bitch, now you and your sister and your mom and dad will live with us until you can find a house in the neighborhood." His arms flailed, and his voice bounced off the walls. "So your mom is close. So she can help the nurses with G'Ma."

"Why can't we live in the attic above you and Gee forever, PopPops?" LeeLee begged.

"Because those son-of-a-bitches are going to have to pay," he yelled, froth oozing from one corner of his mouth.

"Dad!" Mama hollered.

Pops ignored her. "And you'll have a big new house with your own bedroom on the street around the corner, where no imbeciles roam the back alleys like in your old neighborhood, and your sister will be safe walking to kindergarten because old man Johnny the fireman crosses kids at the corner."

But LeeLee liked sleeping in the attic, where she wasn't as afraid of the nightmares. She could inch over and snuggle up to her big sister when they came.

"I don't want my own room," she whined to Daddy.

But Daddy agreed with PopPops that they needed their own home.

"This is only temporary," Daddy yelled and then talked about hell. He said if it froze, they could stay.

LeeLee prayed hell froze. She didn't understand why Daddy and PopPops couldn't live in the same house. They both liked to swing their arms and shout words Mama never used.

Sometimes at night, PopPop's voice drifted up through the floor and woke them. Momma said Pops was venting—like the bathroom—but her sister said he was gulping down the crazy yellow drink with the suds. She said he was angry about and sorry for Gee. Sorry that now Gee had to sleep in the narrow bed with the push button that rolled her up and down, or slump over in the living-room chair with the footrest and the lever on the side to help her lie down.

"A tragedy," PopPops called Gee's situation.

But then the loiterers came and drank coffee in the parlor downstairs, and everyone talked and smiled about how much money PopPops and Gee would get. PopPops said the cash would help pay for the nurses, and that Mama could buy a house one street over.

Until then, her grandparents slept in separate first-floor bedrooms—with the brand-new, wide-doored bathroom in between—and LeeLee's family filled the space between the new walls in the attic with their belongings. They had a big garage sale beforehand and sold a lot of things, like her inside playhouse and Barbie castle. Everything remaining had to be stored far away in the tin garage with no windows, because Pop's garage was "busting at the beams."

"This place isn't big enough for all of us. Pop's dad, your great-grandfather, built this house during the Second World War," Gee told her one day while LeeLee was downstairs in her bedroom, playing on the floor. When Gee talked, LeeLee liked to jump in bed with her and pull the covers to her chin and listen. Gee was a good talker, her voice soft and flowy.

"He wasn't able to enlist due to a boyhood injury, so he worked at the electric company downtown throughout the thirties and forties." She stopped and whispered to LeeLee, "Made a lot of money," then continued in a normal voice, "and he passed out dimes and quarters to the bums, who lined up outside the back door for him on payday. Your great-grandfather was a good man. So is Pops."

"I love PopPops."

"He loves you, too." Gee squeezed her, weakly. "We both do."

"I like living with you and PopPops, Gee," LeeLee told her.

"It's only temporary." Gee's face sobered. "Until your Mama can find a home close by."

"I don't want a new home. I want to stay here forever." She crossed her arms and banged them against herself.

She meant what she said. She loved their new home—until the bad night, that is.

LeeLee had lots of dreams that woke her in the night. But she felt safe in the attic, even when the worst of the dreams came, because the bed she and her sister slept in sat only a few feet from her parents in the next room, and because PopPops and Gee slept right downstairs. Sometimes, when the wind died down in his head and his ears worked, PopPops would hurry up the stairs when she cried. He would grab her up in her blankets, carry her downstairs in his warm arms, and lay her beside Gee for the night. Gee would hold her with her weak arms and stay awake all night, chasing the dreams away.

"Don't be afraid," Gee would tell her. "Close your eyes, take a deep breath, and watch for the feathers of the white angel to come."

LeeLee loved to watch for Gee's white angel.

"The white angel will protect you," Gee would say with a voice as soothing as a gentle summer breeze. "Turn the bad dreams off and think of nice things—the beach and the waves and PopPop's sandcastles—and then count the feathers as they come: one feather, two, three."

"Four, five, six." LeeLee would close her eyes and watch as the wings of the white angel formed in her mind. She had troubled counting the big numbers, but Gee helped her.

"Ten, eleven, twelve," Gee would whisper. "Thirteen feathers, fourteen."

Falling asleep was so easy when Gee chased the dreams away.

LeeLee tried hard to be the dream chaser on her own, in her own bed. "One feather, two, three…" she would whisper as she snuggled up close to her sleeping sister and closed her eyes, "nine, ten, eleven, fourteen feathers."

But she was not as brave as Gee and her sister. So on the night she met fright—after which, she would not dangle an arm over the side of a bed for the rest of her life—she let out a blood-curdling scream that sent both her parents and grandparents into a shaking frenzy.

"Eeeeeek," she screeched. "Help meeee! Momma, Momma!"

"LeeLee." Her mother crossed the short distance to her bed, lifted her up, and cradled her in her arms within seconds of her wails. "What happened, my precious?"

LeeLee gasped for air and, for a long time, struggled to speak. "Momma," she repeated over and over until Daddy turned on the light, and PopPops came up the stairs with the baseball bat.

"My God," PopPops said. "I thought someone was killing her."

"We can't get her to talk," her dad said, his eyebrows furrowed into one long, black line. "Sissy, do you know what happened?"

Sissy shook her head, shrugged her shoulders, and leaned toward her sister. "What's wrong?"

LeeLee raised her hand in slow motion and stammered, "My, my—"

"Did something happen to your hand?" Momma's soft fingers reached around her wrist.

She nodded and sniffed, trying to control her sobs.

"What?" Her father knelt on the floor beside the bed.

"He, he, he—"

"He?" Her dad grew angry. "He who?"

"He, he—" She couldn't bring herself to say his name. "He grabbed my hand."

"Who grabbed your hand?" her dad hollered.

LeeLee turned to face the headboard, wiping her eyes, and pointing one little finger.

"My hand was there." She motioned to the space between the mattress and the headboard. "He grabbed it and pulled, and I woke up and he wouldn't let go."

Her face fell to her mother's arms, and she sobbed dramatically.

"My God." Her father sat back on his legs. "Just another dream."

"No," she hollered, "eyes open. Eyes open."

"LeeLee, darling." Her mother drew her close, stroking her hair and rocking her small frame in her arms. "It was a dream, a bad dream, nothing more."

"No," she screamed and pushed her away. "He grabbed my hand. He pulled me. Bad, bad, bad!"

There was no comforting her. The three of them tried for a long time, repeatedly looking under the bed to convince her no one had grabbed her hand. But she insisted, and they were unable to comfort her. After a time, PopPops retreated down the stairs, and her father stomped back to bed. Sissy lay back down, and their mother slipped under the covers beside them and held LeeLee close, murmuring reassuring words.

When her mother finally fell asleep, her arms still tight around her, LeeLee turned toward her sister and realized she was still awake.

"I saw him," her sister whispered. "The black devil."

LeeLee wiggled down under her mother's arm and moved closer to her sister. "Did you hear him?"

"No."

"He said I'm going away someday." LeeLee tried hard not to cry again.

"When?" Her sister seemed alarmed.

"After the big buildings fall."

"Where are you going?"

"I don't know." LeeLee squirmed closer to Sissy. She sank her head into her pillow. "What's a desert?"

Her sister raised her eyes to the ceiling. "It's a place far away where the sun is hot and the floors are sand."

"I don't like sand floors." She pressed one cheek deep within the pillow.

Her sister lowered her eyes to meet LeeLee's. She bit her bottom lip and quickly wrapped her arms around her and shook her head. "Don't worry. I won't let them take you."

They would not mention that night again until they were much older, and LeeLee would never sleep with a hand dangling over the bed until the day she died.

4 John Michael; dreamer #2

John Michael punched in the first security code on his laptop and answered seven security questions. Then he entered a second code, and a third, and watched as his clearances climbed the screen. Code name. Number. The unyielding words that appeared every time he signed in. Words reminding him of his oath, his duties, and the secret language he had sworn to take to his grave.

Finally, a touch of humanness unfolded. "Hello, John, what can we help you with?"

When the words flashed on the screen, he set his coffee cup down on a stack of uneven papers by accident and nearly sent the mug tumbling. A few brown spots splashed on his hand and his students' essays. Quickly, he jostled the cup to an open spot on his desk, nudging folders aside.

"Damn it," he said, giving his hand a hard shake, sending coffee drops off his fingers to the floor.

For lack of a towel, he wiped his hand clean by swirling it in the pocket of his suitcoat, which shouldered the back of his chair. He glanced behind him, out the tall classroom windows to the campus's dimly-lit cobblestone path, and peeked in both directions. Neither students nor professors sauntered before dawn. He bet Ivy League school paths were littered with footprints by now. He turned back to his computer and typed, "You promised me you would get me out of this hellhole of a town before the next semester. I'm still waiting for orders. What's the holdup?"

A minute passed. He adjusted his glasses. Sipped coffee again. Practiced his patience.

"We set up a transfer to Houston."

Houston? When the hell did a spot open in Houston? He'd begged for Boston. For one brief moment, he couldn't find his fingers.

"But there's been a glitch," came up on the screen. "The transfer was declined."

Of course, he thought, he needn't worry about being transferred to some half-assed dump in Texas. No one wanted to trade for Erie. His shoulders sagged.

"We won't have another college opening until the fall," flashed at him as he tried to catch his breath. "I'm afraid you'll have to make do where you are for another semester."

He shook his hands vehemently to kill the numbness, and the feeling in his fingers came slowly back. If they had sent him to Boston in the beginning, this entire mess of bouncing from college to college could have been avoided. He snapped his wrists in rapid succession until both hands felt completely whole again. The mediocrity of these paltry institutions dragged at him. He hated this miserable little college with its religious overtones and despised the gray words on the pale-blue screen in front of him that chained him here. He deplored the fingers that typed those words and detested the faceless men dictating his life from who knew where.

His anger rose. The muscles in his neck bulged. He picked up his cup, his knuckles white around the handle, and he whirled the ceramic mug against the far wall of his office. Coffee splattered and pottery shattered everywhere.

He typed, "Damn it, you promised me you'd find me another school." He hit "send" and waited in the silent building. Only a few people were there that early in the morning. Maybe Penny, the accounting teacher. She didn't sleep well. And the creepy janitor, whom he knew all too well. God, he hoped they hadn't heard the shatter.

A vibrating noise brought his body to attention. He picked his head up to decipher where the sound came from. His eyes shot toward the floor, his briefcase. Instantly, one hand reached inside, shuffling through papers to reach the bottom. His fingers felt for and found metal, and he lifted his cell phone to his ear.

It was them.

"John, we are working on moving you. Probably Vermont. There's an opening in August," the voice on the other end said.

"I asked for Massachusetts."

"We don't have a unit in Massachusetts."

He sighed. A gift, they called it. Clairvoyance. His sixth sense, premonitions, crazy dreams. This was the fourth college he'd taught at because of that damn so-called gift.

"I have been asking you people for years to get me to Massachusetts. My family is there. You ripped me away from them when I was twelve years old, remember? Said I'd be away for a year. And instead you kept me in that oven baking for eight years, and then pretty much informed me my life was yours—forever—and I should get over it. So now get me the hell out of here like you promised."

"Eventually we will, but it won't be Massachusetts."

"How the hell did Rachel get her hometown?" John Michael felt blood rush across his face. His cheeks burned. "A little favoritism going on?"

The man on the other end hesitated, then spoke slowly, pointedly, "The Erie unit was created because the city is the hometown of two transmitters."

"Of course, Lenny and the favored Rachel." He spat his words into the cell. "I want to get away from them. Call it transmitter disparity and send me back to Minneapolis if you have to. You do that sort of thing, don't you? Give recalls due to incongruence? Get me out of here."

"Minneapolis is—"

"Full." John cut him off. "Yeah, yeah, I know. Four to a team. Twenty-five teams across the country. I stay until there is an opening somewhere else."

"Unless—"

"Unless I go back to the belly of the abyss." John was yelling now, which he didn't do often.

"I'm sorry, John." The voice sounded sympathetic. "It's a lifetime commitment. You know that. We can arrange a holiday for stress—"

"A holiday? For stress? Cut the crap. I went through that once and won't make that mistake again. I'll get by."

"You'll wait, then? For the opening?"

He glanced toward the brown coffee stains on the wall and then extended his arm and sneered at the cell phone. His shoulders tightened, and he forced himself to bring the phone back to his ear. They'd warned him not to break another one. They had replaced five for him already, and their high-security, ultra-encrypted features weren't cheap. He shifted his weight and leaned back in his seat, tilting his eyes to the ceiling and cussing under his breath. What choice did he have?

"I'll wait," he uttered.

"Thanks for understanding." The voice quieted. "And John? You may want to clean up that mess before Lenny sees it. You know how angry he gets."

The call ended.

John Michael composed himself, stood, and put on his suitcoat jacket. He leaned both hands on his desk, took a deep breath, and thought about Rachel and Lenny and Todd and how much he hated them. He straightened, smoothed the lapels of his suitcoat, and picked up his phone. He lingered for a while in an upright, motionless position—attention. Then he rotated one shoulder and hurled his cell across the room, grunting like an animal as the silver slivers of metal and gritty glints of glass bounced off the stain on the wall.

5 Todd; dreamer #3

He wrapped up his meeting with the president of the hospital at ten minutes after ten on a Monday morning. Outside the glass door to the president's office, administrators in suits and dresses and nurses and doctors in scrubs hurried by. Todd Kennedy smiled. He would out-earn every one of them next year—even the finest surgeons. He had just landed a mammoth contract. He could do anything, sell to anyone. He had the governmental punch to back him up and the confidence of Mike Tyson.

Positive thinking. *The Four Agreements. The Secret. The Power of Now.* He'd read them all.

"Thanks, Connie." He lay a contract on the secretary's desk, reminding himself they didn't like to be called that anymore. She was an Administrative Assistant. "Jim said you'd take care of this for me."

"Sure will, Todd," she said, smiling. "I take it your meeting went well?"

"Always." He smiled back, winked, and whistled his way out the door and toward the elevators.

Pharmaceutical sales, he thought, as he stepped outside into the fresh air. Who knew he would make so much money when he was talked into the career—forced, really. But everything had worked out like they said. This year, he had passed the six-figure mark in June, by October the quarter-million goal. Now with the hospital contract, he would make a fortune.

He reached for his phone to call Rachel and then thought again. No, he would surprise her with a gift. He jumped in his Mercedes and sped toward the mall. Once there, he headed to the best jeweler in town and bought the biggest diamond necklace he could find. Then he called a five-star restaurant from his car and made dinner reservations for Friday evening, requesting—insisting upon—a bayfront table next to the fireplace at eight o'clock.

He tested the power of his car as he drove, reveling in the twin-turbo engine sound. He stopped at a few doctors' offices on his way home to check on clients, slap backs, drop off samples, and talk about next year's golf outings. He pulled into his driveway at twenty minutes past one. He had five hours before Rachel got home. God how he loved her. He ripped open a sample pack and popped a pill in his mouth as he thought about her. They'd been married five years, and he still marveled at his luck. As long as he lived, he would never believe she fell in love with him—a nerdy kid from Idaho.

He relaxed into the thick cushions of the couch and opened a different pack. Popped another, let the tablet melt beneath his tongue as he thought back to age fifteen when he first laid eyes on her long legs and auburn hair. How he knew right then—in the middle of that Nevada desert—that she was the one.

As the drugs did their job, words began swirling in his head: round one, twenty-five; round two, seventy-five; hot, dark, dream. He took a bag of cocaine out, a credit card, and a twenty-dollar bill. He stopped and thought for a moment, tucked the twenty back inside his wallet and took out a hundred-dollar bill. He dumped two small mounds of cocaine on the coffee table and formed them into two straight lines with his credit card. Then he rolled the bill, held one nostril closed, snorted both lines, sniffed, and laughed. He would never use a twenty again.

He closed his eyes and tipped his head back, thinking about his past, his future, Rachel, Lenny, and John Michael. But most of all he thought about Todd. He let the colors and the music fill his head, and he drifted into a party in his mind that would last just until he heard the creaking of the garage door as Rachel's Audi rolled into their heated garage. Until then, he would block everything out except the party and Rachel and the sweet sleep that neared.

How he loved to sleep. Wipe his mind clear of everything—something that had never been permitted in those long eight years. But despite how much he hated his time in the desert, his presence there had proved worthwhile—because he had won Rachel's heart. He smiled and thought of her soft skin, enjoying the pill-induced euphoria until, eventually, he slipped into a vacuous, thought-killing world of sleep.

That nothingness was the only thing he loved more than Rachel.

6 Jack

"Good work, Nostradamus. Mark your sister's house." Billy Mack whirled a container of pins at Jack. The clear plastic box bounced off his arm, skidded across the desk, and snapped open. Pins spilled everywhere. "Then tell us no one tipped you off."

"You're a pain in the ass." Jack caught a few pins in his lap with one arm and stopped those bouncing on his desk with the other. He dragged his forearm across the desktop, herding them into a pile, and then leaned over and picked up the container. Loose pins rolled to and fro on ceramic tile. He kicked some away with the side of his sneaker. "A real asshole, Mack."

Detective Bill Mackentire smirked as he passed him. He stopped to thump Jack's desk with the side of his leg. The pins stirred, and Jack jumped. Then Billy continued down the crooked aisle.

"Like shaking a tree with a bear," Billy Mack said out of the corner of his mouth. "I love your sensitive side."

"Cut it out, Billy." Jack ran a hand through his hair, tried to forget the email he'd just received. The home security system could not be installed for a minimum of two weeks.

"Who you gonna call?" Billy laughed as he moved toward the front of the room where the maps hung.

"Shut the hell up." Jack hated the ghost-buster mockery. That innuendo was getting old. He watched Billy skip around staggered desks and effortlessly hurdle a stack of boxes at the end of the aisle that he could easily have walked around.

Trying to make light of serious situations was just one of Billy Mack's many annoying faults.

"Could have caught him, Crackerjack." Billy laughed and punctuated his merriment with a high-pitched whine and jab. "If you ate no fat, that is."

Jack let a deep, throaty grunt escape. Billy Mack was an expert investigator, but a buffoon of a person. A small city like Erie was lucky to have a detective as skilled as him, but sometimes everyone just wished he'd go away. Jack included.

"Ten pounds ago you were almost fast." Billy tossed a glance toward Jack, made a single clacking noise out one side of his mouth and topped the sound with a wink.

Jack shook his head and released another fed-up moan. He didn't need this now. Billy Mack was a stone in his shoe.

Billy's track records taunted Jack from the walls of their high school auditorium, and his state most-valuable-player soccer trophy laughed at him from the showcase every time they entered the school to investigate a heroin tip. Best friends and biggest rivals in high-school days, they lettered in the same four sports, parted ways—Jack to the Army like his dad, Billy Mack to the Marines like his—then reunited on the police force. Billy was more than a pain in the ass, he was Jack's nemesis.

A fine line separated love and hate.

Jack turned his eyes toward the front wall—and Billy. Could he tell him about the note with Mikala's name in it? Trust him to keep his big trap closed? That was his fear. Billy Mack never shut his mouth.

He watched Billy unclip a red marker off the top of the file he carried, bite the cap off, and glance at the maps covering the wall-sized police sketch board.

"This here ol' map needs taken down." The marker top in Billy's mouth muffled his words.

"What are you saying? Take the map down?" He must pay close attention to every word Billy uttered without arousing suspicion. Cops missed important information, acted differently, when the case was personal.

But he didn't have to pretend to be annoyed with Billy. That came naturally.

"Just a feeling we need a bigger radius, is all. Surrounding counties." Billy removed the lid from his lips, stared straight ahead. "But Jesus Christ himself couldn't get the county to fork over a lousy map without charging us a fee big enough to require an ordinance."

With manufacturing jobs long lost and Erie's population plummeting over two decades ago, Jack had thought the ex-rustbelt area would be a perfectly safe, mid-size place to raise a family. Again, Jack's hand rose and his fingers threaded thick hair. Maybe he hadn't thought that through.

Limited resources challenged both city and county law enforcement agencies, but the city had taken the brunt of the economic decline. Pennsylvania's state joke was Temple University in Philly housed more cops than Erie, Pennsylvania. The FBI hated working with the understaffed city force and scoffed brazenly at their facilities.

Jack glanced around the windowless room. If he lived in a bigger city, would he have turned over the note? Trusted the administration had the means to protect his daughter? God knew fancy cubicles and new desks had no bearing on competency. Yet, despite the stellar reputation of the men who shared these seats with him, could he trust a shorthanded, old-fashioned, small-city precinct to keep his daughter's name away from the CIA?

Every item there—save one new desk up front—averaged twenty years' service. To the right and left, staggered desks, some with big dents and only a handful flaunting computers, gave the room a dilapidated, old-school-house guise. Beside those jagged aisles, hooks bearing sweatshirts, gun holsters, and the animal enforcement officer's paraphernalia stretched scrappily along the wall by the room's entrance. Two chipped metal tables, their feeble legs reinforced by old steel files crammed beneath, stood like two decaying tombs dividing the back wall. Each bragged a menagerie of police odds and ends that seemed more lost and found than tactical items. To their right, shot-up flak jackets and worn-out body armor formed a heap in a back-wall corner. On the nicked, used-to-be-white-but-now-grey wall leading away from the garb, officers pinned documents here and there that they felt important. Penciled drawings flanked those pinned pages. None of the sheets or graffiti had meaning. Jack knew the only important item on that wall was the clock they watched when the crime-lab fellows lectured them on protocol. And that didn't work—the clock. It hadn't ticked in six months.

Other than the front wall with the clean, smooth whiteboard and maps, the room was a disaster. But up front, three symmetrical city diagrams hung without a wrinkle. All were printed by City Hall's engineering department and strung across the board like in an old movie. The chief liked ample visibility with big cases. He said seeing the entire city made locating patterns easier.

On the map Billy Mack studied, three pins held three pictures of three little boys in place. Around those photos, enlarged red circles and numbers caught the reflection of one of the room's crummy fluorescent lights, which flickered nonstop, begging for maintenance. Those red glints shimmered like a failing neon light above a seedy hotel. They represented the names and addresses of what both Jack and Billy agreed were the city's biggest scumbags—child sex offenders. In big black letters, "Chomo Coward" spread across the wall above that map. Below, in smaller script, someone had penciled, "Have Mercy on me, oh God."

"So what's your sister-in-law doing these days, anyhow?" Billy asked, his back to Jack and his head bouncing up and down again as he glanced from file to map.

"Can you just leave it alone? For once?" Jack scowled at his backside just as the door to the room opened.

For a moment, the hum of a police precinct filtered in from outside their imperfect but safeguarded sanctuary—the Helen room, tagged for Helen Keller because the walls were soundproofed. The chief, his bulky body taking up much of the doorframe, entered and yanked the door shut behind him. All sound ceased. Only the voices of the men inside could bounce off these old, decrepit walls.

"Gentlemen." The chief nodded as he strode in, then frowned at Billy Mack and headed toward Jack. He cleared a barrage of pins from the aisle with his big foot, shook his head, and dragged a chair out from underneath a desk, falling into it. The metal seat squeaked with the weight of him.

"Okay, let's not prolong this." He took his cap off, stretched one long leg out, and set the cap on his knee. "The truth, Jack. How did you know this guy was at Janice's house?"

"Haven't you heard? His sister-in-law is psycho. I mean psychic." Billy gloated over one shoulder.

The chief leaned back and returned Billy's stare, shooting him a don't-give-me-any-crap frown. Billy turned away triumphantly. He lifted a marker and circled another spot on the map.

"You know what, Mack? Sometimes you can be a real asshole."

"So I hear. I love you, too, Chief."

The chief's lips fluttered as he released a gust of breath. He placed his cap back on his head and shifted his weight.

"I should have known better than to put the two of you on this case." He heaved himself upward with sloth-like slowness and ambled toward the front of the room.

His big strides and thick thighs forced desks aside as he strolled up the crooked aisle. He took a stance behind Mack, feet shoulder-length apart, arms crossed, lumbering body dressed in a heavy, blue uniform that masked seven bullet holes—a Desert Storm door prize. Those seven scars were only part of the reason people revered him. His size and physique were another. At six-foot-three, his squared shoulders and perfect posture resembled those of an Unknown Soldier tomb guard. He seemed much younger than his forty-six years. His eyes, much older.

"I'm still not convinced we're dealing with a pedophile." Jack herd Billy Mack tell him. "Despite what the county investigators or worthless reporters say."

"Any connection, yet? Between the boys?" The chief uncrossed his arms and lifted them away from his brick-hard abs. He rested the big fingers of one hand on the back of his neck.

"None, other than their mothers were raising them alone. Husbandless. We checked them out. All working hum-drum jobs. But one has a nice chunk of change in the bank," Billy responded, his eyes studying the map. In a low voice, he added, "Debutant dee-vor-cee."

"C'mon Mack." The chief let his hand drop from his neck. "Some respect."

Jack leaned back in his seat and let out a long whistle. Acting natural at the precinct was crucial. He had thought of nothing but Mikala for twenty-four hours, so when the opportunity to needle Billy presented itself, he jumped for two reasons. One, Billy expected abuse, and two, Jack welcomed any diversion, no matter how short lived.

Since his separation, Billy had taken a beating at work. He told the guys he and his wife separated for financial purposes. Katie spent cash as quick as blood spewed from a jugular, he said. Then coworkers pounded him with money and divorce jokes. But in Jack's eyes, their breakup had nothing to do with finances and everything to do with Billy being a damn good cop. He had a workaholic mentality, and he had confided as much to Lisa during a weekend drinking jag. He admitted he hadn't been home much after they married, told

Lisa he was afraid he might have lost Katie for good. His heart felt bludgeoned.

Of course, Jack felt bad.

Still, this was Billy. And Jack's chance to twist the knife. Everyone but Billy knew he and Katie would eventually reunite. But Billy dished out so much garbage on the guys that Jack couldn't resist turning that blade to the right and left, drawing a little blood. "What's with you? Catamaran Katie take another vacation?"

Billy's face held steady, but Jack took joy in knowing stifling a reaction challenged him.

"Cut it out, Jack." The chief rubbed his nose with a handkerchief and shook his big head. "Two juvenile delinquents. That's what I've got myself here. Two snot-nosed kids playing detectives."

Billy Mack didn't flinch. He hesitated and continued, "As I was saying, not much in the line of dating for any of the women. The one with three kids is busy. The other two, dull and boring, so say friends and neighbors. All three boys attended different preschools, different day cares. No connections identified."

The thing about Billy was, he had an exceptional detective eye for detail. Again, Jack tempted himself with telling him about the note.

"Except the way they were abducted," the chief added, "and the notes."

"Yes, the abductions were identical. Glass broke, screen popped, chloroform, out the window, and poof they were gone," Billy said. "Which reminds me, Serpico, any note at your sister's house?"

Bang. As quickly as Jack's trust for Billy had slid in, it slid out again.

Glad their backs were turned, Jack cursed the instant sting in his cheeks. He sat helpless as the burning exploded to his temples and chin. He prayed the blush wouldn't betray him.

He thought of yesterday and this morning, and he slid his fingers beneath his sweatpants and jammed a hand into the pocket of his shorts.

He had examined the note a hundred times yesterday, then worked late last night. Slipped out of his shorts long past midnight and stepped back into them this morning, threw sweatpants on top, and took off for the precinct. Hadn't thought of showering.

His fingers felt for the paper, and he shoved the crumbled message farther down into his pocket. "No, no note."

"No time, maybe," the chief responded, stuffing the handkerchief back into his pocket. "What made you scream?"

"No clue." This time he responded honestly. "You react differently when it's your own family."

Feeling the tingle in his cheeks subside, he rose and moved toward Mack and the chief, stood behind them silently contemplating that truth.

"Instincts aren't as sharp when the case is personal." The chief's hands fell behind him. Even his at-ease stance appeared formal, grave.

Jack understood why. They had all witnessed dulled instincts at one time or another. When a co-worker's sister was struck and killed by a drunk driver. When the DOJ came to investigate an officer accepting bribes. When the chief's niece was raped fifteen years ago, and his unrelenting conviction to deliver that rapist into the hands of the DA catapulted him up the ranks to chief.

Jack thought of Lisa, so fragile, and Rachel, so fierce, and stories of the chief's past caged his thoughts. Could he tell the chief about Mikala's name on the note? In a dead stare, Jack focused on the big sheet with the pins and circles and blue-lined streets that spread out in all directions from the three boys' houses, like blood flowing from a heart.

He supposed the map back then had been in the same place as this one. Pins abutting pins. He heard there had been forty-six rapes in all. The case stretched over six years. They couldn't catch the guy. He was too clever for an understaffed investigative division, and the FBI wasn't much help. Then Ben's niece, Ashley, was raped. Number forty-seven. And by the grace of a coworker's sick day, she was the last rape, and Officer Ben Morgan was the next contender for chief.

Jack's eyes refocused on the chief, and he watched him shift his weight and wondered if he was recalling the case, too. Fifteen years was not so long ago. Some wounds mend slowly, and others, never.

The story Jack heard was the city's public relations officer came down with the flu on the day of St. Luke Grade School's "Tribute to Our Police Officers" assembly. The chief at that time needed a fast replacement, and Ben Morgan and his partner had been three blocks away at the Veterans Hospital checking records. The chief called and said they should get their asses over to St. Luke's. He instructed Morgan to spend fifteen minutes saying a few words to the kids and get the hell out.

Morgan's partner at the time later told Jack that Morgan was irate and had glanced intermittently at his watch while delivering the impromptu speech. The entire school applauded when he finished. They handed him a plaque. On the way out, the students formed a line, and he shook their hands one by one. His partner followed along behind, remembered elatedly inching toward the big auditorium doors. He wanted the assembly over, too.

They were a few feet from freedom when Officer Morgan's fingers reached for Rachel Callahan, and her hand slipped into his. He stopped. She wouldn't release her grip. That was the moment Ben Morgan's life took a three-hundred-and-sixty-degree turn.

Jack's image of an auditorium filled with cheering students faded slowly into the quietness around him, drawing him back to the present, to the Helen room. He noticed the chief staring back at him. Their eyes locked, and Jack knew the chief, too, was recalling the past—and Rachel. He could almost see her reflection in his eyes—almost.

"Jack." The chief's big hand rose to his face. He rubbed his eyes forcefully, then spoke quietly. "I could ask you if it was Rachel."

Jack broke eye contact, stepped away. He had prepared himself to field questions about Rachel. Why wouldn't the chief ask about her? Unless—

Damn that Billy. He'd worked with him long enough to know. Billy had checked his phone records. No calls had come from Rachel in the night.

"Give us the truth. Who told you to go to your nephew's house?"

Even Billy Mack stood quiet, his eyes cast sheepishly downward, the fun gone from his game.

Everyone teased Jack about his sister-in-law, but truthfully, they all feared what they couldn't understand. Jack, too. Yet, Rachel Callahan being whisked away at age fifteen to some undisclosed governmental intelligence program and coming back not talking gave gravity to her psychic abilities. The real problem, however, the one no one dared mention, was the rumor that Rachel had taken the heat for her little sister.

The humor in the room killed, Jack walked back to his desk and slumped onto the hard seat. He rubbed his temples with his fingers, and then moved his hands to the back of his neck and massaged the mushrooming kinks.

Lying went against his grain, but he could lie a second time if he thought avoiding the truth would protect his daughter. He had tested high in protective instincts on that human resources test years ago, and he supposed the results were accurate because he'd saved his first partner's life and took a bullet for his second. Word also circulated that he was the most honest soldier and cop to come out of Erie. Sure, once he'd lied to save his partner's behind, but that was back when his gun holster's stiff leather squeaked like only a rookie cop's could. He'd never lied again, until now.

He let his hands slide away from his neck. Could he protect his daughter alone? He must.

Lying to the chief and Mack would haunt him. These two men had his back. He could trust them with his life.

But not his daughter's.

He decided on brevity and caution. He could lie altogether, but they'd never believe him, so he'd sacrifice the safer person—Lisa.

He exhaled an intentional sigh. "No, not Rachel," he said, knowing those three words implicated his wife.

The chief took a step and leaned his backside against a desk. Billy Mack closed his eyes for one brief moment, let out a sigh, and headed toward the door.

"Houston, we have a problem," Billy said, then shot Jack a stare that spoke to him: *You're in trouble now. Sorry, man.*

Billy grabbed a toothpick from a box on a desk near the door and said, "A big problem." Then he left the Helen room.

Jack turned and studied the chief. The chief wiped his face with his big hands again, raised his eyebrows, and tilted his head.

"Go home and talk to your wife, Jack," he said, then his big legs carried him across the room.

The click of the door locking behind him rang in Jack's ears. Eventually, the sound ceased, and Jack relaxed into his seat. He was safe for now, but safe from whom?

The insulated walls around him no longer seemed impenetrable.

7 The perpetrator

Sixteen miles south of the Helen room's door, in a broken-down, two-story home, a light in a basement window turned on: a headlamp. The man there knew no one had been near that house in over a year. Thick foliage sprouted and twisted in a tangled mess along the street and down two sides of the property all the way back to the woods behind the home. That barbed-wire-like scramble stretched as close as ten feet to the sagging front and side porches, making reaching the home nearly impossible.

Out back, giant hogweed and hemlock with waxy purple stems inched even closer. Behind those menaces, a purgatory of intertwined trees crawled a mile downhill to Elk Creek. Hidden within that mile, a one-acre plot of dry land, cleared by its owner two decades ago, could not have been more secluded than an island in the Pacific Ocean. Only God could see that patch of earth. Like a blink of an eye, even pilots of low-flying planes missed the field with its rusty old tractor caught in its middle, like a diseased iris.

Due to a heavily trod deer path wide enough for a man to skirt through, that thirty-five-year-old tractor had received new parts last spring and was fired up late summer. No one heard its sputtering engine. An eighty-year-old man owned the acreage on both sides of the creek behind the property. His hearing wasn't as good as in old times, and he certainly didn't venture beyond the creek these days.

The man in the house, in coveralls and head gear, aimed his light at the old cedar chest, fidgeted with its lock, and lifted its lid.

Yes, this certainly had been a grand find.

He would have killed for a hideaway like this in his youth. A place far from Mother, school, kids, and church.

He sifted through the contents of the chest, thinking about his childhood. He felt for the utility shovel, grabbed the handle, yanked, leaned its tip on the floor, and bent at the waist, slouching his shoulders. The memories of bullying still taunted him. He took a breath, reminding himself that was long ago. Then he stood straight and tossed the shovel in his bag.

As bad as they were, the boys who teased him and the girls who laughed at him hadn't been his worst cross to bear. As a child, he had been molested. Cornered in the church vestibule. Coaxed into the Monsignor's office and coerced into the private bathroom by a trusted church lector. A single old man, retired teacher, had abused him more times than Satan was mentioned in the Bible.

An educator, go figure.

He wondered how many others the old geezer had preyed upon.

When he told the Monsignor about the pederast, he received a paddling—with a belt. When he told his mother, she forced him to suck on a bar of soap and then sent him to his room for a week. Both called him a liar. The old man continued to drag him into that back bathroom until he finally lifted a push dagger from a gun shop in town—no one could catch him back then. He supposed the owner had just been happy he hadn't taken a pistol, because he barely ran after him.

The abuse stopped after one flash of that dagger when the man's pants were around his ankles. He assumed the man had moved on to another victim. However, the ceasing of abuse for him came much too late. His hatred had been cast, and his festering, lifelong abhorrence of Mother and repugnance of religion had given him the whole kidnapping idea months ago.

That and the voices.

But now he had to worry about that damn girl.

Protect my face.

And his plans had been so simple in the beginning.

First, he would start a rumor that the proposed perpetrator, an abductor of young boys, had been molested by a priest as a child.

No harm there.

He would say the perpetrator told him in confidence during their days in the desert.

Easy enough.

He had already gathered the life histories of the other two Project Dream male transmitters—every Tom, Dick, and Harry that ever read scripture or led the flock at their churches. The discovery came as a lucky research break. Both men had attended only one Catholic grade school.

Second, he would provide notes with religious messages. The voices had planted that seed as well. Plus, he fancied old books and movies where killers hinted at Bible connections.

And third, he'd abduct boys living with their mothers. Women with no man to flash their apple in front of. Catholics, of course.

Oh, how I hate mothers, religion.

Yes, this was a notorious find—this home of an Oklahoma-born farmer who had twice lost everything to tornados. This treasure had closed all the loose ends.

His one holdup—well, other than the girl—was that he still debated if he could finger two people in his plan, a sort of co-conspirator scheme, because honestly, they had both made his life a living hell. His hatred fell equally upon them. Actually, upon all three of them if he counted Rachel.

Yet, the voices had discouraged him from going in that direction.

Take one down.

He removed the body bag, bottle of chloroform, and pistol from the trunk, stuffing them forcefully into his duffle bag. He hoped John weighed less than Luke. Hauling that Luke kid through the shrub and out to the storm cellar had been rough.

And the tow would be worse when he was forced to drag a bum through the mess. He'd have to sickle through the path once more for a man, widen the opening a bit.

He glanced at his pant legs, still mucked up by the stream. Dragging Marky Blakley out of this place and dumping his body elsewhere had been an ordeal.

He raised his eyes to the ceiling and thought about the boy.

Unfortunate.

He slipped a hand into a coverall pocket, felt for his keys, and removed the little flashlight keychain. Without looking down, he aimed the light at the ceiling and turned the switch on. Then off. Then on and off again. With his headlamp and the flashlight, he could see the floorboards and the pointy little nails from the hardwood floors that poked through. The house must have been lovely once. Fine and sturdy until neglect ravished it. The owners probably built a house somewhere else. Couldn't manage them both, he supposed.

He flicked the light off and sighed. The answer was clear. One man was an easier task than two.

He conceded, decided which one. He supposed he knew all along who he would choose in the end. The person who had highlighted so many passages in his Bible would be the most believable.

Would that be Rachel's choice? Of course, he knew who she would choose.

She has no idea who I really am.

He slammed the lid of the trunk, clicked the lock, bent, and zipped the duffle bag. He hoisted the sack up, fumbled with the straps, bouncing them just enough to hear a slight jangle from the items inside, and then he laughed.

No idea at all.

His guffaw heightened and then ebbed into a long subsiding whine. He aimed his headlight to the corner of the cellar by the stairs. Four stunned mice scurried away. One hesitated in fear, for a moment, before following the others.

Probably the female.

He reached up and clicked off the light. Moving in the dark reminded him of his nights under the stars—and Rachel.

I really don't hate her now, do I? Her soft skin and amber eyes would entice Satan himself to do good.

Once again, sadness rushed him, but he erased the feeling, stacked the molecules in his brain to build a wall like Project Dream had taught him to do.

"Protect my face from the girl," he whispered, and he stepped gingerly as he climbed the stairs, avoiding the holes and rotted spots despite his blindness.

8 Jack

Off-duty cops leaned elbow to bar, sandwiching themselves among fellow officers sitting on high barstools. Guinness bottles and empty shepherd's pie plates sat on the thick, dark bar in front of them. Molly Branigan's, a stone's throw from City Hall and long the watering hole of Erie's finest, was trimmed in dark paneling and dotted with Irish memorabilia shipped straight from the Emerald Isle itself. The pub was a good place to cool down at in summer and warm up in during winter, just loud enough to block thoughts of the work day. The cops needed Molly as much as she needed their money.

He wasn't much of a drinker, but Jack threw back a shot of Jameson that evening and chased the toss with the daily special, a Killian's Irish Red. The guys tried forcing a Guinness on him, but he let the stout sit on the bar. Eventually, Billy Mack leaned in and grabbed it. For a while, the music blaring from the juke box and the jeers bouncing back and forth between cops distracted him.

The words and phrases he planned to use when he talked to Lisa, slipped in and out of his thoughts. He couldn't make them right. So he stayed longer than originally intended, left after eleven, and by the time he slipped his sneakers off and set them on the matt by the front door in his living room, Lisa was asleep on the couch.

He stood watching her as she slept, loved how she had curled into a little ball. He felt his lips turn upward helplessly as he lay his keys quietly on top of the *Parent* magazine on the coffee table. That was Lisa—always honing her mothering skills. Even in troubled waters.

She was so tiny she fit on half the couch, her frame so thin that when he snuck up behind her while she was doing her hair or making dinner, he could fit his two big hands almost completely around her twenty-two-inch waist. He sat down slowly on the end of the couch and set his hand on her hip.

She was even lovelier now than when they first met. Her blond hair, blue eyes, and slightly-turned-up nose perfect in every photo. Little lines around her eyes were fighting their way out now, and he loved those, too. She would grow old gently, like the women in her family before her, though she was kinder, more fragile, than the other Callahan women. She was a fighter when she had to be, defender of the weak, lover of the poor, hard-working, and a fantastic mother. Yet, when the lights went out, she was afraid of her own shadow, her skin so thin and soft he loved to keep his hand on her all night long. Protecting her. Saving her from her dreams.

He kissed her forehead, his lips barely grazing her, then he leaned back on the couch and remembered the first time he saw her.

"Officer," she had said, tapping him on the shoulder. Mikala's tap always reminded him of that first time Lisa caught his attention. "This is going to sound terribly insane."

He hesitated, then said, "What's that, Ma'am?"

Immediately, he thought, Ma'am? Did I just call her Ma'am? She was his age and drop-dead beautiful, her blond hair, long and tousled. A blue scarf swirled around her thin neck. His second thought was that he had never seen such sexy blue eyes.

"You should go out back." She drew the scarf close to her face, and her breath sent frost spewing into the cold air. Her eyes glanced in both directions and then came back to him. She bit her lip. "Check the garbage bin."

"We already did, Ma'am, I mean, Miss," he stammered.

"Do it again." All insecurities left her mien, and something in her voice drew his attention from her face to her words.

"We checked there this morning and again this afternoon."

"You must do it again." Her eyes turned icy blue.

Just then, a voice came over his shoulder mic. A summons from the chief to head back to the station.

"I'm sorry, I have to go," he said.

She grabbed his arm mightily. He remembered looking at her hand to make sure the grip was hers.

"No." She squeezed his arm tighter, her intention clear. She wasn't going to let him leave. "You need to check again. He came back. Snuck her through the alley."

"Who came back?"

"The boy."

"Did you see him?"

"No, but you must go check again," she said, her eyes fixed and glassy. "She's still breathing."

What happened next he recalled only as a blur. The teenage girl, dumped in the garbage bin by a boyfriend who thought she was dead, was rushed to intensive care and survived. Down at the police station, Chief Morgan asked what made him check the bin a third time.

"A girl," he answered. Then he explained what happened.

"Did she work there or was she possibly a relative?"

"No, she came out of nowhere. Never saw her before."

The chief spoke softly. "A tall girl? Brown hair? Attractive?"

Billy Mack stepped closer and asked, "Rachel Callahan? Is she home?"

"I don't know her name," Jack answered, "but no, she was blonde, big blue eyes. And, yes, nice looking."

"Shit," the chief said. Then no more talk. The silence became uncomfortable.

Finally, Jack spoke. "What's wrong? Should I find her? Bring her in?"

"No." The chief spit tobacco into a Styrofoam cup, leaned, and tossed the cup into a waste can. "No, need."

"Who is she?" Jack asked.

"Lisa Callahan," the chief said, then straightened his cap and left the precinct.

Jack glanced at Billy Mack, and Mack's eyes twinkled. "You just met a witch, Jack. Don't fall under her spell."

But he had already fallen. He took her to dinner three days later, and within three months, he was spending every day with her. Never in a million years had he thought he would give up friends and bar-hopping for a girl. But he had.

"Jack? You're home?" Lisa's voice lured his thoughts back into the room.

"Where were you?" She wiped her eyes and sat up lethargically. "I called after I put the kids to bed. I must have fallen asleep."

"Sorry. I stopped to have a drink with the guys for once. Bad day. I stayed longer than I should have. I knew you weren't home. Geoff called. He's down the street in a cruiser. He's watching our house—along with Janice's. He said you got home a little after ten. How's Mikala?"

She folded her legs Indian style on the couch and yawned. "You know she's fine. Nothing ever affects her. She's like Rachel."

He picked up a piece of her blond hair and let go, then he picked the strands up again, sifting them through his fingers. He didn't know how to tell her.

"Janice is still frantic," she said, yawning and placing a hand on his leg.

"I know. She had to come down to the station today. She and Danny are staying with my mom."

"That's what she said." She lifted her hand and placed her arm around his shoulder. Instantly, he lay down in her lap and stared up at the ceiling.

"This may resurrect them, you know." Her hand fell softly on his chest.

"Who?"

"Janice and Steve. He came over here this afternoon crying like a baby. Said he wanted to move back home, but Janice said no."

"She'll change her mind," he said, lifting his hand to hers and folding his fingers into hers.

"She will. They still love each other." She hesitated, squeezed his hand. "It's sad that it takes a catastrophe for people to realize what's important in life."

"A near catastrophe," he corrected.

"Yes, thank God." She let go of his hand and stroked his chest subconsciously. "You know I hate that Mikala has this gift, but just this once, I said a prayer of thanks."

"Yeah," he said, closing his eyes and enjoying the last few strokes of her affection, "about that gift."

Instantly, he felt her legs go rigid beneath him. She stopped stroking. He continued. He had no choice. "The chief asked me to talk to you."

She stood so abruptly he nearly tumbled off the couch.

"What do you mean he asked you to talk to me?"

"Quiet, calm down."

"Please tell me you didn't say anything?"

"No, no," he said, jumping up and placing his hands on her forearms. "This isn't about Mikala. He didn't mean her."

"No one can know about her," she yelled, her eyes wandering. "They'll take her away. Like Rachel. They can't ever know, Jack. Never!"

"No, they won't, Lisa. That project has been over for years."

"Are you kidding me? You don't know that. You don't know anything more about what projects the American government has than I do, so don't pretend to."

"Lisa, all that is over."

"With Trump? You think now that Trump is the president he isn't going to bring this project back when he hears how successful it was? He's just crazy enough to do that, Jack. Resurrect the whole Project Dream."

"Shhhh. Quiet. You'll wake the kids." He put his arms around her and drew her into his chest, trying to comfort her. He didn't want her to talk. He hadn't swept the house in well over a week. She shoved him away.

"This is why I told you not to involve her." She began pacing. "This is what we talked about after that first time, her first dream. You promised, Jack. You said we would never tell anyone."

He jerked her in closely, sternly, and put a finger against her lips. "It's all right, baby. Mikala's not in trouble."

"But if the chief knows, then it's over," she said, her voice lowering. "I can't go through this. They can't take her from me. I'll leave, Jack. I'll go to Canada or Mexico or some god-forsaken island where no one will find us."

"Calm down, it's not what you think."

"Then what? Why else would the chief ask you to talk to me?"

"He thinks." He paused to lay his lips against her ear. "He thinks it's you."

They moved apart. Their eyes locked and neither spoke another word.

A still and quiet dread crept into the air of their little house. The feeling took on a thick, lifelike existence, swirling around them and ascending the stairs.

On the second floor, Mikala stood in the hallway clad in pink pajamas and puppy slippers, her back pressed against the wall. When the dreadful feeling reached her, she lifted the stuffed animal she held in her hands up to her chin and hugged it tightly. Then she tiptoed back into her room, stepped out of her slippers, lifted her blankets, and slipped into bed.

"I don't know if Mama's going to let me help you, Marky," she whispered in the still room.

9 The boys

They learned quickly not to cry when Monster Man came. If they did, he took down the thick leather strap that hung on the wall directly across from them and heaved one mighty slap toward their chained feet. Mostly, they scurried away in time, and the whip landed in the dirt. Once, the end caught the back of Marky's heel, but Matt and Luke never felt the whip's sting.

The boys also learned, early on, not to eat and drink everything as soon as the bad man left because sometimes he didn't return for days. So they spaced out their meals—rationing, Matt's Daddy used to say. He did that during the war.

One dull lightbulb hung from a wire halfway up the wall behind them, but hardly cast enough light to help them see much. Mostly, the soft glow kept the rats and mice away. Their eyes adjusted to the dark, but Matt was afraid they'd never be able to tell the policeman—when he came to rescue them—what Monster Man looked like because of the ugly mask he wore.

Matt couldn't decide how tall he was, either. Maybe a little taller than Daddy. And he didn't see any distinguishing marks. Momma said the boy who stole her purse downtown at the children's library had a distinguishing mark on his arm—a skeleton head. But Matt didn't know if Monster Man had a skeleton head on his arm because he covered all his skin with clothes and gloves. When he set the jugs down, sometimes Matt could see black hair on white skin peeking between his glove and sleeve, but nothing more.

Whenever Monster Man came, Matt tried to do what Momma said to do when the scary wolves came on the screen at the movie she took him to see last summer—shut his eyes tight and not look. He tried hard to be quiet, too, because Mommy said people at church liked quiet little boys. But Monster Man didn't like little boys no matter how quiet and good they were.

He missed Mommy. He hoped she got there soon. But he didn't know if she would ever be able to find him in this dark, dark place.

Mommy loved him to the moon and back, but she couldn't see underground. And he thought he might be in a hole somewhere. He and Luke and Marky—before Marky went to heaven—could make out the wobbly wooden ladder at the other end of the room. An oubliette, the man called their room, but none of them knew what that was. A basement maybe, Marky had said. But Matt didn't think he was in a basement because as soon as Monster Man entered, a cold breeze hit them. And after he left, he heard a lock click and then dirt, or grass, or leaves being tossed on top of the flat door that fit into the ceiling.

Matt had grown accustomed to Monster Man coming with food. This time when he heard the door squeak open, he felt relief laced with fear. Monster Man had been gone the longest ever. A week maybe? Matt had no sense of time with no light of day, but he knew lots of days had passed because he and Luke had run out of water a while ago.

Instinctively, he and Luke withdrew to the far wall as the man's big feet clumped down the steps. Luke huddled sideways against the wall, face down. Matt scooted in front of him, his back against the side of Luke's arm and leg. Even though he was bigger than Matt, Luke was terrible scared. Matt leaned against Luke's trembling limbs and then hugged his own knees with unsteady arms.

Monster Man quickly dropped the food and water jugs on the ground and tossed a big, empty bucket toward the corner where the other potty buckets were. His toss clanged pail against pail, tipping one over. Urine spilled out, seeped into the dirt floor, and formed a small puddle on top of the ground. The man wiped his nose, swore, and swooped a big, black-gloved hand toward Matt, yanking him away from Luke. Matt frantically reached his arms toward Luke, as if his friend could help. Luke cowered against the wall, eyes shut, hands cupping ears.

"Sit still." The man spit words through clenched teeth, and Matt strained to stop his tremors.

He knew not to cry or whimper, but the man's big hand around his wrist terrified him. Helplessly, he let a sob escape. The man released his grip and slapped him with the back of his hand, sending his face into the dirt. Then he dragged Matt toward him by a leg and plucked scissors from a green bag. Matt nearly lost consciousness from the tingling that numbed the trunk of his body and rushed down his arms and legs and up his neck to his head. Matt was sure he would have wet himself like Luke always did when Monster Man neared them, but Matt hadn't had anything to drink in days.

The man stepped toward him, yanked him by his frayed shirt, ripping the collar, and Matt's body stiffened with a paralyzing fear as he watched the scissors come at him. He closed his eyes and waited for the pain. He heard metal scrape metal and then felt his body smack the ground. For a moment he wondered if he was dead. His cheek was lodged in the dirt and his lips tasted of mud. He opened his eyes and watched two big legs ascend the stairs.

Monster Man had merely cut off a piece of his hair.

When the door closed and the sounds of rubble being shoveled on top of the door ceased, Matt lay still, but Luke lifted his head and slowly crawled toward the food. Usually, the chains on their legs just barely allowed them to reach their meager ration. Luke's chains were a bit shorter than Matt's. Luke inched forward as far as his shackles permitted and then stretched his arms out but couldn't touch a morsel. He gazed toward Matt, the terror in his eyes betraying his desperate thought: what would he do if Matt was dead?

Matt understood the fear in Luke's eyes. They had both watched Marky die.

Slowly, painfully, Matt pushed himself upward and scooted his butt along the ground until he reached the water. He lugged one jug toward him, careful not to spill a drop. He tilted the container toward his lips and drank, then he turned and tipped the vessel for Luke to drink.

"Remember," he whispered, "just a little, this time."

10 Mikala

Children's shouts and squeals mixed with bus-number announcements over loud speakers. The happy chaos of dismissal time echoed down the long hallway outside the open classroom door with the caterpillars and lady bugs flaunting children's names. Inside, Mikala Daly straightened the last seat in the last row, stood back, and nodded proudly at her alignment job. Outside the classroom windows that stretched along one entire wall, big yellow buses inched forward as the roar of one grinding bus engine escalated and its wheels carried children away.

Mikala slipped her arms through her jacket sleeves, bounced her backpack onto one shoulder, and hurried up the center aisle.

"Who's picking you up today, Mikala?" Mrs. Shield sat behind the big desk, holding her red pen. She touched the tip of the pen in front of each of ten numbers on every spelling test she graded, occasionally placing a big X in front of a number and correcting a word. Then she wrote a letter at the top of the page along with a smiley face—sometimes—before turning the test over into her finished pile and beginning again.

"My aunt Rachel."

Mrs. Shield stopped dotting the test in front of her. She rested her forearm on the edge of her desk and glanced up.

"Tell her I said hello. I'm not sure you know this, but your aunt Rachel and I went to grade school together."

"Yes, I know."

"I can walk you out and wait with you if you'd like."

"No, thank you, Mrs. Shield. Mr. Foley is going to wait with me if my mom or aunt are late," she said, dropping her backpack onto the floor, reaching into a side pocket, and removing one of two small cases.

Her classmates had long left the tidy little room with its perfectly-aligned alphabet cards adhered above the front wall's poster-dappled marker board that boasted words, math equations, and homework assignments. Only Mikala and her teacher remained. Mrs. Shield grinned behind her neat gray desk that sported colorful workbooks, penguin pencil holders, and an oversized purse hugging one corner.

"Mr. Foley is a wonderful security guard."

"Yes, he is. I like Mr. Foley." Mikala nodded quickly and felt two streams of hair brush gently against her neck. She lifted one hand and tapped the matching pink bows on top of each pigtail, just to be sure she hadn't lost them. So Momma wouldn't be mad at her for losing another. Then she scratched the back of her neck and continued. "I want to give you something before I leave. For your baby."

She lifted the fingers of her other hand and slid a blue teething ring in a clear plastic container across the desk. She had an exact duplicate tucked away in her backpack. Both were tied with blue ribbons, one for Mrs. Shield and one for her aunt Rachel. She had hoped to hold her aunt's a little longer, but Mrs. Shield needed hers now. Her face hadn't seemed as pretty lately, her lips always sagging toward the ground. So yesterday Mikala had decided to give Mrs. Shield the present.

She withdrew her hand and waited for Mrs. Shield to examine the package with the silky ribbon. Her brothers had received so many gifts when they were born that two, perfectly-good, blue pacifiers had gone untouched. She dug them out of her brothers' closet, found blue ribbon, and fashioned the best little bows her hands were capable of crafting. She couldn't wait to give each of them their gifts.

Of course, she knew Mrs. Shield would never be able to keep the gift a secret, and that would force her to give Aunt Rachel her gift sooner than she wanted.

"My brothers never used this one," Mikala said, gaily. "So I thought you could give it to your baby. Isn't it just perfect, Mrs. Shield?"

She stood at attention. Her tongue repeatedly clicked the one crooked tooth in her mouth crying to be pulled. She could tell from the look on Mrs. Shield's face she had done the right thing. She stopped playing with her tooth and smiled, intentionally making her expression brilliant.

"I'm not sure what you're talking about," Mrs. Shield said slowly, articulately, like when she gave instructions for a test. "You have…a gift…for whom?"

"The baby," Mikala responded, nodding her head confidently. "In your belly. Colin. The gift is for Colin. Aren't you naming your baby after Mr. Shield?"

*****

Elizabeth Shield was taken aback. At a loss for words, again. This wasn't the first time she didn't know how to respond to Mikala Daly, and more than likely, this time wouldn't be the last. That child stumped lots of teachers with her tender-voiced truths, some that should not touch a child's mind. Her resemblance to her mother and aunt grew stronger with each passing day.

But this? Undeniably, Mikala's most shocking revelation.

Elizabeth hadn't told a soul she suspected she was pregnant, not even her husband. They'd been trying for over two years, but an infertility problem fought them. She'd almost given up hope.

Then last week she'd missed her period. She thought her lateness a fluke. But this morning she completed the pregnancy test after her husband left for work. When the little stick showed two lines, she grabbed the sink and held on tight until the woozy feeling passed. Instant euphoria swept across her. She had to calm herself down and refrain from calling Colin and telling him. Frightened that the test might be inaccurate, she took another. The two lines persisted. Pregnant. She thought she'd repeat the test in a day or two before telling him. To be sure.

But now Mikala came with a baby gift. Mikala Daly. Daughter of Lisa Callahan Daly, niece of Rachel Callahan Kennedy. Tears filled her eyes. "My God," she whispered, "I'm having a baby."

Her eyes rose to the package, to the blue ribbon. When had Mikala looped the bow around her gift? Early this morning? Last night? The fact dawned on her that Mikala may have known her dream of having a little boy and naming him after his father would come true before she herself knew she was pregnant.

"It's okay. My brothers never used it. See." Mikala pointed to the package's unbroken seal and the $2.99 tag. "The price sticker is still on it."

"Why, thank you, Mikala," she said, reminding herself to breathe. "The gift is lovely."

Elizabeth watched Mikala pick her backpack off the floor, slip her arms into the straps, and secure the sack onto her back with a wiggle. As Mikala turned to leave, the knapsack knocked Elizabeth's purse off the desk, and items spilled to the floor, rolling in every direction. Breathless and woozy, Elizabeth simply watched as Mikala bent down and quickly scooped up the keys, lipstick, inhalers, vitamin bottle, and other contents that rolled to and fro.

"Sorry, Mrs. Shield," Mikala said as she stood up and struggled to push things back inside the handbag. "My mom says I'm clumsy."

"Oh, no, you're fine, Mikala," she said, still sitting, her head and thoughts spinning.

When Mikala handed her the purse, Elizabeth couldn't resist the temptation to pull Mikala close and hug her affectionately. She wasn't supposed to do that these days. Teachers shouldn't be hugging students, but she simply couldn't help herself.

Mikala stood straight as a pencil, smiled affectionately, and then bounced happily toward the door. As she skipped off, Elizabeth watched the cartoon characters on the back of her backpack hop away, and the thought occurred to her that Mikala may tell someone about the pregnancy before her family knew. She opened her lips to call to her but before she said anything, Mikala stopped and turned back in the doorway.

"Babies are gifts," she said, then hesitated. "It's okay, Mrs. Shield. I won't tell anyone."

She flashed a delicate little smile that made Elizabeth's heart flutter. She loved that little girl. All the teachers did. There was something different, wonderful, and blessed about the child with the keen insights. She smiled back and winked at Mikala.

"I won't tell either," she said, then reached into her bag and felt for her cell phone.

Mikala's smile widened. She waved, turned, and darted from the room.

"No running," Mrs. Shield called loudly.

"Yes, Mrs. Shield," echoed back at her from halfway down the hall. "Is skipping okay?"

"Skipping?" Elizabeth's voice cracked. "Today, I think skipping is fine."

She lifted her phone with sweaty fingers, setting a hand firmly on the desk to steady herself. She listened as Mikala's soft skips rebounded off the hallway walls and faded. She took a deep breath and wiped the tears off her cheeks. Then she punched in Colin's number, hands shaking. Tears blurred her vision as she counted the rings.

"Pick up, pick up." Her fingers moved to her mouth to steady her trembling lips. When she heard the click, she whispered his name before he answered.

"Colin?"

"What's up, Lizzy?"

She broke down. She could barely speak.

"Lizzy? Is something wrong?"

"No, nothing's wrong." She sobbed. "Everything is wonderful."

"Lizzy, are you crying? What is it?"

"I'm pregnant," she whimpered. "And it's a boy. We are having a boy, Colin. You're going to be a dad." Her voice faded, became almost melodious. "I'm going to be a mother."

*****

Outside on the school's front steps, Mikala stopped and thought about just that. Mrs. Shield being a mother and how blessed baby Colin would be. She loved Mrs. Shield, even if she couldn't keep a secret.

Sometimes, you had to do what was right—like putting dishes in the dishwasher or letting Cousin Danny sit in your seat at the dinner table next to your brothers. Sometimes, you had to give instead of take, her mom said.

She glanced toward the school's circular driveway and waved to Mr. Foley. Then she spotted her aunt Rachel's car. Her aunt hovered over her cell phone, eyes downward. Mikala threw a glance over each shoulder. No one stood close. She opened her hand, examined Mrs. Shield's inhaler lying against her palm, and quickly dropped her backpack on the cement walkway. She unzipped a compartment, tucked the inhaler inside, and replaced the knapsack on her back with one swift swirl of hands and arms.

And sometimes, you had to do the taking to make things right.

She cleared her mind by stacking the molecules in her brain, and then she dashed toward her aunt Rachel's car.

11 Rachel; dreamer #4

Rachel Callahan Kennedy stretched her legs on the couch and reminisced while she waited for her sister. Since age four, she had been protecting Lisa. Born seventeen months apart, Rachel stood a full four inches taller than Lisa all the way back to seventh grade.

That year, she "shot up like a bean stalk," her doctor said. "With legs like a model," the frumpy nurse in white loafers added. She'd spit in the woman's face once when jabbed with a flu shot.

Back then, she may have emanated a soft, sensual appearance but, admittedly, Rachel's core had been anything but model-like. Her roughness surfaced long before her teenage years. People called her a bully as far back as kindergarten.

A sweetheart, they said of Lisa.

They were soft and hard, the sisters. Two arrows pointed in opposite directions on a circle. Lisa was blonde. Rachel, brunette. Lisa was book smart. Rachel, street savvy. In school, Lisa had sat up front with the girls, waving her hand in the air to answer questions and staying after class to help the teacher. Rachel sat in the back with the boys, throwing spitballs and cheating on tests.

As adults, Lisa drew artsy alphabet letters for bulletin boards and helped her own kids with schoolwork. Rachel backstabbed business rivals in boardrooms and hired housekeepers and nannies for the house and Jeffrey.

In her opinion, they were like a charm and a heavy-linked bracelet. Alone they were shiny but distinct. Together, they were brilliant.

Their differences continued with their children. But that's where the switch came. At four years old, Lisa's twin boys led the pack at climbing trees and batting tee-balls, and Mikala's toughness surpassed any other six-year-old's, while Rachel's poor little Jeffrey struggled to breathe in all four seasons, wheezing even on clear, windless days. But she knew his problems were temporary. Long ago, her grandmother predicted she would have two sons. Both would be sickly in childhood, she had said, but mighty by their twenties.

She smiled. Grandma Margaret never led her astray; even in death her prophesies lingered like a steady, silent wind.

"Your sons and Lisa's sons, the four boys, will be good-looking. They'll break hearts around the world." Grandma smiled proudly whenever she spoke of great-grandchildren that she knew she would not live to see. "But Lisa's oldest girl, her firstborn, you'll have to help her with that one. Lisa will struggle with raising her. Oh, how I wish I could be here to watch her grow."

"You can be," Rachel scolded. Even with her grandmother, she liked to throw her weight around. "Eat your fruits and vegetables like Mama told you."

Her grandmother smiled. "Ah Rachel, darling, life moves along like a river, bending and flowing and gaining ground as it winds down the hills and past the valleys. The current grows stronger. Once in a while, you find a nice calm pocket off to the side where you can float along peacefully." Grandma had stopped there and whispered, "Your Mama rests in that swimming hole. She doesn't like to feel the current rushing beneath her." Then she continued, full-voiced, "But you and I, we hurry on by those resting places. We enjoy the sheer excitement of the river float, our limbs adrift in the magic of the water."

Rachel loved the way her grandmother's voice, itself, rose and fell like a river.

"It will be you and Lisa who feel the lift and plummet of the raft and the thrash and power of the magnificent current. I'm old now. I pass my scull to you, to Lisa, and you'll pass it to that girl, the one to come after you, and then to her sister after her. But watch the first girl. See how calm she is on the ride. See her acumen, mental fortitude. I see her in my mind's eye and marvel."

Rachel remembered dragging a ladder out of the garage and into the house, so she could climb the wall bookcase and find that old dictionary. She looked up scull and acumen and fortitude.

Now she felt the corners of her lips turn upward. Dang if Grandma hadn't been right about her great-grandchildren.

She placed a hand on her stomach. She supposed it didn't matter that she was pregnant, and Todd was using again. She could certainly take care of two boys on her own. God knew with the government program she would never want for money, but she did hate Todd bringing cocaine into their house.

Her eyes worked across the room, scanning the imposingly large living area with its designer furniture, fine art, and towering windows. Somewhere, his stash hid waiting. Her gaze wandered from corner to corner then rose to the chilly lofty ceiling. She sighed and reached for fruit, grabbing an apple from the crystal bowl perched on the glass coffee table, which a maid had wiped to pristineness an hour ago. She began tossing the round, plump apple up and down.

With each touch of the fruit to her fingers, she turned their situations over in her mind: Lisa and Jack, her and Todd.

How had she allowed what her grandmother warned her of to come true? Lisa marrying a decent guy, and she, pregnant in the midst of a failed marriage? What happened to childhood' street smarts?

"Flogged by the heat of the desert sun," she said out loud. She stopped tossing and took a big bite, chewing dramatically. She wondered how long she had before Lisa figured out she was pregnant.

This was her third pregnancy. Her first had been in the desert. She had miscarried at five weeks' gestation. The Project Dream doctor called the loss a blessing, but she knew the truth. They had slipped something into her food, forcing an instantaneous abortion. Back then, they tracked every molecule of their beings down to the freckles on their skin.

Thank the Lord she had gone instead of frail, little Lisa. She bit the apple again, chomped, slid a hand beneath her head, and thought about her sister and brother-in-law. How marrying Jack had lessened Lisa's brittleness. Jack was her rock—unlike Todd. Todd crumbled at a trifle of tribulation.

"Your first son's health problems will break your husband," her grandmother had told her. "But you needn't worry. You'll find the right medication, and your son will grow up fine."

So far, Grandma had hit a bull's eye on all accounts. Todd left the room every time Jeffrey cried. He couldn't bear their son's suffering.

A noise grabbed her. She heard the click of wheel against driveway pavers, and she swung her legs over the couch and stood too fast. Blood rushed to her head, and she plopped back down onto the couch, swearing under her breath and waiting for her head to clear.

A minute later, Lisa entered without a knock, and Rachel stood a second time, slower. She felt the heat of her face build, and so she stretched her neck away from her tight collar and lifted her chin. She brushed a tuft of hair behind one ear and hoped the breeze from the overhead fan cooled the fire in her cheeks.

Lisa came to an abrupt halt in the doorway and shot her a wrinkled-faced gaze. Rachel stretched her lips into a smile, trying to camouflage her lightheadedness.

Lisa's purse strap dropped from her shoulder to her wrist. Her purse plunked onto the slate floor.

"Really? Now of all times?" The sweet, soft lines on Lisa's pretty face deepened. "You're pregnant?"

Rachel closed her eyes for a moment, then opened them and formed her lips into a pout.

"Record time. How could you possibly know that? I just found out myself."

"Honestly, Rachel, don't we have enough to worry about?"

"Humph, you needn't worry about me—and be quiet. I don't want Jack to hear. Is he behind you?"

"You were in bed two months with Jeffrey," Lisa whispered. "You need to take it easy this time."

And the river bends.

Jack entered, and both Rachel and Lisa glanced his way. He returned their stares, and when neither said a word, he put his hands out.

"What?"

"Nothing." Rachel snickered.

"I just walked through the door. What could I have done?" He raised his hands in the air and then thrust them downward into the pockets of his hoodie. His two fists bulged in front. His head bobbed in bewilderment. "Already? You guys are annoyed with me?"

Rachel stifled a laugh and headed toward the kitchen, Lisa's soft step and Jack's heavy heel tapping behind her.

"Don't worry. It's not you, Jack." She passed the breakfast bar and stepped down into the sunroom.

"Then what? You're annoyed with each other?" He glanced toward Lisa but seemed comforted.

"Something like that," Lisa responded, and as she passed the glass entry table, Rachel watched her sweep up a clothing catalogue and begin flipping pages. She snubbed Rachel's gaze and paced to the center of the room.

Jack shook his head. "I hate the way I feel I've missed half the conversation when I'm with you two."

"This time you literally did." Rachel plopped into a low, plush armchair, and stretched her elbows out on the armrests. "Your wife thinks she's my mother."

Lisa paused her page turning and shot her a nasty look. Rachel scrunched her face and tossed it back. Lisa tucked her chin, shook her head, and continued strolling languidly across the sunroom.

She stepped gingerly onto an ivory area rug, abutting a black brocade sofa, and ten unblemished cottage windows drew the fall colors inside around her. The light called attention to the furniture's little pink and brown flowers and cast mullion shadows on the surrounding china-white walls.

The room, with its fine glass, was an addition to an already lavish house. Todd had insisted on spending last year's bonus on the Florida room Rachel dreamed of. She read there in the evening, watched the tiger lilies bloom through the glass last summer, and now the flakes fall as autumn approached winter. The room's appeal never dulled.

Rachel's gaze settled on Lisa again. She liked how the light fell through the window and framed her sister's small stature. She thought Lisa more fitting for the home's exquisiteness. Her soft blond hair, cut two inches below shoulder length now, swayed with every move she made, and her baby blues bobbed around the room in observant regard. She watched Lisa tilt her head and raise her eyes to the clerestory, not a morsel of envy in her.

"Well, I'll say this, it's beautiful out here. Aren't you glad you talked Todd into adding on instead of moving?" She lowered her eyes, and her chastisement resurfaced. "Now?"

Snap, Rachel thought, the brief, beautiful moment dashed.

"Yes, Lisa. The move would have been a struggle—now." She raised an eyebrow and, for Jack's benefit, added, "Jeffrey being so little and all."

Lisa's face softened.

"How's his asthma, by the way? I almost forgot about it. You haven't mentioned any episodes lately."

"He's good. Great, actually. The doctors at the Cleveland Clinic found the right medication for him."

"What a relief."

"You can say that again." Rachel stood slowly and waved a hand. "And that reminds me. Come outside. I want to show you our new stepping-stone with Jeffrey's handprint. You may want to make one for Mikala and the boys."

In the yard, the first autumn snowflakes drifted lazily downward and disappeared into the long, faded green grass. When their feet hit the edge of the flower garden, Rachel turned toward her sister.

"My battery died." She crossed her arms and lifting her shoulders to warm her bare neck. "So we have to talk out here."

"Your frequency finder? I thought you had two?" Jack snapped.

"Three. One I can't find, one is broken, and my wireless detector needs batteries."

"Rachel." As usual, Jack appeared overly concerned. "You need to keep up on checking your house."

His tone held a frantic quality she didn't like. She tightened her lips.

Years before, she had begun using radio frequency finders to search for bugs in her house. Even when those finders shed no proof that the American government monitored her, she still took important conversations to the yard. Voice recorders, cameras, and microphones could go undetected in high ceilings.

Still, no need for Jack to alarm Lisa.

"No big deal, Jack."

"Yes, it is a big deal."

She examined his seriousness.

"Okay, so what's this really about? I know you too well to think you stopped by—both of you—for no reason."

Lisa and Jack swapped glances, an exchange that made her muscles tighten. "What's wrong? Is this about the break-in? Janice and Danny? I thought you said they were okay."

"They are." Rachel watched Lisa's mien stiffen, too. "But the chief is asking questions."

"Ben?" Rachel filled her mouth with air, cheeks puffing, then exhaled a heavy burst. "I was afraid of that. Does he think it's me?"

"No." Lisa shook her head.

"They don't think it's me?"

"No, not you."

Rachel dropped her chin and crowded her lips onto one side of her mouth. In the next few silent seconds, Lisa's childhood nightmares and panic attacks flooded her mind. She righted her head and spit words through clenched teeth. "You? He thinks it's you?"

"You have to stop being so overprotective of me."

"You can't handle this, and you know you can't. Tell him it's me. Ben and I go way back. He'll believe it."

"We can't." Jack stepped between them. "I already admitted it wasn't you."

Rachel unfolded her arms and fixed the palms of her hands on her hips.

"Just one time, Jack. Just once, couldn't you tell a frickin' lie? Who are you? George Washington?"

"Listen, Lisa's not as fragile as you think. She's come a long way since she started seeing Dr. Jansen."

"Well, correct me if I'm wrong, but she finished counseling months ago. I'm not having her slip back into an asthmatic attack—"

"I haven't had asthma since I was little, Ra—"

"Well, then a panic attack, or worse." Rachel peered at Lisa nastily and then sent a more vicious glare toward Jack. "I want you to march back into that station and tell Ben I'm the one who told you there was someone breaking into Janice's house." She realized she was shouting and lowered her voice. "You need to give the performance of a lifetime because he's going to call you on it. What the hell were you thinking?"

"You think he's stupid?" Jack's brows arched. "He'll know it's not you. He'll talk to Lisa himself, and you know she's a terrible liar."

"You make sure he doesn't. I'll go down to City Hall myself and tell him it's me." Rachel pointed a finger, stepped toward Jack, and jabbed him in the chest. "Do it."

"Stop!" Lisa grabbed each of their arms and separated them. "Stop talking about me as if I'm not here. I don't have panic attacks anymore, Rachel, and I can lie better than you know, Jack. Don't think I can't."

Lisa shoved them and stepped away, her cheeks a fiery red.

"Lisa—" Rachel readied for battle, but before she said more, a glimmer of sadness surfaced in Lisa's eyes, and she hesitated.

She could forever handle abating Lisa's fears, but never in her life could she bear Lisa's disappointment or hurt. Instantly, her heart wrenched. But before she said more, the muffled hum of a garage door rolling over track grabbed her, and she glanced toward the house, abruptly.

"Todd is home," she told them, then turned toward her sister and softened her voice. "We can talk later. Sorry, Lis. Really, I am."

Lisa made a forget-it gesture with her hand, but she avoided eye contact.

"I worry about you." Rachel stepped toward her and touched the side of her arm tenderly. "I'm sorry. I wouldn't hurt you for the world."

Lisa relaxed her shoulders, and a softness fell across her, too. "It's my own doing. I used to hide behind that towering shadow of yours."

"Not so towering." Rachel shrugged. "Believe me."

"Well, I abused it. Your strength."

"I was stubborn."

"You still are," Lisa said, her eyes widening. "But I could never stay mad at you. Not then, not now. I know you'd sacrifice your life for me. In some ways, you already have."

Rachel stretched her arms around Lisa and hugged her. "Let's talk when I get back."

"When you get back?" Jack leaned toward her and talked into her ear as if Todd had already invaded their little meeting, and he didn't want him to hear.

"I'll be in Columbus for training this weekend. I leave in the morning. I'll be home Monday evening."

"Okay, but listen." Jack inched closer, crowding her space. "Don't mention a word of this to Todd."

Rachel released Lisa and moved toward the house. When Jack reached in front of her to open the door, he gestured toward the garage with his head. "The less he knows, the better."

"Agree," Rachel muttered as she slipped past him. "Keep Todd out of this."

In the kitchen, Rachel's eyes focused on the door to the pantry that led to the garage. Its brass doorknob rotated, and Todd entered carrying an envelope and keys. When he saw the three of them staring at him, he quickly stuffed both into a pocket, turned slowly, and shut the door softly, leaning two flat hands against it. He hung there, hesitating long enough to pique Rachel's curiosity and arouse her suspicion before he turned to greet them with that fake, jolly-good-fellow mien she hated.

"So." He forged a smile. "Nice to see the two of you. What's the occasion?"

"No occasion." Jack was curt. "Can't a guy stop to see his sister- and brother-in-law? C'mon Lisa, we have to pick up the kids."

Lisa leaned and hugged Rachel goodbye.

"Thanks for stopping." Rachel raised her voice, trying to coax Jack's unblinking stare away from Todd.

Jack didn't respond, and Rachel nudged him toward the door to prevent him from saying more. She watched him back out of the house, still staring at Todd. He grabbed Lisa's hand when he turned toward the car. Her heart thumped with a twinge of envy as the door closed behind them.

"Why does that guy hate me?" Todd's smile fell off his face, and he pointed a finger at the door. "He never liked me. From the day I met him."

"Don't be paranoid, Todd," she said and trudged toward the living room. She picked up her coffee mug and half-eaten apple and returned to the kitchen. He followed.

"But what did I ever do to him?"

She shrugged, stepped toward the sink, and tossed the apple and coffee in its basin.

"Rachel." Todd stepped behind her and gently placed his hand on her arm. "You didn't tell your brother-in-law about the bank, did you? Because, you know, with this new contract I will be fine."

She shirked his hand and chuckled mildly.

"Why would I do that? Let him know the six-figure sales king is close to bankruptcy?"

She shoved the apple down the garbage disposal, flipped the switch, and the ugly, grinding noise made him flinch. When the sound smoothed, she nudged the switch off and left Todd standing alone in the kitchen. The faint stomping sound of her own heavy foot against the staircase's thick rug runner bounced off the walls.

She didn't say another word, leaving Todd staring at the back of her head as the cold room absorbed her trudging foot thuds.

*****

When she was gone, Todd removed the little box from his inside coat pocket and flicked the lid open with one hand. He stared at the diamonds.

He was always doing that, reacting before he thought things through. Still, how nice the moment would have been—seeing that necklace placed against Rachel's soft skin. He snapped the top shut and tucked the box back inside his coat. Then he called and cancelled the dinner reservations, took out his keys, and headed for the casino.

*****

A half mile away, the tension in the car was nearly as thick.

"Don't tell her," Lisa said.

"For God's sake, it's your sister. If you can't trust Rachel, who can you trust?"

"This has nothing to do with trust. The fewer people who know Mikala is seeing Marky Blakley, the better. Even outdoors or in the Helen room, I don't want Mikala's name uttered."

"What about the car?" Now Jack was just being a smart ass.

"It's clean," Lisa snapped.

"How would you know?"

"Because I checked myself. Do you think I don't know what you're doing? See how you sweep for bugs? Since the day you found out about Mikala's visions, you've been checking our house and car."

"Oh, so now you think you can sweep a house or car?" He laughed dramatically, his eyes squinting and mouth widening. "I suppose you think if I took you down to the precinct, you could examine the evidence and find the perpetrator."

"Maybe I could, Jack, just maybe I could."

Her eyes seemed penetrating. Their blue, icy.

"Not on my watch you won't." He loved her dearly, but she was pissing him off.

"I'll go to the precinct if I want to go to the precinct. Maybe it's time I talked to Ben myself. You can't stop me. You're not the boss of me."

Jack did a double take. He didn't think he heard her right. His eyes raked her face. Was she serious? Mad? He couldn't tell. In that instance, all he could think was how determined she seemed.

He turned his eyes back to the road.

There is no greater warrior than a mother protecting her child, he thought. *Who said that?*

"N. K. Jemisin," she spat at him, and he nearly wrecked the car.

12 1996 - Gee

"Mama says I can't sleep in Sissy's room anymore." LeeLee jumped on top of Gee's bed and pressed the back of her head into the feather pillow.

"You have a big, beautiful bedroom in your new house, I hear." Gee's voice rose. "Don't you like having your own room? Mama said she painted it pink for you."

"I'm afraid the black devil will find it."

"Who? The black devil? Oh, woopty-doo, we're not afraid of any devil. We have the white angel."

LeeLee sifted the silky edge of one blanket through her fingers and thought for a moment. "Gee?"

"Yes?"

"I don't want to go to school." She kicked her shoes off and wiggled down under the blankets, tugging the one with the silk hem to her chin. On Saturday, she always spent the afternoon with Gee. Sometimes they watched movies or played *Old Maid*, but today LeeLee wanted to talk. "What if he's there?"

"At school?" Gee chuckled. "Why, I've never known a devil who liked school."

"Devils don't go to school?"

"No, never, so don't worry that precious little head of yours about that." Gee lifted her arm, LeeLee scooted closer, and Gee tucked an elbow beneath her braided hair and bows. "When you go to kindergarten next September, you are going to learn to read and write and finger paint. Don't you like to finger paint?"

"I guess so."

"Oh, finger painting is fun. You can paint a picture of your teacher, so I know what she looks like. And Sissy will be there to keep an eye on you."

"Sissy punched a boy in the face yesterday."

"Sissy? Punched a boy, you say?" Gee laughed so hard LeeLee watched her chest heave up and down and waited for the cough that usually followed. When Gee finished coughing, she continued. "See there? You won't need to be afraid of anyone with Sissy in a classroom down the hall."

LeeLee watched Gee's eyes move toward the ceiling, and she knew Gee was thinking; she loved the way her lips turned up at their sides when she did. Gee always seemed happy. She never became cross like Mama or yelled like PopPops. LeeLee could tell Gee anything.

"Mama doesn't believe in the black devil," she said, gazing into her grandmother's eyes, hoping Gee would say her mother was right not to believe. "She says devils only live in books, not in attics or bedrooms. She doesn't believe in angels, either."

"Well, some people don't believe what their eyes can't see." Gee hugged LeeLee gently. "Doesn't mean they don't exist."

"I saw the black devil once, when I was little."

"When you were little, you say?" Gee laughed and smiled and stroked LeeLee's hair. "I know you did, my precious."

"You believe I saw him?"

"Well, sure I believe you."

"Did you ever see him?"

"Yes, once. I suppose I did see him one time. In fact, I was about the same age you were when you saw him."

"You were? Did he ever come back?"

"Never." Gee spoke softly. "You only need to see him once to know you never want to see him again. After that, you just don't let him come. You say, baby Jesus protect me, and once you say baby Jesus's name, no devil will ever show his face around you, only angels."

"That's all I have to do?"

Gee always knew what to do. Sissy was like Gee.

"That's all," Gee said, still stroking LeeLee's hair and raising her eyes once again to the ceiling. "You were born with a gift, LeeLee. You see things other people don't see."

"Like Cinder? When she was caught in the pricker bush in the park?"

"Yes, just like Cinder. You saw her in your head, and then you sent Daddy. Told him about her paw being stuck, and how he would find her under the little bridge past the garden maze. I remember everyone shouted for joy when he brought her home."

"And then Mama fixed her up."

"That's right. And someday you'll see other things and help other pets—and people. You'll grow and be the fixer-upper like Mama."

"I was the fixer-upper for the little boy with the big ears, who lives in my neighborhood. I fixed him up before he got hurt."

"Which boy?"

"Little Lenny."

Gee became quiet. LeeLee thought her face looked flushed.

"I helped him."

"You did?" Gee cleared her throat.

LeeLee nodded timidly, not wanting to be proud over something sad.

"How did you help him?"

"I told him to hide when the big kids came down the street."

"Why did he need to hide?"

"They don't like him. They were going to knock him down and drag him across the cement. I saw it in my head.

His knees and elbows and face were all bloody. So I told him to run and hide behind my house."

"And did he?"

LeeLee nodded.

"Well, see then, you already helped someone. You keep an eye out for that little boy. It's a good thing, you helping him."

"But only for now," she said, wiping her nose with the back of her fingers. "They are going to beat him up when Sissy and I aren't around."

"Why don't they like him?"

LeeLee shrugged, meekly. "He looks different than the other boys. And he's little, littler than them. But someday he will grow up to be big and strong. Do you think I will be here to see him grow up, Gee?"

"Why not? Where else would you be?"

"In the desert."

"In the desert? For heaven's sake, child, who put that notion in your head?"

"The black devil."

"The black devil? When he came that one time?"

LeeLee nodded and blinked her eyes slowly and deeply. "The black devil said I am going to go away after the buildings fall."

"What buildings?"

"I don't know. Two tall buildings."

Gee lifted her head off the pillow and looked LeeLee straight in the eyes, then hesitated a moment before laying her head back down.

"And after these two tall buildings fall, he said you are going to go away?"

LeeLee nodded again, her eyes tearing. "To a desert," she said. "That's a place with sand and prickly trees. Sissy and I looked it up."

Gee became unusually quiet. Her lips no longer turned up, her eyebrows furrowed.

"But I don't think he's right," LeeLee said. "I don't think I am going away."

"You don't?"

LeeLee shook her head.

"I think Sissy is going to the desert."

13 Jack

"Something's going on." Billy Mack burst through Helen's doors. He rushed past Jack and the chief, his sneakers muddied, face wet with perspiration, and eyes wild with marvel. "With the Blakleys."

"The Blakleys?" Jack wiped his own face with a towel.

"Yes." The big dimple on the right side of Billy's face betrayed him. He was attempting to squelch a smile. "The father is back."

"Marky Blakley's dad?"

"Yep, moved back home two days ago."

Jack turned toward the chief. From the look on the chief's face, this was new information to him, too. Jack tucked the hand with a towel on a hip. "Temporarily or for good?"

"No clue." Billy Mack rushed toward the front of the room and placed his knuckles flat on a desk, his eyes raking the map. His breath still labored. Sweat ran down his neck and soaked his collar. "That's what happens when you cut out of a run early, Crackerjack. You miss conversation. The FBI surveillance guy said he's been there the last two nights. I don't think the Blakleys are telling us everything."

Personally, Jack hated the FBI guy nosing around, horning in on their morning runs. That was partially the reason he quit early.

Billy Mack pushed off his knuckles, whipped the sweatshirt he was wearing over his head, and tossed it on a desk. His t-shirt underneath was drenched.

"Are you ready for this?" Like a kid with a secret, Billy beamed with excitement. "The Blakleys have not one but two private investigators."

"Is Carlson one of them?" Immediately, Jack's demeanor changed, the calming effects of his run ruined. He didn't need Carlson nosing around.

"Oh, for the love of Jesus," the chief interjected, head tilted. He turned as if he wanted to run from the room.

Mike Carlson's name sickened every officer in the precinct. Born and raised in Erie, he made a name for himself in 1991 on the streets of Chicago. They had a bad summer that year, over one hundred murders in August alone. Carlson worked homicide, earning a reputation for solving the most heinous crimes. Ones involving children, teens, and twenty-somethings were his specialty. Jack heard he single-handedly brought down seventeen murderers before leaving the force and setting up shop as a private investigator.

There were unconfirmed mob-tie rumors. He rescued a three-year-old girl from a foxhole in the backwoods of Mexico, once. She was clinging to life but survived. Her father owned a chain of resorts across the country. Carlson moved back to Erie afterward. Opened an account at a local bank to the tune of three million bucks, one million in cash. Said the funds were a gift from the family—ransom money never retrieved. Erie police checked him out, and Chicago said he was legit. Then Carlson became the biggest pain in the neck to the Erie detective division.

"Yep, Carlson." Billy wiped the sweat from his eyes with the bottom of his t-shirt. "The mediator king muddying up our small-town muck."

"Son-of-a-bitch," the chief grunted. "He'll make sure they don't work with us."

"Think there's a ransom?" Jack lifted his shirt and wiped his stomach and back with his towel.

He, Billy, and three other cops had run five miles at a blistering six-minute and ten-second pace. Beating down his fear over the note and maintaining normalcy was critical for Jack. That meant showing up for morning workouts when he would rather have stayed at home with his sweet little Mikala.

"Has to be." Billy said, dripping. Sweat accumulated on the floor around him. "What else could it be?"

Though Jack had finished his run fifteen minutes ago, he began sweating profusely. That the Blakleys had hired Carlson, and his extra protection for Mikala involved half-assed favors of friends and retired policemen, unnerved him. He needed to tell someone about the note—Chief or Billy? His eyes scanned the room. Was Helen as safe as the chief swore? A rush of heat hit him.

"You're right," he said, wiping the back of his neck. "Had to be they got something from the kidnapper."

He'd be discreet, would choose one of them—probably Billy. But he wouldn't tell him here. For the time being, he had protection for both his immediate family and his sister's. The security wouldn't last forever, but the police surveillance the chief had ordered gave him breathing time.

"Call Eddie for a tap," the chief grunted, catching his attention.

"Why, Chief, that's illegal." Billy Mack smiled, then dropped his towel on the floor and swooshed it around with his foot, sopping up the sweat and dirt around him. "Carlson will serve your head on a platter to City Council."

"I don't give a rat's ass what Carlson does. Get me a tap and find out if there is a ransom note. Three kids are missing, one for several weeks now. We don't have a clue if these boys are dead or alive."

There was quiet. Billy Mack walked to his toothpick stash, grabbed one, and slipped it between his thumb and index finger like he held a cigarette. Then he leaned the palms of his hands and his backside against the desk and squinted. "What do you know, Jack?"

The chief turned, too.

Jack held his expression, wiped more sweat. A burning sensation rose to his cheeks, and he prayed his face hadn't lost the redness from his morning run, so the chief didn't see his blush.

"What did Lisa say?" The chief stepped slightly toward him. "You talked to her, right?"

Unable to speak, Jack sighed and nodded.

"And?"

Sweat began rolling down the sides of his head and dripping onto his shoulders. Yes, he'd talked to Lisa over the weekend. Their conversations had danced between shouting matches and silent treatment. Both of them felt boxed into a corner. Finally, Lisa conceded, and they approached Mikala.

In the quiet of Mikala's bedroom, they talked. Did their magic, voodoo, or whatever they called their conjuring. Jack had sat helplessly watching, thinking if they weren't his wife and daughter he would have concluded they were crazy. When they were done, a few silent tears slipped down Lisa's face. Mikala sat poker straight, no tears. Between the two of them, they were fairly certain.

"Lisa said the kidnapper has psychic abilities," he said. Another lie. Lisa hadn't told him that, but because the note bore Mikala's name, he knew the guy was psychic.

"Is she sure?" Billy shot.

"Yes."

Jack allowed them a moment to digest what elaborated on everyone's suspicions. A team of detectives had analyzed the Bible passages on the notes and determined the perpetrator had some fixation with spirits.

"Are the boys alive?" The chief asked.

"Two of them." Jack swept a hand through his damp hair.

Again, he refrained from explaining. What could he say? That his baby was talking to a dead boy, and he told her the other two boys were alive? And that, try as they may, Lisa and Mikala had no idea where the boys were?

"One boy is dead," he said, dropping his hand and sighing. "That's all they know. Marky Blakley is dead."

"Did you say they?" Billy asked.

His eyes shot to the chief and Billy. My God, he had. How the hell could he have been so careless?

"Yeah, they," he stammered. "Lisa went to Rachel's house last night, and—well, you know—they meditated, or whatever, on the case."

Billy Mack tilted his head. "But—"

He stopped, and Jack held his breath. You never knew what Billy was thinking. What his next question would be.

"But—they don't know where the boys are?" Billy slipped the toothpick into his mouth. He wasn't blinking.

"No, not yet."

The door to the Helen room opened. It was 7 a.m. and time for the morning staff meeting. The chief headed for the front desk, and Jack watched Billy Mack move to the back of the room. Billy leaned a shoulder against the back wall. He was still staring at Jack, twirling his toothpick around and around with his tongue.

Jack turned and faced the front of the room, trying to squelch the growing ache in his belly. He could almost feel Billy's beady-eyed stare burrowing through the back of his head. Why was he looking at him that way?

It hit him. A rush of realization and dread that raced from his head to the pit of his stomach. Did Billy know?

Rachel was in Columbus.

14 The perpetrator

This wasn't how he planned his exit. He had carefully charted everything from the first abduction to the final release and deaths. None of the kids were going to die. Marky Blakley's demise was unfortunate. How did he know the kid had a peanut allergy? Didn't people wear bracelets for that sort of thing?

No, of course a child that little wouldn't wear a bracelet.

He ripped the newspaper in half once, twice, and again and again until only shreds remained. He was tired of all the press that kid was getting. He tossed the scraps into the fire and stirred them with a makeshift poker until every last one had shriveled into ash.

The Erie newspaper had insinuated the boy had been abducted by a pedophile, a pervert. Weren't news articles supposed to remain impartial? And how come they hadn't mentioned the kid's peanut allergy? Or the ransom? He had half a mind to tip them off where the body was, so they could see for themselves he hadn't harmed the boy. He wasn't a monster, after all.

He warmed his hands over the fire in the trash can, glanced around, watched the bums, and thought about the boy's disastrous death.

Not delivering enough food and water may have contributed to the child's unlucky demise. And the late delivery of blankets hadn't helped the situation. September had been colder than usual. October, even worse. Bogged down by responsibilities, he had neglected to bring them their supplies and water on the scheduled date. Now, Marky was dead and Luke was sick.

He blew on his hands, picked up the bottle of whiskey, and watched the guy with the shopping cart.

Often, while lost in his schemes, he forgot the boys existed. He worked through his daily routine, strategizing, plotting, and maintaining this fictitious bungling character—so no one, not even his own mother, would recognize the cool-headed genius he really was—as if he had not abducted anyone and was a normal human being.

But he wasn't normal. He knew that.

Now, such an inconvenience.

Completing the actions according to his time plan had been important: Abduct the four boys on the appropriate dates. Shortly afterward, throw police off track with additional clues, send ransom requests—dead men walking could never have too much money,—set up suspicion that the perpetrator belonged to Project Dream by a note mentioning Mikala, and then reference Rachel and Lisa. (Yet his guide had highly underestimated the kid's abilities.) Finally, murder some insignificant bum with no purpose in life, and end the abductions on an upswing with the death of the perp and his own demise, of course, because everyone knew the only way out was by death.

But he couldn't think on that now. He had chores to complete.

He watched the man and his wobbly cart roll down the street toward the bayfront. He stood and staggered along behind him.

Try as he may, he couldn't keep his mind on the bum. His thoughts kept boomeranging back to the desert and Rachel and the other two Project Dream transmitters. When the vagabond disappeared into the bushes on the bluffs, he stopped and raised the bottle to his lips. He didn't drink. He lowered the whiskey, licked his lips, and then turned their ends slightly upward.

"Revenge," he whispered. "Death is but a doorway."

Some words sounded melodious in whispers. As sweet, euphoric as—

His eyes fell to the pocket with his coke.

15 The four dreamers

The view of the college campus from Thirty-Eighth Street was stunning, especially in the evening light. Rachel poked the CD button on her car's dashboard, and the rap music faded. She quit jiving and cracked a window to hear the last of the chapel's quarter-hour bells toll, amused by how varied her music taste was. Kanye West and Catholic bells tolling? My God, she'd been driving too long.

She drove through the brick and iron gates and up the well-manicured drive. Mercyhurst never lost its appeal. She'd been coming here four years, and still the aesthetics awed her. An alluring English Gothic structure, "Old Main," stood atop the center lane, dressed in fine brick. Lush green lawns with perfectly-staggered light posts and flawlessly-pruned, up-lit trees trimmed the lane's edges.

Built as the school "over the lake" in the 1920s by nuns who migrated from Ireland, the stately, aged college hinted at a clandestine history.

"Clandestine, indeed." She sniggered, turned left, drove along the winding roadway, and found a parking space on the second floor of the school's single parking ramp.

Once her feet hit the cobblestone walkway, she saw John Michael exiting the employee parking lot. Even in dusk's dim light, she recognized his short, quick steps—fast-twitch strides. She hurried toward him.

"Wait up," she called.

He jumped and turned abruptly.

"Hello, Rachel." He adjusted his glasses. "You startled me. I didn't realize you were behind me."

"Don't you know when I'm coming? Isn't that what everyone asks a psychic?"

His expression soured.

"Yes, that and what's tomorrow's daily number? Will I meet the person of my dreams? Etcetera, etcetera."

She put her hands in her pockets and chuckled. John Michael was too serious these days. He had been transferred to Erie against his will awhile back.

They had been friends in the desert but, like many of the kids, his time there had hardened him. When they first met, he was witty, entertaining. They'd shared some fun times. Now he lost his temper a lot, broke phones, told Todd and Lenny off, but he liked her. Maybe tolerated was a better word.

She walked alongside him, quickening her steps and shortening her strides to stay even with his.

"Do you ever do it anymore?"

"What's that?" he responded.

"Give readings to people?"

"No." He glanced toward the ground. "Not anymore."

"Me neither," she said.

"What?" he leaned away from her and smiled. His turned-up lips were a rarity these days. "You and Todd don't want to be the psychic couple anymore?"

"No. Todd gave up the idea when I wouldn't take money for it."

"I bet he did." John Michael opened the door, clicked his heels together, bent his long, lean body at the waist, and waved a hand for Rachel to go inside. With his little round glasses, the movement made him appear Gestapo-ish. "Where is he, by the way?"

"He should be inside." She curtsied and stepped past him, gazing at his shoes, almost expecting muddied army boots. "I just got back from a training for work. Came directly here."

"Well, then." John Michael followed her, adjusted his glasses again. "We shouldn't walk in together, should we?"

She couldn't argue the point. John Michael knew Todd too well.

"I suppose not."

"Go on." He motioned with his head for her to continue down the hall and then, very unlike him, he chuckled. "I'll count to one hundred and follow."

She snickered a bit herself as she made her way down the empty hall, her heel clicks bouncing off hollow walls. She passed through two metal doors of a small reception area and stepped into a dimly-lit room with pale beige walls and no windows. There, the air seemed heavier. The temperature, cooler.

Todd stood and stepped toward her, his lips reaching for hers. She turned her face at the last second, so the kiss landed on her cheek. She glimpsed the facilitator, Doctor Peterson. Thought he may have noticed because his glance darted toward his laptop, the single item atop his metal desk.

"Still waiting for Lenny and John Michael," he said, fidgeting with his keyboard. "Have a seat, Rachel. Get comfortable. They should be along soon—well, look here, John Michael."

Rachel's eyes shot toward John Michael and then Todd. Had there been enough time between arrivals? Todd's facial expression seemed unaffected.

"We may as well begin our prayer." Doctor Peterson clasped his hands. "Lenny can catch up when he arrives. Is that okay with the rest of you?"

Fine, they agreed, and Doctor Peterson recited a blessing followed by an Our Father.

They always began with a prayer, which seemed ludicrous to Rachel when the government insisted on separating God and state so dramatically these days. Yet they had begun this way initially—since 2002 for some, 2003 for others, 2004 for her. The door opened, and Lenny's large body clumped in. He ambled across the room and took the empty seat beside Rachel.

"Glad you could make it, Lenny," Peterson quipped, his annoyance apparent.

Rachel nudged Lenny with her shoulder, winked, and whispered, "How are you?"

"G-g-good." He widened his eyes, opened his lips again, but stopped mid-breath. Rachel thought he was going to return the question, but he clamped his lips and nodded instead.

"And your mom?"

"She's good, too," he responded, head down. Then each of them relaxed into their cushioned seat and prepared for meditation.

Doctor Peterson lit incense, turned his computer to face and record them, and after the four of them meditated and raised the vibration of the room through prayer and recitation, they began.

"Rachel?" A voice from the computer called. "What do you see?"

"Nothing in Cleveland, Buffalo, Pittsburgh," she responded, hesitated, and continued. "I don't see anything in the Big Apple, either. I do get this heavy feeling around Scranton."

"Approximate latitude 41.411835, longitude -75.665245. Zero in, please. Everyone." The voice from the computer sounded methodical, mechanical.

Silence rang for minutes; she had no idea how many. Rachel and the other three fell deep into concentration.

"The numbers 747 on a house come to me," Rachel finally said.

"A plane? A 747?" resonated from the computer.

She thought for a moment, eyes closed. "No, not a plane. It's an address. The house is older. I'm having difficulty seeing the structure through the haze in my head. The pitch of the roof, the windows—it looks like a—" She hesitated long enough for Lenny to step in.

"A Cape Cod. There are young men inside."

"Lenny's right. I can see them. Is there a college in that area recruiting middle-eastern students? These kids are dark skinned but not African American. If you can locate the college, check student computers." She wondered if psychics could be accused of racial profiling. She nearly laughed.

"Anyone else getting that?" the voice from the computer asked.

"Yes," John Michael spoke up. "I see packages arriving in the mail."

"I see them, too. Lots of packages." She winced. "What is that? Looks like—"

"Toy guns," Todd interrupted.

"Yes, they are putting toy guns together." She opened her eyes. "A do-it-yourself gun?"

The voice over the computer acknowledged that possibility. "Rachel, can you see the street sign?"

She wasn't sure why, but lately she struggled to see the images. Generally, a soothing white fog in her mind formed clear visions. Despite never mastering clairaudience—she didn't hear voices,—she accurately interpreted visualizations, and that accuracy had built her a fine reputation.

Today, however, the mist clogged her brain. So she spent time in her mind, wandering streets around the house in her head. Gazing through the mist toward the addresses as she floated.

"I don't know. I can't make the address out. There's an N, C, L. It is definitely 747, but I'm having trouble with the street sign…it says…"

"Lincoln Avenue." Lenny never stuttered when he was confident. "Three houses down from a Rose Street sign. North side of the road. The basement has sliding closet doors. Open them, remove the toys, and you'll find a door to a back closet."

Lenny was remarkable, the best of the best. If only he could see himself in that light. She closed her eyes again and floated through the fog in her mind. Found the basement closet.

"He's right," Todd said, an as-always twinge to his voice.

"Yes, he is." She settled in her seat, wiggled to a more comfortable position, and placed her hands on the arm rests. "I see it, too. A back closet. Guns."

"And other weapons," John Michael added. "Knives, explosives—an armory."

The voice on the computer rang out again. "What's the target?"

Rachel roamed the house, climbed stairs, opened drawers, just as she knew Todd and Lenny and John Michael were doing.

"Train," John Michael said. "I believe they have train tickets."

"I see the number 1272017. Must be the date, December 7," Rachel said after a time. "I can't see the words."

"Philadelphia to Washington, D.C." Lenny spoke confidently.

"That's it," John Michael confirmed. Rachel was sure she heard his head nod. "Philly to D.C."

"Get the bastards," Todd sneered.

"We're on it." The voice on the other end hesitated and then said, "Clear."

Each of them opened their eyes and took a drink of the water Doctor Peterson had placed in front of them, and then they released their energy in their own individual way. Rachel massaged her tight shoulders. Todd stood and stretched. John Michael paced. Lenny rocked.

Rachel inched her fingers upward toward her neck and moved her head in big circles, first to the left, then right. She forced the picture of a blank wall into her mind and attempted vacuity.

She refused to think about the missing boys—or Mikala. She was dead set on keeping her niece's abilities secret from the CIA's Project Dream, a program that ripped clairvoyant children from their mothers' arms for the good of the people.

Remote viewing, they called the phenomena. Accessing information in unconventional manners. Soaking the area around a person with Frankincense, sage, and a silence so piercing that the room's stillness forced them to reach past their own consciousness. Subjects learned self-hypnosis. Were taught to clear their minds, accept images, objectify their impressions, and repeat the process. Years of daily practice created governmental "Star Children" who caught glimpses of future threats to the American government and public. The intent was to avoid another 9/11.

Eventually, the intense training of young minds gave the process a fluidity no one expected. Their flashes lengthened into dreams. Visions.

"Prepare," the voice hailed from behind the computer screen, "repeat."

Rachel stacked the molecules in her brain and, for one brief moment, allowed herself to think the truth. How much more successful this program would be if her sister, Lisa, sat in her seat—or her niece.

Then, if whispering in her mind was possible, she whispered. *They must never find Mikala.*

Her hiccup in time completed, she unstacked the molecules, closed her eyes like the others, and spent time in her mind, hovering over the earth. Moving like the wind above her territory: All of Pennsylvania, Ohio, New Jersey, half of New York and West Virginia, a pinch of Virginia, Maryland and Delaware. She floated, searched, smelled, and zeroed in on potential threats to America or Americans.

Dreamers, the CIA called the participants of the covert operation. The program began in 2002 with twenty-five wayward kids ripped from detention centers. Kids with a sixth sense that scientists thought they could coax visions from. When the project produced results that stunned the White House, the government bypassed the adult remote-viewing programs and searched for intuitive children. They were more easily trained.

They found seventy-five with virgin minds and clean slates. That second round, in 2003, contained no juvenile delinquents who might cause problems. The government scoured police agencies, educational facilities, and psychic websites; hired private investigators; and manipulated, paid, or coerced people into dropping the name of any child with a sixth sense. Covert screenings followed. Lies were told. Contracts were made with families. Children were taken to prodigy camps with the promise of the best education in the world and a lifetime of success. Selection was a gift, government officials said. No child would pay a dime for education throughout their lives, and jobs would be at their fingertips. They would never want for anything. Nor would their families.

The select few children who made the final cut were moved to what the government said was an undisclosed area in Phoenix, Arizona. Every state and federal document listed a Phoenix address. The kids could have no visitors for six months. But after that six-month period, the chosen few were permitted holidays once a month. The government flew families in for all-expense-paid weekends in a plush, thirty-acre resort with a small amusement park, hiking trails, and pools, one the size of a small lake.

Their real whereabouts—a barren land deep within layers of governmental fencing in the state of Nevada—was never to be disclosed. But there, buildings and play yards took form and Project Dream gave birth. The location was far away from civilization, people, normalcy, in a no-fly zone labeled Area 51. Rumors circulated that the government had the body of a Martian floating in a clear tank of formaldehyde twenty miles down the road, but the children would never confirm that story. Often referred to as the "Star" kids, government officials were not permitted to speak of them. Even the children themselves could not disclose the secret affairs of Project Dream. They knew the consequences. Your experience was a take-to-your grave secret. A lifetime commitment that even a twelve-year-old could understand.

In 2004, they sorted out the rough edges, eliminating a few problem participants who produced little results. They replaced seven of the one hundred children. Other than by death, none ever left the program again.

"Let us consider other concerning points." The voice from the computer shattered the room's long silence and Rachel's assessment of Project Dream.

What was the tinny voice saying? Concerning points? She nearly laughed. The person should clarify that question. She could rattle off a barrage of concerns but being a smart ass never went well for a person in Project Dream. Thank the stars she, not Lisa, sat in this seat. Unlike many of the others, she had made peace with the lifetime commitment. It was a chore, like cleaning cat litter. The job stunk but you got through it and forgot the smell.

Until the next time.

So other concerns? Only one. Keep—stack the molecules—her niece the hell away from these people—unstack.

She brought herself back to the task at hand.

"South of Scranton," she said.

"Allentown," Lenny clarified.

"Latitude 40.610306, longitude -75.477104, zero in. Take a look around."

Quiet, then the energy of the room exploded once again.

"Chew and Tenth Street, across from a park," Lenny responded. "Second floor. Dining room cabinet. Bullets in tea cups. Guns in wall cabinets."

He was proficient and remarkable, the most underrated transmitter of the lot. Rachel opened her eyes, then quickly closed them and allowed the room's gyrating molecules of energy to swarm her.

"A separate compartment in that cupboard." She heard Lenny say. "The target is the same, Philly to Washington."

"Train tickets are the same day, same destination," John Michael added.

"Can you locate the tickets in the house?" the voice from the computer echoed in the chilly room.

"A bedroom dresser, perhaps," Rachel said, opening her eyes and straining to count the number of drawers.

"Third drawer from the floor," Lenny whispered to her, and John Michael opened his eyes as if he heard.

"Third from the floor," she repeated, watching John Michel with her peripheral vision. "Underneath the shelf lining. But wait, I see a second ticket, a different route."

Lenny nodded and smiled. She closed her eyes and continued, wondering if John Michael had closed his. She suppressed the temptation to peek and see.

*****

But John Michael had not closed his eyes. He kept them set on Rachel, observing her suspiciously, while asking himself the same question he always asked. Why was Lenny helping her?

And now a second question surfaced. What was wrong with her? She seemed off a bit. His eyes raked her soft features, creamy skin, shapely eyebrows, and perfect lips. The thought struck him that every man in that room might be staring at her, like him, when her eyes were closed. He glanced toward Todd. His eyes were shut. Then he turned toward Lenny. His eyes were open and gloating.

Wait, was Lenny staring at Rachel? Or at him? Why was he smiling? He lost concentration until the voice from the computer uttered "clear" and the time came for them to recharge, once again.

He stood and turned his back to Lenny.

My God, that man is creepy.

A hush fell over the room. Doctor Peterson refilled the glasses, and each of them relaxed their shoulders and allowed the electrical thickness of the room's air to envelop them until the slower vibration of the room rejuvenated them, and they were ready. Once they had raised the vibration of the room initially, re-raising the molecules and finding threats became much easier.

The people on the other end of the computer were quiet and when once again, Rachel spoke first, she sent the vibration of the room into an unmeasurable decibel. John Michael could almost feel the CIA vanguard marveling, pictured them lost in a maze of computers. Big wall screens displaying their faces—his, Lenny's, Todd's, and Rachel's—shadowing them in pale blue. Intelligentsias and squirrels listening, then fingering their location trackers, zooming their satellite cameras, hacking residential computers. All of them talking about the woman on the screen with the plump, red lips and wickedly attractive eyes.

"Morgantown," Rachel said, and he imagined them applauding her.

He opened his eyes and glanced around the room, expecting to see Doctor Peterson, Todd, and Lenny staring at Rachel, too. But, my God, Lenny Emling was still glaring at him.

He felt a cool sensation rush over him, and his hands began to shake. How had he gotten stuck in the same city as Lenny? Ninety-nine of the one hundred Project Dream participants feared that freak.

His eyes moved to Todd and he wondered. Who hated Lenny more? Him or Todd? And who did Todd hate more? Him or Lenny?

Then he remembered the one other time Rachel Callahan's sixth sense fell below the others, and as he did, Todd Kennedy opened his eyes as if he had read John Michael's mind.

16 The boys

Matt held the apple to Luke's lips, but Luke didn't flinch.

"Luke," he said, his voice hoarse and cracking, "try to take a bite."

He pressed a dirty palm on Luke's shirt and watched his hand move up and down with Luke's slow, gentle breaths. Then he sat back and stared.

Luke was dying. Marky had that same glassy-eyed gaze before he died, his unblinking eyes only partially open, his personality lost behind a black stare.

Matt had been careful this time. When Marky first came, they drank the water and ate the food right away and had nothing left for days.

His eyes found the jug a few feet away. This time, plenty of water, apples, and peanut butter remained. He lay the back of one hand on Luke's forehead and the other on his own, like his mother used to do.

What did Mommy do when he was sick? Once she carried him to the bathtub, and he sat in the cool water. She scooped it over him and brushed his hair back. He shivered and cried, but Mommy said, "I'm sorry, sweet boy. We have to bring that fever down."

That was before the big fight, before Daddy packed his clothes and shoes and computer and moved to the small apartment with the big windows and white walls. He wondered if Daddy knew he was gone. That Monster Man had taken him.

He dropped his hands, leaned back, and sat on the back of his calves, subconsciously wiggling his shins around pebbles to softer spots in the dirt. He couldn't think of

Mommy and Daddy and the argument, or he would cry. So he thought about his sick bath again.

"Pretend you are at the beach," Mommy had said as she dumped the cups of water. "Remember when you and your cousins took turns burying each other in the sand? How hot you were? How uncomfortable? Close your eyes and think of the cool water washing away that hot sand."

He missed Mommy's sweet voice, her hugs, the sugary-lemon smell of her skin when she held him, how her hand felt creamy against his cheek when he was sick. He glanced at his own grimy hands. Surely, Luke missed his mommy, too.

He leaned over and studied him, his saggy eyes. Then he flapped Luke's cover off him and scooted on his knees across the dirt. He dragged the jug to Luke, making a squiggly rut in the dirt floor. He tipped the water. Poured a little on the edge of Luke's blanket. Then he wiped Luke's arms and legs and forehead.

Luke squirmed a bit, groaned. His eyes widened a tad and his personality came back into them.

"Luke?"

No answer.

"Are you cold?"

A whimper flowed over Luke's parched lips, no words, but he straightened his head.

"It's okay," Matt said, patting his forehead with the damp corner of the blanket. "Pretend you are at the beach and it's hot. Remember when we were at the beach? You and me, we met there. Remember? We skipped stones and yours went the farthest. That was a hot day."

Luke nodded slightly, and Matt dropped the blanket and grabbed the apple.

"Take a bite."

He placed the apple against Luke's lips, but Luke didn't have the strength to take a bite. Matt chipped a small piece off with his fingers. Some of the dirt from under his nails darkened the fruit. He brushed the grime off and placed the small piece on Luke's tongue. Luke chewed and, after a time, swallowed. Matt broke off another section and then another, and Luke chewed slowly. When a third of the apple was eaten, Matt lay the remainder on the cleanest part of the blanket and tipped the water jug toward Luke's lips. A few drops gently swished into the side of his mouth. Luke slurped, swallowed, and Matt poured again. He counted eight gulps before Luke's head tilted to the side, and he closed his eyes.

Matt sat back. He didn't know what more he could do. He hoped Luke lived.

Why did people have to die? His Papa Michell had died. And his gold fish. And Marky. Mommy said people floated up to heaven after they died.

He didn't want Luke to go to heaven. He felt his bottom lip begin to shake, and he peered across the room to the stairs. He didn't want to cry. Monster Man might be outside, listening.

A memory burst into his mind. A feeling. Another time when he worked hard not to cry. He had run his hand along a deck railing at the beach and gotten a splinter. The pretty camp counselor with the pleasant voice sang to him when she used a needle to remove the tiny sliver.

"Remember the song Miss Stacy taught us?" he said to Luke, even though Luke slept.

He thought to himself for a moment and then nodded his head as he recited the syllables of each word. "It is the song that never ends."

Slowly, the melody came back to him, and he began singing quietly. His voice echoed in the hollow cell. "It just goes on and on, my friend."

He didn't think Monster Man would whip him if he sang, just if he cried. Still, he lowered his voice to be careful. He stroked Luke's forehead with the cool, wet corner of the blanket over and over, and he sang the song they'd learned at summer camp, where he first met Luke and Marky and the other kids from the other day care centers.

"Somebody started singing it not knowing what it was, and they'll continue singing it forever just because…it is the song that never ends. It just goes on and on, my friend…"

17 Billy

He couldn't fathom what would make Jack lie. But he had a theory.

Billy sat in his beat-up old Chevy and cursed himself for giving Katie the spare car when they separated. That 2008 Altima had been in great condition, so plain it could blend in like an egg on snow. But she wanted a mid-size, front-wheel drive for winter. Didn't take her convertible out of the garage if the temperature dipped below forty.

"I have to trust my instincts, and they are telling me don't drive that convertible in snow," she told him as she shifted the Altima into reverse the day she left.

"And you know what I always say," she added as she began backing down the driveway.

"Ah, hmm, I can't recall. You've said so many things you didn't mean."

"There's a reason for everything, Billy."

"Oh, that's right." He slapped his forehead. "A reason for everything."

He remembered the window rolling up past her sad eyes and how bad he felt for being a jerk. But she was always saying stuff like that. Things that meant nothing. At the time, he didn't give a damn about cars.

But now, on the sparsely-treed street, he thought she'd scammed him with those soft brown eyes. Keeping his Chevy out of sight was like trying to hide an ostrich on a pig farm. It was fire engine red. The engine whirred like a fan, the muffler rattled like a roulette wheel, and every metal inch of body clanged once his speed reached ten miles an hour. The car was an antique, built from junk yard parts in his teenage years, and mostly he loved the good-for-nothing heap. Until every time he wanted to work a little overtime without getting paid.

His work car, now that was flawless. A new Crown Vic that he swore could out-run and out-maneuver the old Ford Inceptors or any vehicle he'd ever driven, for that matter. The chief was a stickler about cars. He let Purchasing skimp on the little things, but never on vehicles.

"Only the best for the boys," Billy said to no one. His gaze never left Jack's house. "And that's what I love about you, Chief. You're always thinking about your men."

The curtain in the upstairs bedroom jiggled.

"Now, let's see what your man Jack is thinking about." He inched the car forward a bit and shifted back into park.

The room with the swaying drapes was Mikala's. He was sure. The boys slept in the first room, and Mikala's bedroom sat at the end of the hall. He'd read them bedtime stories once. Last Christmas Eve, maybe? He couldn't remember.

He could find his way on the first floor of Jack and Lisa's house with his eyes closed, but not upstairs. And his familiarity, at all, with their little home was solely due to Lisa. She, never Jack, invited him for dinner, always waving him in while ignoring Jack's objections.

But then, when the chips were down, Jack had been the person who kept him in the game—got him over his funk after the separation. He could never deny that.

And in a stakeout? He'd pick Jack every time to cover his back. No one else.

"So what the devil are you up to, my good man?"

Shaking bushes across the street from their house caught his attention. At first glance, he thought the little old lady who lived there was searching for something in her shrubs. He shifted into drive and inched the car forward. No, too big for her. The figure was masculine, and in a hurry. The man jumped out of the bushes and sprinted down the street, running on the lawns, hugging the houses to keep in the shadows.

Billy turned on his lights, stepped hard on the gas pedal, and high-tailed it out of his parking space to follow him. He drove past three houses, and his car stalled.

"Son of a bitch." He banged his hands on the steering wheel. "Are you kidding me?"

He tried starting the car again, and again. No good. He banged his fists, harder. So much for Katie's everything-happens-for-a-reason philosophy.

This was the first night Officer Filutze had been called away from watching Jack's house, and the perfect evening for Billy to snoop around. The precinct, busy from three o'clock on, had received a tip about a domestic murder, and the chief reassigned Filutze to the park where the purported crime took place. When Jack heard, he'd rushed home, and Billy knew something was up.

As soon as he clocked out, he had driven straight to Jack's house and, just now, when the figure tore off down the street, he momentarily thought Katie was right—God sent him there with reason.

Then his old clunker coughed to a stop, and so died Katie's mantra.

He let the car sit a full thirty seconds, bargaining with God and promising himself if the old wreck would start just this once, he'd scrap the piece of crap as soon as possible. He pumped the gas. The engine turned over.

He shifted to drive and clunked his way toward the house, slowing to see if Jack's car was in the side driveway. The pretty blue SUV sat there, reflecting the moon. He inched forward. The house was lifeless. Everyone inside, sleeping. Yet Mikala's window was ajar. Her drapes fluttered.

He eased up on the gas, and his heap of junk clattered forward another few inches and came to a stop in front of the house. There in the upstairs window, on the far side,

Mikala's face pressed against the screen. She had raised the window and was staring at him.

"Hi, Uncle Billy." Her voice was soft, but he could make it out. "What are you doing out there?"

Son-of-a-bitch, he thought, even Mikala could make out his fucking car. He would go buy another one tomorrow.

"Mikala," he grumbled in a whispery voice. "Get back to bed. And don't tell your mom or dad I was here."

"I won't. Are you chasing bad guys, Uncle Billy?"

"Yes; go to bed."

"Okay," she said, and her hands reached toward the windowsill, but Billy Mack called to her before she closed the window. "Mikala?"

"What?"

"You, ah, didn't see anyone from up there, did you?"

She hesitated just long enough for Billy Mack to become suspicious.

"Nope," she said, then slammed the window shut and closed the drapes.

"Damn it." He stepped on the gas. "She's lying, too."

He drove down the street and turned the corner. The big man was nowhere in sight.

"What the hell is going on?"

18 Jack

"I think he has a thing for her," Lisa said, her blonde hair swirled on the pillow beside her.

"Who?" Jack answered by rote.

Staring at her from his own pillow, the way her tousled hair balanced her perfect profile of pale skin, often sent him into rapt contemplation. This morning, her beauty offered him a minute diversion from protecting Mikala. He had so many safeguards in place they were overlapping, the school security guard was bumping shoulders with cop friends keeping an eye out on his kids, and so he allowed himself one night of peace. Mikala and the boys were but a wall away. His wife beside him, like an epinephrine injection.

A work of art, she's a work of art. And when this is all over, I'll ask my mom or Rachel to watch the kids, and I'll take her to a movie and dinner. Give her the attention she deserves.

"The chief. Ben."

That caught his attention. He snapped out of her spell and rolled onto an elbow, propping himself up in bed, mouth gaping. "Lisa, you can't be serious."

This was another quirky feature of hers that he loved—her wandering mind, which usually resulted in words that took the wind out of his sail. "He's old enough to be her father."

"Barely." She sat up, tugging the covers to hide her nakedness, then she fished on the floor for her nightgown, lifted the garment over her head, and let silk fall over flesh. "Put your shorts on in case Mikala wakes up."

Jack reached to the floor, laughing without making a sound. Where did she come up with these thoughts? He pulled his boxers on. "His wife has only been gone a year."

"A year is a long time, Jack. Plus, a lot of women like older men. What is it? Sixteen years between them? I'm telling you. The chief likes Rachel."

Jack squealed out a long, whining sound that ended in a laugh. "Oh, my God, you are out of your mind."

"Really, Jack, after all these years you doubt me?"

"You're never right when it comes to family. You get your dreams and wants mixed up." He yawned and lie back down. "Can we go back to sleep for a while? What time is it?"

"Almost the time Mikala wakes up when she's dreaming."

She curled up in a fetal position next to him, and he automatically snuck an arm around her waist. She reached behind, leaned across him to the nightstand, and flipped the switch for the electric blanket.

"Turn that off, it's roasting in here," he chided.

"I'm freezing. This house is always cold." She settled back under the blankets.

"Spirits dissipate," he called to the ceiling. "Isn't that what they say? It gets cold when dead people come around?"

"Shut up, Jack."

"Were they watching us?" He flipped the electric blanket switch to off and leaned over her, kissing her neck.

"Turn that back on."

"I'll keep you warm." He slipped an arm around her waist, tugged her close, and rested his chin in a tuft of blonde hair on the pillow. "When does Rachel get back, anyway?"

"She's already back."

"Did she say something to you? About Ben?"

"No, I haven't seen her, yet. I'll see her today."

"Are you going to ask if the feeling is mutual?"

"Of course not. I know she's always had a crush on him."

"Why in the world would you think she likes Ben? She's happily married to—Todd."

"Yeah, right—Todd." She laughed and repeated "Todd" with the same nasal tone Jack used. "Husband of the year. Star child of the century."

"What was with him last week? He was higher than a kite. Literally shaking. What do you think he had in that envelope? Samples?"

"I don't know." Lisa sighed, tucked a hand between her cheek and the pillow. "Rachel has her hands full with him. He's definitely using again—if he ever stopped."

"Billy Mack saw him at the bank the other day. Heard him hollering at the manager. Asked me if he was on something."

"He was yelling? What about?"

"Evidently, how incompetent the tellers were. Made me wonder if his financial woes were back. I thought he was having a good year."

"A good year in Todd world, maybe. He spends money like a billionaire."

"Cops see him at the casino all the time."

"I know. Rachel said he's gambling again. I guess he didn't learn his lesson." She lifted her head off the pillow. Her body stiffened beneath his touch, and he raised his own head to listen. "Did you hear that?"

"Yep," he said. "Batton down the hatch. She's up."

They both laid their heads down and closed their eyes.

The sound of two little slippers shuffling down the hallway hit Jack. Mikala stepped into their bedroom and tiptoed to the edge of the bed, where Lisa had moved to his spot. Her feet stopped shuffling for a moment, and then she crept around the bed to the other side.

"Daddy?"

Jack remained still for a moment and then sprung at her like a tiger. He growled, grabbed her, and lifted her into the bed, tickling her sides.

It was nice to forget his plight, even if only for a little while.

They laughed through a battle, which Jack got the best of. When her giggles stopped, she placed one hand on Lisa's long hair and one on the side of Jack's face.

"Mommy?"

"Yes, Mikala?"

"Don't get mad."

"I never get mad, Mikala, just concerned."

"I need to talk to Daddy about my dreams."

"About Marky?" Jack responded quickly and then cringed. He couldn't see Lisa's expression but, surely, she was scowling.

"No, not Marky. Something else."

"Well, I suppose we better get our coffee," he said. "Downstairs this time?"

"Yes," she answered cool-headedly. "Downstairs is fine. Is that okay with you, Momma?"

"Well-l-l." The sound of that one word from Lisa told Jack their lovemaking had softened her usual Jack-and-Mikala morning-chat annoyance. Eight years they had known each other, and they were still crazy in love. Jack could read her like a newspaper. She never stayed mad long—especially after they made love. "It depends. What exactly goes in that mug of yours, Mikala? Is it coffee?"

Mikala giggled and leaned against her mom, as if glad for her mother's mood. "Mommy, you know it's milk."

"Well, I suppose milk is okay," Lisa responded, then lowered her voice. "But don't let Daddy drink too much coffee."

"Daddy says it's his fuel. He needs caffeine to wake up."

"Mommy already woke Daddy up," Jack said, then he leaned over and kissed Lisa.

"Don't believe him, Mikala." Lisa shook her head. "Daddy woke Mommy up."

"How did he do that, Mommy?"

"Ah, with his snoring, of course."

"Of course." Jack raised his eyebrows at Lisa, kissed her again, and then grabbed Mikala's hand. "Let's go get that coffee."

Their kitchen was small but homey, embellished with stainless steel and black appliances that matched a smart, charcoal-colored granite countertop. Jack flipped the light switch and the black morning dissolved. Mikala dragged one stool out, set a slipper on its rung, and scooched up, knees to wood and elbows to counter. She reached for the mug holder and grabbed their favorites, sliding them across the counter toward her father. Jack poured milk into one and set the other on the counter. He shoveled coffee into the coffeemaker, hit the on button, and waited, yawning as he did.

"I'm a morning person," Mikala said.

"You are, are you?"

"Yes, Momma said so."

When the flow of coffee ceased, Jack grabbed his mug and took a seat next to her.

"What else does Mommy tell you when I'm not around?"

"That you are the best daddy in the world."

"Oh, now, she's right about that." He winked at her and took a big sip from the mug, wincing as coffee burned the roof of his mouth.

"Aunt Rachel thinks so, too. She says Uncle Todd isn't such a good daddy. He likes coke too much."

Jack studied her face. Was she tempting him to say the coke wasn't soda pop?

"Mikala-a-a." He tilted his head and squinted one eye. "I thought we said you shouldn't listen to adult conversations from around corners."

"No, we didn't say that." She sipped milk. "You said that."

"I told you. No eavesdropping."

"I didn't listen."

"You didn't listen in on a conversation or you didn't listen to me?"

"What do you think?"

He could see her squelch a grin.

"Mikala?"

Her lips relaxed into a wide smile. "To you. I didn't listen to you."

He sipped his own drink again and sighed.

"Well, at least you're truthful. You come by it honestly. Heaven knows we Dalys are not good liars."

"Why did you lie, Daddy?"

"Me? Lie? What are you talking about?"

"You didn't tell Chief about the note."

Despite knowing his daughter like he did, she still shocked him occasionally. How she knew the things she shouldn't know never ceased to amaze him.

He stared into his coffee. What could he say?

"Daddy?" Her blue eyes reflected the kitchen light behind him. They twinkled with curiosity. "Is it the same reason you put your phone in the drawer and unplug the computer?"

"Mikala." He attempted to hold his mien. "Who have you been listening to?"

She slurped milk and thought. In that moment, she seemed ten, maybe twenty years older than her six years.

"No one, Aunt Rachel and Mommy do the same thing. They are afraid someone is listening. They don't talk inside Aunt Rachel's house." She blinked her eyes slowly in her typical, deep-in-thought way. "Once Aunt Rachel told Mommy she would never let them take me. Is that what you are afraid of, Daddy? Someone taking me?"

That smacked him. A hundred responses zipped through his head, none appropriate for a child. He could lie to her, but she would know, wouldn't she? His hands began to sweat around his coffee cup. How could someone so small arouse a nervousness in him that he didn't even experience in front of a judge on a witness stand?

For a diversion, he stood, sauntered to the coffeepot, and refilled his half-full cup. When he sat back down, he made eye contact but, still debating how honest to be, he refrained from speaking. Being frightened for and by your own child was a terrible dilemma.

"Daddy," she spoke, more than likely, because he couldn't. The blue in her eyes seemed turquoise this morning, transparent and tropical, as if you could look past them and see into the depths of the ocean. "I won't leave you until I go to college, so don't worry. You can tell Chief about the note."

He felt his face drop and his mouth slump into a frown. What was she doing? Comforting him?

"I promise. The white angel promised." Her little fingers reached across the counter, and she rested them on the back of his hand.

A deep, contemplative look emanated from behind those baby blues of hers. By God, she was comforting him. Was she studying him, too? Watching for some gesture that might betray his thoughts?

He'd been cross examined by senior lawyers with less acumen.

He cleared his throat. "You still see the white angel?"

"Sometimes, when I get scared."

He set his coffee cup down, wrapped his arms around her, and pulled her onto his lap.

"Oh, baby, you don't have to be afraid. Daddy will always protect you." He squeezed her little limbs.

"When you're not here," she whispered in his ear, "she protects me."

The memory of her first words—white angel, pretty—flashed in his head. At thirteen months old, she'd had trouble with their enunciation. "Why ain', prit'," she had muttered. But Lisa understood. Her reaction had been immediate. She covered her mouth with a hand. It took him all day to drag what Mikala was saying from Lisa.

Then the begging for an explanation began. Finally, after hours of nagging, Lisa broke and elucidated. When she herself dreamed, a white mass came to her in a fog. The mass was alive, swirling with an indescribable beauty and knowledge. Her grandmother called that anomaly the white angel. It—she—protected them, showed them visions, brought spirits in, and allowed them to talk to people who had passed to the afterlife.

The concept was all very confusing.

Billy's words sprang from his memory. "You just met a witch, Jack."

Would people call Mikala a witch? His sweet little girl? He didn't believe in witches. He wasn't sure he believed in mediums or psychics either, yet here he sat, holding a child who saw dead people and told the future.

Embarrassed by his own thoughts, his face reddened. Before he met Lisa, he had laughed at and referred to the Lilly Dale residents as wackos.

Alongside Cassadaga Lake in western New York, about an hour's drive away, psychics with self-proclaimed paranormal gifts lived in quaint little cottages in the town of Lily Dale. Palm readers, automatic writers, seers, and mediums walked those streets. He thought they were all crazy.

Then at a City Hall picnic shortly after he began dating Lisa, a wife of a fellow officer mentioned going to Lily Dale to have her fortune told. Another woman, whom he did not know, said she didn't need to make the hour drive.

"Just call one of the Callahan sisters," she had said. "I hear Rachel sees dead people."

Later, after they had dated for a while, Jack asked Lisa about the comment. Lisa said while all mediums are psychic, not all psychics are mediums, and that Rachel was merely psychic.

"So that means?" Her explanation did nothing but confuse him more.

"She doesn't see dead people. Only the future."

"And you?" Jack had asked.

"I see both." A light strawberry hue rushed over her nose and cheeks. "I'm a medium."

She looked so embarrassed that he was sorry he'd asked. So he tightened his arms around her and kissed her cheek. "You look too small to be a medium," he said, and her face brightened.

They didn't discuss the topic much after that. His mundane brain couldn't comprehend esotericism. It wasn't until Lisa likened the spirits-are-around-you phenomenon to radio waves that a smidge of understanding surfaced in him. Just because he didn't see something, didn't mean it didn't exist.

But talking about white masses and dead little boys to a six-year-old? Crazy.

"And Daddy?" She interrupted his scrutinizing of new-age mysticism.

"Yes, sweet pea?"

"Do you want to catch the bad man?"

Ah, back to the mundane. Now this question he could answer.

His eyes rose to the window, and he gazed outside to where the first rays of yellow light streaked the sky. Geoff Filutze had been called off his surveillance of their house last night, but Jack had already taken other measures to protect her.

He had stopped at her school without Lisa knowing and talked to the principal when the chief forewarned him they would be short staffed last night. Yesterday, he spoke with hall monitors, lunch monitors, Mrs. Shield and, more importantly, Mr. Foley, the security guard. He would call Foley again this morning. Remind him to keep an eye on Mikala. And he had told the neighbors on both sides of them, across the street, and two doors down to watch their house. Passed out little cards with his cell phone number. Wrote Geoff Filutze's number on the back and instructed them to call about anything out of the ordinary. If so much as a strange dog ran by, they should contact one of them.

Did he want to catch the bad man? Yes, more than anything. With missing children, you never left your job. Everything reminded you of the case—your kids, a man in an overcoat, a slow-moving car, a child walking alone on an empty street. You kept a notepad on the nightstand in case something hit you at three o'clock in the morning. When you answered the phone, you prayed for a better clue, tip, answer.

He set his cup down and gazed at Mikala's tiny hands, soft features, and cotton-candy pink pajamas. This bastard had let his daughter's name flow off the tip of his pen. Yes, catching him was all he wanted.

"I do. I want to find him, so he stops taking children from their moms. But I can't and won't involve you anymore."

She dropped a hand in her lap, blinked slowly, and nodded.

"But, Daddy?"

"Yes?"

"We need to find Luke."

"We're trying, baby."

"We need to find him soon. He's dying."

"Luke? He's sick?"

"Dying," she said, quite calmly.

"Mikala, how do you know that?"

"Marky," she said, confidently, not blinking. "He told me Luke is going to die soon if we don't find him."

There was something frightening about a child who talked of death so nonchalantly.

"We will find him, Mikala."

"Promise?"

He pictured Luke Anderson in his mind. The boy had malt-ball brown hair like Jaden and John, and his eyes were as honey-comb-hued as theirs. The twins were about Luke's age, same height, and similar weight. If they stood side by side, they would look like triplets from the back.

"I promise."

With that response, Jack shuddered. He must be removed from the case. This was the first time in his life he made a promise he did not know that he could keep.

"We can tell everyone else it's Aunt Rachel and Mamma who see Marky, as long as you tell the chief the truth—that it's me." Mikala scooted back onto her own stool and placed both of her hands on her mug and drank the last of her milk. "You have to tell him, Daddy."

No, he realized the truth then. He would never tell anyone she was the seer, not the chief and not Billy, because he could not bear people calling her a witch.

He cupped her sweet little face in his hands and kissed her forehead. "I'm sorry, Mikala, I won't tell him. I can't."

"Aunt Rachel can," she said softly. "She'll tell Chief."

He thought her wrong. She didn't know her aunt's history. Rachel would risk her life to protect Mikala.

"Honey, Aunt Rachel is the last person in the world who would tell anyone you are seeing Marky, but just the same, we aren't telling her."

He watched Mikala blink intensely like she always did when she didn't believe someone. But Jack had spoken the truth, and if God himself came down and told him Rachel would be the one to tell the chief that Mikala was the seer, he would call Him a liar.

"You're wrong, Daddy. Aunt Rachel is going to tell him."

19 Chief Ben Morgan

The chief knew his intimidating size unnerved some officers and detectives, so as he strolled through the precinct toward the Helen room, he used his size to discourage them from approaching. He held his head high and his torso straight, lengthening the space he filled in the room to 6'4" as he walked.

He was in no mood to be detained. He wanted to get in and out and back to business. So he lumbered through the station like a mama bear with two cubs trailing behind, avoiding all eye contact with anyone in the station unless he felt the need to discourage discourse. One officer approached him and then rapidly rushed away after reading his body language: back off.

When he pierced Helen's doorway and saw three officers perched on seats inside, he nudged his head toward the door, encouraging them to their feet. They dropped pens and grabbed files like there had been a raid, and then they scurried toward the door. Rachel and Jack filed in past the chief, and all three men looked back as Rachel passed and they exited the room.

The chief shook his head, shut the door, and lumbered toward the only new piece of office equipment—the desk in the corner. He dropped his cell into one of its metal drawers, and Jack and Rachel followed suit with their cells. He motioned for them to sit, slammed the drawer shut, and circled the room, jerking computer cords from walls and turning screens.

He dragged a chair from under a desk, turned it around, and lifted one long leg over the seat. He sat down, muscled abs against the back of the chair, forearms leaning on top. Then he watched her, too.

The Callahan girls, on a kind day, women called them witches and men tossed salacious stares as they passed but made no comment. He sighed. Beauty did have its drawbacks.

"We're fine here," he said, his voice deep but cordial. He knew she'd be leery of the location. This was her first time back to City Hall in ten years. With the help of his wife, Lynn, Rachel had successfully avoided a return trip while volunteering as an advisory board member for the County's comprehensive plan. Lynn always sought out the finest young minds to aid in her projects. Lynn loved Rachel. "We sweep this joint every other day."

"I don't know if I'm comfortable here." Rachel tugged the cuffs of her jacket abruptly to straighten her sleeves. "Are you sure? We can talk?"

That hurt him. With a history like theirs, she needed to ask?

"I wouldn't take the chance if I wasn't sure."

She tucked her chin and tilted her head toward Jack. "What do you think?"

"We're fine here," Jack answered.

That she trusted Jack and not him offended the chief.

He felt his lips purse before he turned toward Jack. "You admitted the informant wasn't Rachel."

Jack hesitated long enough for Rachel to perk up and speak first.

"No, but we're going to say it is." She was determined and spoke in a tone no one else—except the chief's secretary, Donna—used with him. "That's the deal breaker. If you want your man, you're going to act as if everything comes from me."

"If I want my man?" He used a cold tone to respond but stifled a laugh. Rachel Callahan's spunk never ceased to amaze him.

"That's right, Ben. If you want your man, you'll accommodate me because—correct me if I'm wrong but—it's been how many weeks? And you don't have a clue who this guy is?"

"Rachel, c'mon, don't start with him." Jack looked particularly tired today. "You need to work with us on this."

She sat down haughtily, folded her hands on the desk, and offered an insincere "Sorry." Then right before she glanced around the room arrogantly, her eyes fell to the floor just long enough for Ben to realize she was uncomfortable.

So was he.

He reminded himself of all she had been through and softened his annoyance. "I understand your concern, Rachel. I do. But the truth is the press will get wind Lisa is the informant."

Jack hadn't been prepared to hear that, and true to form, he sprang to his feet before Ben could continue. "Wait a minute. You both know she's too fragile."

"Sit down, Jack," the chief said. Then he did something he'd never done before. He dug into his pocket, pulled out a cigar, and, right there in the middle of the Helen room, he lit up, took a drag, and offered Jack one.

With a look of confusion first, then one of disdain, Jack dropped back into his seat and waved a hand vehemently. "Saying Lisa is involved is not an option. Period."

The chief squinted, considered Jack's feelings, and gave him time to sulk. He knew lots of men who underestimated their wives' strength. At one time, he'd been one of those guys.

Ben had watched Lynn's fearless charge into the depths of cancer while his big, strong, stocky frame sat silently in the corner. He couldn't mention the "c" word at first. For a long time, he thought, if only the cancer had found him, not Lynn, he could have beat it. But in the end, he realized he was the weaker soul. Lynn's strength took her soaring into the next life. She didn't beat cancer, she transcended the disease. Left a hole in the world where she exited. Her faith unwavering, her convictions unbending, and her love, unending.

Ben glanced at his big hands, opened the one without the stogy and then closed it. Yes, he smiled inwardly, strength could be widely defined. Jack would realize that in time.

He began raising the cigar to his lips a second time, and the thought of how alike Lynn and Rachel were struck him. He glanced Rachel's way. Her expression toughened, and even if those taut cheeks and bold brown eyes hadn't revealed her thoughts, her body language did. It said: really? You aren't going to offer me a drag?

He intentionally put on a pout, but inside he laughed. He handed her the cigar and watched. Thought the way she let the smooth, sweet taste swirl in her mouth seemed unwomanly. He couldn't help but allow his lips to flicker upward on end as she let out a puff of smoke and ran her tongue over her top lip.

"Wow," she said. "Cuban? I haven't tasted a Cuban cigar in over six years."

She took another drag, sent smoke into the air, and handed the cigar back. The chief took the stogy and shrugged. "They opened the border."

Two officers barged through Helen's soundproof door, and the chief threw a glance over his shoulder that would have stilled a charging bull. The first man stopped so abruptly the second guy ran into him. They backed out and closed the door. Whether his stare, the cigar, or Rachel Callahan's presence hastened their steps, the chief was unsure.

Jack broke the silence.

"We need a plan in place to protect Lisa." He crossed his arms and tucked his hands in his armpits, thumbs pointing upward. "I want that cruiser back in front of our house and an undercover cop, too."

"On what grounds?" the chief grunted. The director of finance had already chastised him for exceeding his labor budget.

"On the grounds she's going to help Rachel solve the City's abduction case. And you needn't tell them that. Just say the kidnapper targeted my sister's kid. That's all they need to hear." Jack seemed nervous to the chief. "Put Filutze there. He's the best. I trust him."

The chief and Rachel exchanged glances.

"What's going on? Why are you two rolling eyes at each other?"

"Actually, Jack, I do want everyone to think I'm the informant." Rachel crossed a leg and shifted in her seat. "But I've been thinking about this case long and hard for over a week. We do need Lisa, but she can't work strictly from home."

"You're right," the chief agreed. "Lisa's going to have to come down to the station."

"I'm hoping to avoid that, Ben." Rachel poked her elbows onto the desktop, seemed a bit miffed. "I agreed we have to talk to her, and she may have to visit some places with us, but I don't want her coming here. There are too many reporters hanging around."

"Eventually she'll need to come in."

Rachel sat quiet for a while, tugging at her sleeves again. "You know I'm not comfortable with that."

"I understand. I expect all hell to break loose. But the Mayor and City Council will want the entire department dancing at the press's shindig. So, although we can attempt to keep Lisa's name from them, we should prepare for the worst."

"I don't like the sound of that." Jack shook his head.

"Neither do I." Rachel took a long breath. "I told you, Ben. I only agreed to come in if you promised to keep Lisa's name out of this."

"Wait." Jack put a finger in the air and squeezed his eyes shut. "What did you say?"

Rachel pressed her lips together.

"Did you and the chief have a conversation before today? About my wife?"

She remained still a moment longer, but then Ben watched Rachel's eyebrows lower and the line of muscle beside her high cheekbones tighten. He squared his shoulders and prepared for fireworks.

"That's right, Jack," she said. He was sure her lips hadn't moved. Her teeth were still clenched together. "Ben and I talked about your wife, my sister, and we both agree she needs to be on this case full-fledged." She turned toward Ben. Her lips began moving again. She unclenched her teeth, slightly. "But I said her name must be kept out of it."

"We will try—"

"No," Jack interrupted Ben, hand raised. "I'm changing my mind. If the chief believes the press will expose her then she's out."

"Oh, really? Says who?" Rachel spat at him.

"Says me. Her husband."

"Well, who the hell are you? Her master?"

"Here's the deal. Lisa's name stays out of this, or she doesn't help you, Rachel. You can do this on your own."

"I can't guarantee that, Jack." Ben tried getting back into the conversation. They ignored him.

"I can't do this on my own, Jack. I'm having some trouble."

"What do you mean trouble?"

"Trouble concentrating."

"Because of Todd?"

Red burrowed out of Rachel's cheeks. The chief didn't like where this was going. He attempted to do damage control. "Tread lightly, Jack, you're—"

Rachel cut him off. "It's none of your damn business why I'm having trouble. The fact of the matter is I am having difficulty seeing this bastard. Maybe he's blocking me or maybe it's something else. Doesn't matter. Lisa can help me."

"Well, now I'm saying you do it without her."

"Jack." She stood. "She sees more than I do, and we need to find these kids."

"No, she's done. Do the rest alone."

"She's better than me."

"I don't give a shit."

"It should have been her, Jack." Rachel's voice lowered. "Years ago. They should have taken Lisa. They would have if they'd known she was better than me."

"That's not true." He pointed his finger. "You were the child prodigy, the great psychic, not Lisa."

"No. She was better than me."

"I don't give a damn who was better than who. You were the one carted off to Project Dream. You're the expert, you're stronger than her, and you're taking the heat."

"I already did." Rachel bent at the waist and pounded her fists on the desk in front of her. "I went away for her."

The chief's gaze fell to the ground. As long as he lived, he would feel responsible for Rachel Callahan ending up in that Nevada desert. He had been so callow when he first met her. By all standards, he was the best upcoming rookie, a medaled hero from Desert Storm. He was invincible, unrelenting, so when his niece's name turned up on that long list of rape victims, he worked day and night to find the perpetrator. Yet that his fingers entwined with Rachel Callahan's was sheer luck—for him, not Rachel.

She was an eighth-grader, barely a teenager, but her uncanny sight helped him solve a case the department had called the FBI in on and marked unsolvable. He had no experience with clairvoyant people, but when Rachel Callahan told him where to find the rapist and how to get a search warrant, he started believing the John Edward, Sylvia Brown, and Lily Dale weirdos of the world might not be so off the wall. She was an uncanny find, an investigative Midas.

He bragged her up in front of the Mayor and Chief and mentioned her on the sly to FBI investigators. Said they might consider using her on other cases. He had no idea what was going on after 9/11. That the government was searching the country for clairvoyant kids and plucking them from communities for the good of the people. Next thing he knew, she was gone and the family wasn't talking. The government had ways of silencing people. The Callahans kept their mouths closed and Lisa close to home.

Then Jack came along and drew her out. Poor, helpless, lovestruck Jack.

"And I'll do it again for her, Jack," she said. For the first time ever, Ben saw tears in Rachel Callahan's eyes. Even when Lynn died, she had choked them back for his sake. "But I need her help. I wish to God I could do it alone."

She closed her eyes for a moment and then opened them.

"But I can't." She put a hand on her forehead and sat back down, turned toward him tiredly. "All I'm asking, Ben, is that you promise to keep Lisa's name out of it."

"I could lie and promise, but truthfully? I know her identity will come out."

"Then no." Now Jack pounded his fists on his desk. "Lisa is out. End of discussion."

"C'mon, Jack," Ben reached for his handkerchief. Wiped his nose.

"You think I'm kidding? Use Rachel or—"

"Or what, Jack?" The chief interjected calmly. "You're going to walk away and forget someone's abducting kids? Turn your back on a predator, possible murderer, child abuser?"

"You're damn right I am. I'm going to leave this room and go directly to Human Resources and ask to be removed from the case. I'll tell them my sister-in-law is involved, and it's a conflict of interest."

"You know you aren't going to do that."

"Yes, I am, Chief. This time I'll walk away."

The chief tipped ashes of his cigar onto the floor and brought the stogy to his lips. He took a long drag, swirled smoke inside his open mouth, and exhaled. "You care too much. You won't go."

"You're wrong," Jack pointed a finger, raised his voice. "You don't know me so well. It's Rachel. Rachel alone or I walk out that door and never look back. I don't care how many more children are snatched from their mother's arms. Do you understand me? You put the surveillance back on my family, but you say it's Rachel. Or I go to HR."

"Oh, my God." Rachel slid from her seat.

The chief watched her jump up. She leaned forward, crossed her arms, and dropped her head.

"Oh no, no, no," she whispered. She closed her eyes and began rocking back and forth, the gesture so unlike her.

She stared at the floor, swaying. Much like—who did it remind him of? He thought for a moment. That Lenny Emling guy. The one they were always picking up for walloping juvenile delinquents. A night-walking vigilante. He'd seen him rock that way every time they brought him in. In that moment, it occurred to the chief that Lenny might sway because of horror. Maybe fear rocked his frame, not incompetency, because wasn't that what he was witnessing now in Rachel's eyes? Fear?

When Rachel finally returned his stare, her face was flushed. She looked like she was about to pass out.

"Don't you see?" she asked him. "Why Jack won't allow it?"

He furrowed his brow and shook his head. No, he didn't understand. What was she saying? Her face was pale.

"What is it?" He stood and reached a hand to steady her.

"It's Mikala," she murmured. "Lisa's not dreaming. Mikala is."

Jack jumped to his feet, his fists clenched.

"My God," he whispered. A redness fell down his face like a shade closing. He looked as fragile as Rachel. Stunned, he slumped back down into his seat. "She said you'd tell him."

Baffled himself, the chief barely heard Jack. Never had the idea occurred to him that Jack's child was the seer. He glanced at the freckles on the back of his thick, rugged hands. One was wrapped around his Cuban cigar and the other flat against Rachel's arm. They were getting old, wrinkled. How small they seemed in that instant.

He sighed, then with complete emotional restraint, he stepped away from Rachel, lifted the cigar to his lips, and took one last long drag. He licked two fingers and cauterized the tip of the Cuban with his wet touch. His fingers burned.

"Not this time, you lousy bastards," he said. Then he tramped to Helen's door and grabbed the doorknob. "Rachel, you're our informant. Lisa's our lamb. We'll put on like we're keeping her secret—for everyone's sake."

He heaved the door open, but before his feet carried him away, he uttered under his breath. "They can go to hell."

He didn't give a rat's ass that lying to the FBI was a felony.

"They'll not take another one of our kids. Not as long as an ounce of blood runs through my veins."

20 Rachel

"Mikala sees more than I see." Lisa picked nervously at her fingers. Two or three bled. "I don't want to be like Mom and ignore everything, so I encourage her to talk about what she sees."

Lisa drank the last of her coffee and sashayed to the sink, avoiding several of the twins' toys sprawled on the kitchen floor. She placed her cup in the basin. "She says she will, but then I find out, after the fact, she's told one of her friends to give their dog extra treats because they're going to die or, worse, they better go visit their grandmother."

"You said she gave Lizzy a teething ring?" Rachel fought off a smile trying to work its way out.

"Yes." Lisa bent down and picked up a toy. "Liz promised she wouldn't tell anyone, but you know Lizzy. She never could keep a secret."

Rachel had stifled her laugh as long as she could. She hid her mouth behind her coffee cup, but felt her shoulders shaking.

"It's not funny." Lisa set the toy on the counter.

"Yes, it is. She gave me a teething ring, too."

"You're kidding." Lisa plopped into her seat, leaned elbows to counter and slapped her forehead in a cupped hand. "What am I going to do with her?"

"Nothing." Rachel shrugged. "You can't do anything. She's her own person. But how nice for Lizzy. I heard she was having trouble getting pregnant."

"I'm happy for her. I just hope she doesn't blab it all over town how she found out."

"She won't. I'll talk to her."

"I don't know what to do with Mikala anymore."

"She doesn't know how to control it yet. She trusts everyone. She'll learn. We did."

"Were we that blatant about it?" Lisa grabbed a tissue and pressed it against her two bleeding fingers.

"Are you kidding? Remember our neighbor, Mrs. Hobeck? You said her dead husband was standing behind her, and if she looked inside the vase with the fake flowers, she would find their safety deposit box key." Rachel smiled behind her cup again. "Then you turned to Mom and asked what a safety deposit key was."

"I remember." Lisa laughed. "Mom nearly dropped the dinner she made for her on the floor."

"When Mrs. Hobeck grabbed the vase and dumped the flowers, the key clanged onto the floor, and she fainted."

Their laughter ebbed and then rose and then ebbed again. Rachel loved these sister moments.

"So, you see." Rachel wiped tears off her face. "Mikala will learn to control her dreams, just like you and I did."

"I suppose. You know, I used to read for Mrs. Hobeck after you went away. Mr. Hobeck came through easily. She missed him so much that I felt like I was in the middle of a love reunion." Lisa leaned toward the end of the counter and tossed her tissue in the garbage. "I hope I helped her. She seemed content afterward. When the doctor told her the cancer was back, she wasn't afraid. She said her husband was waiting for her."

Such an abnormal conversation in such a normal setting. Lisa's warmth took the chill out of everything. Her plain split-level home with its neat but dated kitchen, popcorn ceilings, drafty windows, and JCPenney furniture held a charm Rachel could not duplicate in her own chilly mansion.

What was the warmth she felt when she stepped into her sister's home? Love? Energy? The house danced in the ordinary—slightly worn carpets, food spills, TV blasting—

but it was a comfortable place to land. A sanctuary where her sister's family could reenergize and then go out into the world and wring the light out of the day.

She envied Lisa's normalcy. To be so mad about your husband, so in love and happy with your world that you never noticed the fancy cars and designer clothes around you must feel peaceful.

But for the American government, I, too, could have been happy. Que sera, sera.

She felt a grimace squeeze her lips. She hated hormonal self-pity. Usually, she accepted her lot in life. She was born of strength, the matriarch of the family even before her mother passed away.

Yet now, she glanced toward her sister, hadn't Lisa's strength surpassed hers? There she sat, so cute in her t-shirt and holey jeans, while Rachel tried to disguise her own wild demeanor with fancy clothes. Lisa's simplicity mixed with her sensitivity, making her a portal to perception.

Jack was wrong about Lisa, and perhaps she herself had underestimated her sister. Her passion and childlike sweetness made her powerful. And her beauty? Lisa's blue eyes glistened with acuity—even if she didn't know it.

The tide in that old river is turning.

"I never thanked you." Lisa's words flushed the thoughts from her head.

"For what?"

"That day. I know you don't like to talk about it. Every time I bring the topic up, you change the subject, but you knew back then I was afraid to talk to the police, so you spoke to them for me."

"You were younger."

"Sixteen months is hardly an emotional advantage."

Rachel reached across the counter and squeezed her hand. "Seventeen months and forget the past. It's spilt milk. I was tougher than you back then. And, better that you stayed with Mom. There was no question you were the kinder daughter."

"Why don't you ever talk about the desert?"

"Because there's not much to say." Rachel released her hand. Gazed toward the living room where Lisa's computer sat ostentatiously open to the world. She wondered. Would the American government be monitoring her sister's home? She doubted they extended surveillance to siblings. Some transmitters came from families with ten children. Still, a slight burning rose from her stomach to her throat. She couldn't risk anyone finding out about Mikala.

"Let's go for a walk." Rachel had to rethink their conversation. Had they said too much about Mikala? With the television blasting next to the computer, she thought they were safe.

"Sure." Lisa stood. "It's nice out. Jack took the kids to the park. Let's walk there."

They packed a few things, grabbed sweaters, and ventured out. Rachel nodded at the next-door neighbor, and Lisa commented about the woman's beautiful mums. They passed several houses before Lisa turned to her.

"Do you think we said too much?"

"No, I doubt your house is bugged, but when it comes to Mikala, I don't want to take any chances."

"I agree. Jack does check. I'm not sure how often, but he's never found anything."

Yes, Rachel knew. She had suggested Jack check his house shortly after Mikala began having dreams.

"Just keep your computer turned off," she told Lisa. "Cover the camera with duct tape or a sticky."

"Shoot. The webcam. Never thought of that."

"I'm no longer on close surveillance, but I never trust an open computer." Rachel shuffled her feet through crisp leaves on the sidewalk, stuffed her hands in her pockets, and lifted her chin to feel the soft breeze against her face.

"Rachel, tell me the truth. How bad was the desert?"

The truth? Rachel tipped her head back and enjoyed the peaceful November day a bit longer. Then she dropped her chin and wondered how to answer. The cold, hard truth was Rachel hated the desert, especially in the beginning. She had felt, at fourteen, her life was over. Then she noticed Todd.

"Not too bad," she lied. "Once Todd and I started hanging out, time passed quickly. He was tall and lanky, gaunt when I first met him. But he filled out. Grew handsome. And I liked listening to his stories about the freeness of being raised on a farm, tipping cows, hitchhiking to the Sawtooth Forest.

"Todd 's father wasn't around much, so his mother practically raised him alone. She was a religious fanatic. Came from a long line of strict Catholics. Todd told her about his visions once and never again. She threatened to call the priest for an exorcism."

"At least Mom didn't do that."

"I know. Plus, we had each other. Todd and his sister weren't close. She's a lot older. He said he didn't have many friends, either, but he did spend a lot of time at a neighbor's farm a quarter mile down the road. They had six boys, rotten to the core. Their mother, Rashmi, migrated from Sri Lanka and didn't speak much English. Todd thought she might have been a mail-order bride. She was fourteen years younger than their dad and seventeen years older than George Junior. After Todd left for the desert, Junior killed a man during a robbery outside of Boise. He was sentenced to life in a state penitentiary. Todd wasn't sure what happened to the rest of them."

"Those are the boys he got in trouble with, right?"

"Yeah, they were roasting a stolen pig on a spit and smoking marihuana. Todd wasn't sure whether someone dropped a joint or the pig roast caught the grass on fire, but it was small, at first. They weren't worried. Then the wind shifted and the flames rose fast. The Meyer boys took off. Todd ran for a neighbor, Mr. Miller. Woke him. Mr. Miller hurried to wet down the field, but the fire had crawled all around the pasture. He sent Todd to another neighbor's to call for help. By the time the firetrucks came, Mr. Miller had burns over eighty percent of his body.

"Todd was devastated. The old man didn't die right away. His body swelled, and Todd sat at his bedside and watched. The old man suffered for days—and Todd for years."

"That's terrible."

"He only talked about it once and made me promise not to tell anyone. I guess my allegiance to him is subsiding these days. He's not the same person anymore."

"I know. Jack and I suspected he was using again."

"Yeah, he can't kick it. He really got hooked on coke in the desert."

"How did he end up there?"

"Actually, Rashmi told the detention center counselor he was psychic. She was a Buddhist. Believed wholeheartedly in siddhi, the power of the mind, and taught her boys—and Todd—how to meditate. She said both Junior and Todd had visions. The CIA sallied in and tested them. Turned out George was pulling one over on his mother. Todd's gift, though, was confirmed and away he went. They dropped all charges for everyone. A sort of thank you to Rashmi. And then, you know, they made their promises to Todd's family. He wasn't always the way he is now."

"I remember how happy you were when you first met him." Lisa buttoned the top of her sweater to cut the chill of the wind.

"I was." Rachel folded her arms. "He and I used to sneak out with a bunch of kids at night, lie on the ground and watch for shooting stars. One night I snuck out alone, and Todd showed up. He was so sure of himself back then. Said he was going to Las Vegas and play poker when our time was up there. I asked him what Vegas was like, and he made the city sound so dreamy. We would lay under the stars and imagine him playing poker and the two of us opening a side business reading for people—you know, Las Vegas's psychic couple. We were going to give Allison Dubois a run for her money."

They laughed and then Rachel became quiet.

"You loved him," Lisa finally said.

"I did. He had such an imagination and so much energy. He was fun, always joking around. Even our mentors loved him."

"What happened, Rachel? Why do you think he changed?"

Rachel let her hands fall to her side, and she slipped them back into her pockets. "People never expect their life to go bad. You don't know you are on the wrong path until you're so far down the road you can't find your way back. He couldn't kick the drugs. He couldn't get out of the program to go after his dream. He was a good poker player—until the drugs clouded his mind. Then his dream slipped further from his reach when they moved us back to Erie."

"He still plays here and goes to Las Vegas every July."

"Yes, Las Vegas, Atlantic City. Philly. Hits all the weekend tournaments, and really, I'm partially to blame. I like it when he's gone."

"Do you love him at all anymore?"

"I don't know." They had arrived at the edge of the park. They stopped near the iron-gated entrance. "I don't know anything anymore—about Todd or my life."

"I'm sorry, Rachel. Sorry you had to go through everything." Lisa stretched an arm around her sister's broad shoulders and squeezed. "Does it still exist? Project Dream?"

Again, a burning sensation settled in Rachel's throat. "Honestly, I don't know what goes on in the desert, now. I just know I don't want any of our kids involved. I heard they closed everything. We can only hope."

"And pray."

The wind swirled and mixed coolness into the Indian-summer breeze. Rachel tucked her sweater close to her body and glanced around. The cruiser that normally sat outside Lisa's home had followed Jack and the kids to the park. That comforted her.

"This is cruel to say," Lisa interrupted her thoughts, "but if Trump resurrects the program, I hope they take kids from detention centers."

"Me, too. Pluck them from reformatories and leave the rest of us alone. But they probably won't. Some of those kids were god-awful."

"As in?"

"As in there were rumors one committed first-degree murder."

"Oh, geez, how did Lenny get along with them?"

"Lenny stayed to himself. Todd said some kids made the mistake of picking on him in the dinner line their first week. Lenny kicked the living daylights out of one of them. After that, everyone steered clear of him."

"That's good."

"Why did you take to Lenny like you did?"

"Lenny?"

Rachel thought Lisa blushed a little when she spoke his name.

"You always stuck up for him."

"I don't know. I hated kids picking on him, calling him a freak." Lisa glanced away, slowly blinking her eyes.

Rachel loved that habit of Lisa's. The mannerism had fallen to Mikala.

"There is just something sweet about him." A slight grin curved Lisa's lips.

"Sweet isn't a word I'd use to describe Lenny Emling."

"Well, in school he was so small for his age even the nuns couldn't prevent the name-calling in the cafeteria, and the principal was no help. So, I stuck up for him."

"Yes, you did. Sucker punched the boys who picked on him."

"Then you'd step in and protect me."

"I had to. You were little yourself." Rachel's mood lightened. "I thought you were going to get killed that day you slugged Robbie Redgrave for knocking Lenny into a snowbank. So much red came out of his nose it looked like the spaghetti sauce."

"That wasn't from my punch. It was form yours."

"Mrs. Arbuckle threw up her macaroni and cheese lunch." Rachel's husky voice pirouetted into a laugh.

"Well, she was pregnant and there was blood everywhere."

"Thank God Lenny grew twelve inches that year, and you never had to stick up for him again."

"I know. He still stuttered, but the kids were too afraid to say anything to him. Everyone picked him first for football. He probably would have been recruited by a high school coach if he hadn't gone berserk and sent those four kids to the hospital at that festival."

"Those boys deserved it, so I guess you're right. Lenny is sweet in a big-oaf sort of way."

"I hear he's taking care of his mother. I hope life has been kind to him since he's been home. Did you see him much when you were in Nevada?"

"Twice a week for seminars. He asked about you. He never forgot how you stuck up for him. He seemed sad when Dad passed away, and we sold the house. He and his mom still live in the house he grew up in—so I hear."

Lisa reached a hand toward Rachel and stroked her arm. "You don't need to lie to me. I know."

Rachel glanced at Lisa's hand. How did Lisa always know when she was lying? Sometimes Lisa's seriousness sucked the life out of her.

"What do you mean?" she asked, because 'Can't you just leave it alone?' would offend her.

"I know you still meet—you and Lenny—for Project Dream."

"Project Dream was over a long time ago." Technically, that was the truth. What they had now was a spinoff.

"If that were so, you wouldn't be worried about Mikala, would you?"

Rachel said nothing.

"I'm not as fragile as I used to be."

Hadn't Rachel just told Jack the same? Still, Lisa's childhood panic attacks had been disconcerting.

"Rachel, I'll be fine. That was long ago. I haven't had a panic attack in years."

Rachel glanced at her. How did Lisa always know what she was thinking? Had she guessed her thoughts? Or read her mind?

The government's dream program had produced two mind readers, both children. The adult program never produced one. But two kids—out of the hundred, out of the millions of children screened—had been rumored to have that ability. The names of those two individuals remained hidden in the masses. She wasn't completely sure they existed.

Did they? She decided to try something.

"*What do you think would have happened to you if you had gone to the desert instead of me,*" she said slowly, pointedly, in her mind.

Then she waited.

They stood quietly at the edge of the park. After a minute passed and Lisa said nothing, Rachel relaxed, thanking God for the silence. Rumors were swirling amongst transmitters that a mind-reading test program had begun out west. She didn't want the curse of that trait in her family.

She glanced toward the park and searched for Mikala and the boys. Off in the distance, Jack climbed a monkey bar alongside Mikala, and the twins played beside them on a slide and fire pole. She watched quietly until Mikala spotted them, waved, and jumped from the monkey bars, running toward them.

Lisa wrapped her fingers around Rachel's arm.

"I would have crumbled."

21 The boys

"Luke, you look terrible sick."

Luke used to be big and strong. At the beach, his stone skipped five times before sinking into the water. Matt's only skipped two times. Luke had been the bravest boy at summer camp. Swam out the farthest in the water.

But now Luke's skinny body was flat against the ground. Like he imagined that skydiver, who fell from the sky because of a broken parachute, would look Maybe worse.

Matt heard a noise. He listened. A mouse scurried across the dirt. Matt breathed stale air out of his lungs and watched to see if the mouse approached.

He used to be afraid of the mice, but he quickly learned they wouldn't hurt him. As long as the little light on the wall behind him didn't go out, and he kept the lid on the food container tight, they didn't bother him. Four times now, one baby black mouse with a white spot near his nose inched toward him, and Matt mustered the courage to pet his fur. He gave him a lick of peanut butter twice.

A mouse approached now. He squinted his eyes to search for a white spot.

"Itty?" he said. He had named the little one Itty Bitty. "Is that you?"

The little mouse neared, and Matt quickly unscrewed the peanut butter jar, stuck a finger in, tightened the lid, and stuck his hand toward the mouse.

"There you go. Hurry before the others come."

The mouse licked his index finger clean and dashed away. Other mice forged toward Matt, but he stood and kicked dirt toward them.

"No," he hollered, and they scampered away.

He sat back down Indian style next to Luke. He leaned toward him.

"Luke," Matt shook him. "Want some water?"

Matt's lips hurt when he spoke. They were cracked and bleeding, and his throat was so dry he didn't recognize his own voice. He hoped he didn't get sick, too. He saved as much water for Luke as he could. Only drank, himself, when he was dizzy.

Luke made no effort to respond, and Matt picked up the apple he had given him earlier and set it against his lips. Still, he didn't move. He lay cheek to dirt, eyes closed.

Matt grabbed his blanket, scooted across the dirt toward the water jugs, and dumped a bit of water on its edge. He closed the lid tight, moved back to Luke, and once again pretended the corner of the blanket was a washcloth. He dabbed Luke's forehead.

"Luke?" He sat back on his legs. "Are you okay?"

Luke's eyes twitched, and he tried to lift his head, but Matt could see he had no strength left inside.

"I want my Mommy," Luke whimpered.

"Luke," Matt said, happily. "You're awake."

"Momma—"

"Don't cry." Matt patted him twice on the chin. "It makes Monster Man mad."

But Luke couldn't stop. He sobbed, and, to Matt, Luke's weak cry bounced off the dirt walls and sounded as loud as Nana's noisy dog, who you had to lock in the basement when you left the house, or he'd tear up the carpet.

"Don't cry."

The last time Monster Man climbed up the ladder to leave, he said he would be right outside, and he hollered at Matt to keep Luke quiet. He said he'd whip Matt if Luke cried.

Luke moaned, and Matt's eyes shot toward the steps. No one. He wormed onto his knees and stroked Luke's head for a while. When he tired, he plopped into a sitting position as the room whirled in his head.

Time to drink.

He drank water and took a bite of an apple, wondering, hoping, maybe Monster Man would be gone long this time, and Mommy would find him before the water ran out.

Monster Man had lugged plenty down the stairs that last time. Three jugs. And he had filled the food container with apples, bread, and another big jar of peanut butter. He also left blankets, lots of them. One was shiny and smooth and especially warm. Most days were cold now, so Matt was thankful for the shiny one.

Maybe winter was here. He didn't know. He could not see the sun and count the days.

He wondered about his preschool and about Christmas. Did Santa know where he was even if Mommy didn't?

If Mommy were there, he'd sleep in her soft, warm arms, and she'd brush back his hair and tell him everything was going to be all right. That Luke was going to live, and the police were going to capture Monster Man and lock him in jail forever.

He glanced at Luke. Wondered what his momma was like. That's when he realized Luke had stopped crying.

Matt took a breath so deep he could feel the air inside him reach his shoulders. His lips quivered. When Luke cried, Matt's belly ached. But when Luke was silent, pins and needles ran up and down his arms and legs.

He leaned close. Slowly put his hand to the bottom of Luke's nose. Felt his warm breath against his fingers.

Luke's still alive.

He lay his hand on Luke's cheek.

Cold.

He took his half of the shiny blanket and wrapped it tightly around Luke, tucking him in. "Sleep tight," he said.

Then he wrapped himself with blankets and snuggled up next to Luke, allowing one knee to overlap Luke's legs, trying to help keep him warm.

"Don't die, Luke," he said once he settled in.

He thought he would know this time. When Marky died, he and Luke kept trying to wake him. His skin was cold and he wet himself and they poked him with their fingers, but he wouldn't get up. His eyes and mouth were open. His hands were hard.

Matt reached over and felt Luke's cold, soft hand. Yes, he would know this time.

With no window, he didn't know if it was day or night. He was tired. It must be night. He moved closer to Luke, closed his eyes, and pretended Luke was Mommy.

"Now I lay me down to sleep…"

22 Lisa

"Now I lay me down to sleep..." Mikala lifted her head off her clasped hands.

"Go on, Mikala," Lisa said, her own head resting on folded fingers. "Finish up and I'll read a story."

When Mikala said no more, Lisa lifted her chin.

"Mikala?" She leaned on the bed for a closer view. "Are you crying?"

Still, Mikala said nothing.

"Jaden and John." Lisa stood, tugged one hand of each boy until they stood, too, and then placed her hands on the small of their backs. "Go pick out a book and get into your beds. Daddy will be in to read to you in a minute."

She guided them toward the hall, and they ran for their bedroom, hooting like they'd been busted from jail. Lisa hurried to the end of the hallway and hollered down the stairs. "Jack, can you come up here and read the boys a story?"

She waited to hear his "sure" and then returned to Mikala's room, closing the bedroom door behind her. By then, a few tears streaked Mikala's face. Lisa sat down on the bed, and Mikala jumped into her arms.

"Mikala." She brushed back the long blonde strands that framed Mikala's face and caught one of her fingers in a tangle. She twisted it free and stroked the child's wild hair. "Are you all right?"

"Oh, Mommy." Mikala buried her head in her mother's chest.

"What's wrong?" Lisa leaned back, slid Mikala under the covers, and slipped in beside her. She wiped Mikala's cheeks and drew her close. "What's this all about? Why are you so upset? You hardly ever cry."

"Momma, Luke is dying and Matt is scared."

"Luke? The little boy who was abducted? That's what this is about?"

"Yes, Mommy. Matt tries so hard to help him, but he isn't even six like me. Luke needs his momma. You've got to help us. Marky and I don't know where they are. Please, don't be mad at me."

"I'm not mad at all." Lisa kissed her forehead. "I wish I could help you—"

"You can, Mommy. You have to. They are in the ground, and it's cold and dark and—" She lifted her head, and her sad eyes tugged at Lisa's heart. "You have to help us."

Lisa placed a hand on Mikala's cheek, gently brought her face down, and nestled Mikala's head under her chin. A teardrop from Mikala's wet eyes dribbled to her neck. She lifted a lock of Mikala's hair and rolled several strands through her fingers.

This was a crazy life for a six-year-old. Seeing angels and talking to dead people. Lisa wished she could stop this gift-turned-curse dreaming in her family. Denying their abilities had become exhausting. Three months ago, Mikala asking for help would have sent her into a frenzy. Now, she was tired of the lying and pretending.

Here she rested comfortably with Mikala safe in her arms, while another mother ached to hold her boy. How could she not help? Was she afraid of failing? Or succeeding and exposing herself?

Meeting Jack had helped suppress her dreams. She so wanted to be normal for him. Fitting in with people in their neighborhood and community, or at school where she taught or the gym where the kids swam, had been her main objective.

She told herself she wasn't crazy or schizophrenic a thousand times. She denied her clairvoyance. Lied on psychological tests to secure her teaching job. Did she hear voices? Yes, all the time. What would they say about that? Oh, you talk to dead people? We don't care. You see them, too? That's fine. You can still teach kindergarten. Parents won't mind that you aren't normal.

But this was her normal. She wasn't psycho, demented, or demonic. She was just Lisa. Jack's wife. Mikala's mom. A girl who could see the energy that remained of people who once walked the earth.

She twirled Mikala's hair around her fingertips, closed her eyes, said a prayer, and pushed off the river bank with her scull.

"I'll try, Mikala. I promise to try."

"Oh, thank you, Momma."

"You're welcome, baby. Now close your eyes and sleep. Let me worry about Luke Anderson," she said, straightening her fingers and allowing Mikala's hair to fall free.

She slipped out from beneath the covers and tucked the blanket around Mikala. Then she sat on the edge of the bed and sang softly, like Gee used to do when the bad dreams came.

"Stay awake don't rest your head. Don't lie down upon your bed. While the moon drifts in the skies stay awake don't close your eyes…"

When Mikala's eyes closed and her breathing became even, Lisa crept away, stepping cautiously so the floorboards didn't creak. She paused in the doorway to ensure Mikala still slept, then tiptoed down the hall, peeking in at the boys and Jack as she passed.

Jaden's head lay on top of Jack's outstretched arm, and a book lay on the floor beneath Jack's fingers. John hugged the other side of him. All three slept peacefully in a single twin bed. Lisa pulled their door semi-closed and descended the stairs.

Then she called the one person in the world who understood her completely.

"Rach?"

"Lisa? What's up? Everything all right?"

"Is Jeffrey asleep?"

"Yes."

"Does Todd still play poker on Wednesday nights?"

"Yes, why?"

"I'm coming over."

"No, wait, Todd is already home. Must have lost a bundle. He was home before nine. Why?"

"We have to talk. Can we meet somewhere?"

"Can't it wait until tomorrow? After work?"

"No," she said firmly. "It can't."

Silence.

"Okay, hang on." More silence. Then Rachel's voice came back. "Take down this address: 1336 West Twenty-Sixth Street. I can be there in fifteen minutes. Pull in the parking lot. I'll meet you in front of the office marked 103."

"See you there."

Lisa wrote the address on a Post-it note, stuck the paper in her purse, and hung up the phone. Then she called in the white angel.

"Protect us," she said. "Do what you must to prevent that man from seeing us. Baby Jesus, protect my baby."

She picked up her purse and hurried out the door.

*****

Up in her room, Mikala stood beside her bedroom's half-ajar door, hugging the wall and straining to hear her mom. After she knew Momma was going to see Aunt Rachel, she tiptoed to the windowsill and peeked beneath the blinds to watch her leave. That's when she saw the man again. He stood in the shadows across the street.

She squinted her eyes, but she still couldn't make out his face. He had been there before, both at night and early in the morning. She lifted the blinds, lay her forehead against the window, and brought her hand up to the glass. She gave the man a slow, slight wave.

The man took a tiny step forward. His head slanted upward. She waved again.

Slowly the man lifted his arm and waved. Then Mikala heard the garage door of their home opening, and she watched the man step back into the shadows as Lisa backed out of the driveway and sped off down the road. After a moment, the man stepped toward the street again, waved to Mikala a second time, and then hugged the houses as he took off running down the street.

Mikala stepped back and lowered the blinds, tumbled into bed, and drew the covers up to her chin.

"It's okay, Marky," she whispered. "Mamma is going to help us."

She turned on her side and fell asleep.

23 The perpetrator

"Protect my face."

The movie played over in his head like a tune you hum subconsciously: Mikala talks about the boys. She tells someone. Rachel. At least, he thinks the obscured face is Rachel's. She's surrounded by haze. Blocked by whiteness. Is that her? He can't see clearly. He opens his eyes to the black night. Stops the movie that has been replaying in his head for hours. Some force bigger than him is blocking the picture. Literally, mystifying the scene.

He sighs. Then, there in the night, decides. He's going to have to take care of the situation. The note he left at her cousin's home didn't faze her in the least. Her father? Yes, the note had rendered him nearly useless. But her? Nothing. She's a fearless little thing.

"Protect my face."

But right now, he had to concentrate on the task at hand—the bum. He hit his watch and blue numbers glared from his wrist. The vagrant should be coming any minute. He closed his eyes and prepared to perfect his crime.

In the event they were taken into custody—by the KGB, FSB, ISIS, Mossad, MSS, ISI, or any other intelligence agency threatening to out the United States' Project Dream—they'd been trained to control their heart rate, pass any polygraph, and suppress their emotions in any situation.

He did the drill. Breathed in deeply for eight seconds, held his breath for nine, expelled the air in ten seconds, massaged the carotid artery in his neck, and performed the Valsalva maneuver by breathing in and pressurizing his abdomen five times.

Once completed, he hit his watch again, placed two fingers on his neck, and counted heartbeats for fifteen seconds. Fourteen thumps, fifty-six beats per minute. Not bad for a guy hiding in a thicket of brush with a body bag, rag, and bottle of chloroform in a sack beside him; and a shovel at his feet.

He had scouted areas on Erie's lower east and west sides for two weeks, searching for just the right size bum. He'd spotted a few on the east side, but then decided the police traffic there was too dangerous, so he settled on the drunk who spent his evenings snoozing in a patch of foliage just above Erie's west-side bluffs. The area was close to downtown but not too close. It was a low-income, minority-laced neighborhood, with lots of shattered streetlights.

The guy had to be white and the perfect size. Yet, he had to be moveable. Grabbing a kid was so much simpler. He had settled on this particular bum, not only for size and race, but because of his evening resting place. The spot was secluded, despite being a half mile from a broken-down grocery mart with no locks on carts.

Location, location, location. Who knew the adage applied to vagabonds, too?

Still exercising his breathing and massaging techniques, he watched the man stumble across Front Street with the pace of a turtle determined to die by tire. The man's bed was a few feet down the hill in the undergrowth, his blankets hidden in thick brush. But tonight he was dallying at the top, looking down, whistling a little too loud and annoying him relentlessly.

Finally, when he could take no more of the man's irresponsible joviality, he grabbed his shovel, stepped out of the greens, and smacked the guy flat on the back of his head. The dude fell directly into the blankets on the hill.

Nice aim.

He grabbed his bag and slid down to the man. The guy was out like a roofied bitch. He poured chloroform on a rag and held the cloth over his mouth as a precaution. With that, stuffing his unconscious ass into the bag took less than two minutes. He was getting good at this. He lay the chloroform rag on his face to keep him sleeping and zipped him up, leaving a small opening at the top. Then he completed the hardest part—dragged him up the hill and heaved the bag into the shopping cart he had waiting on the path.

He covered him with moldy, ragged blankets, snatched the bottom-shelf whiskey in his cart, poured some on his own cloak—a jacket he had stolen from a different bum the day before—and started along the bayfront, pushing the cart. He sang the very song the bum had been whistling, amused that he sounded so drunk and appeared so seedy. He held up the half-empty bottle of whiskey as he neared two young men, probably Gannon University students headed to cheap apartments. They crossed the street.

Then he laughed and sang all the way to Second and Cherry streets, where he turned into the little dirt driveway of the boarded-up house. Once out back in the fenced yard, he dumped the body bag and all his tools into the trunk of the car he had paid cash for two days ago.

He got in and drove off. Didn't turn on the lights until he was two blocks away, thinking how much he and the bum had in common.

Death was really their only way out.

"Protect my face."

24 Lisa

In the food co-op plaza, next to a massage and cleansing clinic, a colorful sign anchored above a small office door hailed the words: Ellen Wood, Reiki Specialist and Certified Medium. Lisa zipped into one of two parking spaces in front of that office. Her car's headlights lit up the sign and reflected off the fluorescent 103 number above the door. A second light brightened the signage, and Rachel's elaborate car shot into the space beside Lisa's. Lisa cut her ignition and hopped out.

"Perfect timing," Rachel said, swinging her own car door open and stepping out into the night.

Lisa watched her sister hurry toward the building, heels clicking. Rachel motioned with her head for Lisa to follow and then sent a few choice words into the night air as she struggled to unlock the door in the dark. Once inside, she flipped the switch to the reception area, and lively-colored figures jumped at Lisa from the far wall. Angels, animals, gods, and goddesses stared back at her. Salmon-colored, cushioned folding chairs encircled the room. A delicate moon-striped valence and matching sheers rimmed the room's picture window, and angel figurines on an antique cherry-wood desk welcomed her.

Rachel tossed her keys on the desk and locked the door behind them.

"Ellen said I'm welcome here any time she isn't using the place." She headed for the back room.

There, thick, cushiony furniture beckoned Lisa in. The windowless room flaunted an antique library table hugging one wall. Candles and pictures—more angels—decorated the table's elegant lace table runner. Rachel lit the delicate, hand-painted Victorian lamp with the glass-beaded fringe and a soft red glow cast shadows against the walls.

"Make yourself comfortable. I read for people here."

"You do?" Lisa's own surprise-tainted voice startled her. She quickly tried to recover. "I don't mean anything by that. I just didn't think you did that sort of thing."

"Typically, I don't." Rachel seemed unchallenged. "Not for money, at least. But every so often a friend will beg me to tell them their future or help them make a decision, and I succumb. I practically make them sign in blood they won't tell anyone."

Lisa relaxed. "I know what you mean. I still have people asking me if I can see their future, and I haven't admitted to anything in over eight years."

"Admitted?" Rachel struck a match and lit two candles. Lavender and lemon scents filled the air. "That means you still have visions."

"A few." She fell into an overstuffed tan leather chair. "Once in a while, some poor soul hounds me. They stay until they realize I'm ignoring them."

"Like when we were little? When they frightened you?"

"I'm not afraid anymore, but yes, like when I was Mikala's age. Back then, I confused the dead with the living because I could reach out and touch them. I wonder if Mikala can."

"You don't know?"

"No, up until tonight she did most of her talking with Jack. I think she felt more comfortable with him." Lisa lay her arms on the high arm rests, and her eyes scanned the warm room. "She's smart. I think she knows I'm still debating what is best for her."

"You'll figure it out."

"Mom and Dad never did."

"We didn't turn out so bad."

"I suppose not." Lisa ran her hands over the chair's soft leather. "Were you mad at them? For letting them take you?"

"At first, but eventually I realized they had no way of knowing what they were getting me into. How the government would control my life."

"Well, I was mad at them for a long time. They gave your life away. Were you allowed to marry anyone?" Lisa waited for Rachel to plop down in a seat before she continued. "I mean, you married Todd, and Lenny isn't married. Do you have to marry within the system or—what would you call it—your lot?"

"Our lot? That's a good description. But no, we can marry other people. Although the other person in our lot." Rachel made quotation mark gestures with her fingers. "He isn't married either. He works as a professor at Mercyhurst."

"They can do that? Just make you a teacher?"

"No, John Michael has his PHD. He's a smart guy. He was born in the New England area and is dying to go home and teach at Boston College. He loathes Erie. Hates Lenny, Todd, and the program altogether. But if they move him home, I think he'll be fine."

"Why does he hate Lenny and Todd?"

"John Michael and I go way back. We were close. Todd knows, and you know how jealous he gets. And as far as Lenny goes, he beat the crap out of John Michael once, although later they made amends, sort of. Now I think he's just bitter that Lenny and I got our hometown."

"I'm glad you did. After Mom died, I hated being here alone. And I felt awful for you. Like you'd been cheated out of knowing her."

"Don't feel bad. There is a reason for everything."

"Katie Mackentire always says that." Lisa flashed an I-only-half-believe-that smile. "But, well, you left and met Todd and now—"

"And if I hadn't met Todd, I wouldn't have Jeffrey, would I?"

"True." Lisa squirmed backward and settled into the cushions.

"Okay, so let me have it. You didn't come to talk about Todd."

"No." Immediately, dread seized her. "I have to help them, Rachel. The missing boys. Luke Anderson is dying."

She watched the crimson climb Rachel's face. She continued calmly, "Mathew Nuber's mother goes to my church. I can't face her one more Sunday knowing I might have been able to help. And—"

Lisa hesitated and then spoke slowly. She knew how to reach in and grab her sister's heart. "If I don't do something, Mikala will. She talks to Marky Blakely every night. She thinks I don't hear her, but I do."

"Oh, Lisa," Rachel whined and bent forward. She placed her elbows on her knees and fingertips on her forehead. Then she became very still. Eventually, when her hands fell from her face, the lines around her eyes had softened. "What do you want to do?"

"Call in the white angel." Lisa looked her straight in the eye. She didn't blink. "Together."

They shared a quiet moment. Only the shadows from the flickering candles moved in the room. Then Rachel sighed and rose mechanically, sauntered toward the library table, struck a long match, and lit several more candles. She turned down the lights.

"I can't believe I'm saying this, but then that's what we will do." She headed for the door. "I'll get us some water."

When Rachel was gone, Lisa tipped her chin up and relaxed the back of her head onto the top of her chair. She allowed herself a few triumphant seconds. She breathed deeply, thanked God, and then sat up and folded her legs beneath her, shifting to a comfortable position and closing her eyes.

She recited the Our Father, asked for protection, and called in the white angel. She pictured herself physically shedding her worries and bathing in the warmth of the angel's white light. In a short time, she raised her vibration to a level she had not experienced in years, and the cries of a child crept into her mind.

The impact was immediate, which she hadn't expected. She felt the child's paralyzing sobs flow through her and seep out every pore of her body.

The whimpering echoed and bounced off some hollow wall, reverberating with a tunnel-like quality. The eerie sound sent chills over every inch of her, leaving her with a cool, damp sensation that relayed an underground feeling. Out of rote memory, she snapped her eyes open and nearly forced the experience to end. But instead of denying the vision, she stopped, breathed deeply, closed her eyes, and allowed herself to collapse into the scene.

In the white mist of her mind, she floated toward the child named Mathew. She neared his frail, weak frame and became him. She glanced down and watched her hands and arms shrink into a child's as the room around her darkened. She observed her new surroundings: the dark, dank walls across from him, his chained ankles, the body beside him. She smelled urine and feces, heard the boy's heart beating in his ears, and felt his knees lodged in gritty earth.

Mice scurried across the far end of the dirt floor. Straps, ropes, and chains hung from pegs above the varmints. She glanced down at the boy's ankles—now her ankles—and to the other two boys' legs. Her eyes followed their attached chains. Each set led to separate stakes pounded deep in the ground.

Another coldness gripped her. There were four stakes.

He's not done.

The pictures came to her like puzzle pieces, and the fear they invoked momentarily incapacitated her. She reminded herself she was safe. The room existed in her mind. Mikala and the boys slept at home in their beds, Jack with them, Geoff Filutze outside in the squad car.

She felt Rachel's presence in the room again and heard two glasses clink onto the little table in front of her, but she wouldn't allow the sound to distract her. Instead, she listened for the boy's thoughts, using Rachel as her security and usurping her energy. Her courage rose.

"They are underground but not buried," she said. "They exist in a room beneath a pasture. Above them is a door with rectangular pieces of grass."

"Sod?"

"Could be. It blends in with the field, so you can't see the door. The woods surround this grassy plot. It's relatively large, wide. Maybe an acre."

She hesitated to investigate her whereabouts. "There is a man in a long dark cloak that crosses the field, but I can't see his face. He's blocking me from seeing him. This man mows the grass there. It's very dry. He wants to make bales of hay but his tractor, equipment, is old. He does the best he can, but they are lopsided. 'They'll do.' I hear him say."

"I see the field," Rachel said, and Lisa opened her eyes to notice Rachel had closed hers.

"But I'm way behind you. Keep going."

Lisa watched Rachel open her eyes, pick up pen and paper, and click on a recording device. She nodded at Lisa, and Lisa closed her eyes and dove back into the vision.

"He dumps the almost-round bales in several piles around the perimeter."

"Lisa," Rachel said, her voice firm. "Move higher. Can you see where you are?"

"It's dark, so I can't see much at all."

"Try to hover above the area. Like a drone."

Lisa shifted in her seat, placed her hands on the arms of the chairs and boosted herself upward. "I see the lake. And Erie. I'm not in the City, though. I'm farther south because the lake is a good distance away."

"How far away?"

"Far. I'm south of Interstate 90." Lisa strained to see through the white mist. "It feels like McKean Township. There is a house—an old house buried in weeds—and this room that the boys are in is underground in a clearing behind that house. I see a man digging these holes years ago. Putting boards in, cinder blocks, and a roof over top. He didn't cover it with dirt, back then. He was afraid of…of what? Indians? No, tornadoes. He was afraid of tornadoes. He came from Oklahoma. Okay, I understand now."

"Is it a bunker? Some sort of bunker in the ground?"

"Yes." Lisa concentrated. "Inside, I see two little boys, then three. Then two again. One is gone—the boy who died. But then a third one comes. And another after him. Wait. I see that last child descending those steps."

She hesitated, concentrated, watched. She no longer existed in the room with the candles. She floated in that bunker, scrutinizing the scene before her. A man's legs sidled down the stairs, and a child stepped behind him. But something frightened her. The clothing was familiar. She recognized the pants.

She thrust her body forward, drew in an enormous breath, and screamed.

Rachel jumped toward her, slipped an arm around her shoulder.

Lisa's hands clenched the table, its doily wrinkling beneath her grip. "I see…" She gasped for air.

"Walk away from the scene for a minute, Lisa. Calm yourself." Rachel spoke slowly. "Bring your pulse down, your blood pressure. Come back into this room. You're too upset."

"No, no, no, I'm going back down." Her eyes were open, but she couldn't see a thing in the room—only the cellar. "I have to."

"Can you see the boys? Matt, Marky, Luke?"

"Yes, no, Marky is gone. His soul is…" She hesitated. "In Mikala's room. But then Luke comes and then John and then—"

She began sobbing.

"What do you see?" Rachel scrambled to the floor and knelt beside her.

"Big legs then little legs climbing down the ladder. Oh, God, I see who it is!"

"Another boy?" Rachel shook Lisa. "A boy we know?"

"No," Lisa whispered and fell into her arms. "It's Mikala."

25 The perpetrator

He moved quickly. Hurried his meditation because so little time—and yet so many tasks—remained.

He turned the lights down, set the music low, and got comfortable in his favorite chair. Then he cleared his mind and concentrated, calling in his guide or spirit or the devil himself. He didn't know who showed him the visions in his head, and he didn't care. He only knew now, not only must he keep Rachel at bay, he must circumnavigate that damn sister and niece of hers, too.

Unfortunate. His head was getting awfully crowded.

He asked his guide for the means to throw them off course. Lisa's sensitivity pristine, her presence ebbed closer than Rachel's. Holding them off longer was imperative, so he took extra precautions.

"Protect my face."

He needed a diversion to turn their attention while he snatched John.

Oddly, only one John lingered on the long list of children being raised by single mothers. Tapping Mercyhurst's files for them had been simple. Trained extensively in hacking passwords and cracking codes, all four Project Dream transmitters had the names at their fingertips. Only the government could keep hackers out. Jumping security hurdles at a university? He was like a world-class hurdler clearing a two-foot fence.

To date, the cops had not come up with how they all knew each other.

"Idiots." He spoke to the black spirit, then cleared again and suppressed his annoyance.

Rapidly, the black spirit infused flashes, then movies into his head. Homes with easy-access windows and voices inside saying, "John, it's time for bed," or "John, wash your hands." But the actual locations were hard to decipher. Premonitions were so much clearer when two or three people raised the vibration of a room, and with four? The vision acuity was perfected. But alone, he struggled to clarify precisely what the dark spirit relayed.

He opened his eyes. Then his laptop.

"Ah, the brilliance of Google satellite." He expanded Google maps to examine houses and sifted through census tract data to research names. He searched for Johns. Slowly, addresses unfolded. After a time, his body sprang to attention.

A sound. Was that outside or inside? He closed his eyes and saw a dark figure in his mind. A man—more than one. They were outside. He stormed to the window. No one was there. He closed his eyes again and they resurfaced. They were police. They would pay him a visit soon. He must quicken his pace.

More research, more visions, and within an hour, he decided which address to use.

He closed his eyes and opened his mind to the world. Then he filled his head with the number 322, avoiding 417. He did not allow himself to think the latter.

"322, 322, 322."

He turned the number over in his mind until he was ready to leave. Then he built a cerebral wall and blocked his thoughts like he had been trained to do in the desert.

"322, 322, 322." He dangled that number outside his wall like a lantern on a gatehouse, its bridge drawn.

Then his own inner demons caught him, and he lowered his eyes and pulled a bag from his pocket. He squeezed the supple pouch, so the white powder inside moved up and down through his fingers. He could almost feel the fine particles. He lifted the sack to his nose, sniffed, and then straightened and tucked the bag away.

No, not now.

He had to keep his wits about him. He must distract the girls, make a phone call—*322, 322,*—get them to that house, so he could abduct John.

Beads of sweat formed on his forehead and neck, but he squelched his craving by reminding himself of Project Dream's veracity.

The only way out is by death.

26 Chief Ben Morgan

Ben Morgan waited for Rachel Kennedy at the back entrance to City Hall. He watched her pull her fancy car into the parking lot and run tippy-toed through the rain, so her three-inch heels never touched tarmac. As she entered and walked down the long hall toward the elevators with him, the chief remained at her side, step for step.

Despite being back from that Nevada desert for years, this would only be her second visit to City Hall. The last time, Jack escorted her. This time, she came alone. Ben wanted her to feel comfortable.

She was a teenager when she left Erie. He vividly remembered her waving good-bye from a half-open window of the back seat of a black limousine as her family stood helplessly on City Hall's back steps. She was driven to the airport, placed on a plane to Pittsburgh, then on another to Phoenix. Then they shuttled her to Nevada where she spent six years of her life in the desert, and then another four years somewhere out West in a town in California he couldn't recall the name of.

After she returned to Erie, he didn't recognize her when he ran into her at the grocery store. She seemed older than her twenty-five years. Looked foreign-born. Like a movie star plucked from LA more than a small-town girl who had spent formative years roaming backyards in Erie, Pennsylvania. Men stared and, for envy of her charm, women studied her. The high heels, fitted clothes, bulky sunglasses, designer purses dangling from squared shoulders, jumped at you before she spoke. Then, if you weren't yet under her spell, hearing her raspy voice at least knocked your confidence down a peg. Immediately intimidated, most people refrained from talking much when they first met Rachel Callahan. The chief had been no exception in that grocer's nearly four years ago.

And she had struck him dumb a second time when he saw her at the Gertrude Barber Ball. A hand looped lazily around her husband's arm, she locked eyes with him, and her gaze spewed bitterness and blame at him like a sling shot.

He and Lynn stood at the bar with drinks in hand. Lynn, chatting with the bartender. Him, leaning sideways, an elbow on the bar ledge, a long happy smile spanning his face. Lynn's remission had stretched into its eighth month, and they had renewed their vows, vacationed internationally, mountain-climbed, white-water rafted, and made love like twenty-year-old newlyweds. Happiness brightened their faces. In every picture taken that evening, their smiles appeared as fake as the upturned lips of wax-museum figures. Later, when people looked at those photographs, they would swear their grins were phony. No one could be that happy.

But they were.

Ben was in a good place at the time. A new, young chief, with loyal, hard-working officers beneath him and a vibrant wife who had licked cancer beside him. Yet despite those blessings, when he first espied Rachel Callahan that evening, a dread rushed over him. Her animosity reached past the crowd and slapped him across the face. Lynn noticed his gaze.

Dear, sweet Lynn. The only person who truly understood him.

She set down her drink, lay a hand on his arm, smiled, and touched the corner of his mouth with her fingers. Tried to form his lips back into a smile.

"I love you. But I'll never understand how you can look so tough on the outside and be so marshmallow soft on the inside," she said, then took a drink of that fancy French wine he could never remember the name of, her wet lips lovely.

He slipped his hand around her waist, drew her close, and kissed her long and hard, something he never did in public before the cancer.

"I love you, too, Lynn." He smiled and breathed in her salacious scent.

"She's still young, Ben. Someday she'll realize it wasn't your fault." She hesitated, brushed a strand of hair off his forehead. "Will you?"

That memory of Lynn gazing up at him, the corner of her lips lifted by a soft smile, her eyes twinkling, brought an almost unbearable heaviness to his chest. They didn't know then that the cells inside her were multiplying, metastasizing.

He kissed her again, and she shoved him playfully. She grabbed her drink, sipped, set the glass down, and stepped away from the bar.

"Let's go over and introduce ourselves." She walked away before he could object. When he caught up to her, she whispered over her shoulder, "Look in her eyes. She's nervous, the poor thing."

Ben glanced in Rachel's direction and followed Lynn, whispering back, "She looks anything but nervous to me."

"You are completely lost when it comes to women." She smoothed her dress over her perfect form and grabbed his hand. "Imagine being so beautiful that everywhere you went, people gawked at you."

He remembered thinking, *oh, Lynn, do you even know how beautiful you are?* But she tugged him away before he could respond. Led him right toward Rachel. Introduced herself and him. Then she talked fashion, California, and before he had even mustered the courage to say more than "hello," the two women were laughing like best friends, and the animosity in Rachel Callahan Kennedy's eyes had vanished.

Oh, how he had loved Lynn, Ben thought, as he walked that path alongside Rachel. Fifteen years her senior, Lynn took Rachel under her wing. They remained friends until Lynn—like Rachel years before—was whisked away too soon from a life she loved, and Ben was left alone.

But Lynn had laid the foundation for Ben to forgive himself and for Rachel and him to remain friends after her death, so they might help one another. He would not disappoint Lynn. Of course, mistakes had been made, but he knew Lynn would both understand and forgive. He moved to rekindle the quiet friendship.

"I have been thinking about this for a long time. We've never discussed it, and so I want a straight answer. The truth," he said, sitting down and reaching for his coffee mug once safely inside Helen. "Did they have an extraterrestrial body out there?"

Rachel had just taken a sip of coffee, and, instantly, she spritzed the table with a mouthful. The brew even came out her nose.

"Seriously?" She wiped the coffee quickly with a tissue. "You seriously are asking me that?"

"Yes, I want to know."

He felt her eyes studying him.

"You're serious? Really? International secrecy, covert operations, mind-reading games, and you want to know if "My Favorite Martian's" body was swimming in ice down the road?"

He smiled and winked and felt his shoulders shake as his grin bloomed to a laugh. She rolled her eyes.

"Honestly, Ben, you are such a pain in the ass." She was holding in a laugh. "I will never understand how you buffaloed Lynn into marrying you."

He loved that she talked so openly about Lynn. Few people did. He never understood why people avoided talking about those who were gone, especially those who had the most life in them when they were alive.

Because they were alone, he bragged. "She was a woman of exquisite taste."

She grinned. "In everything but men, I must add."

He shook his head. "I'll never understand why that woman took you under her wing like she did. Skydiving, right? The two of you went skydiving with your garden club?"

"Oh, my God, the only reason she isn't coming out of the sky to smack you herself is because she knows I'm here to do it," she said, then shoved his shoulder.

He was surprised at her might.

"You know she would kill you for that remark."

"Why?"

"Garden club, my ass. We were working on the City's comprehensive plan. We went up in a plane to overlook the city and snap pictures, and she got the idea to sign up for skydiving." She shook her head. "I don't know whether I'm more appalled at the garden club or Martian comment."

Ben felt happy. Lynn would be proud. She had lectured him on end about approaching Rachel slowly on important issues. She said people both misread and mistreated Rachel because of her beauty. They didn't recognize her softer side. Lynn wanted to change that.

He gazed down into his coffee cup. Lynn, a modern-day Joan of Arc. When she died, he thought they were going to have to bury him in the ground beside her, but then she had prepared him even for that, hadn't she?

"You're thinking of her, aren't you?"

Her question surprised him. For a moment, he had forgotten where he was. He raised his gaze to Rachel and nodded.

"She was a great lady, Ben."

"And I love how your face lights up when I mention her. You know she wanted to bring you down to the station herself. Tried a few times but said it must not have been time because something always seemed to get in the way. She thought it might be hard for you, since you said goodbye to your family here. 'Bad memories hold on to a place,' she used to say."

"Yes, she told me that, too. I think she planned those comprehensive plan meetings at the County to make me comfortable. I told her I didn't want to go if they were at City Hall."

"She told me."

"After—" She glanced at him.

"It's okay," he said, then pressed his lips into a smile and nodded, giving his approval for her to broach a subject so few mentioned.

"After she found out the cancer was back, well, there was so much she wanted to do."

"And you were just the friend she needed, Rachel. Someone fearless, who she could talk into doing anything."

"She could talk anyone into anything. She had that way with people."

"I'm sorry about that first time back when you came with Jack," he said. "That was tense. If I had known ahead of time you were coming, I would have—actually I don't know what I would have done. I guess what I'm trying to say is I hope this gets a little easier for you as time goes by."

"It's not so hard. I've been back in Erie for a while." Her eyes scanned the room. "Everything looks different, smaller. So while I hated to return, and in the back of my mind I still pictured the old rooms and how I cried so hard when I left with my escort, it's the back parking lot I loathed seeing the most. Getting into that black car with the dark windows was scary. But my life has turned out fairly decent, so I look back on those years differently now."

"They say time heals all wounds. But I'm not sure I believe that."

"Well, I surely would have liked Lynn to be here that first time. But today—" She laughed. "You know she would have loved the Martian question."

Ben's mind-set changed from pensive to proud. "Honestly, I think she put that in my head."

"I understand a little about that." Rachel rolled into another laugh. "Oh, wow, we've come full circle, haven't we?"

Their laughter dissipated.

"We have," he said, and dug into his pocket. "I want to thank you for coming in, and before I forget, your cell?"

He waved his own cell phone and stretched an open palm toward her. She slapped her phone into his big hand, and he took them and placed them in the secured desk drawer.

"Do they ever contact the department like they did back then? Ask if you know anyone with psychic abilities?" She removed the lid from her coffee tumbler.

"No." Ben picked up his own stale coffee from the desk, swirled the hour-old City Hall brew inside, sipped, frowned, and clunked the mug back down. "With all the technology they have today, they don't need us."

"True." She nodded and drank. "Yet, in all its glory, technology still can't locate a missing child."

"Which is why I appreciate your help." He took a seat at a desk beside her.

"I suppose we should get to it. I do have some information for you."

"Did Lisa see something?"

She sighed and twisted her lips into a pout. "And everything was going so well. Did you have to mention her? Can't we pretend it's me? When it's the two of us, let's just pretend."

"You really should stop worrying about your little sister."

"Agree." She wrapped both hands around her coffee and shrugged. "She's just so dog-gone sweet."

"Well, can she, um, help us? I never know how these things work."

"We are both helping. Perception is better with two people. You feed off each other, accomplish a higher meditation state. And, frankly, Lisa is much better at seeing things than I am."

"Is she coming?"

"She should be here any minute. Until then, how familiar are you with McKean? We both get the feeling these boys might be there."

"In McKean? Alive?"

"Two," she said, methodically.

"Two are alive?" He was taken aback by her detached demeanor but hid his judgement behind a straight face.

"We think so. We are fairly certain Mark—Marky—passed away."

"Any idea how?

"Not sure. The cause of death wasn't clear. We didn't see signs of a struggle."

"Any clue where the body is?"

"Not in the bunker."

"Bunker?"

"We believe the other two boys, Matt and Luke, are in a bunker. Lisa had a vision of two boys chained to stakes in the ground. Lisa—" She hesitated, her eyes shot toward the desk with the cell phones.

"We're as safe as we can possibly be, Rachel."

"Lisa saw several street signs. Dunn Valley Road, Stancliff, and South Street. I Googled the area, but there were so many farms and fields. I didn't know where to start searching."

"I'm familiar with the area," he said, thinking. "By south, could she have meant the direction rather than the street?"

"Not sure. We can ask her when she gets here. She did say south of I-90. I believe she travels the route the abductor takes when he drops off a child."

"You believe this is one man?"

"Yes, one man."

"And you think he leaves them there alone?"

"I do. Lisa said she sees the man going down steps to drop off water and food. She also said something else that surprised me. She isn't sure the abductor is a child molester, but that could be hope overpowering intuition."

"Maybe not."

"Why do you say that?"

"Because Billy Mack doesn't think so, either. Can you actually see this place where you believe he has the boys?"

"Not well enough to decipher anything."

Ben sat silent. He didn't pretend to understand the Callahan girls' minds. If he hadn't been privy to Rachel Callahan and Project Dream, more than likely he would have put their files in the "cuckoo" drawer.

"There's something else," she said, slipping a clump of hair behind one ear. "He's going to abduct another child. His name will be John."

"Mathew, Mark, Luke and John," the chief said, nodding.

"Yes, Biblical."

The door swung open, and an officer held the door for Lisa as she hurried in. The private stood for a moment, staring, and then exited the room, closing the door behind him. Ben traipsed to the metal desk and held his hand out. Before he could ask her for her phone, she handed her cell to him, her breath labored.

"Sorry I'm late," she said, unbuttoning her coat. "Jack isn't coming. He had to pick the boys up from day care—the flu of all things. I told him it was more important for me to come than him. I was able to get a sub for the rest of the day and leave early."

She took a seat, tugged her sleeves, and removed her sopping raincoat, tossing it across the desk nearest her. As an afterthought, she picked the coat up and shook it hard. Drops of water flew in all directions. She folded the garment in half and set it down again.

"The thing is," she said, still winded. "We need to get these kids out of there. The bigger boy, Luke, is dying. It's cold and wet, and I'd estimate we have a lot less than a week before he's gone. Any success on Google or any feel for where they are, Rach? How about John? Any idea where he lives?"

Rachel swung her legs to the side of her seat to face Lisa. "Maybe the Glenwood Hills area."

"I'm not in that area at all. I see a man watching a house, but it's not in Glenwood Hills. I'm having trouble seeing everything."

"I am, too," Rachel said. "I'm not sure why."

"Can you girls slow down?" Ben had barely gotten his notepad from his pocket, and already he was behind. "Glenwood you said?"

"No, not Glenwood." Lisa turned toward him, her eyes fixed and staring. "The house I see is not your typical Glenwood Hills home."

"No problem." He flipped open the notepad. "Could you recognize the house if you saw it?"

"Yes." She said confidently. "I'll recognize it. There is a circular room on the corner of her house that she uses as an office. Find that round room, and we find John."

She stood, ready to leave. Her fast pace surprised him. He had always found Rachel to be rather laid back. "You want to go look? Now?"

"Yes, can we use a cruiser, or would that be too conspicuous?" Lisa reached for her coat. "I suppose I didn't need to take this off."

She slipped her arms in the sleeves, flicked her hair over the back, and hustled to the door. When she turned around, Rachel and the chief were still sitting.

"Well?" Her arms remained at her sides, but she turned her palms upward. "Coming?"

The chief glanced at Rachel, arching his eyebrows. Rachel stood and buttoned her own coat, a throaty laugh escaping her. "I've nudged a sleeping bear."

"I see that." He headed for the metal desk. "We can take an unmarked car."

He returned their phones, Lisa left the room, and they followed her outside and headed for Glenwood Hills in a plain black car with no police-surveillance features, save the extra antenna.

The asphalt roads were wet and slippery, and the chief had to lighten his step on the gas pedal. The girls discussed streets, locations. He turned the volume of the car's police scanner down in order to hear Rachel's directions. A difference of opinion surfaced between the two women.

"Are you sure?" Lisa asked twice from the back seat. "Because I'm not getting this."

"I see these streets in my head." Rachel placed a hand on the dashboard as the chief took a turn, and the back of the car fishtailed slightly. "And I have an address, 322."

"Well, okay, if you are seeing them, then let's keep going." Lisa sat back, and the chief watched her through the rearview mirror. That far-away stare resurfaced in her daze. "I'm out of practice."

One fender-bender report after another forced static voices over the car radio. Officers called out street names and addresses where accidents had occurred, confusing the issue.

Black ice on roads stretched across the city like strands of licorice. The chief drove slowly through the icy maze of streets in the elaborate Glenwood Hills neighborhood, turning on Rachel's orders.

When they came to a halt after sliding halfway through a quiet intersection, she said, "I think we're close. But something's not right. The pictures in my head seem—scrambled. Like a bad TV connection."

"I'm having the same trouble." Lisa leaned toward the window and glanced down the street. "This isn't right. These houses are spread too far apart."

"Maybe not. There are smaller homes around the bend. Take a left up ahead." Rachel pointed toward a moderate-sized home on a corner lot. The chief gave the car some gas, drove toward the house, skidded to a crawl, and turned.

Cautiously, he wound down the snaky road with the fancy gardens and stone driveways. Lisa and Rachel gazed from house to house, closing their eyes occasionally.

"Stop," Rachel finally said. "There's 322. That's the street number I'm seeing."

Lisa leaned forward from the back seat. "This isn't the house."

"No? I'm usually good with numbers. I've been seeing 322 clearly all morning."

"There's no circular room." Lisa ducked her head for a better view.

Ben followed Lisa's gaze. A ranch-style home with low trees and thick bushes that hugged its siding sat before them. He inched the car forward to see the side of the house and spotted a round, whitewashed wooden structure in the backyard.

"Could the round room be a gazebo?"

The girls followed his gaze.

"No, I don't believe so. I see the mother working at a desk there. Sometimes her son plays at her feet."

"Maybe she worked there in summer," Rachel said. "It's enclosed."

When neither woman said more, the chief picked up the car radio mic. "Let's see who lives here."

"Donna." He spoke into the mic. "It's the chief. Put in 322 Hilltop Road and let me know whose name comes up."

"You said 322 Hilltop?" blared over the scanner.

"That's right."

In less than a minute, the woman on the other end of the scanner replied, "The name is Forquer, Chief, a Mike and Jamie Forquer own it."

"Thanks," he said, then hung up the mic. "I'll go see if the Forquers have a son named John."

He clutched the door handle, opened the door, and left them alone.

*****

"I have a bad feeling," Lisa said after the chief was gone

"It's like that. Sometimes the visions make me sick to my stomach. I've thrown up and nearly passed out. They can be draining."

Lisa folded her arms to cut her chill.

Officers continued calling out codes, announcing accidents. A car with three children slid off the road. That call grabbed Lisa. She glanced at her watch and reminded herself the car could not be Jack and the kids. The boys were sick. Jack's sister, Janice, would drop Mikala off at home soon. Janice would be shadowed by one of Jack's cop friends, just as she herself had been escorted to school this morning.

Her mind returned to breakfast with Mikala and the boys.

"Wait a minute," she said, mostly to herself. "Mikala told me something this morning, but the boys weren't feeling well, and I wasn't listening. We were late. I thought she was talking about her brother, John. Maybe she wasn't."

Rachel turned completely around. "What did she say?"

"Something about not going to the top of the hill. She mentioned John. The TV was on, and the newsman was forecasting snow. They were showing kids sledding at Frontier Park last year. I thought she was talking about sled riding. You know John. He's always getting hurt. I thought she meant don't let John go to the top of Frontier's Hill."

"Don't go to the hill top?" Rachel asked.

Lisa scrutinized the home outside her window. Studied the 322 Hilltop sign on the front porch. Just then a woman appeared in the doorway.

"Yes." Lisa gazed at the lady with the big frame greeting the chief. "That's not the mother I saw in my dream."

A strange feeling spread through her, a chilly sensation. The weather had turned, and the temperature had dipped below thirty. She had forgotten her gloves. She rubbed her hands together vigorously, shoved them into her pockets, and then glanced down at herself and the upholstery around her.

Suddenly, she wasn't wearing a coat, and those weren't her pockets. A white mist enveloped her, and she no longer sat in an automobile. In her mind, she pictured herself outside standing next to a house. She felt bunched up paper in her right hand and saw herself stuffing a note deep down into a pocket, which was no longer a coat pocket. She wore gym shorts and—she glanced toward her feet—sneakers. Her feet were bigger.

She removed the note, unfolded the paper, but the black letters fell off the sheet. She caught them with her big hands. Jack's hands. She was no longer on Hilltop Road, and she wasn't Lisa. She was outside her sister-in-law Janice's house, and she was Jack. She watched his fingers shuffle the letters and stuff them back into his short's pocket—an M, an I, a K, A, L and A.

"Mikala," she whispered.

"Lisa? Are you all right?"

Rachel's voice pierced the fog, and the white mist slowly disappeared. Colors swirled and rolled until upholstery formed, and she realized she was still sitting inside the unmarked police car.

"What's wrong?" Rachel asked.

Confused, she glanced toward Rachel and then back into her lap. Her hands were no longer Jack's. They were her own.

Just then, the chief opened the car door and sat down. "The woman there has a son."

"Is his name—"

"John." Chief cut Rachel off. "His name is John."

He picked up the mic. "Donna, it's Ben. Call in any detective that's off tonight."

"You already have three units on." The static-laden voice sounded annoyed.

"Leave them where they are. Call three that are off. Tell them to come in now. They'll get paid double."

"You can't—"

"Donna, just call them. I'm in no mood for a lecture. We're going to monitor a house tonight. Call the garage and tell them we need those extra cars."

"The Mayor will have your ass for the overtime. We'll be over our budget for the year."

"Donna, make the calls."

"All right, all right," boomed over the radio.

"And Donna? Call in the phone records for 322 Hilltop." He replaced the mic.

"Phone records?" Lisa heard Rachel ask. "You think this person calls his victims, first?"

"I'm not sure what's going on."

"Why?"

"The woman said a man called her house about an hour ago. Asked if she had a son John."

"Dear God, did she tell him she did?"

"No, she asked him who wanted to know. She thought it was a prank call."

"What was the guy's response?"

The chief threw the car in drive. He looked straight ahead. "He said Lisa and Rachel. Then the call disconnected."

There was silence, then the chief stepped on the gas.

Lisa let the stale air out of her lungs. "He knows us both?"

"He actually said our names?" Rachel asked.

"That's right," Chief said, and the car fishtailed as he rounded the corner.

"My God, who the hell is this guy?" Rachel grabbed a ceiling handle.

"Rachel." Lisa loosened her seat belt, leaned over the front seat, and grabbed her arm, "Who knows about me?"

"What?"

"It has to be someone you told. Everyone knows you have visions, but who knows about me?"

"Well, Todd, Billy, a few others."

"How many others?"

"I don't know."

"Rachel, how many people know I have visions?" She squeezed harder and shook her sister's arm. "How many people have you told?"

"Lisa," the chief shouted, then they felt the car slide beneath them. The back tire hit the curb, the chief's dexterous hands turned the wheel, and they slid sideways into an intersection. He stepped on the gas to avoid an oncoming vehicle. The car narrowly missed them, and they skidded to a stop on the other side of the road.

Lisa broke her grip on Rachel's arm, and the chief tossed a sorrowful glance her way. "Everyone knows about you, Lisa. It's a small town. We've all known for years."

27 1999 – Gee

Gee listened from her bed. The smile on her face was so wide her cheeks hurt.

"Stop calling yourself LeeLee. Your name is Lisa," Rachel scolded, her voice travelling down the hallway.

"No, my name is LeeLee."

"That's a baby name."

"No, it's not."

"Yes, it is. You just want to be called LeeLee because PopPops has two names. Your real name—the name Momma gave you the day you were born—is Lisa."

"Well, you gave me the name LeeLee because you couldn't say Lisa." She made a grunting sound that let Gee know she had stuck her tongue out at her sister.

"Well, now I'm taking it back."

"You can't. People call me LeeLee, and I like it. So I'm keeping it."

"In school they don't call you that."

"Well, Momma and Daddy and Gee and PopPops and all the kids in the neighborhood call me LeeLee."

"It doesn't matter. I'm calling you Lisa from now on. And I'm telling everyone else to. It's time for you to grow up."

"I'm only seven, Rachel."

Their conversation was comical. They had been arguing in the other bedroom for over fifteen minutes.

"You have to learn to be your own person," Rachel chided.

"I don't even know what that means. Be my own person? If I'm not me then who am I? That's stupid."

"Don't say stupid."

"You're not the boss of me. Momma is."

"When Momma's not here, I am the boss of you."

"No, you're not. Gee is," LeeLee said, then yelled. "Gee!"

Gee could hear her little feet tapping the floor as she ran down the hall.

"Gee!" LeeLee burst into the bedroom and leapt into her bed. "Rachel is being mean to me."

"Rachel? Mean to you?" Gee rearranged her pillows and dangled her legs over the side of the bed, moving her feet in little circles to circulate the blood. "I've never known your sister to be mean. She's strong willed, but far from mean."

"She says she's the boss of me."

Gee chuckled. "The boss of you, eh?"

"And she says no one is going to call me LeeLee anymore. She's going to tell everyone to call me Lisa."

"Well, Lisa is a beautiful name. Don't you like it?"

"It's okay." LeeLee blinked slowly. "But I want to be called LeeLee."

"Tell me this. Is your real name Lisa?"

"Yes."

"But everyone calls you LeeLee?"

"Yes, except in school."

"Well, is Lisa the same person as LeeLee?"

"Yes."

"Then why do you care what Rachel calls you?" Gee wrapped an arm around LeeLee. "How about Rachel calls you Lisa, and I call you LeeLee. Is that a fair deal?"

"I guess so. Can PopPops still call me LeeLee?"

"I'd just like to see someone try and stop him."

LeeLee sighed. "All right, then."

"You know someday, your ma and pa and PopPops and Gee won't be around, so you better get along with that sister of yours."

"She's bossy."

Gee thought for a moment.

"You trust me don't you, LeeLee?"

LeeLee nodded, eyes wide.

"Well, I want to tell you a secret about Sissy. Sissy is strong and brave and going to take care of you for a long time. But someday, when the rest of us are all gone, Sissy will need you as much as you need her. You and Sissy will take care of each other."

"I don't want you to leave—ever!"

"Well, it has to be, my precious." She hugged her. "It's the circle of life. People get old and pass on, and new people come in and replace them."

"Then you come back. If it is a circle, you come back."

Gee laughed. "I swear, if there is reincarnation, then you were a philosopher in a prior life."

"What's reincarnation?"

"Well, let's see." Gee stretched her limp arms and settled in the most comfortable sitting position she could. "Some people believe after we go to heaven and swim in the puffy, white clouds for a while, we get bored. Like when you watch too much TV in Gee's room and all of a sudden realize you want to go outside and swing on the swing set PopPops built you. It's like that. We come back here to earth to play and learn and live another life."

"Like the white angel?"

"Oh, no, the white angel is special. Reincarnation is being born as a different person. Like me, Gee, maybe I lived back when Benjamin Franklin went out to fly his kite. You know who Ben Franklin is, don't you?"

LeeLee shook her head rapidly.

"Oh, my." Gee screwed up her lips. "Hmm. Well, maybe I lived in Jesus's time. You know who Jesus is, don't you?"

She nodded. "He is God's little boy."

"That's right, precious." Gee rested an elbow on the bed behind LeeLee. "Maybe I lived a street over from Jesus, in my own house. Maybe one of my sisters lived there with me."

"And your little brother, Timmy?"

"Yes, and maybe Timmy and PopPops. Sometimes we reincarnate with those souls we are closest to. So maybe we lived back then and, after our lives were over, we floated to heaven to play in the clouds. Then, after a long time, we got bored and came back here to be with you."

"Maybe I lived when Jesus lived, too."

"Could be."

"And maybe I was the boss of Rachel then."

"What's that, you say?"

"Maybe I lived with you back then and maybe I was bigger, and I was the boss of Rachel."

"Yes, maybe." Gee laughed so hard she coughed. There was something wonderful about children and their tiny accepting minds.

She scooched back toward the headboard to rest her aching back, pressed the button on the bed's side rail to lower the bed a bit, lodged pillows behind her, and lifted her legs back onto the stiff mattress.

"So let's make-believe now it's Rachel's turn to be the boss."

LeeLee snuggled next to Gee as she spoke.

"Just pretend, mind you, there's no harm in that. It isn't all fun and games to be the boss. When you're the boss you have a lot of things to think about."

"Like what?"

"Like which way we are going to walk to school, if we need our umbrella, grown-up stuff. So, if Rachel wants to be the boss of you—" Gee leaned and whispered, "Don't pay no mind, let her have the worry."

"Do you think when she grows up she will yell like PopPops?"

"No one yells like PopPops, but she'll protect you just as well as he does. She'll help you no matter where you are or what happens to you."

LeeLee lowered her chin, and Gee waited patiently while the child thought. Finally, LeeLee's soft eyes rose to meet hers.

"I was right. She's going to go to the desert for me, isn't she?"

Gee gazed into LeeLee's big blue eyes, and she told her the truth. "That she is, child. That she is."

LeeLee dropped her head again, and Gee watched as LeeLee began to pick the skin on the sides of her fingers. Gee reached out a hand and placed her fingers over LeeLee's to stop her picking.

"Gee?"

"Yes?"

"When Sissy goes to the desert she is going to meet a not-nice boy."

Gee's face sobered. She could not believe what she heard.

"How do you know that, LeeLee?"

"The white angel showed me a movie in my head."

"Well." Gee breathed through her nose and expelled the breath forcefully out her mouth. "She has a mind of her own, that Sissy. Born with it. I expect she will do as she pleases. She may fall in with the wrong crowd, pick the wrong boy."

"And I will have to help her."

"Yes, I suppose you will. I think you are beginning to grow up, my sweet."

"I am?" LeeLee's eyes shot up to Gee, and her expression turned exuberant.

"Yes, you are. Now you see how the river flows. You and Sissy on your rafts, floating up and down past Gee and Pops and all the other people you will meet in your lifetime. And sometimes you will slip overboard and Sissy will pull you back on, and sometimes Sissy will slip and you'll lend her a hand.

"LeeLee, listen carefully. I think you are big enough to know, now."

"Know what, Gee?"

"The truth about your gifts. Sissy is tough and strong and has many gifts. She will go to the desert. It has to be that way. But, LeeLee, you are the stronger soul. Someday, when you are grown and have your own family, that old river will change directions, and Sissy will need you much more than you need her. Promise me when that time comes, you'll take care of her—for Gee."

"I will have to take care of Sissy?" LeeLee glanced at her hands and stopped picking at her fingers.

Gee squeezed her close and rocked her feebly. After a while, Gee stopped rocking and leaned back to examine the girl. LeeLee's eyes rose and the slow and sluggish blinking of pensive thought came as it always did.

"Okay, we can pretend Sissy is the boss of me but, Gee?"

"Yes?"

"No one will ever really be the boss of me."

"No, they won't, and people will highly underestimate you, LeeLee."

"What does underestimate mean?"

"It means no one will know your power."

28 Jack

Jack had cleaned up so much puke he had thrown up himself. The rugs, his clothes, every inch of the house stunk with Jaden and John's regurgitated breakfast. As long as he lived, this afternoon with the boys would remain in his mind as their worst sick day ever. Even the cat had thrown up.

When he heard Lisa's car pull into the driveway, he uttered a "Thank God," and then peeked out the window. Mikala jumped down from the kitchen counter and ran to the front door.

"Go finish your homework, sweetie." He gestured with a fist, his thumb pointing toward the kitchen.

"But, Daddy." She stepped toward him.

"Stay away from me, honey. In case I get the flu."

"But—"

"No really, go finish your worksheets. Give Mom a breather before you tell her about your tooth falling out."

She walked away dejected, and Jack made his way toward the couch and collapsed on the cushions.

"The boys are finally asleep," he said, when Lisa barged through the front door. "You have no idea what I've been through in the past three hours."

"Mikala," Lisa called. She sounded unsympathetic. "Go to your room for a bit but stay away from the boys. I want to talk to your dad."

"But Momma—"

"No buts, go on. Change your clothes, and I'll be up in a minute."

"But—"

"Go," Lisa hollered. Jack and Mikala exchanged glances. Mikala lowered her head and started up the stairs. Jack sat up.

"What's wrong? Did you meet Rachel at the station?"

"Yes, I did. Is there something you want to tell me?"

"As in?"

"As in is there something you forgot to mention?"

Jack put his hands out and turned his palms upward. "Do you want to give me a clue what you're talking about?"

"A little note you forgot to mention?"

A chill crept up his spine. He controlled his breathing and let her lead him. He learned long ago not to put words in someone's mouth.

"Don't want to talk about it?" She crossed her arms.

"Are you talking about the notes the kidnapper is leaving when he abducts little boys? They're Bible quotes."

"What about the one you crumpled up at Janice's house? Where is it?"

She could not know about that. He had hidden the note in a book, *The Art of Racing in the Rain,* and placed that book in a bed-stand drawer underneath several others. Lisa had already read that novel, twice.

"Lisa, I have no idea what you're talking about." He stood up.

"Don't you ever lie to me." She lunged at him so fast, for a moment he thought she was going to smack him.

"Tell me right now what it said, Jack." She was right up in his face. His first thought was he'd never seen her so angry. His second was that she didn't know what the note said, so she hadn't found it in the book. He remained silent.

"We found that boy's house. The John I dreamt about? Rachel dreamt of him, too, and we located his home. The boy was there, safe and sound."

"Well, that's good. Thank God. Don't you agree?"

"The perpetrator, abductor, whatever you want to call him, seems to have called his house."

"He called them?"

"Yes."

"What did he say?"

"He asked if the woman had a son John, and she asked him who wanted to know. Do you know what he said?"

"What, Lisa?" Now he was mad, too. "You want me to guess? Who did he say wanted to know?"

"He said Lisa and Rachel and hung up."

Jack's legs collapsed like the legs on a folding table. He fell to the couch.

"Right before the chief came back and told us this, I saw something. I had a vision of you stuffing a note into your pocket outside Janice's house. Where is it Jack? What did that note say?"

A laundry basket of clean sheets and clothes sat at the bottom of the stairs. She stomped toward it, dumped its contents, and sifted through the linens, arms flailing.

"Lisa—"

She found his shorts. Stuck her hand in one pocket then the other. Turned them inside out and then tossed them back down into the pile on the floor.

"You son of a bitch."

That shocked him. She barely ever swore.

"If that note had anything to do with Mikala, I'll divorce you, Jack."

He said nothing.

"I told you this guy was more dangerous than you knew. But, no, you wouldn't believe me. I begged you to get off this case. But you had to be the big star with the chief and come to the rescue."

"No—"

"Then how the hell does that man know my name?"

She ripped the coat off her arms. He thought a button flew across the room. Then she tossed the coat down and stomped up the stairs, turning halfway up to deliver one final blow.

"I swear. If I find that note and Mikala's name is on it, I'll kill you myself."

She didn't come down again. She stayed upstairs with the boys, and Jack didn't go after her. He grabbed a change of clothes from the laundry, jumped in the downstairs shower and made himself a quick sandwich because he hadn't eaten in over twenty-four hours.

Mikala hurried down the stairs just before he left. She jabbered about a camp she wanted to go to, naming boys in her class who went last summer. He didn't listen. He picked her up and hugged her.

"Daddy has to go, honey. Talk to Mommy about it."

"But Daddy, I want to go to that camp. You learn to fish and skip stones. You go to the beach and meet all kinds of other kids from day care centers and after-school programs."

"I'm sorry, Mikala." He set her feet down on the floor and opened the front door. "Daddy has a lot on his mind. Talk to Mom."

"But Daddy," he heard her say as he shut the door, her little voice trailing away.

When he drove off, he passed Geoff Filutze in the police car. Geoff was now stationed directly in front of his house. He nodded at him and glanced down the street. There was a second surveillance car on the corner, where the officer inside could see both his house and his sister's.

While he wasn't clear why this man had mentioned Lisa, he felt relief that the security at his house had been stepped up. Why hadn't anyone called him about it?

"Damn." He remembered.

He had turned his phone off the minute Jaden threw up. He removed his cell from its clip and tapped the home button. There were eleven messages. He only listened to one. He tossed the phone onto the passenger seat right after he heard Billy's voice say, "Where the hell are you, Jack?

"On my way," he said to no one. "What have I gotten my family into?"

29 Billy

Billy sat, feet propped on desk, ankles crossed, and two fingers turning a pencil over and over, tapping and sliding it from tip to eraser. Files and documents wrestled for space on his desk.

"Where were you?" He bounced his feet to the ground and stopped tapping when Jack walked into the precinct.

He leaned an elbow on the arm of his chair and swiveled his seat back and forth, jiggling the pencil between two fingers. The wall behind him, with the recently replaced windows, had been partitioned off for final touch-up, so sheets of gray drywall framed him. A few asbestos chunks, which fell when ceiling tiles above the windows were replaced, still sat beside his chair awaiting the maintenance man to come sweep them away.

"At home; the boys were sick." Jack sat down at his own disastrous desk.

He, like Billy, had stopped filing over a month ago. More than likely, asbestos hid in the paper creases of every exposed record at his workspace. Jack poked the start button on his computer and shoved papers and files away from his keyboard.

"So you don't answer your phone? What the hell? Did Lisa tell you the guy called the Hilltop residence?"

All around Jack, normalcy reigned. Guys stretched cords on landline phones to reach desktops, scrambled from the evidence room to the front office, sidestepped patches of cracked floor tiles, and chatted around the ancient glass watercooler. No one heard Billy but Jack.

"Yeah, she did."

Billy stopped swiveling, leaned elbows to desk. The corner of his eyes squinted out little lines. He spoke low enough so only Jack heard. "Chief's stepping up security for them—both Rachel and Lisa. And there's something else."

"What?"

Billy leaned back and began swiveling again.

"Don't you listen to your messages? Hell, Jack, what kind of cop are you? We heard back about the tap."

"And?" Jack lifted his shirt collar in back to cut the chill of his still-damp hair.

"We were right. There's a ransom. And the mother isn't talking."

"Carlson?"

"You betcha. He and I had a nice little exchange of affection at the bank. I thanked him kindly for helping me fulfill my citation quota. He left his Mercedes double-parked on State Street."

"How much does that bastard get paid?"

"Enough to make our lives miserable."

"Didn't you mention two investigators?"

"Yep." Billy grabbed a toothpick from a desk drawer.

"How do they have the money for two? She's a bank teller. He's a loan officer."

"The second one is free." He slipped the toothpick into his mouth. "A retired cop from Columbus. Lyndsey Blakley's uncle, or cousin, or some half-assed relative. Wesley Seifert."

"Wesley Seifert. Where have I heard that name?"

"He settled some big case in Las Vegas in 2011. The casino owner's kid."

"Right. Mexican drug wars. I heard he had Erie connections." Jack moved his fingers over the keyboard. He signed in and Googled Wesley Seifert. "You don't think—"

On the monitor, Seifert's resume of drug busts clawed its way to the top of the screen.

"I don't know," Billy said. "But it's official. All three notes had traces of coke."

Jack's eyes left the screen and the scores of drug busts hailing Seifert's name. "The third one, too?"

Billy sifted through the top layer of files on his desk, grabbed one, and handed it to Jack. "If you remember, they only found traces of it on the first two notes, but he got careless. Dust was all over the third."

"Any prints."

"None." Billy twirled his toothpick with his tongue. "Not one on all three. Not sure what they'll find on the fourth."

"The fourth?"

Billy Mack stared. And twirled.

"What you mean is—" Jack stared back. "If and when they find a fourth."

Billy Mack said nothing. The silence lasted so long Jack had to say something.

"Because, you know, we are going to catch this guy before there is a fourth note." The collar of Jack's shirt felt tight, the room warm.

"Now that—" Billy Mack hesitated, tilting his chair as far back as he could without toppling over.

Jack's neck tingled. It took all the restraint he could muster not to shove Billy and that half-assed smirk of his backward onto the floor.

"Would be a miracle now, wouldn't it, Jack?"

Lisa told him.

Jack kept his composure. His face remained stone still. He was a good investigator when he concentrated. Billy was fishing. He had to be because Lisa hadn't known what that note said. Hence, she and Billy had no sound proof a fourth note existed.

"Obviously, Billy, there is something you want to talk to me about." He breathed rhythmically. When it came to his daughter, he could do anything. Control his blood pressure.

Stop sweating. "So talk, Billy. Tell me what you think you know."

There was no reason to tell anyone about the note with Mikala's name, now. Ten days had passed. Seemed like an eternity. But he'd survived without telling. Now the kidnapper had mentioned Lisa and Rachel, and with the added surveillance and security that provoked, he could keep Mikala's name out of the case permanently.

If it weren't for goddamn Billy.

"Jack." Billy stood and stepped toward him. He lay the knuckles of both hands on Jack's desk and leaned in. "You don't know me? You can't tell me the truth after all these years?"

Jack didn't respond.

"Do you trust me, Jack?"

"With my life."

But not my daughter's.

Billy leaned down and whispered in his ear. "I been at your house, buddy. But I'm not the only one." Then he leaned away slowly, and Jack arched his eyebrows.

"You gotta help me here." Billy kept his voice low, so only Jack heard him. "I know Rachel was out of town. That day you said one boy was dead. How'd you know that? Who did you mean when you said 'they' told you?"

"Rachel and Lisa," he answered succinctly. "I told you, Billy. It was Rachel and Lisa."

Billy twirled his toothpick with his tongue. His eyes never left Jack's.

"Who's the guy hanging around your house?" Now Billy's voice was less than a whisper.

"I don't know what you're talking about, but you better goddamn well tell me."

Billy lay a finger on his lips and leaned in again. This time, Jack could feel the stubbles of Mack's chin scrape the side of his face. "You better be straight with me, Crackerjack, because you got a secret admirer hanging around your house watching your family."

As Billy leaned back on his knuckles, Jack straightened. He had no idea what Billy was talking about, so he said nothing.

"Something going on in your family I should know about?"

"You been talking to my wife, Billy?"

"Yep, ran into her out in the parking lot a few hours ago. She seemed upset. We talked."

"About?"

"Well, Katie, of course. She talked to me about Katie because sometimes Lisa picks up on things that men like you and I can't see."

Jack stood and leaned on his own knuckles. The precinct went silent. All movement in the room ceased.

"You been bothering my wife?" Jack annunciated each word sharply. "Coercing things from her she shouldn't be telling you?"

"No coercing." Billy leaned closer. "I expect Lisa told me because she was concerned. Lisa and me, we're a lot alike. We both want to protect the people we love."

"Who you protecting, Billy?"

"I think you know."

The silence was deafening, the precinct so quiet that the ticking of the clock sounded like a fire alarm. Jack felt the eyes in the room on him. Then suddenly, he heard the rhythmic thud of heel on ceramic tile, and Donna Vahey filled the space beside them.

"Oh, for God's sake, what's going on with you two, now?" Donna put her hands akimbo. Her booming voice restarted the room. People began moving again. "You two need to come with me."

"We're not finished here, Donna," Jack said.

"Oh, yes, you are."

"We have some business to settle." Billy's tone matched Jack's to perfection.

"Settle it later. Come to the chief's office. The Nubers are here. There's another ransom."

Donna Vahey didn't stick around for their final exchange.

"You got somebody watching your family, and it isn't one of us," Billy said. "You're not telling us everything."

"And you're not telling me everything. What the hell did you see, Billy?"

Billy stood back, kicked his chair under his desk, and followed in Donna's footsteps. "Until you come clean, I ain't seen nothin'."

30 The perpetrator

He sat for a moment, complimenting himself on the path he had cleared. He'd been busy. But how much easier the widening had made his task. Swinging a sickle through the briar for nearly a quarter of a mile, he'd enlarged the footpath, burrowing a fine tunnel-like trail. Took him hours, his hands were chafed and bruised. But now the path was wide enough to lug more than a child through.

The property's owner lived in Florida. Moved away from the Pennsylvania climate at age fifty-five. He was one lucky guy, a General Electric employee for thirty-two years. They'd given him the golden handshake and sent him on his way. He and his wife moved to a lovely condominium with canal access in Cape Coral, Florida, so they had turned off the house's electricity, gas, and eventually the water. Having no children, they paid the minimal taxes to the township, but made no effort to maintain the house. The dilapidated old homestead was worthless.

Yet the land would someday make their only niece—a doctor of something, working at a college somewhere out in Oregon—a nice inheritance. Until then, the family couldn't be bothered with the land, and no one minded.

East and west of them, neighbors pilfered land on each side. They mowed right up to the dense infestation of gooseberry and black raspberry bushes that had sprung up thirty feet in from the property's border. They didn't care to go farther. There were more than enough berries to be stripped from the exposed branches. The ten-foot high and sixteen-foot wide impenetrable hedges stretched along the property all the way back to the forest. And no one hunted back there anymore.

The hollowed line he had been able to carve with his sickle was impressive. He marveled at his workmanship. Hard labor never frightened him. If you could survive the heat of a desert and the disdain of the government, you could withstand anything.

He sighed and laughed and placed a hand on the back of the man with the bludgeoned head. No heartbeat. He checked for a pulse on the underside of the man's wrist, then on the soft spot beside his Adam's apple. Thank the devil the guy had finally died.

He'd left the old chap in the back of the rented car, gave him water once to keep him alive, then chloroformed him again, and hoped he breathed a day more. The closer he died to the fire, the better. But then tonight, after dragging him in earlier in the day, leaving, parking the car at an abandoned junkyard, and coming back, he opened the body bag, and by God, the old geezer still had a faint pulse. Fortunately, a simple glove resting over nose and mouth did the trick.

He removed his hand, stretched his back, and massaged one shoulder. Placed one hand beside his neck and moved his sore arm in big circles.

He must be out of shape. Carrying weight never used to hurt.

He leaned down and grabbed the edges of the body bag, a sweet pilferage from the landfill. Closing the sides of the bag over the man, he zipped the zipper. Then he grunted as he lifted the bag and dropped the body inside the old cedar chest—the hope chest—and laughed.

"Here's hopin' you're feeling better," he said, then he slammed the lid tight and removed his clothes—stolen from another bum—and tucked them inside a drawer in a bureau next to the chest.

He brushed his gloved hands together. Another task completed. On to the next: John.

"*322. Protect my face.*"

He packed his skintight black garb and appropriate tools in his black bag. While police dallied over the ransom and the women worried about addresses, he would easily nab the boy and take him to the bunker.

He closed his eyes for a moment and concentrated.

"322 *Hilltop.*"

He blocked the other address from his mind and climbed the stairs carefully. He must keep the women hovering above Hilltop Road for a few more hours.

"*Protect my face.*"

The light from his forehead flashed through the steps and sent a mouse or rat on the floor scurrying to a corner. He stepped gingerly on the brittle first-floor boards.

"This place will go up like a gas station," he said out loud.

When he exited the house and strode down into the foliage, he bent down, found the makeshift tunnel, and clicked off his light. He pretended he was that retired man from GE walking blindly away, leaving everything behind—his life, his schemes, Project Dream, and the American government. Sometimes, as he crept through the tunnel, he fantasized that he had the freedom to go wherever he wanted. That he wasn't tied to this godforsaken program, and he didn't have to do what he was about to do.

But then reality set in and he remembered. No one got out alive.

31 Karen Nuber

"I'm going to tell you something, Chief Morgan." Karen Nuber sat on the edge of her seat, spine straight, hands in lap, and chin held high. A thin watery film covered her eyes, but she didn't cry. "My son is not your typical four-year-old. If there is a way for him to survive, he'll find it. Trust me."

Quiet swept across the room. Something in the woman's voice was convincing. Or maybe they simply wanted to believe her.

"The results might not be back yet, but I know my son. That's his hair. You can count on it."

But was he still alive? Jack wondered.

He examined the plastic evidence bag with the ransom note and the hair. The hair color matched Jaden's and John's. He glanced at his watch: Saturday, the eighteenth. Twelve days ago, the perpetrator had left Mikala's name on a note. Since then, his family's protection had weighed on him. Now the security outside their home had intensified and with the twins still recovering from the flu, Lisa and Mikala would be forced to stay at home today, keeping them safe twenty-four more hours. Tomorrow, a cruiser and an unmarked car would follow them to church.

"We aren't dealing with the typical kidnapper either, Mrs. Nuber," he heard the chief say, and his thoughts came back into the room. "But we will do everything in our power to make this drop look like no police are involved. We've wired your car and we'll wire you."

"These new wires are nearly impossible to find on a person," an FBI investigator assured her. "We won't lose you. That you can be sure of."

Karen Nuber looked the man straight in the eye, her gaze so cold it could have caused a brain freeze. "I don't care if you follow me or not. You do what you must do, and I'll do what I must do. In the end? I'm going home to wait for my son. I will see him again. And detective, that is something you can be sure of."

Her surety rendered them speechless.

"Now, if you don't mind, it's been a long day. I'm going home. I'll get up tomorrow and go to church like I do every Sunday, go about my business all day, and at 10:32 tomorrow evening, I'll get in my car and head toward I-90. It takes exactly twenty-one minutes for me to get to Behrend from my house and six minutes to make the walk to the track. I know. I practiced twice last night in the dark and six times today. I'm giving myself one minute to spare. No more. So stay out of my way." She stood. "If I'm required to go somewhere else? I'll do it. I'll travel all around the state of Pennsylvania for the entire night if this man asks me to. And when it's done, I'm going home and wait for my baby, thaw a turkey for his Thanksgiving dinner. He loves turkey and mashed potatoes."

With that, she picked up her purse and left them. When the door clicked shut, the walls seemed to sigh behind her.

One unconvincing FBI agent in an expensive but slightly wrinkled suit said, "Our plan is foolproof. We'll get this guy."

The FBI, state troopers, county and city detectives all had their instructions, Jack included. They would meet at six tomorrow morning and start the day. They'd install the remaining cameras and microphones that hadn't been installed today. By eleven tomorrow evening, they would have covered all bases.

A squeal sounded from across the room.

"This guy is never going to show." Billy's high voice pierced the room. Jack heard chair legs scrape the floor as one agent flinched. Billy finished with "Never in a million years."

"Shut the fuck up, Mack," one state trooper said. "I'm tired of you adding your two cents."

"He'll show." The FBI agent sitting next to Jack sounded annoyed yet poised. "He took the Blakleys' money."

"Doesn't...mean...shit." Billy bounced his head as he spoke each word.

Jack agreed. But he kept his mouth shut. Opinions differed and tempers flared with the tough cases.

He watched the FBI agent wiggle his neck around the inside of his shirt collar.

"You know, Billy." The angry trooper stood and advanced toward Billy. A fellow trooper lifted an arm to hold him back. "We've all had just about enough of your smartass arrogance."

Billy's eyes twinkled. His tongue rolled around his toothpick and he nodded.

"I thank you, kindly. Always good to be known as the arrogant smartass in a crowd of badge-polishing dumb asses like yourself."

Jack jumped out of his seat along with five other City of Erie officers and investigators to thwart two state troopers and one FBI agent from bashing in Billy Mack's face.

32 Rachel

"Rachel?" Lisa slammed the car door. Her heels clicked over the driveway pavers as she hurried toward Rachel. "I'm sure we have the wrong house."

Rachel tossed her purse over the small plastic bag inside the trunk of her car and picked up a gallon of milk and a grocery bag. She stepped to meet Lisa halfway down the driveway.

Sometimes Lisa exhausted her.

She had caught Rachel by surprise today. Showed up at 8:45 on a Sunday morning, all three kids in tow, a cruiser trailing them. No doubt she was on her way to church. She never missed Mass.

Didn't Lisa know she spent her Sunday mornings grocery shopping?

"What?" Rachel asked.

The response was reflex more than question. She felt instant annoyance. A thought surged into her head. A person should never brag about their own strength, because the next thing they knew, they were crying in the corner like a helpless kitten.

And Rachel knew this because she had done so five times. Twice when she was pregnant with Jeffrey, once postpartum, and twice yesterday. Her hormones were dancing like dust in a windstorm.

She inched closer to her sister.

"We have the wrong house." A frown squeezed out lines on Lisa's face. "I think we have the wrong John."

"Where's Jack?"

"Working." She maneuvered around Rachel, coaxed her toward the garage, and spoke quietly. "I don't want anyone to hear. They received a second ransom. I'm not supposed to know."

Rachel stepped inside the garage, wedging her body between Lisa and her car. "Is it possible we can talk about this later?"

Lisa hesitated. "Well, sure. I tried calling earlier but you didn't answer. So I thought I'd stop on my way to church. I wondered if you felt any more. About anything."

"No, sorry."

"Mama," Jeffrey hollered from Rachel's car. He still sat in the back, seat belt fastened. "Out."

"Just a minute, Jeffrey."

"Rach, are you okay? Where's Todd?"

She sighed. "Gone again. Either to Parks in Philly or the Sugar House in New Jersey. I can't keep track. He had business in Scranton and asked if I minded if he traveled down state for a tournament."

"And that was okay with you?"

"Look, Lisa, don't get all prim and proper with me."

"Oh, no, I'm sorry." Lisa's cheeks reddened. She hesitated and then said, "Can I help you with Jeffrey? Or the groceries?"

"Mama!" Jeffrey had turned around in his seat and began to cry. "Out!"

"No, really, I've just been stressed out with work and these missing kids, and Jeffrey is teething again. I'm frazzled, that's all."

"Mama!" Jeffrey stared at them over the back seat of the car. His face was sideways. He had lurched upward in his seat and twisted around so his head inched above his car seat. He pushed with his feet again. His body jerked upward and then down. His chin hit the top of the car seat and he screamed.

Lisa saw him first and ran to him, unclicked the seat belt, and lifted him up and out of the car. She handed him to Rachel.

"There, there, shhh." Rachel bounced him up and down in her arms. "You're fine."

"Hurt!" He pointed to his face with his finger.

Mikala opened the car door and called, "Is Jeffrey okay?"

"Yes, he'll be fine," Lisa hollered. "Watch your brothers for a minute. I'm going to help Aunt Rachel with the groceries."

"You're fine, Jeff—no, Lisa, you go on. Get to church."

Lisa rounded the back of the car and picked up a grocery bag. Rachel hurried toward her.

"I have time," Lisa said, lifting Rachel's purse from the trunk. "Here's your—"

"Lisa," Rachel hollered, sounding frantic. "I can get it."

She grabbed the purse out of Lisa's hand, but it was too late. The clear bag with the white powder sat exposed in the corner of the trunk.

Slowly, the bag of groceries slid out of Lisa's arms and down into the trunk. She picked up the bag and examined it. Her eyes bounced to Rachel and then to the purse in Rachel's hands. Rachel followed her gaze and looked down. A smaller, white-powdered pouch peeked out her purse's side pocket. Rachel threw the purse into the trunk, ripped the package from Lisa's fingers, tossed that down, too, and slammed the trunk shut.

"Rachel," Lisa whispered.

"They're Todd's."

Somewhere far away a train whistled, and closer, the engine of a car moaned. The wind kicked up and rustled the tree branches around them.

Lisa bit her bottom lip with her two front teeth, shook her head, and then said, "Todd's out of town."

Again a train whistle, again the moan of an engine and a brush of wind. Lisa brought a hand to her face and covered her mouth.

Rachel bounced the still-crying Jeffrey in her arms, tucked his head underneath her chin, and began to cry.

33 Mikala

"Are you crying, Mama?" Mikala whispered as the choir at the front of the church bellowed out their finest halleluiah.

"Quiet just a little longer, baby, the Mass is almost over."

"Are you praying for Aunt Rachel?"

"What?" Her mom turned toward her, and Mikala watched her mother shift her weight from one knee to another and finger her rosary. "Yes, sweetie, Aunt Rachel, you, Daddy, and your brothers. I pray for all my family."

"Jeffrey, too?"

"Jeffrey, too. Now be a good girl and sit back and watch your brothers, while I finish my prayers." Lisa wound the rosary beads around her fingers, tightening them, and gestured with her head toward the pew behind Mikala.

Mikala leaned into her mother, looped a hand around her arm, and rested her face against her coat sleeve.

"Okay, Momma," she said, but she remained there for a moment to study her. Think about their morning.

After Aunt Rachel hurried into the house crying, Mamma released her seat belt and the twin's car seat belts and took them inside, too. Mikala and her brothers kept Jeffrey busy in the playroom while Mamma and Aunt Rachel had sister time, making them miss the nine o'clock church service.

Now they sat through the long ten-thirty Mass. Usually, Mamma avoided this service because Jaden and John couldn't sit still that long. They were too "antsy."

Mikala lay her free hand on top of her mother's hand and tightened the grip around her arm. She continued to stare at her. Finally, her mother smiled.

"It's okay, sweetie, really. Sit back so I can finish my rosary."

When she didn't move again, her mother leaned down and whispered, "Go ahead. Everything's fine."

She scooted back onto the cold, hard pew and waited quietly.

When the congregation stood for the final blessing, her mother remained kneeling, her lips moving like an actress on a television set with the volume turned down. Mikala stood and, after the priest made the sign of the cross, the choir began singing again. She watched men in dark coats and women in pretty hats march up the aisle to leave.

Mamma motioned for her to sit down, and Mikala glanced at her beads. She counted them: five, six, seven. Momma had seven more prayers to say. Mikala placed the palms of her hands on the pew behind her and slipped back next to her brothers.

She decided to search for the big white cloud she had seen earlier in the service. She always saw lots of white mist at church. Sometimes, the mist floated toward the priest on the altar or mommies and daddies in the pews, showing her their pretty colors: blue, yellow, purple. She liked to watch for the babies. They had the brightest colors. Momma called them auras and said she shouldn't talk about them. Other people couldn't see them.

But today was different. The white mist was thicker, brighter than the people's auras.

On the altar next to the bright gold tabernacle, she spotted a large warm mist hovering above the marble floor. The hazy form floated sluggishly, expanded into a wide cloud, rose, swirled, and spun into the form of a woman.

Mikala's heart leapt. She had only seen this misty lady with the silver hair and no wings twice before, once when Momma was in the hospital and once in her bedroom when she was scared. The woman looked familiar, but Mikala didn't know her. Both times, the lady brought her a pleasant, peaceful feeling. The pretty lady might be Momma's Gee.

She watched the soft flow of the lovely lady's beautiful hair and white gown as she floated forward and stopped at the third pew. There, she spread her arms out and hovered over the kneeling mother with the slumped shoulders. She encircled the woman with her airy arms and glanced directly at Mikala, smiled, and nodded.

Instantly, Mikala knew the lady she embraced was Mathew Nuber's momma.

The misty lady beckoned Mikala to come to them, then slowly faded into the air. Her shimmering hair and perfect smile folded into the mist last. Mikala was sad to see her go. Afterward, she sat quietly listening to the organ's final melody and staring fixedly at the back of Mrs. Nuber's head. She watched Mrs. Nuber gather her purse and missal and noticed how sad her eyes seemed.

Mikala leaned back in her seat and slid an arm around Jaden. He sat, folding pages of a missal in half, making a half of a paper airplane and trying to get his brother to do the same.

She glanced at her mother. Momma would never allow her to talk to Mathew's momma. She started thinking. People were still filing out of church, but fewer and fewer remained. Momma would finish soon.

She turned toward the back of the church and espied the mother's room with its big glass window. She used to go there with Momma when the twins were little. They liked to play with the nursery toys while Momma prayed.

"Jaden." She tugged his arm, drew him close, and whispered. "Remember the wooden animals that fit in the wooden barn?"

Jaden jerked his head toward Mikala, his eyes wide and mouth agape. Mikala put a finger against her lips to let him know he should remain quiet. Then she pointed toward the mother's room. He turned and saw the barn, his favorite toy right there in the window. He glanced back at Mikala. She pointed to John and then back to the room, nodded her head, and set a finger against her lips again.

Jaden put his missal down, grabbed John's hand, scooted down the pew, lunged into the aisle, and was gone in three seconds flat.

Mikala made a gasping sound and sprang onto the kneeler next to her mother. "Mama, Mama," she whispered. "Jaden went to play with the wood barn."

"What?" Lisa's gaze followed the direction of Mikala's pointing finger, and she glimpsed the mother's room. "Oh, no."

She wound her rosary beads up into her hand and tucked them in her purse.

"Mikala, grab the missals," she said as she snatched the boy's jackets. "Hurry."

Through the glass, they could see Jaden jerking the big barn off the shelf and watched helplessly as all of its pieces fell to the floor. Lisa ran.

"Mikala, come," she hollered over her shoulder.

"Coming," Mikala responded but didn't follow.

Mrs. Nuber was making her way up the aisle. Mikala stepped out in front of her. Mrs. Nuber stopped. Her sad eyes glanced downward to meet Mikala's.

"Hi." Mikala smiled.

"Hello," Mrs. Nuber answered, slowly pulling the strap of her purse over one shoulder.

"You're Matthew's mommy," Mikala said, and watched Mrs. Nuber's throat move up and down with a big swallow. Mrs. Nuber didn't respond right away. She wasn't blinking.

"Are you Rachel Callahan's niece?" she finally asked.

Mikala nodded.

Mrs. Nuber drew her missal into her chest and stooped down, leaning on one knee so they were eye to eye.

"I believe," she said slowly, "I'm not completely sure, but I believe your Aunt Rachel is helping me find my little boy."

Mikala widened her smile and nodded rapidly. Mrs. Nuber offered a bashful smile in return.

"He'll be home for Thanksgiving dinner. I'm making his favorite. Turkey," she told Mikala, her eyes glassy.

"Mrs. Nuber?"

"Yes?"

"Matthew won't be home for Thanksgiving."

Mrs. Nuber's cheeks tightened. The corner of her lips fell.

"But don't worry," Mikala continued quickly. "You can make turkey for him on Christmas. He'll be home by then."

"Mikala!" Lisa hollered. She stood, eyes wide, one hand gripping Jaden's hand and the other clasping John's. Her purse dangled off one wrist and down her leg. "What are you doing?"

"Nothing, Mama." Mikala jumped away from Mrs. Nuber, circled John, and put an arm around Lisa's leg.

Mrs. Nuber grabbed the end of a pew with her hand and stood.

"I'm so sorry," Lisa said. "I hope she wasn't bothering you."

"No." Mrs. Nuber spoke slowly. "I dropped my missal, and she picked it up for me."

Her glance fell to Mikala. "Thank you," she whispered.

"You're welcome," Mikala responded, smiling again.

"Come along, Mikala," Lisa said, but before she turned to go, she stopped. "Mrs. Nuber? I'm praying for you. Every day."

Mrs. Nuber nodded, and Lisa led her children out the church doors. Mikala did not stop looking over her shoulder at Matt's momma until she stepped outside, turned the corner, and her mother unmuted her phone.

Lisa's cell rang.

34 Marky Blakley

The worst happened. Marky Blakley's body was found.

Twenty minutes after Mark Senior identified his son, Jack called Lisa from the crime scene and relayed the horrific news. He told her quite calmly to get home. Two undercover cops were now hidden in their neighborhood. Security had been stepped up.

All around Jack, officers and FBI agents scoured the river banks and nearby areas where Marky's body lay covered in leaves. An indecisive fisherman and his hound dog, Sport, discovered the body while inspecting the ravine for the perfect Sunday morning fishing spot.

Easily, quickly, the team determined the crime scene was not where the murder took place. Everyone anticipated the examination of the body to reveal more, including the cause of death. Finding fibers or lifting fingerprints was not expected. Rumors circulated the man carried the body down the middle of the creek, dumped the cadaver, and left the way he came.

The crime scene was bad, but the scene near the street, unbearable. Mark Blakley Senior stepped over the yellow cautionary tape and trudged toward the police cruiser where his wife sat white-knuckled, and she knew the body was Marky's. Mark Senior's face was white and ragged, his body, bowed. Every ounce of life in his limbs wilted. He needn't say a word.

What occurred next, Jack would never erase from his memory. In the few times he witnessed someone's anguish over losing a child—undeniably, the hardest cross in life—this time was the worst. The tormenting squeals of that mother echoed into the ravine and reverberated for miles down the creek's banks. Her self-blame was unbearable to witness. Listening to her PI, not informing police, would haunt her for a lifetime. Her baby boy was dead.

Jack hoped she would forgive herself in time. A parent had to do what a parent felt necessary for their child, even if that meant lying to police. Jack was no different.

Carlson and Seifert slinked down to the scene with their tails between their legs. Both gave serene statements, their once-poised statures sagging. The two big-time detectives had been reduced to mere mortals.

During Jack's brief conversation with Lisa, he apologized. He couldn't come home. He assured her; however, that she, Mikala, and the boys would never be out of someone's sight until the authorities arrested the murderer. In addition to the extra police, Jack had called Geoff Filutze, two other cops, and the security guard at Mikala's school, Mark Foley, who was a retired thirty-year veteran of the police force. Among the four of them, Lisa and the kids had twenty-four-hour protection.

He informed Lisa that when she arrived home, a white van would be parked in the side driveway. A man with tattoos up and down his arms would be meandering around. She was not to be alarmed. He was installing cameras.

Jack wasn't taking any more chances.

35 Lisa

On Sunday evening, for the third night in a row, Lisa Callahan sat in the quiet of her home meditating. After she dreamed of Mikala's legs descending those bunker stairs, she had called in the white angel, and the spirit had shown Lisa a movie of Mikala growing up, attending college, working, marrying, and having children of her own. The white light had never failed to show her the truth when she was little, and so she believed, hoped, and prayed, her baby would survive this horrifying moment in time.

But now she had Rachel to worry about, and Todd. And, clearly, Mikala knew more than she was admitting because she had overheard her tell Karen Nuber her son would be home by Christmas.

Yet there was no sign of him, and now Marky Blakley's body had been found.

So she said her prayers and called in the white angel on that Sunday evening, and a white mist fell around her and drew out flashes of pictures that developed into a movie in her head.

She watched the movie play:

Karen Nuber drove her black Ford Focus over I-90, turned onto the off-ramp at the Penn State Behrend exit, and drove to the college's parking lot. She walked from the lot to the football field, then counted the trees on the north side of the field out loud. One, two, three… She walked directly down into the ravine and hid the sack of money inside the bush that rimmed the seventh tree down the hill, turned to leave, and never looked back. She drove home and slept peacefully.

Night turned to day, and Lisa saw officers hiding around Behrend's campus, waiting. They stayed long into the morning, after the basketball team sauntered in for their conditioning workout, and the track team showed up to run laps. They remained all day. But no one came for the sack of money.

The scene in her head changed, and Lisa watched an FBI investigator climbing cement stairs and stepping onto a small blue-sided front porch. His index finger pressed the little black doorbell.

"My humble apologies," she heard the man say when Karen Nuber opened the door. She heard him as clearly as if she stood on that porch beside him. "No one came for the money. I'm sorry."

"Don't beat yourself up," Mrs. Nuber responded. "My boy will be home for Christmas."

Lisa opened her eyes, and the white mist floated into nothing.

"Oh, Mikala, what have you done?" She whispered.

36 The perpetrator

This was his finest moment. A breeze. He broke through the window without a sound, cut the screen, picked up the boy at the same time he put the chloroform-drenched handkerchief across his face, and departed the premises in ninety-four seconds flat. A record.

His drive and trek through the woods had also been cut short. And the boy had slept the entire time, right down to when he set him on the dirt floor. The kid didn't wake up when he attached the cuffs to his ankles, the chains to his cuffs, nor when he fastened the chains to the stake in the ground. Three months ago, he'd driven seven hours to purchase those chains. Out of the state. Out of the country. He chuckled in delight of himself.

The best part of the day? Realizing how smart Matt Nuber was. He'd learned to ration his food and water. More than half a jug remained, along with a loaf of bread, the mold barely breaking through, and peanut butter. So while he'd planned two runs with his makeshift sled, he'd been able to do it in one. No need for a second run; the kids had enough water.

"Matthew Nuber," he said, his voice muffled behind his mask. "You are okay."

The boy had nursed Luke Anderson back to health. The gray in Luke's cheeks had lessened. His mother had no idea how lucky he had been to have Matt at his side.

Of course, their survival still depended on how good the girl was, didn't it?

He'd cleared the grass and hay from around the top of the bunker to give them a chance once the flames heightened. After all, he did have a heart.

He climbed the stairs and closed the bunker door. Yes, that Matt Nuber was quite the kid.

He glanced at his fingers, raising and lowering his gloved hand to feel the weight of the bulky padlock he held. Several seconds passed, then he stepped one foot backward and hurled the lock through the air toward the woods. Coolly, he replaced the sod and walked away.

Cutting the chains in time was possible, but cutting that heavy-duty lock, too? Impossible.

Maybe, just maybe, he wanted Mikala to save them.

37 Andy Mesmer

The drop failed, the kidnapper no showed, and another child was stolen from the night while some of the state's finest crime investigators set up a sting around a sack of money no one retrieved, and the best city and county investigators hovered in the bushes around 322 Hilltop where no intruder showed. Simultaneously, the brightest crime pathologists spent the night laboring over Marky Blakley's death.

"How much worse could this get?" Jack thought.

Lots.

He'd gotten no sleep. He'd watched the security camera on his house all night long from his phone. Knowing Filutze could be inside in under twenty seconds, relieved him.

When he let Lisa know about the cameras—he couldn't have her walking around half naked—she said, "Thank God." That alarmed him. Did she know something? Sometimes this gift of hers worked double time as a curse.

Jack closed his eyes, bent his neck backward, and rested his head on the top of his chair. Rumors about psychic involvement were circulating like a viral YouTube video. FBI were showing up like party crashers. He lost count of them. Only recognized a few now, but they all knew him. On three occasions he asked to see badges because they questioned him about Rachel or Lisa.

How Lisa and Rachel's names stayed out of Monday's paper had to do with Ben Morgan's finesse. His keep-this-out and I-promise-better-news deal worked because people in this community trusted him.

Jack sat up, pinched his nose, drank lukewarm coffee, and waited. At ten o'clock the flood gates opened, and the press flowed in.

Men with ties and ladies in skirts juggled pen and paper, rubbing shoulders with each other and raising voices in an attempt to attract Chief Morgan's attention. Despite not sleeping for days, the chief didn't falter. He stood in his stiff, starched blues—that Donna Vahey had picked up from the cleaners that morning—looking more dapper than the Mayor beside him. He answered succinctly. Relayed next to nothing and let the Mayor play political Duck, Duck, Goose with interviewers—ignore, ignore, run around the question but don't answer. For once, the Mayor won, outran them all.

At ten fifteen, the chief exited the room perfunctorily, appearing more machine than man. His feet landed heavily on the tiles. His big, thick shoes clomped loudly away, quieting the room's din. He ignored reporter's sighs. A few tried stopping Jack, Billy, three County investigators, one state cop—the other state investigators still sat in the bushes at Behrend—and an FBI agent as they followed the chief out, but to no avail. No one talked.

At eleven o'clock, seventeen of the now thirty-plus case investigators jammed into a City Hall second-floor office meant for ten. Ceiling fans circulated cool air onto their shoulders, but everyone sweated. Four boys gone and the City, County, and FBI volleyed prime suspects. Jack checked his watch more than ten times in the twenty-minute meeting. Chief Morgan never mentioned the Callahan girls once. Thankfully, neither did any of Jack's coworkers. Either they didn't know, or the chief had scared them into silence.

When the meeting ended, they were no further ahead than they had been after the first abduction. Jack watched the men and women leave one by one. Only a core group remained. A forensics crime scene investigator, Andy Mesmer, joined them afterward with reports.

The abductions mirrored each other. There were no hairs, only a few yet-to-be-identified fibers, and not one fingerprint. They couldn't lift one print from the notes or any of the four boy's bedrooms or windows. Investigators in the evidence room continued to scrutinize a few pieces of evidence: partial footprints, breakage of glass, cocaine on notes, paper and black-ink script, masking tape holding notes, and a trace of chloroform on the sheets. They also reviewed files in an attempt to connect the abducted boys.

Jack, Billy, Chief and four other top investigators conjectured ways the abductor located the mothers living alone with four-year-old, biblically-named boys. But the bottom line appeared to be: these kids didn't know each other.

"Well, it can't be random." The crime specialist adjusted his glasses.

He was a biostatistician turned cop. A whiz kid the chief stole from a local college biology department and occasionally loaned out to other municipalities in the tristate area. He was a neat freak. ADHD. Couldn't sit through a meeting to save his soul. The chief learned early on to bring him in at the end or after the important meetings. He was a workaholic with no social skills, not one. And the big debate about the kid behind closed administrative doors at City Hall was did he have Asperger's? Or was he an autistic savant?

The chief simplified that debate: unimportant, the kid was just damn good. Jack agreed.

"He's not a serial killer. Nor a pedophile. His writing is too light. He capitalizes words he shouldn't. It's planned. Every space and letter. Did the handwriting analysis come back yet? What have you guys been doing?"

"We have the results." Billy Mack shuffled papers, fanning them out on the table. He grabbed and set a stapled report on top of the others and flipped pages as he read. "All notes written by the same hand. High pressure, no slant, crammed, wavy letters. Strokes not typical of a serial killer. Or a pedophile. Indicate creativity,—" a disgusting grunt rose from his throat "—insecurity, emotional fluctuation, instability—no kidding." His fingers released the pages. "The guy is no Einstein but he did grab four kids without a trace. Don't need a writing expert to gather he's not an idiot."

The kid adjusted his glasses. "I worked with you before, Billy Mack."

"That's right. You did, Andy. The Clawson case."

"Domestic violence. Case 74523. John Alexander clubbed Susan Mary with a golf club on August 9, 2016. It rained 2.08 inches that day. He threw the three wood into the pond on the eighth hole of Orchard Pond Golf Course. You went for a swim. Good work."

"Thanks, buddy, have any thoughts on case number—" Billy leaned forward and glanced at the file in front of him. "93214?"

"Abductions are hard. With a clever kidnapper." Andy Mesmer leaned forward then back. He came off his seat and then sat back down, his spine straight, fingers pointing. "You look at the chapters? The day they were abducted? For each kid? The Bible?"

Jack said, "We did."

"Crackerjack." The boy stood and pointed. "You took a bullet for Officer Reynolds. Good Job. If I were a cop, I'd want you to be my partner."

"Thanks." Jack delivered a wink and nod, simultaneously. "Do you know your Bible?"

"Yes. What was the last message? For John."

"For they have gone out in the world." Jack said.

The boy sat back down and looked directly at Jack. "Ah oh. It's part of a passage."

For the first time Jack could remember, the boy had made eye contact.

"That's our guess." Jack studied him carefully, every line on his face from his wrinkled forehead to his smooth chin. "He selects words from passages."

"I bet that one scared you."

"Scared me?" Now Jack wrinkled his face. "Why would that one scare me?"

"Well, you know, because of your wife. She's a prophet."

The kid could not have taken more wind out of him if he shot a cannon in his gut. He felt every eye in the room on him.

Billy Mack rescued him by reacting first. "What are you talking about, buddy?"

"Lisa Callahan. She and her sister are prophets, seers, mediums, psychics, whatever terminology current new-age trends use."

"That's far from the truth," Chief Morgan responded.

"It's okay, sir, I won't tell," he said, placing his thumb and middle finger on the edge of his glasses and moving them up and down. "People don't like prophets."

"So you agree? The passages refer to prophets?" Billy changed the subject.

"Yes, the verse. John 4:1: 'Beloved do not believe every spirit, but test the spirits to see whether they are from God, for many false prophets have gone out into the world'."

Billy Mack brought his cell phone out of his coat pocket and punched John 4:1 into the internet. The passage appeared. He turned the screen to show the others.

"Hell," Billy said, "next time we call Andy. How long did it take us to get the first three passages?"

"Too long," Jack said. "Andy, are you familiar with the other notes?"

"Yes, Mathew 25:41, the devil and his angels; Mark 1:27, the unclean spirits; Luke 1:16, will bring back many; and John 4:1, for many false prophets have gone out in the world. But he's in trouble." Andy lifted his arms, cracked his neck to both sides, and lay his elbows back on the table. "He's in a hurry.'"

"Why is he in a hurry?" Billy asked.

"I don't know why he is in a hurry."

"What makes you believe he is in a hurry?" Jack leaned toward him. Sometimes you simply had to ask Andy the right question.

"Because he didn't wait until the fourth."

"The fourth? What do you mean?" Jack glanced at the file with the abduction dates listed on top.

"Well…the fourth…of November. He didn't wait. He must be in a hurry."

The others in the room exchanged glances.

"Andy," Billy finally said, "what are you talking about?"

Andy shifted in his seat. Moved his glasses up and down. "Well, I thought you knew."

"Knew what?"

"The books are the abduction dates for the first three. Mathew passage 41 of Book 25; Mathew Nuber abducted September 25th. Mark passage 27 of Book 1; Mark Blakley abducted October 1. Luke passage 16 of Book 1; Luke Anderson abducted November 1. John verse 1 of Book 4; John Wickles abducted today, November 19. He should have waited until December 4th. He broke the chain."

Jack's hands shot to the pile in the middle of the table. He turned pages until he found the sheet with the passages.

"You, ah, forgot to mention that to anyone, Andy." Billy sifted through his own notes.

Andy placed two fingers on the edge of his glasses and let them rest there a few seconds before moving his frames up and down again. He blinked intensely. "Well…it was so clear…how could you miss that?"

"Is there anything else you've seen that we haven't? Think hard. Take a look at the map. Anything at all?" The chief asked.

Andy dropped his hand, gazed at the floor, and squirmed in his seat. "I don't…like…being put on the spot."

"Listen, Andy," Jack said. "You are not on the spot. We are. You've given us more than anyone else. No pressure, but if there is anything else you see. Let us know."

"Well, you know about that, right?" Andy raised his eyes and stuck a finger out. Pointed quickly toward the bottom of the map then dropped his gaze toward the table.

"What?" Jack glanced at the map.

"The passage at the bottom." Andy continued staring at the desk.

"The passage?" Billy turned toward the map, stood up.

Again, Andy shifted in his seat. Reached for his glasses, eyes down. "It says, 'Have Mercy on Me, Oh Lord'."

"Yeah." Billy leaned a hand on the front wall, glanced at the passage and then back at Andy. "I scribbled that on the map after the second boy was taken."

"Because of the greyscale on the note," Andy said, his fingers tightening on his glasses, his hand stretching across his face and covering his eyes. "Those are the greyscale words on all the notes."

"That's right," Jack responded. He had to beat down his rising impatience. "The FBI has gone to great lengths to determine who sold the note pad the abductor used. But they aren't having any luck. That particular stationery with that greyscale can be found in every Christian retail store across the country, plus umpteen internet sites."

"Yeah, but—" Andy blinked hard and sniffed behind his hand. "But he chose that one."

"That what?" Billy moved toward the map.

"That passage." Andy dropped his hand.

Jack shifted his chair to face the boy. "What's the significance of that passage?"

"You guys…are just…playing with me, right?"

Playing? A sick feeling worked its way into Jack's gut. Like he was down by a point and the buzzer sounded. The other team's ball was floating in the air, descending toward the net.

"No, partner, we're not playing." He softened his voice, tried to be patient. "We honestly don't know what you are talking about."

"Well…I mean…I know those words are referenced more than once in the Bible, but only one is appropriate."

Jack studied Andy. Waited for the swoosh.

"I thought, well…you mean…you didn't make the connection?" Sweat beaded around the kid's hairline. "That, well…you have to know…it is in reference to the suspects."

"What?" From the tone of his voice, the chief clearly felt the same impatience eating away at him as Jack, but he could no longer contain himself. "We have no clue what you are talking about, Andy."

"Okay…so you…are…playing with me."

"What?" The veins on the Chief's neck were bulging. "No, I'm not playing with you. Why would you ask that?"

"Because you said you had no clue…and actually…that passage on that greyscale…is a clue."

"A clue?"

"Yes, the greyscale passage is your biggest clue."

"Andy," the chief said, "what the devil are you talking about?'

"It's part of Psalm 51. Clearly, the kidnapper is referring to the boys from Area 51. On every note."

The room went silent.

Jack's phone rang.

38 Lisa

Lisa circled number seven on Liam Nelson's test and took a bite of her tuna fish sandwich. How could Liam not understand a seashell belonged with a bucket, shovel, and sand? He had circled a wrench. Hadn't he ever played in the sand at the beach?

She stopped chewing. My God, trying to maintain normalcy with everything on her mind—the note Jack wouldn't admit to, another child missing, one found, Mikala talking to Karen Nuber, and the white angel's continual comfort—she had forgotten to call Jack.

She swallowed her bite, dropped her pen, and dug into her purse for her cell.

Jack answered on the first ring, his voice hushed. "Is something wrong? I can't talk. I'm in a meeting."

"Everything is fine but this is important."

"Okay."

"This morning Mikala told me something."

Lisa had waved to Geoff Filutze as she left for work that morning. Geoff saluted her and followed as he'd done most mornings.

"Mommy," Mikala said from the back seat. "Is Officer Geoff going to follow us to school for the rest of the year?"

"No, just a little while longer."

"Until they find the boys?"

"That's right, sweetie."

"Then Daddy will be home more often, right?"

"Uh-huh." Lisa had adjusted the rearview mirror to keep an eye on the boys. "Jaden, stop fidgeting with your lunch box."

"Momma," Mikala said, and Lisa shifted her eyes to Mikala. She jockeyed them up and down from the road to the mirror.

"Yes?"

"Did Daddy come home last night? Did you ask him about summer camp? Phillip and Brent went last year, and I want to go, too."

"No, I didn't have a chance, honey." Her glance bounced back to Jaden. "Jaden, you need to put that lunch box down right now. Stop."

"Jaden!" Mikala caught Jaden's milk container as his lunch box spilled open. She handed him the milk. "Put this back inside."

"Thank you, Mikala." Lisa smiled into the mirror.

"Momma, do you think Daddy will say no?"

"No?"

"About summer camp?"

"Oh, I'm not sure. I think he might be okay with it."

"But what about the bad man?"

"What's that?" Lisa said. "Jaden, I swear if you open that milk carton, I'll stop this car and take your goldfish out of your lunch."

John squealed and laughed. "Take them, Mommy. Give them to me."

"John leave him alone. Mikala, what did you say? About the bad man?"

"The missing boys that the bad man kidnapped went to summer camp, so I thought Daddy might not want me to go."

"How do you know that?"

"I saw it."

"Another dream?" She had been trying to listen to Mikala, but Jaden and John were tugging Jaden's milk carton back and forth. "Oh, gosh, you two boys are making me mad."

"Yes," Mikala said.

"Mikala, what are you saying?"

"I want to go to summer camp. Mrs. Shield passed out a pamphlet. Didn't you see it? Kids go to the beach every afternoon."

"What does that have to do with the missing boys? John let go of Jaden's milk right now. This is your last chance."

"Because the camp is at Mercyhurst, and the missing boys went to camp there last summer."

Lisa saw Jaden's milk container rip open in the rearview mirror. The spill appeared to happen in slow motion. Milk slopped over both boys. The first chance she got, she pulled to the side of the road and took towels out of the trunk; however, her attempt at sopping up milk proved useless. She had to return home and change them into dry shirts and pants. She arrived at her school twenty minutes late and had completely forgotten her conversation with Mikala until right now when she crossed out the wrench on Liam Nelson's paper and circled the seashell.

"Jack, on the way to school this morning, Mikala told me those missing boys went to a summer camp at Mercyhurst together," she said. "Is that true? Do you know?"

There was a long silence. Then Jack responded, "I'll call you back when I can."

He hung up the phone.

"Well, you're welcome," she said, setting down her cell and picking up her pen and tuna sandwich.

She reminded herself, one more time, what the white angel had told her last night. She and her children were safe.

*****

Down at the precinct, Jack lay his cell on the table. "We have a connection. Mercyhurst summer camp."

A half hour later, Ben Morgan's Mercyhurst contact confirmed the information. Their educational department gave hands-on experience in the summer to college students enrolled in their Early Education Program. Various day care centers across the Erie community enrolled students in the Mercyhurst "Great Beginnings" Summer Camp for four and five-year-olds.

Marky Blakley, Mathew Nuber, Luke Anderson, and John Wickles had been enrolled in last summer's camp by different day care centers. All four of their mothers had applied for the single-parent discount Mercyhurst offered.

The chief contacted Rachel, and she confirmed what they all suspected. John Michael, Lenny Emling, and Todd Kennedy had Mercyhurst University logins. The possibility of any one of them breaking into the college's digital files was high. They had the training and the wherewithal.

Ben sent officers to interview all three suspects and met with the investigative team members who were not currently monitoring the money sack at Behrend or traversing the hillside along the creek where Marky Blakley was found. Investigators pulled surveillance tapes and assembled evidence, then Ben sent those who hadn't slept in two days home for two hours of sleep, including Jack.

The Area 51 names jumped to the top of the suspect list.

39 Jack and Billy

Jack and Billy declined the chief's offer to sleep. Instead, they drove toward the highway. Jack sat in the passenger seat fidgeting with the compartments of Billy's rental car and fighting yawns. He opened and paged through the car manual, stuffed it back in the glove compartment, and ran his fingers through his hair, feeling anxious.

As annoyed as he was that Billy had to pick up his new car today, last night he had arranged for the school security guard, Foley, to remain at Mikala's side until her choral practice was over, and he and Billy arrived. At the same time, Geoff Filutze would follow Lisa to the boys' swim class and the grocery store, and although going home for a few hours of rest sounded tempting, he doubted he'd be able to sleep. Plus, he didn't dare change plans and scare Lisa. For some reason, he wasn't sure why, she had let up on the note issue. He relished the easing.

A quick stop at a coffee shop revived him like a shot of cortisone. With his mind freshened, his desire to mull over Mercyhurst surveillance tapes and to study John Michael's and Lenny Emling's behavior at work the day after the abductions heightened.

"Can't you pick your car up Friday?" He sipped coffee and frowned as Billy drove up the south-bound ramp onto I-79.

"No way. They'll charge me for the car they loaned me if I don't get there by closing today."

"I'll pay for it, you cheap bastard."

"Keep your pants on. It's only a twenty-minute drive. Let's review the facts as we drive, Crackerjack."

They spent the time immersed in heavy case discussion, so when Billy pulled into the lot, his sleek black car sitting out front offered a brief diversion.

He had completed the paperwork over the weekend and only needed to check the finishing touches. Jack waited patiently. Within fifteen minutes, they drove off the lot and headed back down the highway toward Erie.

Their conversation danced between the case and the car.

"Chief said tonight we're going to chart the routes between Marky Blakley's house and the suspects' homes and jobs. You know, your brother-in-law claims he was out of town on the night of the Blakely abduction," Billy said, rubbing the leather on the steering wheel with his fingers.

"I heard. I'm sure he was gambling. I hate the guy, but I don't feel he'd abduct and murder a kid. And he certainly doesn't have it in him to devise a scheme like this."

"Well, they're checking his whereabouts on the abduction nights. Lenny's and John Michael's, too. Lenny was clocked in at Mercyhurst on the night of the Blakely abduction, but the way that guy can run? Who knows what he could do? And who is this John Michael person, anyway? Do you know him?"

"Not really."

For a few minutes they rode in silence. Jack considered the suspects as the soft purr of the engine hummed like background music. When they exited the interstate, Billy placed a hand on the dashboard. "Do you feel this thing?"

"No."

"Exactly." He smiled at Jack. "Ain't it pretty?"

"Nice, Billy." Jack placed a palm on the dashboard himself, then withdrew his hand. "What did they learn about John Michael?"

"He came in with the desert's first crew." Billy pulled his own hand back to the steering wheel. "And he and Lenny don't get along. There's some bad blood between them. The guys coerced that out of a Professor Peterson at Mercyhurst."

"To be honest, I don't know much about Lenny, either. Only that my wife says he's a nice guy."

"Yeah, well, why do we keep picking him up for beating the crap out of kids if he's such a nice guy?"

"No clue. But Lisa insists he is. They grew up together."

"Maybe he stuck up for her."

"No, Rachel said Lisa used to defend him. He was small for his age until sixth grade."

"That's about the time they sent him to the detention center, wasn't it? When he beat those kids?"

"That's the story." Jack grabbed the roof handle when he realized Billy wasn't slowing for the approaching turn.

"I heard he pulverized four boys, but that they had it coming. They dragged a young girl into the bushes. But one of their daddies was a big shot, and no charges were filed."

"I heard that, too. Hey, slow down, this is our turn coming up."

"No thanks, Crackerjack. I'm going the long way. That road has too many potholes."

Jack glimpsed his watch. "We have time."

"That daughter of yours could talk a fisherman out of his fishing pole." Billy laughed, then hit a button and watched all four windows roll down and up. "She's going to love this car."

Jack studied the front seat, running a hand over the leather on the passenger door.

"It's a fine car, Billy."

"Ain't it?"

"Now that the drive is over, I feel privileged you let me ride along to pick it up."

"It ain't you, and you know it. It's your kid."

"Well, seeing as how I didn't get to watch you cry like a baby when you said goodbye to that souped-up buckboard, I feel honored."

"Hey, have some respect. I loved that old car. Although, truth be told, I didn't think the heap would make it out of my driveway the morning I traded it in, let alone all the way to Meadville. But I wasn't going to a dealer in town. They all push undercoating." He slapped the dash with a hand. "Don't want no bugs in this car. Did Chief tell you? Our lines are being tapped."

"By who?"

"The FBI, CIA, Trump cronies. I don't know who. The word around town is they're searching for departments that aren't prosecuting illegals or cigarette-stealing immigrants."

Smack. The wind went out of Jack. His worries about Mikala never subsided for long.

Billy slowed the car, flipped on the turn signal, and entered the school's driveway.

"Get in line up there." Jack pointed. "Behind the white CRV."

"Do you see her?"

"Not yet. Foley will walk her out."

"Ah, Foley, good man. Retired a year ago, right?"

"Two."

"Time flies." Billy pulled behind the CRV.

Jack strained to see past the rush of children and find Mikala.

Billy Mack inched forward in line. His cell rang, and he answered, uttering an "uh-huh" here and there and ending the call with, "Got you. We'll be there by six-thirty, Chief."

"What's up?" Jack asked when Billy replaced his cell in the car's slick cell-phone cranny.

"Phone taps worked. Mark Blakley and Wesley Seifert mentioned the payout on the phone. Wesley Seifert made the drop."

"So they confirmed the ransom?"

"Yep, confirmed. The kid was supposed to be home in bed by ten last Thursday. His mother's birthday."

Jack rolled his window down and jutted his head outside. "Any determination on the voice."

"Nah, he used a voice changer."

"Did the chief say how much ransom?'

"$325,000." Billy glanced at Jack, raising an eyebrow.

"Wait a minute—wasn't that?"

"I think so, Crackerjack."

A child ran to the car in front of him, and the car pulled out of line. Billy drove forward, inching closer to the curb. "Reach back and grab my briefcase while we're waiting."

"What am I looking for?"

"Just get it. On the floor behind you."

Jack turned and lifted the case by one handle. The ragged grip ripped off on one side, and Jack grabbed the bottom of the case with his other hand. "Geez, Billy, how much did Katie take you for? Where did you get this? Out of a dumpster?"

"Shut up and look inside." Billy turned on the overhead light.

"For what?"

"My Blakley notes. A black spiral notepad."

Jack grabbed the pad. A price sticker fell off and stuck to his jeans. "Nineteen cents? You gotta' get another job, man."

"Tell the chief I need a raise."

"Well, at least we know you're not on the take."

Billy motioned toward the pad with one finger. "Just look for numbers."

Jack spent a few minutes turning pages, reading a line or two out loud while occasionally peering through the dark to see if Mikala was coming. When he read the sentence about Ann Blakley's uncle passing on, Billy told him to stop.

"Well, looky here." Jack was ahead of him. "Ann Blakley came into an inheritance last July."

"What was the payout?"

Jack ran one hand over each line; Billy Mack's pencil fetish turning his fingertips black. He stopped on the third page when he located a dollar amount. He lifted his chin and whistled before saying, "$1,050,000. Paid in three installments."

"Bingo. Three $350,000 payouts, my good man. You know, I heard a rumor two drops went down. Maybe we didn't get wind of a third."

"I heard grumbles about a second drop, too. You and Mesmer could be right. Maybe we're not dealing with a pedophile." Jack could feel his blood rushing through his veins.

One mulligan for Mikala.

Just as the note flashed in his head, he spotted her bolting away from the security guard. Jack waved, and Foley nodded just as Mikala reached the car. She swung the back door open and lunged inside.

Immediately, she leaned forward, wrapped her arms around her dad and planted a kiss on his cheek. She hugged Billy Mack from behind, too, and plopped into the leather upholstery. She ran one hand over the soft surface and fished for her seat belt with the other.

"Nice car, Uncle Billy," she said, her eyes darting around the back seat. "This will help you catch lots of crooks. Did you catch the bad man yet?"

Billy Mack cast a sideways glance at Jack. Jack sighed.

"She's your kid." Billy shook his head. "Not yet, Mikala."

"You will. You and Daddy are the best detectives that ever lived."

"You think so?" Billy gazed into the rearview mirror. "And I hear you are the best singer in that entire school.

Someone told me you are singing in the Christmas play this year. A duet, I hear."

"Oh, are you going to come? I'm singing Rudolph with Elizabeth Morton. It's just the two of us. Can you come? Oh, please, Uncle Billy?"

"I wouldn't miss it if an earthquake swallowed me up. I'd climb right out and mosey on in," he said, eyes jockeying from the street to the rearview mirror. "Even though I wasn't invited."

He raised his eyebrows and shot Jack a crooked smile.

"I'm inviting you, and Momma is inviting you," she said, opening the little compartments on the side of the door and lowering the middle armrest. "Gee, this car is nice."

She opened her book bag, picked out the package of ribbons she had brought to school from home and dropped the bundle inside.

"There, I left you a present."

"You did?"

"Yep, ribbons."

Billy laughed. "Why ribbons?"

"They're pink. Didn't you buy this car for Aunt Katie? She loves pink."

Jack squealed, and Billy reached over and smacked him on the arm. They both gazed into the rearview mirror. Mikala smiled like she'd told a good joke.

"You put her up to that," Billy said.

"I swear," Jack laughed. "I didn't."

As Billy drove, Mikala monopolized the conversation. She told Billy about her brothers throwing up and ruining the basement carpet and about her best friend, Emily Jillian, inviting her to a sleepover.

"And next month we have officer appreciation week. Can you come, Uncle Billy?"

"Well, sure I can." He smiled at Jack.

Jack turned around to face Mikala. "What the heck?"

"You can come, too, Daddy. Will you come in your new car, Uncle Billy, or in a cruiser?"

Jack sighed and turned, shot a frown out the front windshield, and his own annoyed reflection bounced back at him.

"Which do you want me to bring?"

"That's a tough choice," she said, then debated out loud which car would impress her classmates more.

"Oh, I have something for you, Uncle Billy," she said, when they pulled into the driveway behind Lisa's car. "Can you wait while I get it?"

"Momma's home, sweetheart, and Billy and I have to get back to work."

"I will only be a minute," she said as she unbuckled her seat belt, whisked up her bag, and scurried out the door. "I'll be right back."

The garage door was open, and Lisa was unloading groceries. She set a bag down, held a hand over her eyes, visor-style, and gazed through the dark at Billy's car. She strolled toward them.

"Oh, my God, I can't believe it," she said. "Don't tell me. You finally scrapped your car?"

She sauntered to the driver's side, leaned in, and put a hand on Billy's forehead. "You must be sick."

"All right. It's bad enough I have to put up with your old man. Now I have to take abuse from you, too?"

"You deserve all you get, Billy Mack," she said, nudging him on the shoulder, then standing back. "But it sure is fine. Isn't this the car Katie said she—"

"You just get back and unpack the groceries. Get in the kitchen and make your husband a good meal."

"Touchy, touchy." She laughed and ran a hand across the car. "How much did they give you for that old clunker?"

"Nothing," Jack said. "He had to pay them to take it."

"All right, all right." Billy adjusted the rearview mirror. "I don't know why I come here."

"Well, since you're here, why don't you guys come in and get something to eat before you go back." She curtsied. "The little misses put goulash in the crockpot before work this morning."

"Goulash? No, thanks."

"It's good," she said as she headed toward the back of her SUV.

She reached in, picked up a grocery bag, set it in the crook of her arm, and reached for another. "Jaden and John are inside. They'd love to see you, Billy."

"Wish I could, but I can't," he hollered. "The chief wants us back. Already going to get an earful for being late."

"Okay, well, thanks for picking up Mikala." She grabbed a third bag and shut the top of the trunk with an elbow. "How late do you think you'll be, Jack?"

"I'm not sure. I'll let you know."

Mikala burst from the front of the house, opening the door so quickly that its autumn wreath swayed to and fro, almost dislodging. She tore across the yard, rounded the car, and bolted toward the driver's side with one hand swinging and the other protecting something tucked beneath her arm.

"You need to read this, Uncle Billy." She handed him a book through the window, eyes wide, and then took one step backward. She was out of breath. "It's a story about cars and driving."

"Driving?"

"Yes. Now that you have a brand-new car, you need to read it." She was talking to Billy but staring at Jack.

"I do, do I?" Billy Mack smiled.

Jack stifled a laugh. Billy would rather poke out an eye than read fiction.

"Yes, the man in the book knows how to drive in the rain."

"Thanks, princess," Billy uttered, and Jack glanced past him to Mikala's beautiful blue eyes, her mother's eyes. What was that he saw in them?

His stomach flopped.

"You're welcome," she said, then darted toward her mother and wrapped an arm around her leg.

Oh, no.

His eyes fell to Billy's hand. His face reddened, and Billy's smile faded.

Billy was holding *The Art of Racing in the Rain.*

40 Jack, Billy, and Ben

Jack and Billy joined several other city investigators and the logistics team to chart possible routes from the three main suspects' homes and places of employment to the Blakley house. The chief summoned the city's best engineer to evaluate most probable routes and confirm the logistics team's time estimations. Those times would be compared to phone records, witness's statements, and suspect interviews. The chief would personally drive the credible routes and search for street and business surveillance cameras along the way.

The chief divided investigators into teams of two and assigned several tasks. Jack and Billy were to retrieve landfill and casino tapes from several key days and bring them to City Hall. Reviewers would watch the recordings all night long, while Jack and Billy rode the routes with the chief.

Billy called ahead for the videos, they retrieved them quickly, and rather than head directly back to City Hall, he dropped Jack off at home. Billy said he needed to stop and explain to Katie why he wasn't able to spend the evening with her, and that after he did, he would come back for Jack. Jack hoped he wasn't lying.

Jack hurried from the car and stormed through his front door.

"Where's Mikala?" He barely had the door open when he hollered.

"Asleep, why? What's wrong?" Lisa sat on the couch grading papers.

When Jack ignored her and stormed up the stairs, she jumped up and followed.

"Mikala?" he hollered.

He hadn't been able to pry *The Art of Racing in the Rain* from Billy. The more he asked for the book, the more suspicious Billy became. He locked the paperback in his trunk.

"Jack, it's late." Lisa's voice was forceful but hushed. "Don't wake her. She had a bad day in school."

"She was fine when Billy and I picked her up."

Upstairs, Jack barged into Mikala's room and stomped toward her bed. Lisa caught up to him and placed a cold hand on his arm.

"She found out her best friend may be moving away," she whispered. "Emily Jillian. Her father was offered a job in Utah. Please let her sleep. She was upset."

"I bet she was."

He positioned his hands on his hips, leaned over her, and watched for signs she was awake, but her blankets rose and fell with her slow, even breaths. Immediately, his annoyance waned.

Lying amidst the soft white sheets, her pink pajamas peeking from behind her satin fleece blanket and fluffy quilt, she seemed so sweet, angelic. Her still face showed not a wrinkle of remorse. She slept peacefully.

Tiredly, he bent down, and gently, he brushed the hair from her face. He couldn't wake her. He'd talk to her later about the book. How she knew the note was inside baffled him. He stared at her little fingers curled around the silky edge of her blanket, one bare foot protruding from beneath the quilt, and a stuffed animal, his face half worn away, tucked under her arm. He pulled the covers over her exposed leg.

He loved her more than life itself.

"Jack, come downstairs," Lisa said. Her hand had grown warm. She still clutched his arm. "I have to talk to you."

He sighed and conceded, turned, and his hand found the small of Lisa's back. He led her out of the room, but his gaze remained focused on Mikala. He half expected her to open her eyes. When she didn't, he followed Lisa out of the room, down the hall and stairs, and his thoughts turned from his baby to his wife.

He hoped this wasn't about the note again.

He wandered toward the couch, dreading another battle. He plopped down and his body sank into the cushions, and his back slumped against the pillows. He watched Lisa take a seat across from him, the cushion of the wingback chair barely sinking beneath her weight. He was so exhausted he couldn't see straight, yet the simple descent of her slight form warmed him. She didn't look angry.

Despite his anxiety, trepidation, and utter fatigue, her stunning blue eyes grabbed him. For one brief consoling moment, he forgot the book, the case, and the suspects. Lisa sat straight-backed in her sloppy blue sweatpants that he swore he hated but secretly loved, and comfort washed through him.

Yet in her simple loveliness, she seemed tense. Her posture was so perfect that she looked like a balloon ready to pop.

He remembered his nightmare.

"I only have a half hour," he warned. "Billy dropped me off. He's stopping home and coming back for me."

"This will only take a few minutes. I've actually been toying with telling you everything."

"Now what?"

She looped her hair behind one ear, which was never a good sign. He didn't know how much more bad news he could handle.

"There is no easy way to say this. The gist of it is: I may take Jeffrey for a few weeks."

"You're kidding, right?"

"No, I'm not. I know it's bad timing, but it can't be helped."

"I thought you promised Janice you'd watch Danny next weekend. So they could get away."

"I did, but this can't be helped. I'll have to watch them both."

His shoulders dropped. He gave up. Arguing with Lisa never ended well. And really, what was one more kid in the house? Like turning on a fan during a hurricane.

"What's going on with Rachel and Todd?"

"It's Rachel. She's going away for a while, and I refuse to allow Todd to watch Jeffrey. I don't trust him."

"Where's she going?"

"That's what I have to talk to you about." She wiggled to the edge of her seat. "Here's the thing, Jack. You can't tell anyone."

Great, another secret.

"Tell anyone what?"

"Well, there is simply no other way for me to say this. Rachel needs to go to rehab."

He sat up and took a long look at her, wondering if he had heard her correctly. "What do you mean she needs rehab?"

"She's using, Jack. Cocaine. Not much, but she knows she can't do this because—" Here Lisa closed her lips and swallowed hard. "She's pregnant."

"She's pregnant?"

"Yes."

"And she's snorting cocaine? How far along is she?"

"Four months. She's only used twice since she found out. I caught her by surprise yesterday and took it from her."

"You have it? Here?"

"Yes, I was hoping you could take it to the chief. He's the only one we can trust to tell."

"For God's sake, Lisa, you can't bring cocaine into this house."

"Well, I couldn't let her keep it."

"Yeah, but here?" His eyes scanned the room. He hoped no one was listening.

"I shut the computer off," she said. "And I searched the house with the frequency finder. As usual, nothing."

"What is she thinking?"

"Jack, you need to lower your voice."

He positioned his elbows on his knees and clasped his hands together in front of him. "Just what else is going on in that household? Do we have to call social services and have Jeffrey removed?"

"They wouldn't do that."

"Who wouldn't do that?"

"The government."

"What do you mean? They know?"

Lisa tilted her head back, closed her eyes, and sat back in her seat. She looked as tired as Jack felt.

"They were all addicted."

He waited for her to continue. He didn't have the energy to ask another question.

"Every child that went through Project Dream was hooked on cocaine or some other substance by the time they were twenty. Rachel said some of them weaned themselves off after they were out, but while they were there, the government kept them happy."

He shook his head, disbelief and belief struggling for position. He thought of past cases, City Hall, and the politicians that the chief had to keep at bay to do his job. On numerous occasions, his precinct had been forced to dance around side deals and bow to City Council members' demands. Nothing should surprise him about the government. There was dishonesty and deception at the local level. Who knew how much corruption hid in Washington?

"So the CIA provided drugs for them."

"Yes. They could have what they wanted. She said the United States helped South American countries—I'm not sure which—fight their drug wars. They pilfered enough for the kids and probably hundreds of other people in programs we don't know about."

"But, Lisa, she can't use while she's pregnant."

"No, she can't, and most of the time she's fine. But every once in a while, everything gets to her. With her hormones and Todd's unending supply, she relapsed."

"So what now?"

"There is a program in Ohio. She will spend two weeks there, then come back to an outpatient clinic in Erie for the remainder of her pregnancy and beyond. So we need to take Jeffrey for the two weeks."

"Well, yes, of course."

"I can drop him off at the sitter in the morning and pick him up when I'm done at work. But I know some of this will fall on you."

Yes, some would, and he didn't need that right now. But how could he say no to Jeffrey? "There is nothing we can do. We have to take him. We'll manage."

"Thank you, Jack." She moved to the couch, put her arm around him, and kissed his cheek. "I know this case has consumed you."

Yes, this case gnawed at every inch of him. Yet now his brother-in-law had crept into the prime suspect box, and he may soon be removed from the investigative team.

"Are they all still using? Rachel, Todd, Lenny and this John Michael?"

"Rachel isn't sure how much Lenny and John Michael use anymore. She said none of them got as hooked on it as Todd. And honestly? I don't care about Todd. I just want Rachel clean. I wish she'd get rid of him."

Her eyes teared, and Jack raised an arm over her shoulder and drew her close. They squirmed into a comfortable position, and Jack rested his head on top of hers. He didn't care about any of them—including Rachel. He only cared about protecting his family.

He closed his eyes and felt the soft lines of her body pressing against his. He forgot about Billy coming back and relaxed in Lisa's warmth. He dozed and dreamed the case was solved, and they were making love.

Then he awoke with a start and remembered the abducted boys and the man who inked Mikala's name on a slip of paper. A murderer who wrote words on a Christian notepad and demanded a ransom for a dead child.

Every inch of his body screamed for sleep. He could count the hours he had slept in the past five days on the fingers of one hand. He squeezed Lisa into him and fought slumber, but his determination waned and his consciousness slipped away.

When he heard a horn blast, he jumped and squinted at his watch. Billy had dropped him off fifty minutes ago.

"Is that Billy?" Groggily, Lisa leaned away, taking her warmth with her.

"Do you believe him?" He sat up. "Is he really laying on the horn?"

Lisa stood and hurried to the door. She swung it open and held up a finger. "He doesn't have kids, Jack. He hasn't a clue he may wake them."

She stepped one foot outside. "He's coming, Billy. Give him a minute."

Jack rushed to the kitchen sink, threw water on his face, and shook his head forcefully. He dried his head with a dish towel and wiped up the counter around him. He went to Lisa. Hugged her long and slow, wishing this was over, and he could carry her upstairs and love her all night long.

His mouth found hers, lingered, and then he went out the door.

Outside, the wind hit him. He zipped his jacket and headed toward the car. In front of his house, he noticed a second cruiser behind Geoff Filutze's.

Down the street on the corner, the unmarked car—with the officer watching both his house and his sister's—still sat, lights out. He snapped his head back toward the two hugging squad cars in front of his house, and his neck tingled. *A third surveillance car?* He waved. Both Geoff and the other officer returned the wave.

As soon as he sat down and closed the car door, he heard a voice from the shadows of the back seat. "Hello, Jack."

He turned and looked directly into the face of Chief Morgan, and then he glanced toward Billy.

"Did you think I'd keep that note secret?" Billy shook his head. "Are you crazy? Mikala's life is in danger."

"You told the chief? Lisa doesn't even know what the note said."

"What were you thinking? Why didn't you tell us?"

"Because I'm not having some FBI or CIA crony show up at my front door and offer me the deal of a lifetime if I send Mikala off to some fucking covert school."

"You don't trust me, Jack?" Billy yelled so loud that Jack's eyes shot toward his house. Lisa still stood in the front door.

"Calm down, boys," the chief said.

Jack waved to her. She waved, stepped back, and closed the door.

Another nerve-bending moment passed, then Billy broke the silence. "You trust me, Jack?"

"With my life." This time Jack said it out loud. "But not my daughter's."

Again, silence. Jack shifted in his seat. Billy tightened his grip on the steering wheel.

"That was evidence, Jack," the chief said. "I could park your ass in jail for not turning that in."

"There. Are you happy?" Jack scowled at Billy Mack. "I'll be in jail, and my family will be here alone. Satisfied?"

"Nobody's going to jail." Billy threw the car in reverse, backed out of the driveway, and peeled out.

"Slow down," the chief yelled. "You want everyone to know we're here?"

Billy Mack reached the end of the street and turned. He didn't slow down.

Jack gabbed the ceiling handle as the wheels squealed. When the car straightened out, he let go and ran his hand through the hair on the back of his head. The ends reached halfway down his neck now. He needed a haircut. He needed a drink. He needed to find this bastard.

"Well, now aren't you boys just tickled pink I got me this fine new car, so our cold-hearted, lying asses can get a little warmth and comfort? Because there sure is a whole lot of double-dealing going on around me," Billy said, and Jack felt the car speed up. "Maybe some of us are a little too close to the fire to realize the grass around us is burning up."

"Just drop it, Billy. For tonight let's scout these guys, call in our favors, and in the morning I'll talk to Jack about the conflict of interest."

"Okay, Chief." Billy tossed a sour expression toward the back seat. "I'll play. Jack's the only person dancing on the coals. Everything else? Copasetic."

Jack felt the car surge ahead again. He watched the speedometer's blue number turn from 83 to 84 and keep rising.

He waited for the chief to yell, but Ben didn't say a word.

41 Mikala

Upstairs in the house, Lisa peeked her head into Mikala's room.

"Momma, is that Officer Geoff out in the car?"

"Yes, sweet pea, what are you doing up?"

"There is another car now. Two police cars. Why are they watching our house?"

Lisa walked to the window, leaned over Mikala, and peeked outside. She was quiet for a moment.

"Sometimes police officers watch other police officers' houses."

"You mean because of the bad man who broke Danny's window? Because they didn't catch him?"

"That's right, honey."

"Are the policemen afraid the bad man will break John's window? Because the bad man wants a Mathew and a Mark and a Luke and a John."

"Where did you hear that?"

"I heard Uncle Billy and Daddy talking." That wasn't a lie. She had heard them—in her head.

"Oh, Mikala." Her mother sat down on the edge of her bed and wiped her face with her hands. "How do you know the things you know?"

"Momma?"

"Yes?"

"It isn't your fault."

"What's not my fault?"

"About John on the hilltop not being the right John." Mikala put her hand on her mother's arm. "Or about Aunt Rachel, or Jeffrey not having a good Daddy."

Mikala studied her mother. Her face looked tired, her eyes droopy, her expression as blank as a marker board without a mark. "Momma, you look like a hiccup."

"A hiccup?"

"When Mrs. Shield calls on a student, if they lost their place in their reader or didn't hear her question, she says they are having a hiccup in time."

Mikala waited for her mother to recover from the hiccup.

"It's past your bedtime, honey," her mother said after a long pause.

"Momma, are you afraid Monster Man is going to take me?"

Even through the dark, Mikala could see the spark of red in her mother's cheeks.

"Monster Man?"

Mikala nodded.

"No, sweetie." Lisa bent down and hugged her tightly. "No one will take you—ever."

She held Mikala for a long time, then straightened and placed a hand on her own forehead. She closed her eyes, brushed hair behind one ear, and took a step toward Mikala's dresser. She leaned two flat palms on its surface and swayed a bit. Mikala sprang from her bed and lunged toward her, slipping her arms around her mother's waist.

"Momma? Are you all right?"

Lisa breathed in and out slowly, turned, and leaned her backside against the dresser.

"You look like Aunt Rachel."

"Aunt Rachel?" Lisa pressed the back of one hand on her forehead and then her cheek.

"Yes, Aunt Rachel. Are you having a baby, too?"

"What?" Her eyes were glassy. "Oh, no, honey, Momma's not—"

She stopped. Her eyes fell to Mikala, and her hand slid from her cheek to her mouth. Her other hand found her belly.

"Momma, is your hiccup gone?"

They shared silence for a moment, but Mikala didn't mind. She stared up at her mother's soft face. She thought her mom might be the most beautiful mom in the whole world.

"Yes, sweet pea, my hiccup is gone." Lisa pushed gently off the dresser. "Now you need to sleep. You don't want to miss school tomorrow, do you? Isn't it your turn to check the computers? Turn them off when the bell rings?"

"Oh, yes, that's my favorite end-of-day chore."

"I know. Hop over and get into bed."

"Are you feeling better?"

"I am."

"Okay, Momma." Mikala's bare feet slapped the floor as she took a few steps and hopped into a mass of blankets. She assembled them into a heap on top of herself. Lisa straightened them out, leaned, and kissed her forehead.

"Momma?" she said as Lisa strode to her bedroom doorway.

"Yes, Mikala?"

"The bad man can see inside my head."

Mikala never saw her mother stand so still. The hall light behind her made her look like a black shadow.

"Monster Man." Mikala clarified.

"Why would you say such a thing?"

"Because he can, Momma."

Mikala listened to the wind whistle against her window while her mother stood thinking in the doorway, her dark form like a silhouette. Mikala had learned about silhouettes in art class when they traced each other's shadows on white paper. Momma's shadow looked just like hers, only bigger.

Finally, her mother spoke. "Mikala, did you learn about molecules?"

"Oh, yes, Mrs. Shield says everything has molecules."

"That's right, sweet pea, and tomorrow I'm going to teach you how to take all those wonderful molecules and that smart head of yours and build a wall with them."

"So Monster Man can't see inside my head?"

For a moment, Mikala thought her mom was going to cry.

"So no one can ever see inside your head."

"Okay, Momma." She didn't tell her she already knew how to do that. Building walls in her head with Momma would be fun. "I love you."

"I love you too, sweetie. Don't worry anymore about Monster Man."

"I won't."

Lisa disappeared from her sight, and Mikala listened to her footsteps as she walked away. Her mother halted for a second, and Mikala pictured her leaning against the wall in the hall to catch her breath. Maybe she was thinking about the blue pacifiers Mikala had given away. They had talked about that last week. Momma said she shouldn't do that again, but Mikala knew Momma didn't need those blue pacifiers.

Eventually, she heard her mother continue down the hall and stairs. She tossed her covers aside and tiptoed to the window. She lifted the blind a bit to see if he was still there.

Her eyes roamed over the dark forms across the street until she found him, the shadow man.

She lifted a hand and moved her fingers, waving cautiously. The man waved back right before he slithered down the street, bobbing from yard to yard and disappearing into the black night. Then she let the blinds slip from her fingers and bounced into bed, thinking how nice it was going to be to share a room with a little sister.

42 2000 – Gee

"Hold the picture above me, so I can see it."

"Can't you swing your legs over the side of the bed anymore, Gee?"

"Well, sure I can, just not today." Gee tugged the covers aside. "Come here and show me that drawing of your new teacher. What's her name?"

LeeLee climbed into bed beside Gee and held the picture for her to see. "Mrs. Dodson. Sissy says she is the best teacher in the whole school."

"Well, if Sissy says so, then it's so. How lucky you are."

LeeLee nodded, opened and closed her eyelids pensively, and Gee knew some deep conversation would follow.

"I like babies. Do you like babies, Gee?"

And LeeLee never disappointed her.

"Oh, who doesn't like babies?"

"Mr. Dodson."

"Who's that? Your teacher's husband?"

LeeLee nodded.

"Oh, I'm sure you're mistaken."

"No, he doesn't like babies. I saw it in my head."

"What did that pretty little head of yours show you?" Gee wrapped a weak arm around LeeLee. Oh, how she loved her.

Although death hovered closely, Gee wasn't afraid. Determinedly, she had declined dialysis. But she was nowhere near prepared to leave this little one. There were things she had to tell her first. She hoped her health held out. If it didn't, her letters would offer LeeLee clarity in the future.

She had written several letters to each of her granddaughters. Notes that explained their gifts and other important facts. And, not sure her daughter would deliver them at the appropriate time—or at all, even—she gave them to a friend for safekeeping.

Still, oh, how hard it was going to be to leave this sweet child with her bright blue eyes and pristine mind.

"He changed the baby's diaper and wrinkled his nose. His hands were shaking. He almost dropped her. I watched him, Gee. He wouldn't go near the baby again. He doesn't like her."

"There is something you must learn about men and boys. They shy away from things they fear." She released her hold on LeeLee, coughed, and then spit into a hankie. "They aren't afraid of much, mind you, but when they are afraid, they build a big wall in their mind to block it out, so they don't have to see what's right in front of them."

"A wall in their mind?"

"Yes, men don't like to think about things that worry them. So they build walls and block everything out. With a baby that tiny, sometimes a daddy worries he won't be able to take care of her. So he tries not to think about everything that could go wrong, because he loves her."

"And then his hands shake?"

"Sometimes, yes."

Gee replaced her weak arm around LeeLee.

"You know, LeeLee, you can build a wall in your mind, too, so that the black devil never sees inside your head."

"I can?"

"Yes, you can. I do that all the time, just in case he or some other bad spirit comes near."

Gee and LeeLee rested quietly in the room for a time.

"Can I try?" LeeLee finally asked.

"You can, yes. Go ahead." Gee squeezed her gently and watched her close her eyes. "You can make your wall black or blue or even bright white. Picture the molecules of your wall vibrating faster and faster and closer and closer together, so nothing can get through. Did you learn about molecules in school yet?"

"Yes, everything has molecules."

"That's right, darling, now build that wall, molecule by molecule."

LeeLee tightened her eyelids.

"What color are you making your wall?"

"Pink. Bright pink. Like Momma's old Care Bear."

"Oh, that's a pretty color."

LeeLee opened her eyes and raised them to Gee. "I can't do it. The other pictures keep slipping in."

"It takes practice. Someday you will be able to build your wall and tear it down at will."

"At will?"

"Whenever you want." Gee squeezed again. "Until then, just take note of the pretty pictures you see in your mind. It's a gift, LeeLee, a gift that will stay with you all your life. And you'll pass it down to your children."

LeeLee's eyes shot toward Gee. "Will my husband like babies?"

"Oh, you are going to have a fine husband. And he will like babies."

"How many babies will I have?"

"Hm, I think four. Yes, four babies." Gee lay her chin on the top of LeeLee's head. "Two girls and two boys. The girls like book ends—the oldest and youngest."

"Will Sissy have babies?"

"She sure will."

"Will the boy she marry like babies?"

Gee hesitated. It wasn't right to tell a child everything, but she must tell her some.

"Not near as much as the boy you marry." Gee had roamed through the pictures of the future in her head, and she was fairly certain.

"What will his name be? The boy I marry?"

Gee chuckled. "Don't know, darling. I'm never good at names."

"I think his name will be Crackerjack."

Now a laugh burst from Gee's lips. Her stomach shook, and she coughed uncontrollably. When she regained her composure, she said, "That's a funny name, but just the same, your two sons will be his best friends, and the girls will wrap him around their fingers."

Gee's glance fell to the window, and she gazed across the street and down the road at the houses and people outside. How she wished she could see this little one grow.

"Will my belly get big like Mrs. Dodson's did?"

"It will."

"What is it like to have a baby in your belly?"

"Oh, feeling a baby inside you is the greatest feeling in the world."

"Did you know Momma was a girl, before she was born?"

"Ah!" Gee tossed a hand in the air, palm upward, and chuckled. "I did not! And that is something you should know, of course. I almost forgot."

"Forgot what?"

"You can't see the pictures in your head clearly when you have a baby in your belly. They become jumbled and confuse you. Something in your body—they call them a nasty name, hormones—well, those little buggers mess up your mind. You must remember that LeeLee. It is important."

"So the pictures won't come when I have a baby in my belly?"

"They will come, but you can't trust the pictures as much." She shook her head and sighed. "The one and only time I couldn't see them clearly was when I was having a baby. You must remember that. You and Sissy both."

"Okay, I'll remember."

"Yes, you remember and tell Sissy, too."

"How about I help Sissy see when she is having a baby, and she helps me see when I am having a baby?"

"Well, now I think that is a good idea. You can help each other."

Gee couldn't imagine being away from the little girl wrapped in her arms. How could she leave her?

She decided then and there to fight to stay for as long as she could. She would reconsider the dialysis. Call that doctor this afternoon. A person could live a year or two even if their kidneys weren't functioning.

"Gee?"

"Yes?"

"What if Sissy and I both have babies at the same time?"

"Well, that would be special, wouldn't it?"

LeeLee nodded. "My friend Megan has a cousin who was born on the same day as her. His name is Michael—that means 'like God.'"

"Michael, you say? Means like God?"

"Yes. Megan says they named him that before he was born."

"Well, good he was a boy because Michael just isn't fitting for a girl."

"No." LeeLee lowered her eyes and fingered the silky end of Gee's soft blanket. "But they could have named her Mikala. Maybe when I grow up and have my little girl, I can call her Mikala."

"Mikala." A picture of a pretty little girl, much like LeeLee, popped into Gee's head. The child had milky-white skin, wavy hair that messily edged her face, and Caribbean-blue eyes that could look through a person. "Well, Mikala is a fine name. Fine, indeed."

"And someday I can teach Mikala to build walls, too."

Gee contemplated this idea and then said, "How about I teach her how to build walls in her head before she is born?"

43 Jack, Billy, and Ben

They drove toward John Michael Turnbull's condo, noting security cameras, checking distances, and exploring back alleys.

John Michael's bayfront suite required card access at the community's security gate. The blacktop road that his building sat on jutted into the bay a quarter of a mile and, surrounded by water on three sides, the gazebo at the end of it offered some of the best sunset views in Pennsylvania. With condo price tags exceeding a half million dollars, only the wealthy eyes caught the sun going down over the bay from that pier. The condo was too pricey for a small-town college professor but easily managed by a Project Dream transmitter.

Chief Morgan phoned the condo's maintenance man, and he met them a half of a mile from the gate. The chief cracked the back window, and the man slid him a card. No words passed between them. Two nods served as a thank you and you're welcome.

Billy drove to the gate, waved the card over the scanner, and proceeded down the lane, his engine purring like a mute black leopard. He cut the lights and reduced his speed to five miles an hour, slowing even more and coming close to a stop when they reached John Michael's condo. He recorded the mileage.

"I see several security cameras." Jack peered out the window, squinting his eyes to see through the dark. "Do we know how long they keep their tapes?"

"Ninety glorious days." The chief turned to watch John Michael's building slip behind them. "Park near the pier,

Billy, and take a walk. Place a camera facing his balcony door like we discussed."

"With pleasure." Billy drove to the end of the lane. Barely a sound squeaked out as he turned the car around, cut the ignition, and exited the car.

"He loves this part," the chief said. "Has a ghost-in-the-graveyard mentality. What do you know about John Michael, Jack? Your sister-in-law talk much about him?"

"No, never. I didn't know his name until a few weeks ago. Has anyone reviewed the camera tapes from this place?"

"Order is in. They begin tomorrow. Would have been done three weeks ago if Andy had told us about Psalm 51, or you had given me that note."

Jack cringed and changed the subject. "Did Mercyhurst have their tapes?"

"Yes, I have two guys watching them as we speak. I'm going to pull two more investigators off the homeless man disappearance and send them to help."

They discussed case issues for a few minutes, Todd's drug problems, Lenny Emling's misdemeanors, and how John Michael seemed to keep to himself. Then the door opened, and Billy jumped inside. "Let's get out of here."

"Something happen?" The chief asked.

"Someone saw me. Who takes a walk in the middle of the night?" Billy turned on the ignition.

"Was it him?" the chief asked.

"No clue."

The strong bay wind outside surged and shook the car. Billy stepped on the gas so quickly, Jack slammed backward in his seat.

"What are you doing?" Jack yelled.

Billy sped down the driveway and crashed through the gate, turning the car onto the Bayfront Highway and peeling out to the right away from the City. Then he laughed. "Fuck you, ya' bastard."

"You know I'm going to have to replace that gate," the chief said when they were far enough away to catch their breath.

"No, you won't. I grabbed this." Billy reached on the floor and tossed his license plate into Jack's lap. "And your maintenance man isn't going to squeal. Plus, a cop wouldn't crash a gate."

The chief sighed. "A cop with a brain."

"You're going to have some dents," Jack warned.

"The police garage is going to smooth out my grill. I'll ask Ronnie to do it. He does real nice work."

"This is why the mayor is always on my ass," the chief mumbled.

Billy laughed and the chief reached into his pocket, pulled out a cigar, and lit it. Before he inhaled, Billy stretched an arm back and grabbed it. He cracked his window and tossed the stogy from the car."

"That was a twenty-five-dollar cigar, Billy."

"And this is a thirty-eight-thousand-dollar car."

"Thirty-eight?" Jack's mouth gaped. "Holy shit, maybe you are on the take."

"Well, one thing is for sure. No one will suspect police inside this baby," Billy chuckled.

But from the depths of the back seat came the voice of reason. "No one but a psychic."

"Didn't think you believed in them, Chief." Billy Mack's eyes glanced in his rearview mirror.

"I didn't," the chief said, placing a second cigar in his mouth. He lifted one big boot, struck a match on its bottom, and plopped the shoe down. He lit the stogy. "Until I met Rachel Callahan."

Billy reached back, but the chief avoided him.

"C'mon Chief," Billy squealed.

"One cigar isn't going hurt your little toy."

Billy Mack let out a tirade of profanities but didn't reach in the back seat again. He stepped on the gas and headed for the victim's house and then to Mercyhurst. He drove up the front path and around back to Lenny's maintenance room and John Michael's classroom. They recorded the mileage, considered alternate routes, planted microphones and portable cameras, and discussed where they would install additional heavy-duty cameras. Then they drove to Lenny's house and repeated everything.

By quarter after seven in the morning, the chief was satisfied they had comprehensive notes on and accurate distances for the routes between John Michael's condo, Lenny Emling's home, Mercyhurst, and the Blakley home.

Jack was fairly certain they would not invite him when they checked Todd's house and possible routes.

"That's all for now, boys. We need to mosey over to the DA's office and meet with Stan Walkiewicz. Afterward, we will talk in my office."

"What time is the meeting with Stan?" Billy asked.

"Seven-thirty."

"Shit," Jack and Billy said in unison.

44 Stan Walkiewicz

Stanley Walkiewicz had investigated childhood deaths for so many years that a permanent disgust now hardened his once fetching face. Today no one noticed his callous appearance. Every eye in the room was cast toward the space on the desk in front of him. Each person sitting at the table gazed at the crime report at Stan's fingertips with the anxiousness of an artist waiting to see the Mona Lisa at the Louvre.

His report lie flat between his two forearms as if he protected the piece. A professional photograph of Marky Blakley was clipped to its top. To the right of his forearms, the most important crime scene pictures lined edge to edge up the desk, like checkboxes on a college criminal justice test. To the left, a manila envelope hid the goriest photos like a maximum-security prison shrouding the worst convicts from the public eye.

The report ruled out blunt force trauma, but the child had been bound by his wrists and ankles. The kidnapper used masking tape around his hands and three-eighths-of-an-inch pitched chain near his feet. No other substantial scars marked the boy. He was not stabbed, shot, drugged, poisoned, and had no water in his lungs.

The chief, Jack, and Billy trusted Stan's judgment, but Billy asked anyway. "Stan, are you saying you think this kid died of natural causes?"

Stan exercised the habit of staring silently without blinking when he was pissed off. He was doing that now. However, Stan had never once raised his voice at work, not in the eighteen years in the investigative division nor the eight years before that in juvenile probation. People respected his flawless professionalism.

But Billy had made a fatal mistake by adding the words "you think" to his question. Stan never "thought." He knew.

In the silence of the room, Jack—and probably everyone else at the table, even Billy himself—hoped Stan would let loose a stream of profanities to prove his humanness.

"You know, Billy, I'm forty-eight years old," he said calmly, still not blinking. "I don't know how much longer I can do this job."

Those words sent shivers up the spines of the three of them, the DA, the County coroner, two county detectives, and the FBI rep who sat listening. Stan talked slow. Some might mistake him for theatrical, but those who knew him knew he was anything but dramatic. His job evaluation described him as a realist, a perfectionist. The absolute best person for the godforsaken childhood investigator position.

Secretly, they all feared he'd quit. None of them had the guts to take a job examining dead kids, and they knew no one else in the county, nor all the counties in Pennsylvania, would be able to provide the accurate findings Stan did.

"I looked the body over more than any other child's body I ever examined because I, myself, couldn't believe it. But yes, Billy, I'm certain the boy died of natural causes."

"I believe you, Stan," the chief cut in. "I don't think any of us doubt you. But we are struggling to believe an abducted kid, his bedroom screen slashed and his body carried away in the middle of night to God knows what hell hole, died a natural death."

Stan wiped his forehead. "Rob, Gary, tell these guys how hard I worked on this case, collecting evidence at the scene; reviewing sketches, diagrams, and pictures at the lab; examining the body at the morgue."

Surprise wrinkled detective Rob Edmund's face. He squirmed into a straight position in his chair. "All day yesterday and all night long. I've worked with you eighteen years. You were thorough."

There was quiet in the room again. The clock on the wall in the county district attorney's office ticked annoyingly. When he couldn't take the ticking any longer, Jack spoke.

"Stan, give us your best guess," he said, leaning in, clasping his fingers together, and resting his forearms, elbows out, along the edge of the conference table. "What do you think Marky Blakley died of?"

All eyes turned to Stan.

Again the ticking hit Jack—like Chinese torture.

Stan cast his eyes to the table, to his right hand, which fingered the upper corner of his report. He brought his other hand forward, grasped the left corner, tilted the report toward him for a moment and then, allowing the pages to slip from his fingers, he reached for the crime scene pictures of the boy. He scooped them up with one fluid stroke, like a card dealer gathering cards at the end of a hand. He lowered his glasses from his forehead, where they always rested until needed, to his eyes. He leaned close to the photographs. Fingered them one by one, reviewing each briefly, and then he turned back to the report. Shuffled through the pages.

After a time, he pushed his glasses up to his forehead again and his seat back. Stan's second nasty habit was lifting the front legs of his chair off the ground and balancing on the two back legs. For years, people had waited for him to fall. He never did.

After a moment, Stan let his chair fall forward, back onto four legs with a clunk. He glanced around the table, eyeing each person individually.

"Gentlemen, if I had to guess." He pinched his nose, wiped his eyes, and set his hand back down on top of his report. "I'd say this boy died of a peanut allergy."

45 Lenny Emling; suspect #1

"Tell me again what the nice police officer said."

"S-someone's breaking in the s-school. Th-they are talking to all the employees." Lenny flung the quilt aside and placed his mother's robe around her shoulders.

"At home? It seems odd they would come here."

"They d-don't want to talk at school. It m-might be someone there."

"But Lenny," she said, gripping his arm, a frightened look spreading across her. "Where do you go some nights? You don't bother the boys, do you?"

"No, Ma. I do my l-long run. T-t-ten miles." Lenny helped pull the robe over her arms.

"At night? Before work?"

"I sh-shower at Mercyhurst and I like to r-run at night. N-no one can see me." Lenny placed a hand under each of his mother's arms and hoisted her out of bed. He held her until she steadied.

"Oh, Lenny, you must get over that. You've outgrown so much of your teenage awkwardness."

"It's okay, Ma."

She touched his chin, lifting his face so their eyes met. "Promise me you haven't gotten in trouble again. Promise me and I'll believe you."

"I p-promise, Ma." He moved aside and waited for her to take a step. Mornings were her worst. She wouldn't take her medicine until after breakfast.

She winced and then smiled quickly, attempting futilely to mask her pain. She barely complained, but he knew the rheumatoid arthritis had flared with a vengeance this time.

"D-did the doctor say he would have you t-try another medication?"

No one would imagine the woman leaning on him was only in her sixties. Her face was plain but pretty, hardly showing a wrinkle, yet people seldom noticed. They only saw her thin, crippled body.

"The doctor said there is a new drug on the market he wants me to try. He expects it to be available sometime in the next six months. It's very expensive."

"W-what about m-medical marihuana? You should try it, Ma."

"I told you I won't do that, Lenny. I don't even like taking the sleeping pill at night."

He led her across the room, and she slumped into her day chair in the corner near the window and raised a shoulder, wiggling her fingers. She shifted in her seat, so her bent arm and hand were positioned over the dainty porcelain cup with the painted flowers. She lifted the tea and sipped. "Thank you, sweetheart. What would I do without you?"

"You w-want me to bring your breakfast upstairs?"

"No, I'm going to sit and do my exercises, loosen up, and then I'll be down."

With the money the government paid him, Lenny was able to provide his mother with the best of everything. He had offered to build her a totally accessible house, but she didn't want to move from her childhood home. This is where she had grown up and where she had raised Lenny. She would never leave, and with his money, she never had to.

Instead, he installed handrails throughout and a motorized chair on the stairs. He remodeled the kitchen and altered both the upstairs and downstairs bathrooms, adding walk-in showers. If his mother wanted to stay in the house, Lenny would make it happen. The renovation costs had been a mere drop from his watering pot.

"M-Margaret's not downstairs, yet. She left a message she's running late. Should b-be here soon. You want me to t-turn on the TV?"

"No, I have my Kindle if I get bored," she said, her eyes raking him. "Did you call that sweet girl yet? What was her name, Danielle?"

"N-no, Ma. I've been busy."

She became quiet. He hated the way she did that. He knew what was coming.

"I worry about you. You need to go out with people your own age, not be cooped up in this house with me. That's why I allowed you to bring in Margaret and the nurses. So you would stop worrying about me, get out in the world, and live your life. Why don't you give Danielle a call? Take her out again. She liked you, Lenny."

"Ma, stop."

She sipped tea. He watched her from the corner of his eye. He knew she wouldn't stop. She would never stop.

"Make me another promise," she said, then reached her bent arm toward him and slipped her contorted fingers into the palm of his hand. "That you'll call her. I spoke with her on the telephone last week. She called and gave me the name of that pain doctor she mentioned when she stopped by last month. She said she had a wonderful time on your dinner date. I'm sure she was hoping I'd tell you. Why don't you call her?"

"I t-told you. I've been b-busy lately. At work."

"Oh please, Lenny, give her a call."

He took a long breath, and his lips quivered as he expelled the air with a great sigh. She wasn't going to drop the subject.

"All right, I p-promise, Ma. But I'm n-not taking her out this week or next week, either. I'm too busy."

"Well, then tell her that and set a date for the following week."

The doorbell rang, and they heard the rattle of a doorknob and the squeak of the front door opening. "I'm here," a voice hollered from the bottom of the stairs. "Mary? Lenny? I'm here."

"I'm still upstairs, Margaret," his mother called.

"I'll put the groceries away and be up."

"All right. Lenny brought me my tea, so take your time."

Lenny clomped toward the door to leave.

"Lenny?"

"Yeah, Ma."

"One last favor." Her voice softened. "Tonight?"

"Yeah?"

"Don't go to LeeLee's house," she said, her face seemed desperate. God how he hated to see the hurt in that woman's eyes. "Stay away, Lenny. Please? For me?"

He left the room without responding, descended the stairs and grabbed his jacket from the front closet, hurrying. He refused to allow his mother to get to him. He had fallen behind. For weeks he had shirked his yard chores, and now a good six inches of withered brown leaves blanketed his grass. Today he must rake and bag them and set them out at the end of his driveway for the last city leaf pickup tonight.

When he stepped onto his porch, his frequency finder made a noise.

46 Todd Kennedy; suspect #2

"Rachel, I love you, but I hate that you don't trust me enough to tell me what's going on between you and your sister."

She had set her cell phone down on the counter the minute he walked into the house. He was sure she'd been talking to Lisa. Lisa was always butting into their business, and Jack? He'd grown to hate that man and his arrogant, curt remarks. But when Rachel turned to face him, his thoughts raced away from Jack and Lisa and fixed on her pout. She appeared particularly annoyed.

"Just like you won't tell me what's going on with you." She folded her arms. "I know."

"You know what?"

"I know the police called."

He sighed and set his keys on the counter. "Is your sister putting things in your head again?"

"No, Todd, contrary to what you believe, you're not the center of our conversation. When you didn't answer my calls, I checked our phone account to see if you were alive. I saw the call."

Todd Kennedy had lots of secrets, none of which he intended on telling his wife. So this morning on his way home, he had asked himself what a man who didn't have secrets would say.

"It's nothing. They had questions about a pharmacy break-in. Now what did Lisa want when she called? You looked worried."

"None of your business."

He hadn't slept a minute last night and cajoling her was going to be a chore this morning. He almost liked it better when Jeffrey's asthma worsened, and she preoccupied herself with doctor visits.

"It is my business. You're my wife." The abruptness of his own voice surprised him. He almost never snapped at her, but his eyelids felt like lead bearings and weary thoughts nipped at his nerves.

"It's not about you. Lisa and I were discussing something else."

"She's upset you. You're pale."

"Look." She narrowed her eyes. "Everything in life doesn't revolve around you."

"After all these years together, you won't tell me what's going on? You haven't been yourself lately. Something's up with you and Lisa."

She shook her head and turned away. Her long frame appeared thinner. She may have lost weight.

"Rachel, do you think I'd betray your confidence? You don't know how much I love you? I don't want to upset you, especially now that you are having my baby again, but if something is wrong—and the way you've been acting lately makes me believe it is—you need to let me help you."

That's what he had come up with—what a man without secrets would say. When she told him she was pregnant again, he forced himself to act happy. Her spite was the thanks he got.

He leaned the palms of his hands on the counter and hung his head, trying to appear forlorn. When he pushed off the counter, his sweaty palm imprints stared up at him.

He needed a fix.

His glance darted toward Rachel. Had she noticed him sweating? No, she stood with her back to him, and so he proceeded with his second thought-out move. He careened toward her, wrapped his arms around her from behind, and buried his face in the nape of her neck. He drew her close, exhaled a warm breath on her shoulder, and tried not to allow his mounting frustration to upset the moment—because that's what always happened when the drugs wore off.

"Where the hell have you been, Todd?" She turned and shoved him away before he could speak. "Another weekend God knows where."

"I told you. Parx." He forced a smile. "I made a bunch of money this time, babe. Really, I did. Cash."

"Stop. I can't take the lying anymore. I don't believe a word you say. You're not the same person I married."

"I'm sorry, Rach." He tried to fake sadness, but what he really wanted to do was head to the guest bedroom bathroom, grab his stash from the linen closet, and feel the adrenaline rush through his body. Instead, he continued whispering, "I'm always worried they are watching, so sometimes I put on an act. But I really do love you."

He stepped toward her and stretched his fingers over her stomach. "My God, another baby. Do you know how happy that makes me? How lucky I feel?"

But her having another kid didn't make him happy. The turmoil in his life, mixed with the euphoria he experienced over the weekend, had enticed him to stop, foolishly, at Erie's casino. Now he couldn't bear to hear her bitching. He hoped the bank withdrawal hadn't hit their checking account yet. Who knew three hours at the raunchy, small-town casino would strip him of his manhood? He had lost two hundred thousand dollars to a twenty-two-year-old girl. She had come out of the woodwork like a spider, rappelling down a web so thin you couldn't see the sticky, silky strands. She was a reject from a tournament. Who knew a tournament loser would do that well at the cash tables? He felt swindled but didn't really give a damn. He just wanted to avoid a lecture.

He tugged Rachel toward him and kissed her lips.

"I'm still in love with you, Rach." That part was true. My God, how his emotions seesawed when he didn't get his fix.

"Enough." She rejected him again, shoving hard and stepping away. She began nonchalantly loading dishes into the dishwasher. "You're still high. I smell alcohol, too. How can you drive like that? If you kill someone, how will you live with yourself?"

"Babe." He leaned toward her and looked directly into her eyes, so she could see his pupils were barely dilated. "I hardly had any. Just a little last night."

She slammed the dishwasher door.

"Babe," she spat. "Three months ago you made a promise you would change, give up the cocaine, go to gambler's anonymous, and make your whereabouts known at all times. That lasted less than a month and in that short time, I foolishly let my guard down. Now I'm pregnant."

"Well, okay." He stepped away from her, untied his tie, and let it dangle down his shirt. He dropped his hands to his side. "Regardless of everything, thank you."

"Thank you for what?"

"For the deposit."

"What deposit?

He gazed at her, unbuttoned the top button of his starched white shirt that had long lost its luster. His eyes roamed the kitchen. He wondered if anyone listened.

"You know, for the money. In my gambling account."

Her mouth dropped open, and she squinted her eyes. "Todd, I didn't even know you had a gambling account."

He turned, slipped the tie from his neck with one snap and stuffed it in his briefcase on the floor. Then he stood and stared at her.

Was she kidding? Did she actually think anyone would believe she didn't know about his account? You never knew what Rachel was up to. She was so smart, so gifted. You couldn't tell if she was telling the truth or lying. His gut turned, and he could feel his eyes glazing over. His hands began to sweat again. He didn't have time to deal with her. Not now.

He leaned in and whispered softly but pointedly. "Don't play coy with me. I know they're listening."

He leaned away. She appeared surprised.

"Sure you did, honey." He smiled. "Don't pretend you don't know. Thanks for your generous deposit. I'm sure you know I'll pay you back."

"What are you talking about?"

He presented his cell, tapped a few icons, and an account statement from PNC bank flashed on the screen. He faced the cell toward her and thumbed down to the line with the deposit. She gasped.

The time stamp said 5:02 p.m. on Monday. $325,000 had been debited to Todd Kennedy's private account—transferred from Rachel Callahan Kennedy's private account.

47 John Michael; suspect #3

"Mom, I'm not going to make it home for Thanksgiving."

"John Michael," the voice on the phone said. "You promised. Your sisters are coming. They're bringing their kids."

"Maybe Christmas." He adjusted his glasses and swore under his breath. Oh, how he loathed the feeling of guilt she so easily provoked.

"You know Julie won't be able to come then. Her kids are too little. They need to wake up in their own house on Christmas morning."

"Well, I'll find time to visit her over the Christmas break. I have a few weeks off."

There was silence on the other end. Then she plunged the knife in his belly from five hundred miles away. "You promised when George died you would come home more often."

George, his stepfather; to this day he still hated that man and how he had scrounged off his mother's money and favored Julie and Isabelle, his prima-donna sisters. No one was happier the cancer took its time with him.

"I'm trying, Mom, but I'm busy. Universities require research and publication of their professors these days."

Then she withdrew the knife and plunged the dagger's sharp blade back into his gut a second time—deeper.

"What about Boston College? The English department?"

He closed his eyes and squeezed his lips together. He had hoped to avoid that subject. Keeping Project Dream information from her meddling had been a problem since its inception.

"John Michael? Are you there? Didn't you get that job?"

"No, Mom, I didn't get that job. The professor decided not to retire. I'm first in line when he does."

He stood from his chair and raised his eyes to the ceiling, one hand squeezing his hip, the other holding the phone snugly against his ear. He paced.

With the turmoil around him, he had no time for his mother's badgering. He must hang up, return the officer's phone call, and get to Mercyhurst—something about a bug.

He laughed out loud and shook his head.

"I really have to go, Mom. I'm sorry. I have a stack of papers sitting in front of me that need grading. They're due tomorrow, before the long weekend."

"Well, when are we going to meet this girl you are dating? Will you bring her at Christmas?"

Oh, that lie. He'd cursed himself a thousand times for telling his mother he dated Rachel Callahan. In a weak moment, he had succumbed to his mother's dating questions and, to get her off his back, made up a story about a long weekend away with Rachel. Ever since, she wouldn't leave the subject alone.

"No, I won't. We broke up. Now, I really do have to get going."

"You broke up? But I thought she was—"

"Mom, I have another call coming in. I have to go."

He clicked the phone off and set it on the table. Then he sat down and put his head in his hands, waiting for the buzz. It came. She called again. And again and again. He peeked over his hands at the table in front of him, the applications, the correspondence, the jobs he couldn't apply for.

His cell vibrated one last time. He picked up the new, encrypted Boeing smartphone and hurled it across the room.

48 Jack

"A desperate person resorts to desperate means." The chief appeared burly, even behind the enormous mahogany desk.

Jack ran his hands over the soft leather of the big chair he sat in. Noise from outside the chief's office door filtered in, and a muffled cell-phone vibration hummed from the chief's pants pocket beneath his desk. Jack heard neither. The chief's words had captivated his thoughts. What was the killer's desperation?

"And if someone wanted out?" Next to Jack, Billy Mack swiveled slowly in his own imposing chair. "If they wanted out of Project Dream?"

"The only way out is by death," the chief answered. He sat across from them, his elbows perched on his desktop, his fingers interlocked in front of him.

"So what the hell is going on?" Billy stopped swiveling. "Jack?"

Jack's mind came back into the room and caught up, processing the last few seconds of the room's sounds and digesting the chief and Billy's words.

"I'm not sure. But I know one thing. Rachel had nothing to do with that ransom."

"Not here." The chief stood from his chair. "Let's take a walk. Go see Helen."

The chief's scant two-room office on the first floor of City Hall had been scheduled for an overhaul when he first accepted his position. Maintenance workers said that with the teardown and buildup of a wall here and there, they could combine the chief's office with the empty office next door and create space deserving of a wartime hero and the youngest chief ever to reign in the City of Erie. But as a new chief, Ben had had other plans. The dimensions of both his room and his reception area remained the same. Ben Morgan spent his redecorating funds building the Helen Room.

Passing through the reception area, the chief's longtime secretary, Donna Vahey, stopped them and asked the chief to sign a federal grant application and neighborhood association letter. She handed him both, and he signed without review.

"Chief." Donna smacked a flat palm on a stack of papers on her desk. Jack was sure the slap hurt. "Don't you want to read it?"

"I trust you, Donna."

"But—" The lines on her face sagged. "I spent quite some time writing this. You ought to at least know what the darn thing says."

After Lynn's death, Donna had begun mothering the chief like a koala whose Joey climbed out of her pouch too soon. Jack watched her stand and put hands akimbo. He shuffled his feet to clear a path for her as she rounded her desk.

"I'm going to put a copy of this in your office, and you're going to read it when you get back. Do you hear me? I understand your fixation on the missing boys, but you have to know what's going on with the neighborhood block associations. They're arguing. Everyone is up in arms about protection. No one wants this abductor showing up in their neighborhood. Tomorrow night you have a meeting with them. The press will be there, and you are dog-gone going to read this letter, so you don't look like a big buffoon standing there when John Deter and Dave Villa hammer you with questions. Because they have every right, you know, to be informed of the additional officers on duty, the neighborhood policing, the extra surveillance cameras you installed, and the grant you just signed, applying for more camera funds. Did you even know you were applying?"

"I knew about the grant, Donna."

"Well, do you know that you have fifteen cops working double shifts at this very moment? That Starsky and Hutch here—" She pointed at Jack and Billy. "Haven't had a day off in a month and neither have I?"

"Donna." He stopped and stood tall. "Is this about overtime, the Neighborhood Watch Association, or the fact I wouldn't bartend at the benefit last night because you had invited every single woman over the age of forty to work alongside me?"

"You said you'd be there."

"I said I'd be there if I could. I have too much going on right now."

"Well, I never." She crossed her arms. "Go on. Get out of here. But you know, Ben, you could have some fun once in a while. Laughing is good for the soul. Even for a big mossback like you."

"A mossback? What the hell is a mossback?"

"Just get out of my office." She snatched the papers from his hand.

Billy Mack's eyes found the floor, and he headed for the door, almost running smack into Jack. The two of them hurried away, rounding the corner and allowing the reception-area door to slam behind them before the chief could escape. They hustled to Helen's keylock. Jack punched in the code, swung the door open, and waited for the chief.

When Ben stomped down the hall to Helen's doorway, Jack stiffened to attention and held the door for him.

"What the hell are you looking at?" The chief asked him.

"A war hero." Jack saluted him. "A man who fears no one."

The sound of muffled laughter ping-ponged down the hall. In Jack's peripheral vision, he saw people gathered in the police barracks at the end of the hallway. No doubt, they had assembled to hear why Donna Vahey was reaming out the chief again.

The chief's gaze shot down the hall. "Do you guys have something you want to say?"

The cops that were clustered in the entranceway scrambled out of sight.

"I thought so," he said under his breath, then he pierced the doorway, tossing Jack a don't-say-another-word glance.

Once inside, they automatically placed their cells in the metal desk. The chief removed his hat and sat. He wiped sweat from his forehead and stuck two thick fingers between his neck and shirt collar, tugging it back and forth.

"That woman's trigger is touchier than a recalled Remington." He shook his head and dragged a big hand over his face. "Man, her husband is a saint. Talk to me. Tell me what you know. I have to get the ring of her voice out of my ears."

Jack and Billy sat down but didn't respond. Jack faced the wall, attempting to conceal the smile that had battled to spread across his face and won.

Donna Vahey held a union job. She had worked at City Hall since age eighteen. Her longevity kept her feet planted firmly in the chief's office. The few people who could bump her didn't want the job. And Jack knew even the Lord Himself couldn't have picked a better woman to be Ben Morgan's secretary. Donna was smart, quick, and didn't give a damn how many stars decorated Ben's shoulders. She'd raised five kids. No one intimidated her. She wore the pants in the precinct.

"All right, laugh it out and get it over, so we can move on," the chief finally said.

They laughed hard, and it felt good to Jack. Billy Mack flung a few jabs at the chief before they quieted and settled down to business. Then Billy tossed the PNC bank records in front of him.

"The deposit was made early Monday morning," he said. "Into Rachel's account. Then transferred later in the day into Todd's. They're examining the EFT."

"Do the feds have access to Kennedy's personal cell?" The chief asked.

"We don't know," Jack answered. "We talked to our contact there this morning but couldn't get a clear answer."

"What does Rachel say?"

"She's the one who told us about the deposit. She called me as soon as she could. Said she doesn't know what's going on." Jack had actually never heard her that shaken. "And I believe her. You can't fake panic."

"You know we are going to have to excuse you from this case, Jack."

He knew.

"Chief," Billy said. "That could have been this guy's plan all along. Getting Jack and—well, getting Jack off the case and away from information."

"Who's at your house at night?" The chief lifted his chin toward Jack as though trying to recall.

"Filutze, Briggs, and Morrison," Jack answered. "Filutze in a cruiser, Briggs in an unmarked car, and Morrison in the second cruiser."

"Well, you've got the best." The chief hesitated. "Let's take a ride to John Wickles' house and talk to the mother."

The three stood, and the chief put his hand on Jack's shoulder.

"Not this time, Jack. Go home. Spend a few days with your wife and kids. You're off the case."

He didn't argue. He felt relieved. Now he could guard Mikala twenty-four hours a day until they caught this guy.

And he could keep an eye on Todd.

49 The perpetrator

He trudged through the woods and hurried toward the house to remove the bum's teeth. There could be no glitches. He must wrap everything up before his face materialized in Mikala's mind. The voices had warned him she would soon see him.

"Protect my face—a little longer."

The final step, nabbing the scapegoat and drugging him, would be simple. He had already set in motion the lacing of his cocaine with Ambien. He knew his runner, not the government guy, but his private provider. The coke the government supplied was pure, a gift from South America that was obtained straight from the makers—fewer hands, less tampering.

Thank you, America, for your help tracking cartel planes.

He'd learned much about the CIA while in the desert. His time there seemed so long ago, yet the ample doling out of cocaine, so unfading. They trained transmitters to raise their vibration level by more than meditation and prayer.

Que sera, sera.

He'd be gone in a day. Two at the most. A sad ending for Project Dream, and if Mikala or Lisa or Rachel got in the way? An even sadder ending.

But if Mikala was as good as the voices proclaimed, maybe they would all live, even John. Asthma choked up that kid's lungs. Unfortunate. But he had needed a John to support the perpetrator's detestation for Catholicism and lure the cops and feds in his direction.

When they checked suspects? They would undoubtedly check Bibles. And when they got to the scapegoat's Bible, they'd nail him as the perpetrator by the scandalous blasphemies in the margins of his worn New Testament. There were chastising words written right beside the four passages he had used on the notes when he abducted the boys. He, himself, had seen those admonishments with his own eyes years ago. Words written by a mother trying to dissuade her son from his evil ways.

Blasphemous spirits, devils, psychics, and mediums all suffered in hell's fire if they didn't atone. He could almost hear that mother's reprimands.

In another life, the two of them may have been good friends. You could sympathize with a child whose mother tormented him. And that they both had been molested would have tightened their friendship. If you didn't feel sorry for a kid because of his harsh upbringing, then certainly you could sympathize with him for his molestation. What was that film where the murderer didn't kill the girl because of her molestation scars? He couldn't remember. But when he did, he'd re-watch that movie.

Then again, maybe not.

No time for doubt. He must hustle. The clock ticked mercilessly and, his plan nearly complete, restitution dangled perilously.

Once inside the house, he turned his headlamp on and proceeded to the basement, to the chest. He positioned his mask over his face and lifted the lid.

My God, the smell was nearly intolerable.

He went to work quickly, extracting teeth. The pliers were all the salesman expressed they would be. To ignore the smell, he busied his mind with thoughts of Project Dream, Mother, the Catholic Church, his impending suicide, the boys, and whether Mikala would find the hollowed-out path before the flames reached the bunker and the fire consumed the boys.

If not? Their parents could blame the American government for their children's deaths. They wouldn't be the CIA's first victims. Six of the kids that left Project Dream had mysteriously vanished. Maybe all seven by now.

He yanked the man's last tooth.

By rights, this guy was Project Dream's victim, too.

He placed the last tooth on the floor and then heaved the body back into the chest. He left the lid open this time. Doused both the body and the chest with gasoline.

He'd be back tomorrow night with his Project Dream friend. Now that the end neared, his desire to scare and torture the man had subsided. He simply wanted the killing over.

The ending to their lives was sad, really. They could have done so much more with their gifts. But the government had treated them so poorly that killing the guy was actually doing him a favor. Maybe he should have killed them all. Blew them up at a Project Dream meeting. He might have done it, if he hadn't long been under the spell of a Callahan.

Witches had a way of getting under your skin. Like scabies. They hatched their eggs and multiplied. It was impossible to rid yourself of the itch they roused.

Yes, he was doing the guy a favor.

Death is our only way out.

50 Billy

"Lenny Emling passed the lie detector test." Billy Mack stared at the report in his hand, scrutinizing it earnestly.

"I heard they trained them to pass in the desert." The chief shifted his weight from side to side, nodding as he spoke.

"I heard that, too." Billy's eyes shot to the map on the wall.

Billy and the chief stood at the front of the room amid utter chaos. Behind them, people entered and exited a no-longer-recognizable Helen room. The State Police, County, and FBI had needed a central location, and now the room was littered with mounds of evidence. The FBI fancied the chief's gigantic map in the soundproofed room and had moved in like couch-surfing freeloaders. It took them exactly one hour to ransack the place.

Now desks flaunted duffle bags and jackets like an FBI gift shop. Toward the back of the room, their tables were stacked with printouts, and a chalk board with a suspect list had been erected on the side wall. Currently, the DA had awarded Lenny Emling the number one spot. But chalk dust from writing and erasing and writing and erasing littered the floor. So much dust had accumulated that the tiles were slippery, but no one mopped it up. Everyone knew the juggling of names might not be over.

The canine division of the state police brought in dogs to scour the areas up and down the banks of the creek where Marky Blakley's body had been discovered. So far, they hadn't located any other child.

Faces of the three remaining boys, which already decorated posters across the city, began showing up on telephone poles and storefronts across Erie County and beyond. News of Marky Blakley's death made its way to the Today Show. NBC, CNN, ABC, and CBS parked mobile towers outside. Pulling into the ramp of City Hall's parking garage became difficult. Annoyed investigators navigated around news trucks like the cautionary flag waved and wreckage littered the road.

"I don't think it's Lenny Emling." Billy lifted a hand and twirled his toothpick. "I'm not sure it's Todd Kennedy, either."

"Me either."

"What do you know about this John Michael character? Has Rachel talked about him?"

The chief cleared his throat, and Billy watched his big Adam's apple rise and fall.

"She said he's an odd fellow with a short fuse. Athletic."

"Athletic? Are you kidding me? He's frail looking. Tall but squirrely."

"Rachel said he's fast like the rest of them."

"They're all fast?"

"All of them. Evidently, when they selected the initial one hundred, they narrowed it down by strength and speed."

"You mean to tell me Todd Kennedy is fast and strong?"

The chief looked Billy Mack in the eye. "Drugs wear a person down. Rachel said no one was stronger than Lenny, but speed wise? Todd could keep up with him."

"Did she tell you that this morning?"

The chief shifted his gaze back to the map. "No, she told me that awhile back."

"Uh huh." Billy dropped his hand and twirled the toothpick with his tongue. "I just bet she did. Well, maybe we have been asking Lenny Emling the wrong questions."

"What's that?"

Billy pulled the toothpick out of his mouth like it was a cigarette butt.

"We've been asking him suspect questions. Maybe we ask him a few witness questions. Then bring Todd in."

"Impossible."

"Why is that?'

"Rachel doesn't know where he is. We don't know where John Michael's been the last twenty-four hours, either."

"Shoot," Billy said. "And I was going to spend the entire night at Katie's cottage."

"Well, how's this? You got until midnight." The chief glanced at his watch. "That gives you five hours. I have to spend some time with the feds, then I'm going home for a little shuteye. An hour, max. I'll meet you back here at midnight."

"Make that one o'clock."

The chief leaned away from Billy and raised his eyebrows. "And if I don't?"

"Then I'll be an hour late."

51 Mikala

"Is Jeffrey sleeping, Momma?"

"Finally." Lisa wrapped an arm around Mikala and planted a kiss on her forehead. "Thank you, sweetie, for keeping an eye on your brothers while I got him to sleep. And for frosting the cookies."

"Will you give this one to Geoff tonight? He comes soon, right?"

"I will. He should be here—" Lisa glimpsed the kitchen clock. "Oh gosh, it's late. In less than ten minutes."

Lisa scrambled to the sink and washed her hands. "Jaden and John, go up upstairs and brush your teeth."

"We want cookies, Momma." Jaden sat across from Mikala, his face mottled with white frosting.

Lisa glanced over her shoulder and laughed. "It looks like you already had enough."

"Look, Momma." Mikala tilted her cookie upward. "Do you like Officer Geoff's police hat?"

Lisa stepped toward the kitchen table, drying her hands with a towel that flaunted a cartoon turkey. She lay one hand on the back of Mikala's chair and bent to examine the cookie. "I think we have a little artist in our house."

"Look at this one." Mikala showed her another. "I made this for Uncle Billy. Can you give it to him tomorrow?"

"You can give it to him yourself, but that reminds me." Lisa straightened. "I have to start the sausage."

"The sausage for the dressing?" Mikala broke into a wide smile. "Is Uncle Billy going to bring Aunt Katie to Thanksgiving dinner? She loves your stuffing."

"Hmm, I don't know." Lisa hurried to the counter and dragged a pot from the top shelf of the cupboard.

Mikala slid the plate with the blue icing toward her brothers. "Here you go, Jaden. You can finish your blue hat for Daddy, now."

Jaden's eyes widened. Mikala glanced at her mother and saw Lisa sorting through plates and bowls in the cupboard. Her back faced them. Mikala nodded at Jaden. Jaden scooped icing with his hand and plopped a clump on his head. Then he used his other hand to grab more, and he patted John's head with frosting.

John laughed. "Now we have a hat like Daddy."

"No!" Mikala raised her voice but laughed, too. "Jaden, not on your head. Momma!"

Lisa turned and nearly dropped the glass dish in her hand.

"Oh, no, Jaden." She only half hollered. "Not now."

She set the bowl down and reached for Jaden's hand before he globed more on his brother's head.

"John, get up." She pulled Jaden's arm to make him stand and grabbed John's hand, tugging him into a standing position, too. "Oh gosh, I didn't have time for this. You two are going to have to get back in the tub. Mikala, leave everything where it is. Daddy should be home from the store in a few minutes. Don't touch anything."

Blue icing fell from John's head to the floor. The boys laughed and jiggled, trying to sling more frosting from their heads. Mikala covered her mouth with a hand and snickered.

"Jaden, John, stop," Lisa said, but it was no use. Blue clumps spewed in all directions. "I mean it. Stop shaking your heads or you won't have one single cookie tomorrow. Do you hear me?"

Both boys moaned, but the remainder of the frosting stayed caked in their hair as they trailed out of the room.

"I'll cover the cookies, Momma," Mikala hollered.

"Thank you, Mikala," Lisa called from the stairs. "Try not to step in any blue, honey. You'll track it through the house."

Mikala placed Billy's cookie back on the plate and ran to get the foil on the counter and a baggie from a drawer. She stepped carefully, trying to avoid the blue globs as she hurried toward Jaden and John's seats. She gathered the cookies, even the ones her brothers hadn't frosted, and placed them on the platter. She selected four small cookies and slipped them into a baggie. Then she covered the plate with the foil, dragged the stool over to the sink, and washed and dried her hands.

Once done, she tiptoed into the living room and peeked out the front window, waiting.

The time had nearly come. The last few nights, before Officer Geoff arrived, the officer in the first police car would get out and walk toward the officer with the long blond hair in the second car. Mikala would watch the officer's ponytail bounce back and forth as the first officer leaned in the car window. They remained like that until Officer Geoff's car rounded the corner.

As soon as the officer in the first car opened his door, Mikala darted to the front closet. She took her coat from the hook, slipped the baggie of cookies in one pocket, and fell to her knees. She reached into the big tub on the floor. Hurriedly, she shuffled through the gravy mix pouches that she had taken and hidden earlier. She found her hat and mittens. Quickly, she slipped them on, knowing Daddy would be home from the store with new gravy bags soon.

She stood, put on her coat, and checked her other pocket to make sure Mrs. Shield's inhaler was still there. When she saw that it was, she closed the closet door and scurried through the house. She opened the back door slowly and stepped into the night.

Once she descended her back steps, she raced across her backyard and ran through her next-door neighbor's backyard, dashing up his driveway because the streetlight in front of his house had been burnt out for days. She peeked toward the police car. The tall officer was still bent and leaning in the window. She darted across the street to the neighbor's yard and hid behind a bush.

She stooped down breathlessly, wondering when her uncle would get there. Hoping he would come before Daddy got home. She had to give him the inhaler for John. Marky had told her that John was struggling to breathe in the cellar. Mikala hoped Mrs. Shield's inhaler was good enough. She was too afraid to take Jeffrey's. Scared he'd have an attack and die. Mrs. Shield had so many she didn't know what to do with them, she had said.

Mikala was only there a minute when she saw Officer Geoff's car come down the road. The policeman standing outside started back toward his car. A second cruiser followed Officer Geoff. The officer with the ponytail started up her car. Farther down the street, the plain surveillance car pulled onto the corner between her house and her aunt Janice and cousin Danny's house.

With the officers distracted, she sat and waited patiently. She hoped she could give her uncle the cookies and the inhaler and get back inside before Daddy got home.

She didn't hear his footsteps. Suddenly, he was behind her. She gazed up at him. He looked like a giant, much taller, bigger now that he stood beside her. He bent down.

"Hello," she said.

"H-hello," he whispered.

"I have an inhaler for John," she said, removing it from her pocket. "He needs it."

He nodded.

"And here are three cookies for them. And one for you."

He nodded again. His lips didn't curl upward like she expected. He seemed sad.

She smiled at him anyway. But he didn't say anything more. In her head she saw Momma and Daddy and Officer Geoff and how frantic they would be. But she knew now that he squatted beside her, she was going to have to go with him. The movie that played in her mind rolled fast forward and became clear.

She handed him the cookies and the inhaler.

He glanced toward the police cars, lifted her up into his arms, and began running.

52 2007 – PROJECT DREAM

Sissy's knees buckled when she hung up the phone. Her body slumped to the ground. She remained on the floor for minutes, sobbing until the headmaster came and helped her to her feet.

The night was long past midnight. Her building director said a car would be dispatched in the morning, but she begged for them to come right away. She wanted to go home to her mother, to LeeLee.

"Impossible," he said, then clutched her elbow and led her to her room where she packed and cried until Todd came and held her and gave her the cocaine to snort, so she could forget. And she did. She forgot and dozed and woke and remembered and cried over and over in the night.

Gradually, the others heard her cries and awoke. Throughout the night, people knocked on her door, entered, and sorrowfully wrapped their comforting arms around her. Lenny, John Michael, her closest girlfriends, Izzy and Sonnie, Paul, Marcus, and an endless line of other classmates drifted in to say they were sorry. Everyone knew Rachel loved her grandmother.

Not long after dawn, they summoned her to the headmaster's office and sent the others to classrooms. The headmaster provided her with a travel itinerary and instructed her to wait in the entryway. There, she sat catatonically down on a stiff chair, her hands folded in her lap, her heels pressed together, and her suitcase square beside her.

A heavy regret of snorting too much cocaine hit her immediately. Her head throbbed and misery wandered in and out of her mind like a slowing cuckoo clock in need of a wind. She couldn't concentrate. The drugs muddled a faint echo of voices down the dismal, stingy-windowed hall that stretched from the entryway and offices to the classrooms. She didn't realize an argument had ensued.

When the big hall clock tolled the hour, she lumbered to the side window of the foyer door and gazed out at the scorching day, oblivious to the erupting ruckus down the hall. Unable to peel her eyes from the narrow dirt road that led out of Area 51, she could process nothing more than she had to get home.

The world swayed and the sun bent through the window and beat down on her. Finally, she saw dust rise in the distance. A slight, swirling sandstorm formed. Umber particles whirled toward the sky, trailing after the turning wheels of a car. A car coming for her.

She didn't hear the footsteps behind her or know he was coming.

"You still have feelings for him, don't you?" the skewed voice uttered behind her.

She turned abruptly, her vision blurred. Now tears, not just the coke, distorted her world. She barely recognized him. "Todd?

"You care for him, don't you?"

"Who?"

"You know who I mean." He sounded breathless.

"I don't—I don't know what you're saying." Unsteady on her feet, she pulled a tissue from her pocket and dabbed her face. "I want to go home. I don't want to come back here—ever."

She felt his arm encircle her waist. He rested his forehead on hers. "I'm sorry, Rachel."

She let his arms hold her, because his sweet scent soothed her, and his muscular frame steadied her. She felt safe in his arms in that instant.

"Why don't I know when the people I love are sick? With all my dreams, why can't I tell when someone close to me is dying? First my dad, now Gee."

"Rachel—" Todd swayed back and forth, rocking her in his arms. "I'm sorry. It was seeing you cry and the cocaine. I had too much. I didn't know what I was doing."

She didn't understand. They'd both had too much. Now the world swirled as the car approached, and the loud voices in the hall neared. Someone shouted, and she turned and saw a trail of bloody footprints on the hallway floor. Had there been a fight? Her eyes traced the path of the crimson red steps. Were those Todd's footprints?

She heard a sound outside, and she glanced through the window glass to the road. The car was almost there.

"I'm going home, Todd." She said, moving toward her suitcase. "I just want to go—"

Finally, she looked at him, really looked. His face bled profusely. Bloody patches reddened his clothes. She glanced down to where his shirt had met hers. His blood had turned her black dress blacker.

"What did you do? Why are you bleeding?"

She tried to focus. If only she hadn't taken so many pills on top of the cocaine. Since yesterday morning when LeeLee called to say Gee was in a coma, she had filled herself with any pill she could score to deaden her grief.

"I couldn't stand it when they all started putting their hands on you," Todd said. "Steve, Marcus, and especially John Michael. You know he still loves you."

"What are you talking about?"

"First Steve put his arms around you. Then Marcus. You know I hate the way they coddle you. Then—"

"Todd, no. It's just my grandmother." She closed her eyes, remembering Todd's jealousies. "They were sorry for me."

"But you don't see it, Rachel, how beautiful you are." His hands tightened. She tried to push him away. "How much they all love you. Every one of them. Lenny, too."

"Oh, Todd, not now."

"Rachel," he said, leaning and whispering in her ear, "Marcus and John Michael both admitted they still love you. So, when they passed you from arm to arm as you were leaving, I went crazy. Kept hitting them. Lenny stopped me and—"

She freed herself, stepping away. If only she could clear her head.

"Lenny?" She put a hand on her forehead. "What are you saying?"

"I lost my mind." He wrenched her back into his arms, murmuring words she could not comprehend.

"Todd...what?"

"I—" He buried his face in her shoulder.

Down the hall, she heard footsteps. Big, loud footsteps coming closer. She tried wiggling loose, but Todd held firm.

"What did you do?"

"I swung the poker at them. Hit Marcus. John Michael, too. He came at me, and we fought. I...I...hope he's not dead. Then, Lenny—"

"John Michael? You beat John Michael? And Marcus?"

"I get so jealous," he whimpered. "Then Lenny came and—I stabbed him."

In that instant, the approaching footsteps halted and Lenny appeared beside them, the front of his shirt covered in blood.

"Lenny." Rachel turned. "Are you all right?"

"I-I'll be o-okay," he stammered. "B-but John Michael is hurt bad."

Todd jerked Rachel around. Stood between her and Lenny. "Get out of here, you flunky."

"L-l-let her go. Sh-she needs to go home."

"Lenny, you need help." Rachel reached a hand over Todd's shoulder toward Lenny, but Todd shoved it back.

"Get away from us, freak." Todd led Rachel out the front door and tried to slam it shut, but Lenny stopped the closing door with one hand.

What happened next occurred in a flash. Lenny skirted around them and shoved them both back inside the building. Then he reached through the doorway and ripped Todd's hand off Rachel's arm, dragged him outside, and slammed the door shut. Rachel heard Todd's back thumping against the big wooden door as Lenny banged him several times. She heard knuckle against bone and knew Lenny's big hands were landing fist after fist against Todd's face.

"Don't hurt him, Lenny, please," she screamed.

She fumbled with the doorknob and banged with her fists. When the door didn't budge, she fell against it, forearms and cheek flat on wood. Her face and body felt the vibration of each punch, and she begged and pleaded for Lenny to stop. But the wooden tremors continued and when she could take no more, her weary body slid to the floor.

"Please, Lenny," she whispered.

After a few more strikes, she heard the click of running feet both inside and outside. Someone hollered. The bouncing of Todd's body against the door stopped, and she felt the warmth then—the tepid, wet floor. She gazed down at the blackish-red trickle of fluid and realized the balmy substance was blood, Todd's blood oozing beneath the door. That gore was the last she remembered of the morning.

She traveled home the next day, and they allowed her one week for the funeral and grieving. When she returned, John Michael and Marcus had been moved to a hospital. Todd, to the infirmary, and Lenny to building twelve, where the worst kids lived. When Todd and John Michael recovered, each were transferred to separate living facilities. Marcus never returned. Someone said he died. Rachel hoped his death was a rumor.

Todd never talked to her about the incident again, but Rachel heard from others that he had vowed to kill both Lenny and John Michael. They said John Michael had reciprocated with a vow to kill Todd.

Lenny made no such threats. He didn't have to. Everyone knew murder was not beyond him.

53 Billy

The cottage that Katie had rented sat on a gradually-sloped hill beside a small lake in the college town of Edinboro. The Boro, as students had tagged the community, sat twenty-three miles south of Erie and abutted the little town of McKean. Its quaint downtown attracted students and residents in all four seasons. Billy Mack thought he might like living there. But then, he'd like living anywhere as long as he woke up beside Katie in the morning.

Three months ago when Katie said she was leaving, for the first time in his life, he had nothing to live for. He went on three weekend drinking binges, where Jack fished him out of the gutter, and Lisa nursed him back to life.

He'd survived a lifetime of anguish in one month. Then, he cut the drinking binges and cleaned up his act. Asked Katie out to dinner. It took some cajoling, but finally she accepted.

"I don't mind your hours, Billy. I knew I was marrying a dedicated cop. Your work ethic is part of what I love about you." Katie dropped that seed of hope on that first date after the separation. His hope shot up like a bamboo shoot. They had met at a little Edinboro pub and shared a pizza. He could barely think of anything other than she still loved him.

"What I can't live with is the lack of communication."

Smack. She lopped off a shoot but didn't kill the stalk. He still had hope. He could change.

"Life can't be fun and games and jokes all the time. I need someone I can count on in the rough times."

"I know," he responded, because he did know. He had done some self-evaluating. "I'm not the most demonstrative person—"

"No, you're not," she interrupted. Her tone had been anything but forgiving. He wasn't out of the woods yet.

"Well—" He surrendered. Said something he never thought he'd say. "I love you, Katie. So I'm willing to try. I'll go to counseling."

He reached across the table for her hand, cupped her fingers in his, and kissed her knuckles. Katie raised her eyebrows and widened her eyes.

"Did you say counseling?"

He dropped his head and laughed, but then raised his chin and squeezed her hand. "I'll go to counseling this time, Katie. I'll take dance lessons. Trim the hedges like you asked me to do. Paint the fence. Wash the dishes. I'll do anything. Just never stop loving me."

She cried. Right there in the pub. She wasn't the least bit embarrassed. That always amazed him about her. How unaffected she was around others. And how she loved him totally, whole-heartedly, not caring about vulnerability. He'd taken advantage of her unconditional love, never thought she'd leave, and when she did, the selfishness in Billy died.

"We can sell the house and move out here, where you're closer to your work. There's no ban on where we cops live any longer. The mayor eliminated that requirement."

"I do love you, Billy," she said. "But let's slow down a bit, shall we? Let's start with the counseling. See how that goes."

And they did—one week later. Afterward, they went to dinner and a movie. The following week they went dancing and later they'd made love. She fell asleep in his arms. He didn't sleep. He stayed awake all night, afraid he'd wake up and his arms around her would all be a dream.

There had never been anyone for him but Katie. He fell in love with her before he enlisted in the Marines and asked her to marry him on his first leave home. She said no. He persisted, asking her on every leave. One year before his discharge, he upped his ante. He bought a diamond ring the size of a dime and eighteen months later, two months after he took the police officer's oath, they married, and he began taking her for granted.

Tonight she had agreed to move home. Turned out she had only leased that cottage for six months. So, sitting in McKean just past midnight, he felt like the luckiest man alive. He would see this counseling through for a lifetime if it meant he could continue wrapping his arms around the only girl he had ever loved.

He adjusted his rearview mirror and saw his reflection. He was smiling again. There in the middle of the night, the face staring back at him looked downright elated. He turned his eyes onto the road and chuckled. As long as he had Katie, he'd be happy anywhere, even in downtown McKean.

Realizing he had been sitting there lost in thought for over fifteen minutes, he turned his wheels and inched toward the car in front of him to get a closer view. A late-night construction bottleneck halted traffic in both directions. Two workers held up stop signs as other workers raked limestone off a dump truck and into fresh tar.

He turned his wheels back in line and sat for a moment longer, thinking about that evening. The way Katie's messy hair had framed her face. Her brown hair whirling from the wind when she cracked a window to hear the engine roar as they rode back from dinner. My God, had she always been that beautiful?

She had even felt badly that he'd given up his old banged-up car. Said she would miss it. Then she rolled her hands along the dashboard of the new one and whined, admitting she loved it. He winked at her. Months before, she had mentioned that particular car was her favorite, and he fully intended to give it to her when she moved home.

This thought aroused a new worry. Tar and chips? He couldn't let that happen. He turned his wheel, edged up the berm of the road, and turned onto a narrow side street.

There, he found himself lost on a country road and, being so late, there was no one to offer directions and no visible addresses to see. He grabbed his phone. Missed phone calls filled the screen. Mostly from Jack. Some from the chief.

"Not tonight, boys." He laughed, then watched the texts disappear as he punched his code in and opened Google maps. "Be there by one, Chief. No sooner."

He entered City Hall's address, waited for directions, and then turned right on a dirt road as instructed. No doubt other drivers were avoiding the construction also, because a few oncoming cars kicked up dust as they passed. He slowed. Didn't want to dirty Katie's car.

At one point, the road narrowed so dramatically that he had to drive onto the edge of someone's property when a car approached. Branches and leaves touched the passenger window, and he cursed. Further down the road another automobile sped toward him erratically, swerving side to side. When the car was fifty yards from him, the driver turned abruptly to the right to avoid coming straight toward him, and Billy caught the soft glow of a cell phone lighting up the automobile's front seat.

"Damn it, get off the phone," he hollered. Then against his better judgement, he drove closer to the branches. "Slow down, mister."

Billy stopped his car completely, grabbed his spotlight, and aimed it at the driver. As suspected, he was just a kid, probably with a Cinderella license.

Billy glanced at his watch. 12:11.

"Shit," he said. He couldn't have a kid killing himself on the back roads of McKean. He threw the car in drive, pulled away from the trees, and turned around. His wheels squealed, but the car's stability was magnificent. The salesman had been right. He could turn on a nickel.

He reached for his red light. He hated sticking the portable emergency light to the front of Katie's car, but he had no choice. When he caught the kid's car, the boy braked so quickly that Billy nearly ran into his back end. Billy slammed his car into park and watched as the front door of the car he was trailing thrust open. The kid started getting out.

"Jesus," Billy said, then drew his gun and yelled, "Get back in the car."

"Yes, sir. Yes, sir." The boy fell back in clumsily and closed the door. His voice was so young it still cracked.

Billy kept his gun raised. He got out slowly and inched his way up the side of his own car and then alongside the boy's. He could hear a second voice. Was there someone else in the car? He stopped. No, the voice was muffled. Was the kid talking on a cell phone? He approached slowly and listened.

"No, Greenlee. I'm on Greenlee. I drove up Tileyard Road to avoid downtown. I saw the guy there."

Billy kept approaching, gun drawn. He peered into the back seat. The boy was alone.

"Dad, where are you?" The boy said. "It looks like a cop. I hope it's a cop."

Billy reached for the car door just as he saw the cell phone in the kid's hand.

"Step outside, son."

"Yes, sir. Don't shoot me, sir."

"Danny?" A voice from the phone called.

"Who's on the phone?"

"My dad. He's coming."

Billy glanced around at the dark woods and then toward the street ahead and behind him. There was nothing to the north, but to the south, headlights approached in the distance.

"Is that him?" Billy, two hands under his pistol, motioned with his gun.

"Dad?" The boy was frantic, looked like he was about to break into a cry. "Is that you? Can you see me?"

"Yes, I'm coming, Dan."

"Yes, that's him, my dad. He's coming." A sigh followed the boy's tang of relief. "Hurry, Dad. Just hurry."

"Why is your dad coming out in the middle of the night?"

"I called him. I saw this huge guy over on Tileyard. I almost hit him. His car was parked, and I didn't see it."

"You been drinking, kid?"

"No, no, working. I've been busing tables at the Marriot. We had a banquet. Then on the way home this mammoth guy stepped out of nowhere. I didn't see him because it was dark. I almost hit him."

"Almost or did?"

"No, I didn't hit him."

"Did you stop?"

"Huh? Stop? No. I wasn't going to stop. I never seen anyone walking that road at night."

"You take it often?"

"Yeah. Every time I work late. This guy scared the daylights out of me. And he had a kid with him, standing on the side of the road. It looked like he shoved the kid out of the way. I almost hit them. Who does that? Who walks along Tileyard Road in the middle of the night with a kid? Dad? Is that you?"

"I'm coming, Danny. I see you. I see the cop's light."

Billy didn't like this. He had no mic to call for assistance.

"Get out of the car, boy. Tell your dad to stay in the car until I come for him."

"Dad—"

"I heard him, Danny. Just do what the man says. I'm here."

The car slowed to a stop, and Billy commanded the boy out and onto the ground. Then he edged his way toward the second car.

"Officer, my name is Larry Feldman," the man said.

"Keep your hands where I can see them."

The man kept them on the steering wheel. "My son called me. He saw a guy in the woods with a kid. Almost hit them. He was afraid. I jumped in my car to meet him."

Billy positioned himself so he could see both the man in the car and the kid on the ground. The boy picked his head up.

"Keep your head down, son."

"Danny, just stay still. Officer, he was afraid the guy was going to come after him. He was frantic."

"Do you live around here?"

"Yes, just over the hill on Stancliff, 4456 Stancliff. I hopped in my car as soon as he called. He's only sixteen. Hasn't had his license too long."

"He told you he saw someone with a kid?"

"Yes, a guy on Tileyard Road. It's pretty desolate there."

Billy took one hand off his gun, reached into his pocket, and pulled out his phone, still eyeing the father and son. Obedience wasn't always a sign of innocence, but Billy had a hunch these two were harmless.

He lifted the cell and took his eyes off them to glance at his phone. More messages from Jack lit up the night. The first thought that entered his head was he couldn't mess with those now, he needed to call and check this Larry Feldman out. He punched in his code and turned his eyes back on the man.

Something flashed in his mind. Words. Like a neon light that brands your vision and stays with you after you look away. His brain recalled the letters and phrases, the texts on the cell phone screen. *Urgent. Help.* And the third message he could not fathom.

His mind left the father and son, and he focused on his cell. One finger found his text message icon. He hit it and scrolled down and saw the most frightening text he would ever see in his lifetime.

The text was from Jack. *Mikala is missing.*

Those three words sucked the air from his lungs. He lowered his arm.

"Is it okay to get up, sir?"

"Officer?" The man in the car asked. "Can my son get up?"

"Get up." He motioned with his head and the revolver in his hand. "Where did you say you saw that man?"

"On Tileyard."

"Where's that?"

The boy pointed down the road. "Take a right on the next road, Greenlee, then Tileyard is a left turn about a mile down. If you get to Hamot Road you've gone too far. The turn is hard to see at night. Lots of trees and no sign."

"He was on foot?"

"Yeah. Had a car parked along the side of the road. He was walking—ah, north—yeah, north. That is, if he's still there."

"And he had a kid with him?"

"Yeah, a kid."

"Girl or boy?"

"I'm pretty sure it was a girl."

"Blond hair?"

"Yeah, I think so. It was dark."

Billy backed away. The kid got up and inched toward his father's car. By the time his dad got out and hugged his son, Billy had turned his car around and peeled out. He headed toward Greenlee Road, words Katie had uttered earlier that evening playing over in his mind.

"There is a reason for everything, Billy." She was always saying shit like that. "We never know what incidents in life help lead us down the right path. God has a plan. There is a reason we had to go through this separation."

"I pray you are right, Katie." He pressed harder on the gas, and the back of his car fishtailed in the dirt.

He hit the Bluetooth button on his steering wheel and said, "Call Jack."

By the time he heard the first ring, his speedometer blinked eighty-one and kept rising. By the time Jack's frantic voice howled over the phone, he realized if Katie hadn't left him he wouldn't be on that dirt road headed toward the little girl who had to be Mikala.

"Jack!" He hollered into the phone. He braked to turn right onto Greenlee Road, and he realized that if he hadn't been so in love with Katie, so distraught over her leaving him, he never would have traded his hunk-of-junk car in to buy her the best damn car he could find.

When his wheels skidded toward the cliff on the edge of the road, he realized Katie spoke the truth; everything had a reason. His old car would have plummeted down that hill into the ravine. His steering wheel would have locked and that rattletrap would have fallen apart as it rolled over and over down the hill. No one would have found his body for days.

But instead, the car skidded onto two wheels and bounced back down onto the road, and Billy forced the gas pedal to the floor.

54 Jack

Earlier, Geoff Filutze, a rifle butting his shoulder, had told Jack he would not leave the house until Mikala personally handed him her homemade cookie. Then he shook Jack's hand and slipped keys to an unmarked Crown Vic—the fastest the department had—into his palm.

"Monroe Drive. Straight behind your house. Go through the backyards," Geoff said.

Jack exited the back door, running.

The cop who watched him leave said, "I ain't seen nothing," when the FBI agent arrived and asked where Jack was.

Jack went to Todd's house first. Entered with a key, searched, but Todd wasn't there. He prayed for guidance. Begged God to see any infinitesimal clue that might hide within the walls of his brother-in-law's house. He found nothing and headed to John Michael's bayfront apartment.

He jumped out of his car at the gate and ran down the street. The light in John Michael's window peeked through the edges of drawn drapes. He called John Michael's phone. Knocked on his door. No response. He busted the door open with one abrupt kick. Empty.

The security alarm sounded like an air raid alarm. He flicked the lights on and rummaged through the apartment. Prayed. But found nothing. He left the door wide open when he exited. Tipped his hand upward in a simple wave at the cop who had arrived and was getting out of his cruiser. The officer nodded at him, shut his door, and walked silently toward John Michael's apartment. Jack kept running toward his car.

He took the Bayfront Highway, turned south, and flew through every red light on State and Thirty-Eighth streets until he turned onto the Mercyhurst campus. There, he checked John Michael's classroom, Lenny's maintenance area, and Doctor Peterson's office where Project Dream was rumored to meet.

With no sign of anyone, he headed to Lenny Emling's house. By then the blue lights on his car glowed 11:45. He knocked but didn't ring the bell. Lenny's ailing mother wouldn't make her way downstairs quickly enough for him, so he busted that door down, too, calling her name as he ran through the house. He found her sleeping upstairs, drugged, no doubt. Empty room after empty room coaxed him in.

He left and headed for the casino.

"Where the hell are they?"

He called Lisa and asked if Todd had contacted them yet. He hadn't. Lisa had talked to Rachel, and the chief had sent a car for her, but she wouldn't arrive home for hours.

"Find Mikala," she said, her voice quivering.

"I will. I'll find her. Keep the boys close."

"We're fine. Geoff is here."

Jack pictured Lisa slumped in a single bed, her rosary beads in her hand; Jeffrey, Jaden, and John huddled together in a matching twin bed two feet from her; and Geoff Filutze downstairs, sitting in the living room, a Glock 26 hugging one leg, a Cold Steel four-inch knife strapped to his other, and the rifle straddling his knees. Three cruisers were parked outside.

"Yes, you are. I'll be home with her. Before morning."

He had no idea why he said that.

"Yes," she whispered. "Bring my baby home."

He disconnected. Immediately, his cell buzzed. He glimpsed the number and answered.

"Billy?"

"Jack, I think I know where she is."

"Where are you, Billy, did you hear?"

"Yes, yes, and some kid just saw a big guy with a little girl."

"Where?"

"McKean."

"I'm close. Robison road. I was headed toward the casino." The tires on the car squealed as Jack changed direction. "Where in McKean?"

"Some backwoods street, I turned off a road called Greenlee onto Tileyard Road. Some kid said he saw a man and a little girl on Tileyard."

"I've been there." Jack punched Tileyard into the GPS. Five miles came on the screen. He stepped on the gas.

"I'm on my way. Be there in three minutes."

"Can't wait, Crackerjack," Billy said. "I see the car. I'm going in. I'll leave a trail."

55 The Zenith

A faint moonlight cast vague shadows on Tileyard road, and even those obscure forms were minimal. Clouds scuttled by, dimness fighting black.

Billy slunk along the edges of the dark road.

"Where did they go?" He whispered to the moon. "How did he get through this shit?"

His flashlight bounced between a wall of vegetation and the street's berm. Brown and green thicket bordered the road, hanging out into the street at spots. He couldn't find an opening.

During the war, his sergeant had nicknamed him Zenith. Made him the first man in their front line, bragging to higher-up officers that the Zenith was telepathic. Said he could avoid devil eggs, mines, on his own merit. Billy had located twenty-two on one trek through Iraq. His name floated up to the highest ranks in the Marines. When they found out, they sent him everywhere: Iraq, 59 landmines per square mile; Afghanistan, 40; Iran 25. He'd heard senior officers took bets on the month and year Billy Mackentire's legs would blow off.

But Billy knew his gifts had nothing to do with telepathy and everything to do with his senses. He had the nose of a mine-detecting dog, perfect vision, and superb hearing, and his ability to focus on detail was stupendous. He could zero in on minute deviations.

Now he walked along the black road and stared at the base of the black woods. He could be patient when duty engaged him. He slithered along the thicket's edge, his feet as light as a dancer's. Then he spotted the inconsistency. A powder of foliage crumbs on the edge of the road. He stopped and aimed his flashlight upward. There, one long slit in the middle of the vegetation had been made. He reached a hand in and looked inside. Someone had sickled a path.

His mind searched his attire. He had nothing to mark the opening. Then he remembered.

He darted toward his car, the back seat. Opened the middle compartment and pulled out Mikala's ribbons. He ran toward the opening and looped one pink band to mark it.

He heard movement far ahead of him. Hesitated for one second and then took off toward that sound.

No one could move through tangled brush faster than him. Once during a training run in the Marines, his commanding officer forced him inside the edge of a forest, insisting every platoon needed a scout good at traversing thick terrain. Really, the guy was punishing Billy for running his mouth all the time, so Billy made the jaunt a game. Ran like a cheetah in a jungle. When his troop finished their three-mile run on the flat, barren path that bordered the woods, Billy stood waiting, clothes torn and body bloodied, a grimace curving his lips. That officer hated him after that.

Everything happens for a reason.

He skirted through the brush, and the foot sounds neared. He moved quickly. When he trekked into a clearing where a house sat, he stopped, sniffed, felt the air against his face.

Gasoline. Dynamite.

A dim light flickered in the window, but he resisted the temptation to run toward the old farmhouse. He kept his cool and listened. He heard movement ahead in the trees, only a hint of sound from the house.

One person in the house. Another running through the brush—a big man. Was he carrying something? A child?

He hurried toward the woods behind the house. Spotted a three-foot path, trampled by deer, widened by man. He hung another pink ribbon.

Behind him on the road, a car screeched to a stop, and Billy knew Jack had arrived. He texted four words. *Avoid house. Follow ribbons.* Then he rushed the deer path.

Within minutes the trail widened, and he stepped into a clearing in the woods. Off to one side, a haystack smoldered. Smoke billowed toward the sky and drifted across the meadow, and the dark night crowded him. He could barely see a few feet in front of him. Then the clouds opened as if God Himself spewed His light down on the ground, and Billy saw them—the little girl and the big man. The man hovered over something on the ground.

Billy lifted his revolver, curled his finger onto the trigger, and aimed. Moonlight fell on the shape of the big man's head and Billy recognized him —Lenny Emling. And just as he was about to pull the trigger, he saw Mikala. She was unbound, leaning toward Lenny, calmly watching him.

In that split second, he knew. He dropped his hand with the gun and took off running. He watched Lenny thrust open what looked to be a door on the ground and saw Mikala disappear into the ground after him.

With the smell of gasoline and smoke teasing his nostrils, Billy Mack ran toward the rabbit hole that had sucked Mikala Daly and Lenny Emling into the ground. By the time he reached it, he knew, even if no one else would ever know, he had just broken a world record.

56 The perpetrator

Two hours before anyone arrived, he removed six dynamite packs from a wooden crate and strategically positioned them around the inside of the house. Outside, he tucked four more packs into the mesh sacks that he had crafted that afternoon. Those sacks hung from the four corners of the house. He placed three more packs in thick brush fifty feet from the road and slipped a couple into two of three bales of hay positioned at the edge of the clearing in the woods—away from the bunker to give Mikala a fighting chance.

He doused the rope that led to the dynamite hanging in the mesh sacks and those near the road and traipsed through the woods, soaking the two long ropes that lead to the bales of hay in the clearing, drenching them at the points where he had tied them together.

Now he stood in the center of the house and took a long, slow much-needed breath. Inhaled the stringent chemical aroma in the air around him.

Soon McKean would wake up to fireworks of Fourth-of-July distinction.

Death is the only way out.

He placed the transmitter's body next to the bum's. Positioned a sledge hammer between them and bound the bum's hands, wedging a mallet between his tied wrists as if he had grabbed it to defend himself. The hobo should appear to go out fighting in case, by some miracle, the explosions, gasoline, and fire failed to obliterate all the evidence.

He observed the scene with pride.

If more than ash survived, if the fire was somehow extinguished before the charred bodies completely disintegrated, surely the coroner would conclude there had been a fight. He had smashed their jaws, bloodied their bodies, and, finally, cut the fingers off the transmitter, so it appeared he set off the dynamite.

I will not go out as the bad guy.

Then he soaked the bum's body, his face and hands especially, with gasoline. He, at least, must be charred beyond recognition.

He felt no remorse for the murders. His single regret was not being able to deliver his long-practiced speech to his nemesis turned perpetrator. Time had closed in on him. He couldn't sober the man up to explain that he'd dreamed about killing him since their time together in the desert.

But he was dallying.

He moved forward, slit his wrist, and paced, allowing a good amount of blood to seep into the hope chest and nearby parlor floorboards. In the kitchen, he smeared his DNA onto the appliances. Then, by the backdoor, he let his blood drip into the toolbox where the mallet had been. More than likely the flames would obliterate it all, especially the old, brittle hardwood floor by the bodies, but he wasn't taking chances: he would be the victim.

With that, the time had come. He had dreamed of this day for weeks, months. His guide had provided the day's timeline in the usual manner—a movie in his head. First, Lenny Emling and Mikala would come, then the Mackentire cop, and finally, Jack Daly.

This was the last fucking dream he would dream wide awake.

"Bye-bye, Project Dream."

As he wrapped tape tightly around his wrist to stop the blood flow, he imagined his family's phony sentiments when they heard of his demise. How they'd cry on camera for reporters, especially his mother, sick woman that she was. He had never forgiven her for letting them take him away—another sin he would take to his death.

"Forgive, lest ye be forgiven," he said, forgetting himself and sneering. Laughing as loud as if it didn't matter.

Then he remembered and quieted. Glanced out the window and turned back to his task.

He picked up the near-empty gas can, dumped the last of its contents around the house—closer to the bum, of course—and made his way by headlamp to the window. There, he medicated himself with a bit of cocaine for calming purposes, cut his headlamp, and drew back the curtain.

He liked the dark of night, felt most comfortable there. He supposed that fondness had grown in the desert where he would hide in the black shadows to watch Rachel. The way she slid her glass window aside late at night, lay her bare arms on the sill, and glanced up to the sky. She liked the black night, too, deep down inside her.

That would be the most beautiful memory of his lifetime. Embossed in his mind for all eternity: Rachel peeking past the window, her home-made macramé necklace dangling over her sports bra, and her auburn hair framing her perfect facial features, cascading downward over adobe brick. Magnificently designed, she was.

He turned his face toward the two bodies on the floor, their ugliness. Well, no use toiling over the past. He'd never see her again.

Death is the only way out.

He tapped the side of his watch, and a faint blue light bled into the room. They should be coming soon.

He shuffled to the back door, snatched and opened the box of matches. He gazed down at the tiny yet powerful sticks, cracked the door, and waited anxiously near the gasoline-drenched ropes that led through the woods to the hay bales. The first bale going up would merely scare everyone. Hurry them along. He'd stuffed damp newspapers inside that one to create a lot of smoke. With a little luck, the Mackentire cop would be rushed, shoot Lenny Emling in the back, and run for Mikala and the boys. He should be able to cut through several chain links by the time Jack arrived. Between the two of them, they might have time to herd all four kids to safety.

Then again, maybe not all four—maybe none.

Well, what did Rachel always say? Que sera sera.

Car engines roared in the distance. First one then another. Far apart yet muffled together like a duet between mother and child, one loud, one soft.

He leaned over, inspected the ropes, and turned his wrist to see his watch, tipping the match box too far. Quickly, matchsticks tapped against wood floor. A few spilled out the door and into the yard. He snapped his wrist back and felt inside the box. He thought enough remained, but just in case, he knelt and gathered a few together, picking them up and dropping them back into the box. Sweat beaded on his forehead and dripped profusely off his face.

My God, was he nervous? Sweating like a convict on death row? He thought he was above that.

He struck a match. It didn't light.

Are my hands wet? Sweaty?

He struck the match again and released his breath when he saw the blue and yellow of igniting flame. He lit the first rope and watched the red ember snake along the ground. He made sure the crawling glimmer squeezed between the trees and careened toward the field. Grass caught fire here and there as it slithered. A minute passed before the creeping glow disappeared into the woods, and several more lapsed before the bale of hay caught fire, and he saw the smoke rising. He turned to complete his other tasks.

But first, he hurried to peek out the window. He couldn't help himself. He watched as Lenny's long legs sailed by.

The scene was just as he had dreamed. He waited to see the cop—the great Billy Mack, friend of Rachel's family, best detective in the tristate area—and then he left the window and returned to the back door.

Small fires dappled the left side of the woods behind the house, and a gray mushroom of smoke hovered above the trees in the distance. Three minutes more. He had to wait three minutes for Jack, the voices had warned. Then he would light the long rope, and the dynamite in the bales would blow four minutes later. The dynamite in the house would explode thirty seconds after that, and the dynamite near the street, ninety seconds later. This had been timed to perfection.

When he heard the sound of Jack Daly running by, tangled with the snaps and sizzles of the small fires growing near the first rope in the woods, he bent down to light the next fuse. He struck the match. No light. He struck a second. Nothing. He felt into the box. My God, the cardboard was damp. The matches were wet.

He had to think quickly. There was another pack. He switched on his headlamp and ran toward the living room. He hurried around the bum to the old bureau, kicking teeth left and right. He yanked the top drawer and reached inside, his fingers sifting. Nothing. He searched the second, third, and fourth drawers. They were nowhere. He dropped to his knees and crawled to the chest, rummaging through it.

By the time his fingers found them, he was shaking like a detoxing junky. He rose and hurried toward the door, glancing at his watch. How many minutes had passed? He struck the match. No light. His entire body trembled. He struck another and another and, finally, one lit. He bent down and ignited the rope, and the orange glow of the flame serpentined along the ground toward the two bales of hay with the dynamite.

57 Jack

Billy climbed out of the foxhole with Mikala in his arms.

"No, don't run, Uncle Billy. Daddy is coming." Mikala tightened her grip around Billy's neck. Her eyelids flickered from the black smoke. She pointed a finger toward the thin orange line crawling away from the one bale of hay that was smoking. "Stop the fire."

Billy Mack blinked his own eyes as the smoke wafted toward them.

Wet newspaper.

He sniffed.

Burning rope. Gasoline.

He glanced south toward the two remaining bales of hay—he bet those weren't filled with newspaper—and then north toward the creek. He could run north and get her out alive but, he looked again at the long line of flames snaking toward the bunker's opening. If he didn't extinguish the approaching fire, the dry grass around the bunker would catch fire, and Lenny and the three boys would be trapped.

He hustled back to the hole, stepped onto one rung halfway down the ladder, and jumped to the bunker's bottom. He set Mikala's feet in the dirt.

"Throw me that blanket," he hollered. "The shiny one."

Lenny dropped his cutters to toss Billy the blanket, and Billy ascended the stairs, ran toward the fire, and snuffed it out. Then he sprinted farther away and smothered two slower-moving blazes. He hoped that gave Lenny a few more minutes to cut the chains.

When he jumped from the ground back down onto the bunker floor, he heard two little boys whimpering and then a snap of a chain link. He picked Mikala up just as Lenny fastened the wire cutter around another link.

"Go," Lenny turned and yelled. "Get her out of here."

Billy placed one foot and one hand on a ladder rung and hesitated just long enough for Mikala's scream to knock him back into consciousness.

"No! Daddy is coming," she screamed, and he forged up the ladder.

"See there," he heard her say, but he had started running north and wouldn't have stopped if he hadn't heard someone shout his name.

He turned and saw Jack running toward him. He met him halfway, handed Mikala to him, and pointed north. "Go toward the lights. You have to get Mikala out of here. Lenny Emling is cutting the boys free."

"But, I—"

"No," Billy hollered right before he jumped down the hole again. "There's dynamite. Get her out of here."

"I'll come back," he heard Jack holler.

Down in the bunker, Lenny's big frame hovered over the boys.

"It's okay," Lenny was saying in a voice too soft for his big face. "I am going to get you out of here."

Billy watched Lenny squeeze the bolt cutter with both hands and snip another link on the chain around the boy's ankle.

"I want my momma," the boy said.

"You'll see her soon, little fellow," Lenny said. The boy wheezed dramatically. "Can you take another breath for me?" Lenny pulled an inhaler out of his pocket and placed it in the boy's mouth.

The boy nodded and breathed in the vapor.

"That's a good boy. Now you hold on to this with your hand, and I'll cut you free."

The boy took the inhaler, and Lenny picked up the bolt cutter and snapped the last link. One half of the chain clanged to the ground, the other dangled against the boy's ankle. The child wheezed again.

"You b-better get this one out of here." Lenny lifted him up and handed him to Billy. "I'll get the other two."

"I'll wait, but you'll have to move faster."

The boy, John, began coughing badly. Billy removed the inhaler from his hand and made him inhale again. Lenny took a bandana from his back pocket, wrapped and tied it over the boy's nose and mouth.

"Hold that close to you, buddy. Can you do that?"

John reached a hand to the scarf and nodded, and Lenny motioned for Billy to go to the ladder.

"Get him away from the smoke."

When Lenny's headlamp cast light on the boy's face, Billy saw the gray skin. For a split second he was uncertain what to do.

"I c-can carry these two," Lenny told him.

Billy Mack thought quickly. His eyes scanned the thick chains. He had never left a man behind in a dangerous position, not in work or battle. He glanced at the bolt cutter lying in the dirt, at Lenny's thick biceps, and at the two boys still chained. This wasn't about valor. It was about who could cut through the chains quicker, and who could run faster with the boy with the asthma.

He knew the answer. Clearly, Lenny must stay and he must go. Still, Billy Mack could not desert a man and two children.

Lenny took a step toward him and put a hand on his arm.

"You're g-gonna have to trust me. I can get them both. I promise you. You have to get that one away from the smoke."

Billy wasted one more second thinking and then made a decision.

Trust.

He turned and grabbed a ladder rung.

"Run north toward the light," he told Lenny. "The bales of hay will go up fast. As soon as I find Jack and Mikala I'll come back for you."

"No need," Lenny said, turning from him. "I-I'll meet you at the l-light."

Billy watched Lenny stoop toward the boy he recognized as Mathew. He wasn't sure there was time to save both boys. His mind danced. He hoped Lenny meant the light in the north—not in the sky.

"Now let's cut your chains," Lenny told Mathew.

Billy heard the snap of the first cut as he started up the ladder, and right before he exited the hole, he heard Mathew Nuber's young voice.

"It's okay, mister, you can take Luke first. He's terrible scared."

With those words echoing in his head, Billy ran toward the light, dodged trees, jumped bushes, and slogged through mucky stream toward the light.

"Strength and speed, Lenny," he whispered into the night. "God give him the strength to cut those chains faster and the speed to get both Luke Anderson and Matthew Nuber to safety."

58 John Huegel

John Huegel sat at the back of his barn on Dunn Valley Road sucking in the sweet taste of his cigar. The two back garage doors, for his tractors, had been rolled to the ceiling, and his floodlights lit up both his yard behind the barn and his property across the creek.

Fifty-five years ago, he'd purchased the old farmhouse and barn along with the land that stretched across the water and deep into the south woods. He loved to sit out back and reminisce about the good times he'd had and the people he'd entertained there over the years.

He had trouble sleeping these days, and this was his insomnia go-to spot. He liked to drag out a lawn chair, sit and listen to the soothing sound of water nudging rock, gaze across the creek, and watch for deer and critters while he smoked.

At eighty-three years old, he still had the nose of a hound dog. Tonight there was a fire somewhere. Smoke smells crept through the trees from the south. He took a long puff on his cigar, held it out, and examined its tip. Well, he thought, the fire smell would soon find its way to the house—and Linda. He better put out the cigar. If she caught him smoking after his bypass, she'd puncture an eardrum.

A cigar never tasted the same if you relit it, so he stamped it out on the bottom of his shoe and flicked it into the creek. He hated squandering ten-dollar cigars, but at his age, he thought he had supply enough for a lifetime. He'd light up new tomorrow evening, though he was sorry he hadn't opted for a cheaper stogy tonight.

He leaned over for his glass of wine. Now that she wouldn't deny him. A connoisseur herself, the two of them had been drinking wine longer than they had been married. He swirled the glass to evaluate the legs. They'd been making wine nearly as long, and this last carboy held what might be his finest Delaware vino. He and Linda aerated the juice to perfection, had mastered that art. Women loved the fruity, bubbly taste.

He raised the glass to his lips and sipped. There was nothing better at this time in his life than wine on a windless autumn evening. He thanked the good Lord for bestowing decent health on him for another day, so he could tend to his farm. This insomnia annoyance was nothing.

He sipped again and looked out across his yard toward the swinging bridge that crossed Elk Creek. He and sixteen friends had run the cables and clamped the boards on to construct the magnificent hanging walkway. His stepson had fallen in the creek upside down over its greatest height during the task. He chuckled at the memory. Thank God the wine had loosened the boy for the fall.

It was a fine sight—that bridge, the moon pushing its shadow onto the quiet stream below. What a beautiful night. He sipped again, raised his eyes above the trees to the stars and caught the faint sound of rustling branches in the distance. The tops of a pack of trees moved in the shadows.

Must be a big animal coming through. He strained his eyes to see the creature. Watched for the foliage to open up, expecting a big-racked buck to barge through. But what emerged from the woods on the other side of the water was not an animal. It was a man and a child. The lean man carried a little girl.

Calmly, slowly, he set down his glass and reached for his gun. He cocked it to make sure the gun was loaded and then picked up his drink and snapped the gun back together. Not a drop of wine spilled from the glass.

The man with the child vaulted down the hill at a fast pace. John could tell he was an athlete. So he sat watching and waiting for the man to reach the swinging bridge.

He had seen that Amber alert on TV about the little girl and, having raised three children and five stepchildren, he wouldn't take the chance of allowing a man to steal a child. So he waited calmly, confidently.

The cables bounced, and John knew the man had stepped onto the bridge. He let him walk a ways, carrying the girl. The bridge was eighty-five feet long, and the man surprised John by crossing to the halfway mark sooner than expected. Good shape, he thought, great balance. John leaned toward the wall between the two garage openings and flipped a third switch with the rim of his glass. Floodlights hit the swinging bridge, and the man stopped.

"Good evening," John aimed the shotgun at him. "Don't make a move. Careful not to drop the girl. And, so I don't have to shoot you, tell me what you are doing on my property in the middle of the night—carrying a baby in your arms."

*****

The sudden light bounced off his pupils, and Jack nearly dropped Mikala. He stopped, tightened his arms around her, and looked toward the old man sitting in the barn. Was that a shotgun he was aiming? It was hard to tell with the blinding light.

"I'm Officer Jack Daly, and this is my daughter, Mikala. There is a fire and another officer coming behind us."

"Daly, now that name seems familiar. Is that the Daly on the Amber alert?"

"Yes, Mikala is my daughter."

Jack knew better than to move, but it was imperative he get her to safety and go back to help Billy.

"Your daughter, you say?"

"Yes, call 911. Jack and Mikala Daly."

A figure emerged from the east side of the barn. A woman with hair as silvery as the moon. She wore a short jacket over a long white nightgown.

"John, who are you talking to out here?" The woman sported a twenty-two. She followed the direction of her husband's gaze, and her stare met Jack's.

"Oh," she said. "Hello."

"Now, darling, why don't you go back on in the house and call the police."

"Ma'am." Jack straddled his feet on the bridge to steady its sway. "I'm Officer Jack Daly. This is my daughter, Mikala. She was abducted. Held in a bunker on the other side of the hill. I need to get her to safety and get back there. There are others."

"John?" The woman kept her gun pointed toward Jack but looked in the direction of her husband. "Do you believe him?"

"Not yet."

The smell of smoke magnified when a gust of wind found them. The woman shifted her gaze back to Jack. "There's a fire somewhere."

"I believe there is," the man with the gun responded, calmly, even quaintly.

"Sir, ma'am, I'm calling my chief. Just removing my cell phone."

"Slowly." The man motioned with the tip of his gun

Jack managed to pull his cell from his pocket, hold its button and say, "Call Chief."

"Did you hear that?" The woman lowered the tip of her gun a bit. "Sounds like he said call chief."

The chief answered instantly. "Jack—"

"I have Mikala." Jack spoke before the chief said more. "Somewhere on—I think I'm on Dunn Valley Road."

"Is she okay? Is Mikala all right?"

"Yes—"

"We tracked your car to Tileyard. Almost there. Can be on Dunn Valley in less than a minute."

The silvery-haired woman strolled toward Jack as he talked into the phone. "Look for lights. Lots of lights out back behind a house."

The woman stepped closer still, placed one hand on the bridge cable.

"Little girl," she said. "Is that your daddy?"

"Yes." Mikala raised her voice. "What is your address?"

"My address?"

"Yes."

"Who wants to know?" The woman's voice sounded apprehensive.

Mikala's voice turned soft. "Gracie."

The woman's jaw dropped, and her voice became nearly inaudible. "Who?"

Her husband stood, lowered his shotgun. "Did you say Gracie?"

"Yes, Gracie said you should give my daddy your address."

There was a moment of silence in the dark. Even Jack was confused.

"3411 Dunn Valley road," the woman yelled. "Now get that child over here, young man."

"Chief, 34—""

"11," the chief said. "I'm almost there."

59 The archangel

Jack made a split-second decision when he heard the chief's squad car siren.

"Can you take her?" he asked the woman. He would start over the bridge without letting Mikala out of his sight. When the chief arrived, he'd take off running toward Billy.

"Surely, go," the woman said, holding out her arms and wrapping them around Mikala. "She'll be fine with me. Go."

Red lights blinked against the tops of the trees, and Jack headed for the bridge. When the chief's car emerged from the side yard, bouncing over rutted terrain, Jack stepped onto the bridge.

"Daddy," Mikala screamed.

He glanced back. She lengthened her arm and pointed an index finger toward the bank on the other side of the creek. He turned and saw Billy forging down the hill. Jack backed off the bridge to get out of his way. Billy surged across, lay the child on the ground, removed the bandana from the boy's face, and held the inhaler to his mouth.

"Is he okay?" Jack leaned and felt the boy's forehead.

"I think so," Billy answered. "Call an ambulance. I have to go back for the others."

"I can do that." The woman stepped beside him. "Now, go. I raised eight children. I can take care of two."

Mikala wiggled out of the woman's arms, fell to the ground, and wrapped her arms around her father's legs.

Billy turned to Jack. "Stay with your daughter."

Before Jack could object, an explosion lit up the south sky like a volcanic eruption. The ground shook and a second eruption sounded, followed by a third and a fourth. Billy was knocked off balance on the bridge and fell to its boards. Jack lay Mikala down and crouched over her while the old woman covered the boy with her robe.

The night lit up like daytime and the evergreens, like Christmas trees. Flames rose in the distance as a cloud of smoke barreled toward them. Billy crawled off the swaying bridge, and the others hit the ground, faces to dirt, as a cloud of smoke infiltrated the air around them. They coughed and choked, but like a fleeting thunderstorm, the wave passed, dissipating into the vacuous black sky above and the misty night around them.

Fire trucks sounded, some close, some far, some on this side of the hill and many on the far side from which they had come. A fifth or sixth explosion—Jack lost count—rattled the ground, and a ball of fire rolled straight up into the sky. This last one was bigger, brighter, than the others. When Jack hoisted himself off the ground, Mikala scrambled to her feet, and grasped her father's legs once again.

"Don't go back, Daddy. Don't go."

"My God," the woman hollered from the ground. "No, don't go. No one could survive a blast like that. You say there were others? Kids?"

Chief Morgan ran to Jack and Mikala. He placed one hand on his arm and the other on Mikala's shoulder. His big hand nudged her toward his knees protectively. A wind escaped his lungs.

"Thank God," he uttered, squeezing Mikala's shoulder gently.

Three breathless officers ran up beside him, darting from side yards, their cruisers scattered somewhere along the dark country road to keep clear for the engines. Two big red fire trucks arrived, bobbing and bouncing around each side of the barn, and a cruiser sped across the lawn, clipping the edge of the Huegels' garden fence and riding right up to where the chief was standing.

"You stay, Crackerjack." Billy's voice battled sirens.

"Billy, you can't go back there," the chief yelled, pointing. They turned toward the bridge. The smoke had slithered in, crossing to the halfway point and obstructing all vision of the other side. The woods had turned to a wall of gray below black sky. Far behind and above the wall, orange-flamed tentacles peeked through the gray and reached toward the sky. "Let the fireman do their job."

"Lenny Emling is in there. And two little boys." Billy wiped his eyes with his sleeve. "I told Lenny I'd be back, and I'm going."

Jack picked Mikala up and kissed her. "I'm going with Uncle Billy. I'll be back, I promise."

"Jack," the chief said. He shook his head. "You can't go in there. Look at the smoke, the flames. There's no one left."

Jack set Mikala on the ground. "There are two kids there, Chief. We have to."

It was simple.

Jack stepped toward Billy, but Mikala clung to him, "Daddy!"

He grasped her wrists, nudged her gently away, and then leaned down one last time, so they were face to face. "I'll be okay. Promise."

"But." She broke one hand free from his grip and pointed a finger toward the bridge, which was swaying now just a bit. "He's coming."

Jack's eyes snapped toward the two big stumps where the bridge's cables were secured. The cables bounced a little and then a bit more, but there was nothing to see but smoke. No one was there. He gazed back at her, sadly.

"There's no one, honey. We have to go."

The old man and the woman stepped toward them.

"Why, no one could survive such a blast," the woman scolded. "Look at the smoke. You can't go back there. You were lucky to get two out."

"We have to," Jack said, his voice a whisper.

"No, you don't, Daddy. He's coming." Mikala's youthful voice struck Jack in that instance. How young and sweet and innocent she sounded. How hopeful.

How sure.

Her eyes met his, and her voice turned soft, too. "He is. He's coming."

Jack turned toward the bridge again. There was nothing on the other side of the creek but thick smoke. Yet the sway of the bridge had picked up. Was it wind? Ripples from the explosion? He turned back to her. "Who's coming?"

"Uncle Lenny."

"Who?"

"Uncle Lenny. He's coming across the bridge."

Once again, she pointed

"Uncle? Lenny?" His eyes shot like an arrow along her arm toward the smoke. He rose slowly and squinted his eyes. Billy, in front of him, squinted, too.

The cables bounced and squeaked.

"That's impossible." John Huegel staggered forward. "There's someone on my bridge."

And out of the smoke walked Lenny Emling. All who witnessed would later say he looked like an archangel emerging from hell. He strode mechanically. Stepped plank to plank as the bridge swayed, no hands on cable, his balance perfect. He was black-faced, clothes-singed, and carrying a child under each arm.

60 2002 – LeeLee

"Come here, darling, I have some things I want to talk about."

LeeLee thought she was too old to be called darling by anyone but Gee. She sat down on the edge of the bed.

"Do you want to swing your legs over the side, Gee?"

"Not today."

LeeLee scooted up beside her, lay her head on the pillow, and took Gee's hand in hers. "What is it?"

"Well, you and I spend a lot of days together, and we are close, but someday—not right now but in a year or two, maybe more—I'm going to have to go away, so there is something I need to tell you."

LeeLee's heart leapt. She felt pain. She didn't know where the pain resonated, but she could feel the hurt ricochet through her body and cover every inch of her. Like when she stuck the fork in the toaster, and Sissy had to yank its cord from the socket.

Tears filled her eyes.

"No," she whined. "You can't leave me. PopPops already left me. Stay here with Mommy and Daddy and Sissy and me. Who will I tell my secrets to?"

"That's what I want to talk to you about, my precious, our secrets. I have one to tell."

LeeLee couldn't hold the tears in; they began streaming down her face. Gee reached slowly for a tissue and handed it to her. LeeLee wiped teardrops away. "I don't want you to go. Take me with you if you have to go."

"Take you with me, you say?" Gee laughed and coughed. "Now you have a whole lifetime of fun in front of you."

"I don't want to be here without you."

"Oh, fiddledeedee, why would you want a bedridden-old Gee slowing you down? You have so much of life ahead. Don't you want to go to college? Teach children, someday? You want to be a teacher, right?"

"Right." LeeLee's glance fell to her fingers, and she blinked slowly.

"And don't you want to meet a boy?" Gee put a hand on LeeLee to stop her from scratching at a hangnail. "Get married and have children? What name did you decide for the girl? It was like Michael."

"Mikala."

"Yes, don't you want to have your sweet little Mikala?"

"I suppose. But I want you to meet her."

"Oh, I'll meet her, all right."

"You will?" She glanced up at Gee, hopeful.

"Sure." Gee gave two weak squeezes of her hand. "I'll see her in heaven before she is born. I'll tell her all about you and Sissy and how you came to sleep with us in the attic and then moved into the house around the corner with the pink bedroom. I'll teach her about the dreams."

"Will she have dreams?"

"She sure will. I'd just like to see someone try to stop her." Gee paused for a moment and coughed into her handkerchief. When she regained her composure, she continued. "She will dream wide awake, just like you and me and Sissy."

"Will she see the black devil?"

"Maybe. Yes, I suppose she will. Once maybe—like you and me."

"Will she be scared?"

"Well, that's the thing. We don't want her to be afraid of that nasty old black devil. Because, you and me, we know he can't hurt us. So I will go on up there and tell her not to be afraid. How if he comes, she should close her eyes." Here

Gee tilted her head back and closed her eyes. "Call for the white angel and speak Baby Jesus' name for protection. I will teach her everything before she is born, so she is strong, never afraid."

"Yes, she should know that."

"And that's why I have to go. I have to get there and tell her all about how we in our family are special. About our dreams. Now you don't want her to be scared when she comes here, do you?"

"No." LeeLee's response was lost in a whine. "But I don't want you to leave. PopPops is there. Can't he tell her?"

"PopPops, you say? Tell her about the white angel?" She laughed. "Why, he would just mess it all up. No, I will go and tell her. I'll hold her in my lap and teach her all about how to say her prayers of protection and count the feathers of the angel, and she will be stronger and smarter than both of us because when she is born she will already know all about the dreams."

LeeLee thought quietly.

"You know what else?" Gee tucked her hankie inside her sleeve.

"What?"

"I'm missing PopPops."

LeeLee's eyes widened. She hadn't thought about Gee missing Pops. She watched Gee tilt her head back and stare at the ceiling. Her voice would turn soft and flowy now. LeeLee lifted Gee's arm over her shoulder and settled in to listen.

"PopPops is waiting for me. Sometimes in the morning I look out the window and see him waving his hand, calling me to come. I tell him I don't want to leave my LeeLee, and do you know what he says?"

"What?"

"He says it is beautiful there. That my mother and father and sisters are waiting for me. And that no one is ever sad or hurting. Everyone has tea and cake every day."

"Cake?"

"Uh-huh. Pops says you can have anything you want on the other side."

"Is Pops with his momma and daddy and grandma and grandpa?"

Gee's face turned sober. "Yes, he is, sweet pea."

"And you will be with yours?"

"That's right."

"And your sisters, too?"

"I will."

LeeLee considered this for a moment—Gee's two sisters being in heaven. And she thought about her own sister, Sissy. How Sissy protected her and always knew just what to do.

Maybe—someday—Gee should go, so she could be with her sisters and brothers. Gee told lots of stories about the mischievous boys in her family. Especially her baby brother, Timmy, born fifteen years after Gee. Gee said he was a pest, always underfoot, following her so close she tripped over him night and day.

Gee's face always lit up when she talked about Timmy.

"And will you be with your brothers? Uncle Timmy?"

"Yes. That's right. I'll be with Uncle Timmy, and that's just the person I wanted to tell you about."

"He died in a car accident, right?"

"He did. He was hit and killed by a drunk driver before you were born. It was one of the worst days in my life. A tragedy." She placed her hands on the mattress and propped herself up in the bed. "But that's not what I wanted to tell you about Timmy."

LeeLee looked up in anticipation. Gee had the best stories.

"Many years ago, before Timmy went to war—"

"The Vietnam War?"

"That's right, sweetie. Before Timmy went to the Vietnam War, he met a girl. She had soft eyes and chestnut hair. Was tall and slender but only fifteen years old, so Timmy couldn't date her. She was too young. But they became good friends. Worked at McDonald's downtown. Have you been to the McDonald's downtown?"

LeeLee nodded.

"Of course, it was different then. It had two big arches and chocolate shakes you had to eat with a spoon. We kids used to meet there after dances and basketball games. But that's neither here nor there. The story is, Timmy and this girl worked there together every Saturday night and, well, I'm pretty sure they fell in love."

"But then Timmy had to go away."

"Yes, he did."

"Did they write to each other?"

"For a while, but then Mary Alice, that was her name, moved away from Erie when her Daddy died. Her mother moved home to Kentucky to live with her family."

"Ohhh, this is a sad story isn't it, Gee?"

"Yes, it is. And it is a story about how sometimes people do foolish things when they love someone."

"What did Mary Alice do?"

"Well, Mary Alice's momma became real sick. She had what they called rheumatoid arthritis, which is very crippling. And that sweet Mary Alice, she stayed with her mamma until the day she died. Took care of her."

"Did Uncle Timmy go down to see her?"

"Oh, no, Uncle Timmy didn't know where she was."

"Is that why he married Aunt Wendy?"

"Yes, I suppose it is."

"Did he love Aunt Wendy?"

"Uncle Timmy did love Aunt Wendy, but he always wondered what happened to sweet Mary Alice. And then one day, he ran into her at the grocery store. Mary Alice's poor mamma had passed away, and Mary Alice had come back to Erie. Uncle Timmy recognized her right away. Said he dropped a jar of pickles on the floor, and it shattered into so many pieces they had to close off the aisle.

"After a stock clerk came and mopped up the pickle juice, Mary Alice and Timmy started laughing and couldn't stop. They laughed so hard they decided to go sit for a spell, grab a coffee. And they had a real nice time. So they decided to meet back at that same coffee shop a week later. And then they returned the week after that and the next one, and before you knew it, they became real good friends again."

"Did Uncle Timmy still love Mary Alice?"

Gee took a long breath in and released it slowly. "He did."

"Did Aunt Wendy cry?"

"What's that? Aunt Wendy? Oh, no, Uncle Timmy and Mary Alice were good people. They didn't want to hurt Aunt Wendy. Then I expect the good Lord took care of that problem."

"How did he do that?"

"Why, he called Uncle Timmy to heaven, child, and Aunt Wendy never knew anything about Mary Alice. Still doesn't."

"How did you know?"

"I saw them in that coffee shop once, so I talked to Uncle Timmy about Mary Alice and he broke down and cried. Said he couldn't hurt Aunt Wendy, but he was in a terrible way because he still loved Mary Alice after all those years."

"Did Mary Alice love Uncle Timmy, too?"

"She did. Very much."

"What happened to her?"

"She went back to her old neighborhood for a ride one day, and it just so happened her mother's house was for sale, so she bought it, got a job—at the big insurance company downtown—and still lives there today. I expect she wanted to be close to Timmy even if he was married to Aunt Wendy."

"But then Uncle Timmy died."

"Yes, he did. My, my." Gee shook her head. "That was such a bad day."

"Did Mary Alice cry?"

"She did."

"Did she move back to Kentucky?"

"Well, here's the thing. She was sad, but she couldn't leave. Because in her belly, there was a little baby growing, a baby boy. And I expect she just felt he should be raised here in Erie, where his daddy had grown up."

"Uncle Timmy's baby boy?"

"Yes, child, Uncle Timmy's baby."

"Where is he now?"

"Well, he still lives with his mama in that old house. He's not much older than you."

LeeLee knew. Instinctively, she knew.

"Has the gift, just like Uncle Timmy and me." Gee squeezed her gently. "But that is our secret. Just yours and mine."

"Can I tell Sissy about him?"

"No, child."

"Why can't Sissy know?"

"Here's the thing about Sissy. She's smart and strong and the best big sister in the whole world, but she can't keep a secret like you and me, never could. She might let it slip accidentally, so you can't tell her. It would break Aunt Wendy's heart—especially since she and Timmy never could have any children of their own. So, no, you can't tell a soul—not even Sissy. The time isn't right."

"Will the time ever be right?"

"You just ask the smartest questions. Yes, someday the time will be right."

"Mikala will know when to tell, won't she? Because you are going to tell her."

"That's right, honey. When I get to heaven, I'm going to talk it over with God. Find out what to do about it because a boy shouldn't live without a family forever. And now you understand why I must go."

This perplexed LeeLee. She understood the gravity of the situation, the importance of the secret. The dilemma was that she was losing Gee. Her heart sagged, but she knew Gee must go and she must stay.

"It's Lenny, isn't it, Gee? The boy with the big ears. Lenny is Uncle Timmy's boy."

"That he is, child. That he is."

61 Lenny

"Momma?" Jack watched Mikala place her fork on her empty plate and reach for her spoon and pudding. "Can I always sit next to Uncle Lenny?"

"You sure can."

"Good," Mikala said, then looked up at Lenny. "Did you like our Christmas turkey, Uncle Lenny?"

"I did. It was very good."

"I'm so glad you're my uncle." Mikala leaned toward him and rested the side of her face on his shirt sleeve. She looped her free hand inside his arm, and Lenny smiled.

"We're all glad." Lisa smiled, too.

Jack watched that smile light up her stunningly beautiful, makeup-free face.

She had risen early, polished her grandmother's silverware, squeezed twelve fine china place settings elegantly onto their mid-size table, and cooked all morning. Her unwashed hair sat limp on her shoulders. She leaned her elbows on the table and clasped her bare fingers together. Her wedding rings still sat on the windowsill by the kitchen sink. Jack could see a small spot of silver polish caked on her forearm.

Not only had she not had time to shower, she hadn't changed her clothes. Only Lisa could appear sexy in a gravy-stained t-shirt.

"Yeah, we're all glad." Jaden hollered from across the table, drawing Jack's stare from Lisa.

"Try the pudding, Uncle Lenny," John added, a wreath of chocolate decorating his chin.

Jack's eyes skated across the table from the twins to Lenny. For some reason, his family's expressed affection for the guy irked him.

"Yes, yes, we are all glad. But I have to say one thing." Jack folded his napkin in half.

"Oh, no," Billy Mack grunted, then reached to the table behind him and grabbed the bottle of bourbon. He poured some into his glass. When the chief raised his glass, Billy poured into his, too.

"I know. I know. No one wants to hear this, but it has to be said." Jack wiped his mouth and pointed at Lenny with his napkin. "Really, Lenny, you have to stop chasing those boys from Peach Street."

Jack watched the exchange of glances around the table. He could almost read the thoughts behind the annoyed expressions: *Leave it to Jack to ruin a good party.*

"We know it was you," he exhaled and tried to imply he was sorry to have to bring the fact to light. "I just had to get that off my chest. So I'll drop it from here, but you have to stop knocking the crap out of those kids."

"Lenny!" Mary Alice lifted one hand to her mouth. Her other hand dropped her fork against Lisa's good china.

All eyes in the room darted first toward the china—nothing broke—then to Lenny.

Lenny's eyes circled the room and landed on his mother's. His cheeks reddened.

"B-b-but they were breaking in stores, Ma." He rocked slightly in his seat.

"C'mon, Jack." Lisa removed her elbows from the table and let her hands fall into her lap. "Just drop it."

"I can't, Lisa, it's the law."

"Crackerjack," Billy whined, took a swig of his drink, and made a grunting sound that appeared to alleviate both his bourbon burn and his exasperation with Jack. "Leave the guy alone. He's a hero."

"He can't be doing that, Billy." Jack glanced at the chief, but Ben merely raised his eyebrows, shrugged, and drank.

"Well, I won't say it again. It's just, you're going to hurt someone, Lenny."

"They are b-bad kids."

"We know." Jack poked his elbows onto the table. "But let us do our job. Stay out of it."

Lenny's big face tilted downward, and he lowered his eyes toward his plate. The silence in the room made everyone uncomfortable. Finally, Lenny cut through the quiet.

"O-k-kay," he said. Then when silence had its turn in the room for a few more uncomfortable seconds, Lenny Emling, Lisa's cousin, added, "C-C-Crackerjack."

The room stilled, eyes bandied about, and then laughter erupted. The jeers rang so loud Jack thought the neighbors on both sides would wonder what game the Dalys were playing around the Christmas Eve dinner table.

Billy poured more drinks and clanged glasses with Ben again as Lisa stood and scurried around the table. She stopped behind Lenny, leaned down, and wrapped her arms around his thick neck. Kissed his cheek.

"You tell him," she whispered loud enough for Jack to hear.

"What?" Jack withdrew his arms from the table. "My own wife? You take his side?"

Mikala took the opportunity to become the center of the room's attention. She bounded out of her chair and jumped into Lenny's lap, smiling at her dad. Loud squeals erupted again. Jack tossed his napkin on the table.

"That's it. Mutiny. My entire family." He rose, took his plate, and stomped toward the kitchen, setting his plate down clumsily in the sink.

When he turned his back to them, he began to laugh. Maybe Mikala was right; he just might like this Uncle Lenny guy.

62 Jack, Billy, and Ben

One week after Christmas, the final results came in. The findings confirmed Todd Kennedy's and John Michael's ashes were mixed in the rubble. Their remains unrecoverable, the coroner, FBI and—because of the deceaseds' affiliation with the government—CIA reports all substantiated what the dental forensic pathologist had gathered from the meager remains: Todd and John Michael were dead.

"Can you keep the other information out of the paper?" Now that the case was done and Mikala safe, Jack's compassion for his sister-in-law reemerged. "Rachel's having a terrible time. She's still staying at our house with Jeffrey."

"I'm trying. I have a call into Texas. The newspaper bigwigs reside there. But I have a few connections."

"Thanks, Chief."

"Don't thank me yet. I don't know how long I can keep them at bay. Couldn't have kept the details out of the paper this long without the help of the CIA."

"Finally, something Project Dream is good for." Jack felt some gratitude for the CIA's involvement in the case, if for nothing more than they quickly eliminated any suspicion that Rachel was involved in the kidnapping. They now concentrated on protecting her identity.

"You got that right," the chief agreed.

The FBI disclosed the Blakleys had deposited $325,000 in different bank accounts on three separate occasions, including the one to Rachel Callahan's account. That deposit, transferred to Todd Kennedy's account, caused an inter-agency stir. The FBI and CIA volleyed and deflected accusations and theories. The first two payments had been deposited in bank accounts out of the country, which began a maze of transfers between various accounts at European and South African locations, the Caribbean, and one small city in Jordan. The CIA continued to trace those.

"The FBI is studying Todd's financial activity last spring. He hit it big at Parks in Philadelphia last May, and two days later he was in New Jersey. Drew down over $300,000. No record of losses."

"Yeah, I heard, and that's odd," Jack told the chief. "Rachel said Todd claimed he had been mugged in Philly. Stopped at a donut shop early in the morning. Someone hit him over the head and stole over a half million dollars."

"Cash?"

"Of course, always cash."

Jack and the chief shared a few silent moments. Each tossed glances toward the back of the room where Billy Mack stood quietly, one hand holding an elbow, and one bent leg propping a sneaker flat against the wall. His other hand twirled that damn toothpick.

"Did he ever call in the mugging? Is there a report?" Jack turned back toward the chief.

"No, so we're not one hundred percent sure there was a mugging. He could have lost that money at some other casino. The CIA sent Kennedy's picture to every casino within a thousand-mile radius. Police agencies are checking past videos, but some smaller places don't have May's any longer. So we may never know."

"Rachel never believed he was mugged."

"Who knows what Todd Kennedy did with his money." The chief sighed.

"Well," Jack said, "he went through it like a pig through mud, that's for sure. What about John Michael?"

"The FBI is heading the investigation on him but, well, there's not much incentive investigating a case when you're sure the culprit is one of two people, and both of them are dead."

"Can any of the boys identify the kidnapper?"

"No," the chief sighed, took a hankie out and blew his nose. "Not a one of them."

Quiet found the room again. Loud ticks divided the silent seconds, and Jack realized maintenance had finally resurrected Helen's wall clock. He examined the room. They had fixed that damn flickering light, too, and replaced the old, stained ceiling tiles. Helen had gotten an overhaul, and he hadn't even noticed.

But then he had been busy, hadn't he? And he had succeeded in protecting those he loved. His family was safe. The CIA had credited Lenny Emling with locating the boys. Only a handful of people knew Mikala and Lenny, together, had found them, and Jack knew all of those who knew would take that secret to the grave.

Of course, Jack owed a shitload of favors to cop friends, but he would return each and every one unquestioningly if called upon. He owed them his daughter's life. His toiling and worry had paid off in the end. But…

He listened to the clock tick. What else had slipped by him while he labored over Mikala's safety?

"Could be Todd Kennedy was one bad poker player." Billy's voice obliterated the ticking and shattered Jack's thoughts.

Billy removed the sole of his shoe from the back wall and approached them. "Or could be the guy who hit him over the head was the luckiest son-of-a-bitch in Philadelphia."

Billy Mack stepped up beside the chief, stopped, and locked eyes with Jack.

"Or." The end of his toothpick twirled. "Could be someone socked that money away somewhere."

Quiet infiltrated Helen once again. Then her door sprang open, and a line of officers filed in. Along with them, a distracting din arose and didn't dissipate even as officers took seats and turned toward the front of the room. The tall hand on the clock hit twelve. It was 7 a.m. Staff meeting time.

Up on the board, a city map printed by the Engineering department sat below the words "Trevor Somebody." One red pin shimmered from a point on Erie's bluffs. With the settled kidnapping case and departure of the FBI, it was back to small-town Erie business: the missing bum.

Jack Daly and Ben Morgan and Billy Mack lingered at the front of the room. Ben swallowed so hard his Adam's apple looked grapefruit sized. His guys were staring at him, but it appeared he couldn't find his voice, so his lead investigator on the missing bum case spoke for him.

"We've identified the missing person's full name. He is Trevor Higgins and the last time anyone saw him…"

Jack's concentration slipped away. He ran his fingers over his head, half through air and half brushing bristle. He had forgotten his weekend trip to the barber. His eyes rose to Billy, and he noticed Billy was staring back. His eyelids seemed stuck to his eyebrows. He wasn't blinking

Billy Mack tossed his toothpick in the garbage. He didn't reach for another.

Epilogue

Halfway across the continent, in a small building alongside a sunny beach somewhere in the Virgin Islands, a doctor removed the last bandage from his patient's nose. Trevor Higgins took a step toward the mirror, held his chin in his hand, and stared at the fresh scars. Even though the swelling wasn't completely gone, he could see the workmanship. The doctor had done a magnificent job. Carved some bone away from his cheeks, narrowed the nose, enlarged the lips slightly, even the brow lift looked good.

"Marvelous." Trevor released his hand and stood back, glanced toward the surgeon and then back in the mirror.

My God, he was handsome. The facial reconstruction along with his $150,000 smile made him appear ten years younger. He couldn't stop staring. "You've outdone yourself, Doctor."

"Why, thank you. I pride myself on giving people what they want, especially men. You know women can get all they need in the way of plastic surgery, but cleaning up a man's face is an art. Not too many doctors get it right. Combine the sharp lines of surgery with masculinity. A lot of patients come away with feminine features."

"Well, we certainly didn't want that." He reached into his pocket and took out the long white envelope. "Here you go, Doc. Your last payment. Cash. And worth every dime."

"Why, thank you, Mr. Higgins." The doctor placed the envelope in his own pocket. "It's been a pleasure."

Trevor shook the doctor's hand, placed a baseball cap on his head and nodded. "The pleasure was all mine."

He stepped outside into the bright sun, reached into his pocket, and removed a second envelope. He ambled slowly toward the building's shaded side alley, turned the corner, and glanced in both directions. No one. He snagged a bill from his money clip, stooped, leaned on a leg, dexterously rolled the white powder into the bill, held one nostril, and sniffed.

"Finally," he said out loud, dabbing his nose gently with a monogrammed handkerchief. Then he stood and headed down the beach toward his suite.

He'd spend another week there and then fly to Switzerland where an exquisitely-renovated home and new job awaited him. He snickered. He'd never want for money again. Would live off the interest of his 3.5-million-dollar nest egg, all planted and grown by the American government, gambling winnings, and a tad from the Blakley family.

Unfortunate about their boy.

But the others had lived. Good for Mikala. And although Lenny Emling living irked him—damn that lucky flunky junkie—he would never see any of them again, so what did it matter?

He strolled into his complex and meandered through the outdoor kiosks where the natives beckoned him to buy over-priced island t-shirts and jewelry. He purchased a souvenir shot glass, island cigar, and Cruzan rum, which he planned to open later that evening in celebration.

Closer to his suite, an enclosed booth with a moon and star-striped curtain caught his attention. He stopped to read its A-frame sign: Madame Duvessa, Sorcerer of the Islands.

"A fortune teller?" He cackled. The tone of his voice flaunted both delight and surprise.

His chuckle caught the attention of the woman inside. She jerked the curtain aside and eyed him pensively from her seat. The chair across from her was empty.

"I was waiting for you," she said, quite confidently.

When she stood, her body ascended straight up like the slow launch of a rocket. She wore layers of skirts made with thin, silky material.

"I bet you were." He crossed his arms, amused. His hand reached and touched the skin above his lip. Old habit.

"You want your fortune?" She hesitated, then added, "Sir?"

"I already have my fortune," he said, a wave of happiness washing through him.

The woman gave her head a slight tilt and stared oddly at him. His elation subsided and curiosity replaced his warm rush. What did he see in those beady, hollow eyes of hers?

"I think not," she said pointedly.

Inside, he laughed at her—an amateur. She had no idea who she was dealing with.

"Are you afraid, Mr. Americano? Afraid of… having your fortune told?"

"Afraid of wasting my money on a swindler is more like it."

The woman's eyes raked him up and down, but not a muscle of her long, thin body moved. She looked like Edith, turned to salt. He stilled his own body. Sharpened his glance.

"Then for you, sir," she finally said, the hand at her side jerking part of her skirt behind her for effect. "I read for free."

Her gesture made him relax his shoulders and snicker. She was a performer, not a soothsayer, and he was never one to turn down anything free.

"What the hell," he said and stepped inside, laughing when he noticed the crystal ball.

"I've never seen one of those. You tell the future with these, do you?"

"I do," she said, unable to hide her Caribbean accent with even the smallest of sentences.

He took a seat and her skirts swirled, talked to him, as she rounded the table and sat down opposite him. She leaned her elbows on the table and came to a calm, serene resting position.

He analyzed her: observed her breathing, listened to her native prayer, and watched as she waved her hands over the ball in an almost seductive fashion. Impressively, she began quite quickly.

"You're running from something."

Again, he chuckled. "I assure you, I run from nothing and no one."

She glanced strangely at him and then resumed her caressing of her crystal ball.

"What this mean?" A puzzled look fell across her. "No way out except death."

"Well, now, that was fairly clever." He raised his eyebrows then lowered them quickly. His brows still burned with movement. "Not bad. Not bad at all."

"And you love someone."

"Now that could not be farther from the truth."

"You love someone."

He could sense her defiance.

"Is this the person you run from?" She looked into her ball, swirled her palms over the top of it. "Wait. No. You run from another."

He sighed. "You'll have to do better than that if you want a tip, woman."

She gazed deeper into the ball. Leaned forward and turned an ear as if the translucent globe talked to her. "This person you run from is young."

Her head jerked upward. "And you are a sorcerer as I am."

"A sorcerer?" He wrinkled his nose, felt a twinge of pain. "Not a sorcerer."

Her head dropped, and her face inched closer to the ball. A change fell over her. He witnessed fear surfacing in her eyes. She swallowed hard, ran her hands over the ball, and then dropped them to her side, leaning her back against her chair.

"There's no more."

Now he leaned forward, tilting his head to see into the ball. "No more?"

She had his curiosity.

"No more."

He stared for a moment. Sighed. He couldn't believe he was going to allow this woman to swindle him, but he couldn't resist. He dug into his pocket, felt for the envelope, removed a one-hundred-dollar bill, and slapped Benjamin Franklin face up on the table. Her gaze shifted from him to Bennie and back again, but she didn't move a muscle of her body.

He kept his eyes on her as he laid another bill on top of the first. The two hundred dollars called to them from the little round table, coaxing them to look, but neither broke eye contact.

The woman barely breathed.

Finally, he let a long breath escape to convey this was it. The last bill.

"This is more than you earn in a year, woman." He tossed another on top of the other two.

Her eyes fell to the money, and she tipped her head slowly backward, reached a hand to the table, and her fingers fell lightly on the stack of bills. She dragged them off the table and down into the depths of her skirts.

"I thought so," he said, already feeling duped.

"So what do you see?" he asked, frowning.

"You run from a child."

That made him sit straight.

"A child?" He glanced around the dark room.

"Why—you're crazy woman." He hesitated. Reached up to finger his mustache again and then slammed his hand on the table when he remembered his new face. The crystal ball jiggled.

"Be careful, sir."

"Do you really get paid to do this? You're mad."

"Not mad. You run from a child." She raised her chin with confidence. "A girl. And someday—she will find you."

"She will find me? This child?"

"Yes." Her eyes narrowed. "I'm certain. She will search for you, and she will find you."

"Why would a child search for me?"

"I do not know."

"Well, then it isn't so."

"Truth. My crystal ball tells only truths. There is a girl, far away, and someday she will find you."

He lost his composure, looked at the table and all around, searching for some small item to throw. But there was nothing in the makeshift room but the table, its cloth, and the glass ball. The woman leaned in, bent at the elbows, and stretched her arms around her crystal ball as if she knew what he was thinking.

"You run from a child," she said, and he noticed it then. No separation between her irises and pupils existed. Her eyes were black.

"Why would I run from a child?" He spit the words through clenched teeth.

The woman's eyes glassed over and for the first time, he recognized something authentic in her. Something he had seen in the mirror on occasion, in his own eyes.

"Because she knows your name."

"My name?" He swallowed. "And what is my name?"

"John Michael."

A word about the author…

CJ ZAHNER is a digital-book hoarder, lover of can't-put-down books, runner, author, and Mensa wannabe. That last trait explains the inspiration for her first novel, *The Suicide Gene* (The Wild Rose Press).

Her second book, *Dream Wide Awake*, was inspired during long runs on Presque Isle State Park in her hometown of Erie, Pennsylvania. She is a proud mother of three and an even prouder grandmother of one.

Before becoming a novelist, CJ worked as a grant and freelance writer. Her articles varied from business to women's health to the paranormal. Her most popular articles can be found on her website at www.cjzahner.com.

In 2015, she began looking at life differently when her brother and his wife were diagnosed with dementia and early-onset Alzheimer's. At that time, her husband pulled her aside and said, "Quit your job. You're a writer." After twenty years of service, CJ picked up her purse at work one day and quietly walked away.

Now, she rises before dawn, writes, runs, and smiles much. She completed *The Suicide Gene* and *Dream Wide Awake*, and is nearing completion of two other novels, *Within the Setting Sun* and *The Dream Snatchers*.

A hard worker and story lover, CJ Zahner is determined to read, write, and run happily ever after…

10506343R00211

Made in the USA
Lexington, KY
27 September 2018